Support and Defend

AN ALLISON QUINN THRILLER
BOOK ONE

VANNETTA CHAPMAN

SUPPORT AND DEFEND

Copyright © 2023 by Vannetta Chapman

• **ASIN** : B0BW2GW1MS

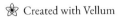 Created with Vellum

"I, Allison Quinn, do solemnly swear
that I will support and defend
the Constitution of the United States
against all enemies, foreign and domestic;
that I will bear true faith and allegiance to the same;
that I take this obligation freely,
without any mental reservation or purpose of evasion;
and that I will well and faithfully discharge
the duties of the office on which I am about to enter.
So help me God."

Her Solemn Oath

AN ALLISON QUINN PREQUEL

Allison Quinn was the first to arrive at the emergency meeting of Seattle Division's Joint Cyber Task Force, more commonly referred to as the JCTF. The calendar had barely turned on a new year and here they were—still trying to stop Armageddon.

Donovan Steele dropped into a seat beside her. "Still getting here first I see."

She leveled her gaze on him, but didn't answer.

"Still sitting at the back, near the door."

Donovan was big, obviously strong, and he carried himself with the poise of a well-educated, well-seasoned agent. He was six foot, two inches, Black, good-looking with a smile that he tossed around too readily.

He was also FBI, which in Allison's mind was a strike against him.

"Same as you, Donovan."

"First in. First out." He arched his eyebrows as if he'd solved some great mystery.

What he said was true, but she also wanted to be able to watch the other agents. Size up the people she would be working with, and in the process, be as inconspicuous as possible. It wasn't that

1

she didn't trust them. It was that she was careful. Always. Very. Careful.

The conference room was cramped with too many chairs and quickly filling with too many people. It was ensconced in the sub-basement of the Seattle Federal Office Building, which covered a full city block near Seattle's Pioneer Square. All digital devices including cell phones and computers were left in locked boxes on the ground floor. This room was supposed to be cyber-secure.

Allison wasn't sure there was such a thing.

The single laptop at the front of the room was in a hardcase—essentially a small Faraday cage. It was also air-gapped. In theory, it couldn't be compromised.

"Looks like everyone was called in." Donovan shrugged when she turned to study him. "Must be a verified threat."

Allison did a quick head count. Eighteen agents had crammed into the small room. They'd been yanked from whatever they were doing in order to be present for this update. Which meant this was the real thing. She sat up straighter and locked her full attention on the front of the room. She hadn't lovingly embraced the idea of a joint task force, but then she was still a junior special agent with DHS. No one had asked her opinion.

The task force consisted of agents from the FBI and Homeland Security. Allison had been with HS since graduating from DePaul University eight years earlier. She was considered a rising star. She didn't care about that. What she cared about was justice —both in general and personally.

Allison had a vendetta—a very personal crusade.

She would find the persons who killed her father.

But she also had a job to do. It just so happened that during some ops, she was able to do both. This was shaping up to be that kind of op.

"Here we go," Donovan said.

Kendra Thomas stepped to the front of the room. She stood nearly six feet tall, had recently turned forty-two, and was earning quite a reputation. Everything from her straight hair to her straight-lined, black clothing screamed *don't mess with me*. She was two levels above Allison, and she was in line for a promotion. If Allison was a rising star, Kendra was a comet burning bright.

"We are here because of Justin Knox, AKA Worm. We received this video an hour ago."

She nodded to a technician who doused the lights and tapped a few keys on the laptop.

Running less than a minute, the video clearly conveyed Worm's intentions. Planes and trains crashing. Traffic a snarl of accidents. Fires. Packed emergency rooms. And behind it all, iconic Seattle images—the Space Needle, Pike Place Market, Pioneer Square, and of course docked cruise ships.

Widespread destruction.

Not a ploy with a huge financial payoff.

Destruction.

"He thinks pretty highly of himself," Donovan muttered.

"We received other...evidence...that indicates he has the knowledge and resources to do exactly what he's threatening. Our analysts believe he'll use an EMP. Casualty estimates are in the thousands. Higher if we can't restore the grid quickly."

Allison's attention was split between what she was seeing, what Thomas was saying, and the possibility that this perp could tell her something about her father's killers. Though she had only seen one man in the woods that day, she suspected it had taken at least two to carry out the killing. The only clue she had at this point to the identity of the murderers was that the guilty parties were deeply involved in the dark web.

It was an extremely cold case. Finding the perps and bringing them to justice had been her goal since she was old enough to have a goal. Unfortunately, two degrees in cybersecurity and a nearly decade long career with Homeland Security hadn't brought her much closer to finding the persons.

But she would.

She was nothing if not patient.

Though she'd rather be chasing down leads in the cold Seattle day than sitting in a conference room.

Among themselves, the agents on the task force referred to it as the PT, or Punk Taskforce. The men and women they sought to apprehend were cyberpunks.

"As you read in Knox's file, he scored significantly above average on intelligence tests and—before he went off the radar—he exhibited a tech savviness that bordered on the edge of being considered a savant. He's thirty-two years old. Every indication is that he's well acquainted with the Seattle area."

Some of the terrorists they chased considered themselves radicals who sought to rid the world of government surveillance or capitalistic intrusion. Others were simply greedy, sending out their cyber-poison and then offering a cure for a steep price. In the majority of those cases, the entities involved were willing to pay that price rather than lose precious dollars due to "network down" complications. Even admitting to such an attack could cause a company's stock to plummet.

Because of that, JCTF had to work diligently to be aware of current threats in the private sector. Public entities weren't as circumspect. JCTF was often on the scene within hours.

Then there were the cases like this one, where it seemed that few in the local area were even aware of the impending attack. Allison had checked all the local news feeds earlier that morning. There was nothing about an impending attack.

"Two hours ago we intercepted what we believe to be his signal for a very brief moment. That signal confirmed that he is in the Washington area, but we don't know where. To complicate matters, the JCTF has fewer than two dozen agents in Washington State."

"Best of the best," someone muttered.

"I have no doubt that you are." Thomas scanned the room, as if to assure herself. "More agents are flying in, but we suspect they will arrive too late to do much good. They might be able to help pick up the pieces, if we don't manage to stop Mr. Knox."

"We'll stop him," an agent near the front promised.

"We don't know if he's working alone or has associates. We don't have any historical data connecting Knox to prior attacks, so we have no way to know how far he's willing to go. If he's prepared to set into motion a cascade of events that will cause what you saw in that video, then he's probably willing to put a bullet through a few government agents."

Now she had everyone's attention.

"From what we've been able to put together, Knox is planning to deploy an EMP over Seattle. His goal is to take out the entire northwestern sector—communications, transportation, power grid. He wants to bring down all of it. As I noted earlier, estimated casualties are in the thousands. That number only rises if we are not able to get systems up and running within twenty-four hours, which we will not be able to do."

The casualty estimations never failed to surprise Allison.

Cell phones stop working. Traffic lights fail. The electrical grid goes down. And that kills thousands? How was that possible? But she'd dug into the analytical charts many times, and she knew the projected numbers were accurate. Nearly every aspect of their society depended on technology. When that technology was suddenly and completely stripped away, chaos ensued.

Allison silently vowed that they would not allow that to happen. She had taken an oath to support and defend the Constitution of the United States against all enemies, and she would do that. She would protect the people of Seattle against Justin Knox, aka Worm.

"The entirety of your training and career has prepared you for this. You will find this man, and you will stop him. The weather forecast shows deteriorating conditions across the Seattle area. You can expect high winds and one to three inches of snow. You'll be issued snow suits, which you can pick up in the supply room, as well as rifles and ballistic vests."

An agent close to the front raised his hand. "What does local law enforcement know?"

"They've been made aware of the bare bones of the situation, of course, and they're on standby. We're doing our best to keep it out of the media. The only official photo of Knox is ten years old. He went off the grid at the ripe old age of twenty-two. Our best sketch artists have worked to bring that photo up to date. It's been forwarded to your mobile devices and shared with local law enforcement."

There were no other questions.

Allison had the sense that the men and women around her were as eager as she was to hit the streets.

"Assignments are posted in the hall outside this room. You will stay with the partner you've been assigned and keep to the grid we have set up. I hate that I have to repeat this…" She pierced Allison with a very pointed stare. "You will not go off on your own."

Any other time there would have been snickers in the room, but not today. Today everyone in the room understood the stakes. This was not a drill.

Only one person beat Donovan Steele to the assignment board—Allison Quinn. Donovan had never worked directly with Allison Quinn before, though he'd known her for a few years. She was focused, intense, and competent. Okay, more than competent. She was quickly becoming a damn legend.

As she found her name next to his on the board, a groan escaped her lips.

"Could be worse," Donovan said in a low voice. "You could have been paired up with Peyton Schultz."

Peyton was a cowboy with a deep, southern drawl and a fondness for chewing tobacco. That and his tendency to stream George Jones music on the radio made him a less than ideal partner.

Allison sighed heavily, then turned to scowl at him. "Let's go. You're driving."

"Supplies first." He tossed her a grin which she did not return.

Unlike most female agents, Allison Quinn didn't try to hide her femininity. Her hair was a mess of brown curls that reminded Donovan of the chocolate icing his mother put on every birthday cake. Quinn was thin, muscular, all business. She was also completely unapproachable.

They were the first in line for supplies. Both had service weapons on their hips. Donovan accepted the rifle case. Allison accepted the two snow suits, and they each were issued a bullet-proof vest.

When they reached the Range Rover Donovan had requisitioned, they threw all of the gear in the back except for their personal handguns.

Donovan buckled up, but before he started the engine he asked, "What are you carrying?"

"A Glock. You?"

"Sig."

"And that rifle?"

"The Bureau issues the H-S Precision PLR."

"With a thermal scope?"

"Universal Night Sight."

"Then we're good to go."

"You've got the map."

They were assigned the ferry crossing to Bainbridge Island, then the area north and northwest of Seattle, ending at Hurricane Ridge atop Olympic National Park.

Since it was half past ten on a Friday morning, the morning rush hour traffic had abated somewhat, and the queue for the Bainbridge Island ferry was short. As they waited for the 11:25, Donovan attempted to engage her in conversation with no luck. Finally, he settled for sipping vending machine coffee and studying the light snowfall that obscured the view of Elliott Bay.

Once the ferry ride was underway they questioned employees

and passengers, showing them Worm's photo on their mobile. No one had seen him.

They had disembarked the ferry and were on the 305 before she spoke. "I'd rather be downtown."

"Why's that?"

"Because it's the most likely place to find Worm."

"Maybe. Maybe not."

Now she turned to study him. "You're kidding, right? I'm being penalized for going off on my own in Memphis..."

"Maybe, but you caught the guy."

She didn't answer that.

The snowfall was increasing, so Donovan focused on the road. A few minutes later, they pulled into the parking area for the Suquamish Clearwater Casino. It was small by casino standards, but the location was great. The expertly landscaped grounds were located on a peninsula situated between State Highway 305 and the Agate Passage. It would be a perfect spot for Worm to deploy an EMP.

Thirty minutes questioning the hotel manager, casino manager, check-in clerks, and valet yielded nothing.

They grabbed a sandwich to go, jogged back out to the Range Rover, and sat in the vehicle eating their lunch. Donovan reviewed the weather updates while Allison studied the map.

Ten minutes later they were on the road again. The 305 skirted the peninsula and then merged onto WA-3N. A sign indicated that Bangor Trident Naval Base lay in the opposite direction.

Allison jerked a thumb back toward the base. "A naval base must be like catnip to this guy."

"I'm sure they have their own people on it. Plus, it's not easy to get onto a naval base with forged papers."

"Yeah, but he doesn't have to be on the base, does he?"

"Nope. He only needs to be close." Donovan shifted in his seat. He'd had this conversation a dozen times with other task force people. He was interested to hear Quinn's opinion on it. She tended to analyze situations on a completely different level. "How do you think he'll do it?"

"Drone."

"Most people don't believe they have an EMP device that's small enough for a commercial drone, and a military drone... well, it's doubtful Worm has one of those."

"If you and I can imagine it, they've already developed it."

"Whoa. That's a negative take if I ever heard one. Maybe we should just join the survivalists in their bunkers."

Which at least earned him a smile—and also a hand gesture that was less than polite.

"It's what they do, Donovan." She glanced at him, then returned her attention to the road, as if she'd spot Worm traveling on the highway next to them.

"Sure. I get it. Technology is what they're good at."

"It's more than their bread and butter though. It's literally the one thing they live for." She paused, then pushed on. "I assume you played football in college."

"Ouch. It's that obvious?"

"On game day, what did you think about?"

"Winning."

"Exactly. You weren't thinking about who you might take out on a date the next day or what assignments you'd missed the week before."

"I didn't miss any assignments."

"Your single focus was to win, and that's how cyberpunks operate. They don't have any other interests. They don't live a balanced life. The one reason they exist is to bring down the grid for financial gain or to stop Big Brother or for the simple fun of it. The *why* doesn't matter."

"All right. They're focused. So are we."

They didn't speak again until they were on the other side of the Hood Canal Floating Bridge. The snowfall remained steady, visibility continued to drop, and Donovan could feel the wind pushing against the Range Rover.

Allison crossed her arms and glared out the window. "I heard an interview with one of the social media giants. He said that when you're sitting down at a computer, maybe scrolling social media or whatever, that it's you against massive computers all capable of Artificial Intelligence. His take was that you can't hope to win against AI. It's simply not possible. You're just one guy."

"Yeah, but I've got you for a partner, Quinn. I'd say our odds are at least fifty-fifty."

Which again brought the ghost of a smile, but nothing more. Donovan was of two minds. They were either getting close, or they were on a wild goose chase. Either way, once they reached Hurricane Ridge, they would run out of road.

Olympic National Park was over nine hundred thousand acres with six main entrances and scores of access points. They approached the entrance via Port Angeles, the largest city in Clallam County...though the word *city* was being used loosely in this case. To Allison, it looked more like a small town.

Donovan pulled into the parking area of the visitor center.

Allison was unbuckling her seatbelt before the vehicle had come to a full stop. "I'll go in."

"Want me to go with you?"

"Can't be more than three employees in there. I think I can handle it."

"Fine." He held up both hands in surrender. "Just don't ditch me by escaping out the back."

"And go where? Hiking through the snow?"

"Hell, Quinn. For all I know you could have hired an Uber driver and told him to meet you behind the building."

She didn't want to smile at Donovan Steele, but she couldn't help it. "I'm desperate to get rid of you, but not that desperate. Just check the comms, okay? Maybe someone has seen something. Maybe we'll get pulled out of this deserted sector."

She slammed the door, pulled up the hood on her parka, and jogged inside.

Five minutes later, she hopped back into the Range Rover, using both hands to pull the door shut against the howl and the force and the savageness of the north wind.

"Road's closed."

"Yeah?" Donovan Steele didn't sound convinced.

"Heavy snow, blowing winds, plummeting temperatures." She waved outside the window. "I'm sure you've noticed."

"Sounds like we hit the jackpot."

Since their assignment included Hurricane Ridge Road, the fact that it was closed was only a technicality. He wiggled his cell phone back and forth. "Weather forecast says this will only get worse. What do you want to do?"

Allison glanced over at Donovan, who was peering through the windshield and down the road. "You requisitioned the Range Rover. Might as well put it to use."

Donovan grunted and turned the heater up another notch.

She held back the anger and fear and desperation that were threatening to choke her. She never could abide a terrorist's fascination with mass destruction. She abhorred violence. She'd been the victim of violence, and yet here she was...a gun on her hip and a rifle within arm's reach.

She kept her voice even, calm. "Do you think the video Worm sent was legitimate?"

"Yup."

A cyberpunk in a hoodie. The arrogance and gall of these people never ceased to amaze Allison. Now Worm was brazenly declaring his intentions, and she didn't doubt for a moment that he'd purposely let them intercept his location.

Why?

What could he gain from that?

Notoriety? Or was he trying to distract them while one of his cohorts led the real attack somewhere else?

It didn't seem to make any difference how long she worked on the cyber task force, the sheer level of destruction these people aimed for was difficult to contemplate.

"You think he'll actually do it? Explode an EMP over the Seattle area during the five o'clock rush hour?"

"He wants the biggest bang for his buck." Donovan hadn't slipped the Range Rover into gear.

They sat in the parking lot as the storm bore down on them. They didn't rush. It made no sense to run off in a half-cocked reaction to the threat. Instead, they methodically and thoroughly considered the situation. She appreciated that about him. At least he was patient. That was rare in a partner.

"The collision rate alone is predicted to kill hundreds." And now a little of the fear did creep into her voice. Not for herself. She'd passed that point long ago. But her fear for the average citizen sometimes seemed to weigh her down to the point that she felt as if she'd be frozen into an immobile lump of clay. If she wasn't very careful, the terror would consume her.

They'd both seen the slideshows.

Sat through the briefings.

Understood the casualty numbers.

The great majority of the people they protected had no idea what might happen if the task force failed in their mission. But Allison had an idea. Allison had the nightmares to prove it. It was imperative that they find and stop Worm.

An EMP would render all traffic signals useless, deactivate a good percentage of the cars, create havoc with the trains, planes, and metro-buses. Cell phones wouldn't be able to connect to cell towers. Most would be fried at the moment of detonation. Anything dependent on the internet would stop working, and that was nearly everything at this point.

"Nothing on the news," Steele said. "Looks like Thomas managed to keep a lid on it for now."

"I'm always a bit conflicted about that. On the one hand..."

"A panicked populace is bad."

"And on the other..."

"They deserve to know."

"I agree, but then we're not the ones making decisions."

"Give us a few years." Steele once again offered the wolfish smile.

Allison had hoped that Worm was trying to rattle them.

She'd hoped he didn't have the capability to do what he'd threatened to do. But Thomas had claimed they'd received proof that obliterated those hopes. Worm had the ability and apparently the intention to do exactly what he said.

"Worm must be feeling good about himself," Donovan said as he shifted the gear into drive and drove out of the parking area. "He recently graduated to the FBI's list of top ten most wanted cybercriminals."

"So we'll give him a t-shirt, after we put him behind bars."

"How do you think he'll do it?" Donovan was as experienced as she was. He'd read the same memos she had, been briefed on the latest advances in cyberwarfare. The problem was that by the time they were briefed on an attack strategy it had changed. "You said before that you think they've improved the technology, but do you actually think he'll use a drone? Why not a rocket launcher? Or maybe he'll hire a helicopter, sit in the back with his laptop, push the button."

"Hard to drive around with a rocket launcher in your vehicle. As for the helicopter, it might crash when he detonates the EMP. He wouldn't risk that." She didn't understand why she was so certain, but she was. "He'll use a drone."

"Maybe he stole a military one."

"You know as well as I do that anything is for sale on the dark web, as long as you're willing to pay. An EMP-equipped drone and a laptop. That's all he needs."

"Yup." Donovan pulled up to the guard house and motioned for the man on duty to raise the mechanical arm that stretched across the road.

The ranger opened the window. "Sorry, sir. This road is closed."

"We need through. Now." Donovan flashed his credentials.

The ranger shrugged and pushed a button that raised the gate.

Donovan drove through and glanced at Allison. "Could the park director even tell you if anyone was still up there?"

"Negative. They're compiling a list now, but it isn't as easy as you'd think."

"Uh-huh. And this road we're on, what's the elevation gain?"

"Eight hundred and sixty feet."

"Distance to the top?"

"Seventeen miles."

He glanced at her, offered a crooked smile. "Rabbit, rabbit. Here we come."

She didn't respond. Everything about Donovan grated on her nerves, and he seemed to know it. He was too casual. Too confident. Not rattled. She thought you needed to be a little rattled if you were going to face this type of attack and survive.

The area they drove through struck her as a deserted winter wonderland.

They didn't pass anyone else. The road twisted and turned as they gained elevation. The sheer drop reminded Allison of the day her father was murdered, but she pushed that thought away. She was no longer a child. She was an experienced agent, and Worm was an asshole who would not escape.

Her plan was to find him, stop the impending attack, and then question him about the murder of her father. He might know nothing, but suppose he did? It was always a possibility. The world of cybercrime was a small one, and her father had been killed by a cybercriminal. She was certain of that.

If Worm knew anything, he would tell her before she turned him over to the federal authorities. How she was going to pull answers from him with Donovan looking over her shoulder was another question entirely, but she'd deal with that problem when it was in front of her.

She'd deal with that problem as she did every other obstacle she'd faced—directly, without hesitation, and regardless the personal cost.

———

"You're kinda small for an agent. I'm guessing five foot, five, and one twenty-five?"

She didn't even bother looking at him. "I'm big enough to shoot you."

"And all that attitude. I've heard about you, Quinn."

"Okay."

"Heard that when you're on the trail of a cyberpunk you're like a bird dog on scent."

Now she did pull her eyes from the winding road. "I find that comparison mildly offensive."

"I also heard that you have some sort of personal score to settle."

She didn't even bother denying it. He almost laughed. She was smart, tough, and pretty. He'd nailed her height and weight, and he hadn't dared to bring up her curves. That would earn him a slap on the wrist from the higher-ups and a day in sensitivity training.

It was her eyes, though, that could mesmerize a man—dark and deep and soulful.

He'd do well to stay clear of her. Get through this op, kill or capture Worm, move on. Donovan had a career plan, and it didn't leave much time for romantic liaisons.

He nearly snorted at that thought.

Quinn wasn't known to date co-workers. The phrase he'd most frequently heard to describe her was *hard-ass*.

Kudos to the man who had the courage to ask her out.

She had returned her attention to something outside the window. The snow continued to fall, but it didn't yet obscure their path. It would. He'd checked the weather forecast while she'd been inside the director's office. Plus, he could feel it in his bones. Donovan had grown up in upstate New York.

He understood cold weather.

This storm was going to be the real deal.

Snow, high winds, plummeting temperatures...those things could be an obstacle. Or maybe, maybe they could use them to their advantage. Hard to hide a track in the snow. Hard to disappear without a trace.

Donovan picked up on the fact that Quinn wasn't interested in conversation. He pushed on anyway. Maybe because he needed to, or maybe just to gauge her reaction.

Know your enemy.

Know your partner even better.

It was something they hammered home in the Bureau. Of course, Quinn not being with the Bureau, she might not be on that same page.

"I heard about your dad too. That had to have been tough."

"Don't want your sympathy."

"I get that. Still wanted to offer it though—us being partners and all."

"Temporarily."

"Well, yeah. Unless you get lucky and get assigned to me permanently."

"You're a piece of work. You know that, right?"

"Thanks."

"Not a compliment."

But he thought he saw the ghost of her smile again. Or it could have been indigestion from the lunch they'd consumed in under ten minutes.

They finally pulled into the Hurricane Ridge Visitor Center parking area, and Quinn practically leapt from the vehicle. Donovan stood next to the vehicle taking in the deserted lot. Worm didn't walk up here. He didn't sprout wings and fly. He wasn't dropped through a cyber portal.

The guy would have a vehicle.

Donovan jogged to catch up with Quinn, then followed her around the main building. The Visitor Center was a large structure. It was also devoid of life, other than the two of them.

"Locked up tight." He rattled the door, then cupped his hands to knock off the glare and peer into the main room.

"I doubt Worm's in there," she said.

"Could be though."

"You think?"

"He could be hiding out in the boy's room, sitting on the floor with his little laptop, cackling with glee as he contemplates his power to shut down the northwestern sector of the country."

"Thanks for painting such a detailed picture, Steele."

"Anytime, Quinn. Anytime."

They walked a circuit around the outbuildings and saw nothing.

"We didn't pass him." She stood there, hands on her slim hips, turning in a circle, ignoring the snow and wind and danger. "Maybe he's not here."

"Yeah, but I think he is."

"How do you figure that?"

"I think that signal we intercepted was something he wanted us to see. He enjoys the attention. Likes the thought of us all running around trying to find him. Likes being on top."

Quinn nodded toward the mountain range. "Lots of different places to be on top here."

"Not many roads though. This spot is perfect. The higher the elevation the greater the range of destruction."

"So you did pay attention in cyber class."

"I always pay attention."

She finally looked at him, really looked at him, and Donovan realized that was the thing they had in common—they both paid attention. Nothing slipped by Allison Quinn. He could count on that.

"Why didn't he just walk out on the deck of the Needle, release his drone from there? Send it up and hit the button."

"I don't know. You can ask him when we apprehend him."

The parking area was large. Looked like it could have held a couple hundred vehicles. Donovan figured that any other time of year, this was a popular tourist spot. Today it was deserted, the blacktop covered with a fine layer of snow. The wind was blowing so hard they had to lean into it to make their way back across the parking area. They climbed into the vehicle. He started the motor. Once again slipped the gear into drive.

"What did your father do, for a living I mean?"

"Worked for the Agency."

He was surprised she'd answered him. "Yeah?"

"Cybercrimes."

"Huh."

"Wasn't even a division then, just some guys in the basement with a few mainframe computers and no budget."

"Got him killed though."

"It did." Her voice was flat and factual and fierce in its ability to be those things.

He'd continued inching the vehicle around the perimeter of the parking area until he'd joined back up with their earlier tracks in the snow.

"My daddy was a math professor, but on the weekends, he liked to hunt." Donovan pulled to the right of the deserted road and parked. "Got him."

Donovan hopped out of the vehicle, walked to an adjacent road Allison had dismissed as being inaccessible and crouched down to study something in the snow. Standing, he waved her over toward the gravel road and a sign that read, "Obstruction Point Road. 8 miles. Road not suitable for trailers or motorhomes."

Allison spotted what he'd seen immediately, though how he'd seen it from the Range Rover was beyond her, since it was already nearly obscured by the falling snow. "Tire tracks."

"Yup. Rabbit, rabbit, here we come."

"Where is this guy going?"

They jogged back to the Range Rover. Allison buckled her seat belt, made sure it fit snuggly around her torso and lap, then reached for the safety bar above her window.

Donovan took off a little faster than she would have liked, but then they were chasing a cyberterrorist bent on widespread destruction that could result in the death of thousands. She understood the urgency of their situation. She just wished he would drive a little more carefully.

"Wouldn't mind you slowing down on the hairpin turns."

"What? You don't like travelling down a winding mountain road in a snow storm as we chase a terrorist?"

"What's not to like?" She gritted her teeth and focused on her breathing.

"Atta girl."

"It would help if you were a little less patronizing."

Donovan tapped the brakes as they slid around another curve, downshifted, and checked that he'd engaged the four-wheel drive. "I was aiming for encouraging."

"Couldn't tell."

They rode another mile in silence. One moment, towering trees rose above them on both sides. Then they'd slide around a corner and there would be a sheer drop that the tires of the Range Rover seemed to kiss. Allison wanted to put her head between her knees.

She worried it would make her look weak.

She knew it would.

She was a Homeland Security Agent who was afraid of heights. Not just afraid of them. She'd suffered from acrophobia all of her life. It was something that she managed. Something that she'd spent many hours in counseling to learn to cope with. She no longer actively avoided such situations, but driving on a winding mountain road in a snowstorm still set her teeth on edge.

The trick was to focus on the mission at hand, which meant talking to Donovan.

It was only marginally better than throwing up.

"Why down this road? Why not just set up in the parking lot back there?"

"He hopes we're coming. The chase gives him a little thrill. Plus, this is secluded."

"As was the parking lot at the Visitor Center. He didn't have to go down a gravel road to the middle of nowhere."

"Maybe he liked the symmetry of it." When she didn't answer he added, "Obstruction Point...world's most sophisticated EMP...the snowstorm was just an added bonus."

"What's his escape plan?"

They skidded around another hairpin turn, throwing up a cloud of snow. She closed her eyes. Focused on breathing in and out.

"Once he activates the EMP, he'll ditch the computer...maybe bury it in the snow. With all comms out and GPS down, we won't have the capability to track him. He can wait for the storm to pass, then hike or drive out. Maybe he considers himself a Houdini."

"I think it's more than that."

"There needs to be more?"

"His dad was a Boy Scout leader."

"Seriously?"

"Yeah. Didn't you read the file?"

"I don't think that was in the file, Quinn."

Maybe it wasn't. She always did a little extra research on her own, and she kept dossiers on top cyber criminals. She traced their history back to see if it intersected with her father's. The small details she learned about them were an added bonus. They showed her what buttons to push in order to get the information she needed. "Our boy Worm was your typical childhood tech genius."

"So, daddy tried to balance out his life with Boy Scout trips."

"Exactly. Only Worm wasn't having it. At Philmont he started a fire that landed him in juvie."

"I did read the juvie part."

He slammed on the brakes and slowly backed up.

Allison had thought travelling down a gravel mountain road in a snowstorm going forward was bad. Moving in reverse was exponentially worse.

But she'd also seen the truck.

The question was whether anyone in the truck had seen them.

It had to be Worm's. No one else would be here in this weather.

"Did you see if he was in the vehicle?"

"Nope." He'd backed up a couple hundred feet.

"We didn't exactly creep up on him."

"The snow and wind might have silenced our approach."

"If he wasn't in the truck, where is he?"

"We're about to find out."

———

They stood at the back of the Range Rover. Donovan held the rifle with a thermal scope. Allison had her Glock with two extra clips of ammunition. They both wore bullet proof vests under their snow camouflage and communication pieces in their ears. They'd tried to call their status into the Ops Center, but their phones and radios didn't work. That could have been due to their location or the weather or it might have been something that Worm had already done.

Donovan was all business now, the cocky smile finally gone. "Ready?"

"Yes."

"Stick with the plan."

"For as long as we can."

She knew her adrenaline was surging because she was no longer irritated with him. She also was no longer worried about falling off the mountain. "Just don't kill him. I have some questions."

"Uh-huh. I've heard about your Q&A time." He checked his weapon and peered around the Range Rover. "You're famous, Quinn. I thought you knew that."

And then he was gone, climbing up the mountainside, before working his way back toward Worm's truck.

She waited, per the plan.

The wait felt interminable. Her mind slipped back to her father. They'd been camping in northern California, camping on a ridge not so unlike this one though there had been no snow. It had been a dazzling fall day.

He told her to run.

He told her to hide.

She ran, but not far.

In her nightmares, she still heard the shot that killed him. Nightmare didn't begin to cover it. She'd wake shaking, sweating, reliving the worst day of her life.

Her radio crackled, jerking her back into the present.

"I'm in position. No sign of him."

How was that possible? Where could he have gone? They were on a remote road in a snowstorm. There was nowhere to go that she knew of. But maybe Worm knew something they didn't.

"Moving."

Per the plan, she dropped below the ridge to the right, following a parallel path toward the truck. It might have been an animal trail, or it might have been nothing. With each footstep she expected the snow to give away and her body to begin its final plumet.

She didn't exactly fear death.

She'd been aware of it since she was nine years old. That didn't mean she wanted to end her life this day, in this way, because of a prick named Worm.

When she was certain she had drawn up relatively parallel to the abandoned truck, she tapped her comm unit. "I'm in position."

"Still no Worm in sight."

Allison peeked over the edge of the road. She'd come out a little past the truck. It looked like a Chevy S-10 with a faded paint job and nearly bald tires. He'd driven down the mountain in that? She was even more convinced that the man was an idiot.

Allison climbed up, approached the vehicle in a crouch, and confirmed that it was abandoned. She circled the truck again, more slowly this time, and found the tracks. "He's headed northeast."

"On foot?"

"On foot."

Donovan was at her side within two minutes. "Why would he walk away from the truck?"

"I suppose the *why* is less important than the fact of it."

"We don't have to follow him. We could wait here. He's bound to come back."

"True, but that might be after he pushes the button."

"Fair enough." Steele jogged back to the Range Rover, pulled out two white packs, and brought them back.

After they'd both shrugged their arms through the straps, they set off following the tracks which led at first through a stand of trees, then around a bend and finally down what might have been a side trail. The snow wasn't deep—yet. An hour later, they followed the tracks into the middle of a clearing where they abruptly ended.

They inexplicably ended.

"Anything in your independent research that suggested he was a mountain goat or possibly a crow?"

"No. And something isn't right here."

"I'm pretty sure he's jerking our chain, and I gotta tell you...it pisses me off."

The first shot shattered the silence.

Allison and Donovan dropped to the ground. Worm couldn't

see them as long as they stayed down and stayed still. It was why they wore white snowsuits. At the same time, they couldn't just lie there. The whole point of being in this ridiculous position was to apprehend Worm and stop the attack.

"Unless he has a thermal scope, we're good," Donovan said.

"If he had a thermal scope, we'd already be dead."

The snow howled. The wind roared. Moving her eyes to the side, Allison could barely see Donovan, and he was only three feet from her position.

"Shots came from that stand of trees," he said. "To the west."

"I'm going to cross this meadow on three. Draw his fire. One—"

"No. You're not."

"Get closer while he's tracking me. Two—"

"Quinn. Don't—"

"Three." Allison focused on speed and direction away from Donovan. She sprinted for three seconds...three strong heartbeats, then dropped again.

A shot rang out, close enough to send a plume of snow over her.

"Run, Alli. Hide." It was her father's voice in her ear.

Her father's killer threatening her life.

She rose again, nearly slipped on the snow, sprinted for three more seconds, dropped into a prone position.

He couldn't see her.

If she kept her head down, he couldn't see her.

With her face pressed into the snow, she held her breath. Counted to five this time. Sprinted. She threw her body laterally, hit the snow as the bullet ripped through her left shoulder, lay completely still.

She needed to lay completely still or he would shoot her again. Shoot and kill her.

"Run, Alli. Hide."

Her heart thumped.

Sweat dripped down her face.

She thought she should feel the pain from the bullet. Was it good or bad that she didn't? Adrenaline? Frozen? In shock maybe?

More importantly, had she given Donovan enough time?

She heard the sound of a rifle shot, a different sound from the bullets that had been aimed at her. Donovan's rifle. That had been Donovan's rifle. She didn't know whether to sit up or lay there. She couldn't simply lay there. She turned her head, saw the blood from her wound staining the snow, knew that if Worm was still alive, if he was still watching, he would see the blood too, and then he would finish her.

Donovan confirmed the kill, took two photos to run through the Bureau's database once they had reception again, then sprinted down to Allison. She was lying perfectly still.

Too still.

He dropped next to her in the snow.

"Did you get him?" She lifted her head, groaned as he assessed her arm.

"I got someone, but it wasn't Justin Knox."

She looked confused for a moment, then she looked mad. Sitting up, she scanned the area. "Damn it. Would it have been too much to ask that he was working alone? All of our intelligence points to cybercriminals being loners."

"Yeah, well you know what they say about intelligence."

"Information is not knowledge."

"I don't know who said that or what it means." Donovan had unzipped his pack and pulled out the medical kit.

"Einstein. It means..." Allison wobbled slightly.

"Doesn't matter." He unzipped her suit and worked it off her shoulders, then tore open a package of clotting powder and poured it on the wound.

She let out a hiss, but he didn't slow or waver. The first few

25

minutes after a gunshot wound were critical. He couldn't afford to hesitate. "You're body temperature is dropping and you've lost a significant amount of blood. Hold this compress."

She nodded once, and then with a shaky right hand, she held the compress against the wound. Her complexion was as white as the snow. Her gaze was locked on some distant point.

Donovan ripped open a package of gauze and wrapped it up and around her shoulder. He had some idea how much pain she was in. He'd suffered a few shoulder injuries in college football. They weren't for the faint of heart.

"Don't pass out on me, Quinn."

"And let you get the glory alone? Not going to happen."

"Atta girl." He pulled the snowsuit back up, helped her push her right arm into the sleeve. "This is going to—"

"Hurt. Yeah."

He stuffed her left arm back into the suit as quickly as possible, heard again the hiss of pain that escaped through her lips. He yanked up on the zipper, trying to calculate how much blood she'd lost, how low her body temperature was, what his next move should be. Finally he took another package of gauze and wrapped the outside of the suit where the fabric was marked with blood. "Wouldn't want you walking around like a target."

"Gee. Thanks."

He tried the SAT phone one more time. Still nothing. Pushing all of the supplies back into his bag, he pulled Allison to her feet. "Can you walk?"

"No way I'm staying here. Yes, I can walk."

"You remind me of my momma—feisty."

She shook her head as if she'd been insulted but offered a shaky smile.

By the time they'd made it back to the Range Rover, his watch read two minutes before four—one hour until detonation. Worm's truck remained parked a few hundred feet in front of the Range Rover. It wasn't as if he could take it anywhere. The only way out was backwards, which would've required pushing the

Range Rover over the edge. The small truck didn't have the engine for that.

Donovan helped her into the passenger seat, then ran around to the driver's side. That's when they discovered that Justin's talents weren't limited to disabling networks. He was also pretty good at disabling cars.

The engine didn't start.

Donovan popped the hood to discover the battery cables were cut. He checked Worm's truck and saw that he'd slashed the tires.

"What kind of asshole disables his own vehicle?"

"An arrogant one—the only kind we seem to go up against."

She was shaking again, her teeth chattering together.

"It's the shock," he said, pulling her toward him.

She stiffened. It was rather like holding an ironing board.

"We have to get your body temperature up," he murmured.

Allison nodded, but it still took several moments before she relaxed.

"Try the SAT phone again."

"Right." He pulled it out of his pack. The green light came on, but that was it. No service. Not even static.

"Fifty minutes." Allison had stopped shivering. Now she leaned forward and began rifling through her pack with her right hand.

"What are you doing?"

"Pulling out what I need."

"You're not going anywhere. You know that, right?"

For an answer, she only gave a quick shake of her head.

"You are one damn stubborn woman. Hard-headed, impossible to reason with—"

"Thank you."

"Not a compliment."

She stopped then, her Glock in her good hand, her eyes meeting his. "We have forty-eight minutes to stop him. Now let's go."

Following Worm's trail wasn't difficult. This time he hadn't bothered to cover his tracks. Even with the amount of snow that had fallen, Donovan could tell he'd passed this way recently. The indentions of his footsteps—in Donovan's mind—shone bright as a neon light.

He might as well have left bread crumbs for them to follow.

The question was why.

Maybe he realized he was running out of time. Worm's mission clock was ticking. He wanted to push the button at rush hour. Or it could be that he had miscalculated, figuring that with one agent injured they would both stand down.

They weren't standing down.

Donovan had a feeling that giving up was something Allison Quinn never considered.

———

Allison had never been shot before. The degree of pain was excruciating—easily a fifteen on a ten-point scale. Instead of making her want to curl into a ball, it fueled her anger. She would stop Justin Knox before he had a chance to endanger and maim and kill.

She'd stop him or she'd die trying.

She wasn't a fatalist.

She rather enjoyed her life. And then there was the matter of finding her father's killer. That had been her catalyst through many a dark night.

But just as equally, many years ago she'd simply accepted that dying might be required. It was either that or drive herself crazy with the fear of the thing. That was no way to move forward.

As they walked back toward the visitor's center, the trail had widened a bit and the ground to their right rose steadily until it towered over their position. When Worm's trail petered out, Donovan pointed up.

Allison didn't see it immediately, then she understood what Donovan was pointing at. Broken branches every few feet as

Worm pulled himself up, up, up to the top. There was no way Allison could pull herself up that ridge, not with one arm, and both she and Donovan knew it.

Donovan pointed in front of them, made a motion for her to go that way, where there must be a more gradual slope, then work her way back.

She didn't like it.

She didn't really have a choice.

Donovan gave her that wolfish smile she was becoming used to, then he began to climb. Allison moved forward as quickly as possible, keeping close to the rise on her right, not wanting Worm to catch a glimpse of her if he happened to peer over the edge. She walked a quarter mile, before she found a more gradual way up. She followed it to the top and then reversed direction.

Donovan should be in position.

Approaching Worm from two different directions wasn't a bad idea, though they would be in each other's line of fire. She thought one gunshot wound for the day was quite enough and hoped that Donovan wouldn't shoot her.

Worm wasn't armed that she knew of. She'd read nothing of a history with fire arms in his file. Many cybercriminals avoided getting their hands dirty. They preferred crime in the virtual world. Intel was rarely complete though. It was more like looking at a thing through a kaleidoscope. The truth was there, but it was distorted.

When she reached the top, she stopped a good three feet back in the trees.

Even wearing camouflage, there was a risk he would sense her presence. She had no problem seeing him.

Worm sat on a fallen tree. He must have scouted the area on a previous trip because it was the perfect spot to launch a drone from. On three sides, forest rimmed the clearing, which was fifty yards across and probably twice as deep. In front of him was an unobstructed flight path, probably all the way to downtown Seattle. As she watched from her position in the trees, he tested the drone. It rose a few feet, then hovered. He stared down at his laptop, and a smile spread across his face.

He liked what he was seeing.

He liked what he was about to do.

He smelled success in the air.

She moved through the trees as silently as the snow fell from the sky. When she was directly behind him, she positioned her body in an isosceles stance—feet shoulder-width apart, body squared with the target, arms straight with locked elbows.

"Step away from the laptop, Justin."

His fingers stilled immediately. He raised his hands above the keyboard, as if he was eager to show his compliance. Allison was aware that the drone maintained its position in front of them. Death and destruction and chaos hovered only a few feet away.

"I was hoping Otto took care of you."

"Otto is dead."

"You killed him?"

"My partner."

"I brought friends too—well, acquaintances. Our passion for saving the world from government surveillance sort of binds us together." A rifle shot shattered the silence of the snow and the forest. "That would be Carmen's rifle—I'd know that sound anywhere. A pawn for a pawn. I suspect you're on your own now."

Worm continued to hold his hands a good twelve inches above the keyboard, his fingers flexed out straight.

Allison and Worm both understood that one keystroke would deploy the drone. That same keystroke would end Worm's life. He wasn't ready to die yet. He still thought he could have it all.

"Carmen will come for you next," he said. "And she won't miss."

"Place the laptop down in the snow. Be careful to keep your fingers away from the keys."

She was surprised when he did as she'd instructed. He turned to face her and a small part of her wanted to believe it had all been a mistake. He might have been thirty-two years old, but he looked like a kid. How was it that this slight man with acne on his face and just a whisp of a beard adorning his chin could possibly want to cause such destruction?

Why?

And was he past redemption?

"What happened to you?"

"To me? I'm not the one stalking around in the forest with a gun." He nodded toward her Glock. "How about you put that thing down? It makes me nervous."

"Keep your hands up."

He did.

"Step away from the laptop." She nodded to her left, and he again surprised her by following her instructions.

"Who do you work for?"

"Who do I work for? That's your question?" He shook his head, but kept his hands high. "Maybe I don't work for anyone."

"I rather doubt you have the resources to purchase a military drone."

"You don't know anything about me." His eyes shifted, only slightly—either trying to check his drone, or perhaps...

Was Carmen coming up behind her?

It didn't matter. Allison kept her focus on Worm.

"Who paid for the drone?"

"It's not like we use real names."

She waited, though now she was aware of the pain in her shoulder, the blood pulsing with each heartbeat, the torn flesh and cartilage reminding her that she was not one hundred percent.

"You government people are all the same. You think if you know our date of birth, social security number, IP address, that you can stop us, but we're bigger than that. We're bigger and better than your net that captures information."

"Give me a name, Justin. We can all walk away from this."

"You'll never stop us because you still believe that things

operate IRL. They don't. Virtual reality has surpassed that."

"Save the lecture. I want the name of the person who funded your little enterprise." She had the idea to use his moniker, hoping it would provoke him. "Give me a name, Worm, and you can live to fight another day."

"Don't call me that."

"But it's who you are. Worm. A grub, pinworm, tapeworm..."

"Stop it."

"A self-contained and self-replicating computer program."

"I said, stop it."

"AKA Justin Knox, thirty-two years old, former Boy Scout turned cybercriminal."

She was suddenly aware of the wetness of her shoulder wound. Maybe the blood had seeped through Donovan's wrap because Worm glanced toward her shoulder and smiled slightly.

"That's got to hurt."

Allison was trying to decide whether to handcuff him, how to maintain a bead on the criminal in front of her and disable the drone, where Donovan was, how much longer she could stand there with blood dripping down her sleeve. Those thoughts were careening through her mind when three things happened at once.

Worm reached into his coat pocket.

The drone lifted higher.

And Donovan burst through the tree line.

She'd been trained well. She didn't hesitate. Three shots to the chest, a perfect grouping. She pivoted to her right, toward the drone, aware of Donovan positioning himself on the other side of the clearing. The drone had lifted to a height of twenty feet, accessed its flight directions and moved away—toward the drop off, out of the range of her handgun, toward the mountains and Seattle.

Donovan raised his rifle, calculated height and speed and direction. Then he fired.

The drone shattered into a dozen pieces.

Donovan shouldered the rifle and hurried toward her, ignoring Worm's body, ignoring everything but the woman in front of him.

"What did you do to my bandage, Quinn?"

She shrugged, or rather she tried to. Her left arm had started to tremble and her complexion was as white as the snow.

"Sit."

She shook her head, holstered her weapon and walked over to Worm's body. Kneeling beside it, she stared at the young man's face. His chest was a mess of blood and bone.

"Nice shot," he murmured.

"I thought he was reaching for a gun." With her gloved hand, she opened his right fist.

"Remote detonator."

"He was focused on the laptop when I first came up behind him."

"He would have set direction, speed, deployment commands via the laptop."

She finally met his eyes, then her gaze darted away, studied the pieces of drone that littered the area between them and the drop-off. She took a moment before she looked back at him and nodded once. "You stopped it. Stopped the attack."

"We both did."

"Help me." She unzipped Worm's jacket, checked his neck, his torso, and finally his arms. She found what she was looking for on the inside of his right arm. Pulling out her phone, she snapped a picture of the tattoo.

"We're going to lose the light. Let's go back to the Range Rover."

She shook her head. "We should walk out."

"You wouldn't make it half a mile, Quinn. I know you think you're Superwoman..."

She shot him a look that cut off his words.

He waited a second, then two. He gave her time to evaluate their situation.

Finally she nodded. "Okay."

He took a few pictures of Worm to confirm the kill. The bodies would be retrieved as soon as their team could get through, but he'd had bodies disappear on him before. No sense in leaving it to chance. There were black bears and cougars in the area—though it was rare, if they were hungry enough they'd probably take an easy meal.

"Check his other pockets. I'll document the drone."

"What's left of it."

Which was the first sense of humor Donovan had seen from her since she'd killed Justin Knox. He considered it a good sign.

Ten minutes later they were making their way back toward the vehicle, retracing Quinn's steps because he knew she'd never make it via the shorter, steeper route.

Once she was in the Range Rover, he said, "Back in five."

He moved around Worm's truck, checking it for signs of explosives, boobytraps, motion-sensor cameras. Two of the tires had been slashed. They wouldn't be driving the truck anywhere, but maybe he could at least turn it on. Maybe he could at least get her body temperature up. He raised the hood on the engine. "Damn."

He slammed the hood back down and fought his way back to the Range Rover. The snow and wind had morphed into a blizzard. Visibility was dropping, as was the temperature.

He climbed into the Range Rover and turned to face Quinn.

"Find anything?"

"Nothing useful."

"It wasn't enough that he slashed the tires?"

"Apparently not. He cut his battery cables like he did ours. Which means that he either planned to walk out..."

"Doubtful, since he had no snow shoes."

"Or someone was supposed to meet him."

They both looked out the window. If someone was coming

34

for Worm in this storm, they'd need a snowmobile to get there—something they would hear from miles away.

"Let's rewrap that arm."

It was awkward in the vehicle. There wasn't a lot of room to maneuver. Donovan was suddenly aware of the smell of her hair, the smallness of her, the intensity of her gaze as she watched him rebind the wound. He knew it hurt, but she didn't cry out. Of course she didn't. Even here, with no one else to see, Quinn couldn't bring herself to show any sign of weakness.

Which was how they'd all been trained.

He pawed through the medical kit, trying to find something strong enough to knock back her pain. Finding three syringes, he held one up. "Got some diazepam."

She shook her head—once. Definitively.

He dropped the syringes into the kit and set the kit on the floorboard. She might change her mind before morning.

"Be right back." He attempted a confident smile, but the moment he stepped out of the vehicle the snow and cold enveloped him. They were lucky the full force of the storm had held off as long as it had. He trudged to the back of the Range Rover, opened the cargo area and fumbled around until he found the bag he needed. Then he slammed the hatch shut and fought his way back to the driver's door of the vehicle.

"Honey, I'm home."

"Feels like you just left."

"Does that mean you missed me? I think you missed me." He pulled two bottles of water from the pack, grateful to find they hadn't frozen yet. Uncapping one, he pushed it into her hands. "Drink it all."

"If I drink all of this, I'll be looking for a ladies' room in a snowstorm."

"I'll bet you've roughed it before."

She drank a quarter of the bottle.

Next he pushed an energy bar into her hands.

She didn't even argue.

They sat there as the snow built up around them. The wind howled and the temperature plummeted and he refused to calculate her odds of survival.

He didn't need to.

She was the famous Allison Quinn. She was a rising star at DHS. They'd stopped the terror attack. Tomorrow they'd be sitting around a conference table, drinking coffee, regaling their coworkers with tales of their heroic adventure.

Only, Quinn didn't seem like the kind of person to tell tales.

She was the silent type.

He pulled the emergency blanket out of the first aid kit and tucked it around her. The mylar material was covered with a thin sheet of metalized polyester. "You look like a space creature."

She opened one eye, but this time the smile didn't follow. Instead she fell into a shallow sleep.

He could inject her with the diazepam while she slept. The stuff acted like valium. He knew it would take the edge off the pain. He nixed the idea. She'd find out, then she'd find him and kick his ass. So instead, he rooted around in the emergency kit, found the caffeine tablets, and swallowed two.

It was going to be a long night.

Allison's dreams were filled with terrorists, drones, gunshots, snow, her father. She was occasionally aware of Donovan beside her—insisting she drink more water, pushing food into her hands, offering the diazepam. Twice he had to help her outside and into the trees.

He held her steady as she pulled down the camouflage suit.

Turned his back while she took care of business.

Practically carried her back to the vehicle.

Both times she was asleep before he'd settled into the driver's seat.

When she woke next, her watch said it was past two in the

morning, and she was shivering so hard that her teeth knocked against each other. Donovan climbed out of the vehicle, trudged through the snow to her side, and helped her into the back seat. He walked back around the vehicle, hopped in next to her, pulled her next to him, and wrapped his arms around her.

"I'm not interested in a re...re..."

"Relationship? You should be so lucky." He pulled the mylar blanket more tightly around her.

Slowly she felt his body heat seep into hers. The shivering lessened, then disappeared completely. She stopped fighting it, rested her head against his shoulder, stared at the back of the front seat. Though she felt as if she could sleep for a week, sleep eluded her. She sighed and Donovan pulled her closer.

"Tell me about your dad."

And suddenly that was exactly what she wanted, to share the burden of her history, to describe the scene that so often replayed in her head.

"He was with the agency."

"You said—in the cybercrimes unit."

"Yeah, the criminals were only steps behind the developers."

Donovan's whistle was low and appreciative. "That would have been...what...1980s? 1990s?"

"Late 80s. Early 90s."

"Rumor has it he was killed."

She nodded. She'd spoken of this to no one except her Aunt Polly. "We were camping in northern California."

"You and your mom and dad?"

"No. It was just the two of us. Mom...mom died when I was young—car accident. I was only two. Barely remember her." Except for the scent, the essence of her. Those were things that she clung to. Things she never wanted to forget.

"How old were you...when your dad was killed?"

"Nine." She swallowed against the ache that rose in her throat. How could something that happened so long ago still cause such pain?

"You saw it?" Now his voice was low, gravelly.

"He told me to run, and I did. Maybe if I'd stayed..."

"If you'd stayed, you'd be dead too."

"I didn't go far. Hid behind a tree. Maybe he didn't see me. I'm not sure."

"You're certain it was a him?"

"I heard his voice. Heard him demanding something from my father. Heard my father trying to reason with him, trying to defuse the situation."

"And then?"

"The shot."

Donovan didn't respond immediately, and Allison appreciated that more than anything he might have said.

"Hell of a thing for a child to see. What did you do then?"

"After I was sure that..." She licked her lips, the words, the memories making her throat inexplicably dry. "After I was certain he was dead, I walked out. Found some rangers."

She thought maybe he'd fallen asleep. She was almost glad he didn't say any of the things people say.

I'm sorry.

It's just so sad.

It shouldn't have happened.

She sat there, huddled against him, wondering if this was how her life would end—bleeding out in a blizzard. Not a terrible way to go. There were worse. The pain had become like a third passenger in the car. She stared out the window into a night that was as black as her nightmares. It had been so long since either of them had spoken, that she startled at the sound of his voice.

"I suppose that explains why you are the way you are."

Allison didn't answer that. She didn't know how.

"You're becoming a legend, Quinn. Passionate. Focused. Smart. Relentless." He adjusted the blanket around her. "You're trying to make up for what happened to your dad. It's made you a hell of an agent."

"You're wrong."

"Yeah? What part?"

"I'm not trying to atone for my father's death."

"No? Explain it to me then."

She closed her eyes, breathed in the smell of him, for a moment forgot about the pain. "I'm going to catch his killer." And then she once again dropped into a restless sleep.

Their team came at first light.

A helicopter landed in the clearing where she'd killed Justin Knox. Allison remembered little about the flight, the emergency room, or the doctors. Donovan was waiting in her hospital room when she came out of surgery. He looked rugged, handsome, rested.

"They tell me you're going to make it, Quinn."

"Thanks to you." She wouldn't back away from that truth. Never one to depend on another person, she understood that she would have died in that Range Rover if he hadn't been there.

"Yeah. I guess you owe me." The wolfish smile was back.

"You stayed awake all night?"

"Of course I did. What kind of partner would I be if I fell asleep?"

"What did the team find?"

"Other than the bodies?" Donovan shrugged. "Couple snow mobiles on the other side of the ridge. I suppose that's how they planned to leave."

"And the EMP? Did it take out any part of the grid?"

"Nope. Apparently it only took out our comms. The team was out looking for us in the storm, but the snow had erased our tracks. They found us though—obviously. We're here. You're on the road to recovery. All's good."

"Until the next time."

"Yeah. Until the next time."

She noted the go-bag on the chair next to her bed.

"New assignment?"

"Pittsburgh. Apparently some goon with a laptop has figured out how to hack into the water system. He's demanding twelve million dollars, a private jet, and protected airspace out of the country."

"Is that all?"

He stepped closer to her bed, reached forward, brushed the hair out of her eyes. "You're something else. You know that, Alli?"

She batted away his hand, which only caused his smile to grow until his eyes crinkled into slits. His laughter, when it came, was deep. Beautiful.

"Later."

"Yeah, later."

They released her the next day. She had an Uber driver take her from the hospital to the field office. She didn't have to wait long to be ushered in to see Kendra Thomas.

The woman rose, shook her hand, then motioned toward the chair across from her desk. "Good job out there."

"Thank you."

Thomas studied her for a moment, then steepled her fingers together. "I'm not going to give you another assignment right now. You're on required medical leave for the next month. I've spoken with your director at Homeland. He concurs."

Allison was afraid of that.

She knew that to argue would be futile, but that wasn't really why she'd come to Thomas's office.

"The tattoo?"

"Yeah. The tattoo." Thomas reached for a folder, opened it, pulled out an eight by ten glossy photograph, and pushed it across the desk to Allison.

Branches of a tree. Roots that turned into a sword. Writing in another language circling the top two-thirds of the image.

"The text is Elvish, apparently."

"It's what?"

"Elvish." Thomas didn't laugh exactly, but she clearly found it amusing. "You know—elves, druids, that sort of thing. *Lord of the Rings.*"

"Wow."

"Exactly. Since it's not a real-world language, we can't be entirely sure what it says."

"*Lord of the Rings.*"

"Identical tattoos were found on the other two bodies."

So it wasn't a particular interest of Justin Knox. It was connected to the group.

Which wasn't much to go on. But it was something, and she'd take it. She had a feeling that during her month of medical leave she was going to become very familiar with the works of J.R.R. Tolkien.

"Mind if I snap a picture with my phone?"

"Be my guest."

She thanked Thomas, walked out of the office, accessed her Uber app. The driver would arrive in seven minutes. She stepped out into a crisp, cold Seattle morning. The power grid was intact. The emergency medical system continued to work. Cars and buses and people moved up and down the street, oblivious to what might have happened.

It was a victory of sorts.

One disaster averted.

Tolkien. Elves. Tattoos.

There was nothing to indicate this group was connected to her father or the people who had killed him. But it was all she had to go on, and she wasn't one to back away from a challenge.

Because one way or another, she would find the persons responsible for her father's death. It wasn't a matter of revenge. It was about restoring balance. Setting things right. Moving forward.

She would only do that when they were behind bars.

Or dead.

Support and Defend
AN ALLISON QUINN NOVEL, BOOK 1

Chapter One

Allison Quinn was not, technically, a national park ranger.

Pretending to be one was another matter.

"I can't thank you enough. I could have died back there." The young woman, Shelby Thompson, dropped her gaze to the trail. Her blonde hair hung in front of her face. She was dirty and tired and her left ankle had swollen to the size of a grapefruit, but she'd live.

"You wouldn't have died. Rangers patrol these trails, especially South Kaibab and Bright Angel. Someone else would have found you if I hadn't."

"I guess. Still, it was a stupid thing for me to do. I can see that now."

"A rim-to-rim run is something you train for, Shelby. And you should never—"

"Do it alone. Yeah. Got it."

Allison hoped the lesson stuck. "The Grand Canyon is a place of unparalleled beauty, but it must be—"

"Respected." Now Shelby looked up and smiled. "I'll respect it now. What seems pretty easy with two good ankles, isn't easy at all after you get injured."

Allison had been hiking up from Phantom Ranch when she came across the girl at the 1.5 Mile Resthouse. There was nothing to do but help her out of the canyon. Allison couldn't exactly proclaim her identity as a special agent for the Department of Homeland Security's Cyber Task Force, explain that she was undercover to catch a cyberterrorist, and hike past her.

Nope.

She had to do the rangerly thing.

Which meant she would be arriving up top later than she'd hoped.

"I guess you've hiked the canyon a lot, since you work here."

"At least once a week." Thirty-five years old, five foot, six inches, and one hundred thirty pounds, Allison was probably in the best physical condition of her life.

"And you live at Phantom Ranch?"

"There's lodging for workers at the bottom. On days off, we head up top or go off site."

"I tried to get a reservation at the ranch, but they were filled up."

"It's a popular destination."

"Which is when I got the idea to do a rim-to-rim. I wasn't going to do it alone, but my boyfriend dumped me. I guess I was feeling like I needed to prove I could do it without him."

"Maybe next time join a hiking group."

Phantom Ranch sat at the bottom of the Grand Canyon. Reservations were always filled a year in advance. Fortunately for Allison, she didn't need a reservation. She'd been undercover there as a seasonal park ranger for the past six months. Unfortunately, she wasn't even one step closer to catching the terrorist known as Blitz.

She would catch him though.

They had solid intel that he would make an exchange in the canyon, and she planned to be there when he did. As she helped Shelby through the lower tunnel, her thoughts turned to the two days she'd spend up top. She was looking forward to a long, hot shower, a meal, and ten hours sleep—preferably in that order.

When they approached the upper tunnel, both women paused and turned to study the view. The Grand Canyon never failed to inspire—a chasm 277 miles long, 18 miles wide, and one mile deep. Considered one of the seven natural wonders of the world, Allison wasn't at all surprised that Blitz would choose it for a terror attack.

Everything about Blitz and the terrorist group they suspected he worked for indicated they enjoyed making a big splash. What single place did Americans feel safest from high-tech terror attacks? A national park. Hell, much of the area within the canyon, you couldn't even get cell service. Shelby had been shocked that her cell phone didn't work. She hadn't read any of the warnings on the website or at the trailheads. She was invincible.

Or she had been before she turned her ankle.

A terror attack? None of the guests at the canyon were thinking about that. What would you end up with but a bunch of rocks in the Colorado River?

Allison understood that cyberwarfare had grown more complicated than bringing down a network and demanding a ransom. Blitz was planning something far worse. Something that would kill thousands.

She helped Shelby across the parking area and to the first aid station.

"Thanks again." Shelby looked rather forlorn sitting on a cot, holding the clipboard of medical paperwork.

Allison expected this was not exactly the celebratory finish she'd envisioned.

"No problem. Take care, Shelby."

Allison walked over to the visitor center and behind the counter. No one questioned her. She did this every week. A few workers nodded hello, but most were busy with tourists. Allison pulled the reservation book toward herself and studied the list of people who had hiked down earlier in the day.

Quite a few males were listed. None were the right description for Blitz. They had ascertained his age, size, build, even ethnicity. The hiking log contained information about each hiker, but none of it matched up. He wasn't in the morning group that had gone down, or the previous day's, or any scheduled group for the upcoming week.

She sighed and returned the book to its shelf.

Next up—a shower, a hot meal, and bed.

She was in bed and asleep moments after the sun slid below the horizon.

Allison was once again nine years old.

Frightened, confused, and—like every time before—helpless.

Her legs trembled, as she pressed her back against the tree. In front of her the pine-covered ground dropped away to beach and ocean, but there was no path, only a precipitous drop.

"Run." Her father had spat that one word in her direction.

So she had run, but not far.

Her breath came out in gasps.

Her heart raced from fear more than exertion. She had stopped where their campsite was still within sight, but she didn't look at it. The towering redwood she'd chosen to hide behind was wider than their jeep. It kept her from seeing, but it didn't prevent her from hearing.

"You shouldn't have tried to stop me."

Bang.

The sound echoed through the old-growth forest. Allison squeezed her eyes shut tight. If she couldn't see the man in the ski mask, he couldn't see her.

Her heart pounded an even faster rhythm.

Sweat dripped down her face as the bark of the tree bit into her hands, her legs, even through the fabric of her Dora the Explorer shirt.

"Run."

"You shouldn't have tried to stop me."

Bang.

The three moments played in an endless loop, until she feared that her heart would literally slam through her chest.

Like every time before, she waited—shivering, terrified, and certain that her father would call out for her, assure her that the man in the ski mask was gone, tell her that she was safe.

Like every time before, that did not happen.

Instead, she heard the chirp of a bird high above her head, calling incessantly, insisting that she look up, that she reveal her hiding place. She inched forward, only enough to tilt her head back and spy the bird.

And that was when he stepped in front of her.

Bang.

———

Allison sat up with a gasp, her hands flying to her night shirt, to her chest.

The dream.

She'd had the dream again.

She swung her legs over the side of the bed and dropped her head between her knees, willing her heart rate to slow. Only then, when she had convinced herself that the terror she felt was unfounded, did she realize the bird from her dream was still chirping.

The bedside clock read twelve minutes after eleven.

She'd been asleep less than two hours. Snatching her cell phone off the stand, she checked the name of the caller and pushed the green button.

"Quinn."

"Parking lot. Five minutes."

Donovan Steele was the last person she wanted to see. They shared a history that she did not have the time or inclination to explore, and she'd managed quite successfully to push him from her thoughts. She did not want to meet Donovan in the dark of the night.

Since they were supposed to be cooperating on this op, she pushed aside those childish thoughts. Pulling on her clothes, Allison holstered her Glock, snatched up her cell phone, and hustled out of her room.

She'd reserved an upstairs room at the end of the hall of the Grand Canyon's Yavapai Lodge. Now she pushed through the door that led out onto a small landing and hurried down the stairs. She should have grabbed a jacket. September nights on the South Rim brought temperatures down to the fifties. A light breeze carried the smell of rain.

She jogged down the walk and toward the parking area. Coming around the corner of the building, she nearly collided with the man that was alternately her friend, arch-nemesis, and partner. Five foot eleven and built like a linebacker, he should have been easy to see, but the blackness of the night melded with the color of his skin, leaving merely the impression of a shadow.

Steele held up his rather large hands to stop her from running into him.

An unprofessional squeal escaped her lips before she managed, "What's happened?"

Steele nodded toward a black SUV parked ten feet away. As they walked toward it, he cast more than one glance her direction. Allison felt him assessing her—rumpled night shirt, hair a short mess of curls, her dark brown eyes blinking rapidly as her mind caught up with what his call must mean.

He didn't speak until they were seated—doors closed, windows up, no chance of anyone eavesdropping.

"The situation has changed."

"How?"

"Blitz hiked down to Phantom Ranch today."

"That's impossible. I looked at the guest list." They didn't know a lot about Blitz, didn't know his real name or have an actual picture of him, but Homeland Security had created a composite description based on intercepted emails from his associates. They'd never hacked Blitz. So far, that didn't seem to be possible.

The profilers had fed every piece of information they had into the mainframe computer, which then created a sketch.

Nearly six feet.

Late 20s.

Wiry build.

Pale complexion with straight black hair.

That was it. That was all they had to go on, but it would be enough. That sketch told Allison that Blitz was too young to be the man who had killed her father, but he might know that man.

Allison shook her head again, forcing her attention to the mission at hand. "There was no one in today's group that matched his age or description. I went over the guest list twice."

For medical reasons, the list of people hiking into the canyon included a basic description, age, and level of fitness. She would have known if Blitz was in the group, no matter what name he used.

Instead of answering, Steele passed her his phone. She scanned through the photos, her anger growing with each swipe of the screen. A rental car on the side of the road—red Subaru Outback. A body behind the car, lying on the ground. A close up of the body.

"Where did this happen?"

"Twenty miles from here. Mr. Harris had a reservation to hike down. When he didn't show—"

"Because someone killed him."

"Blitz was there waiting to fill his spot."

Allison sat back against the leather seat. The scenario was possible. Slots to stay at Phantom Ranch were filled a year in advance, but when a person didn't show, someone else waiting at the visitor's center could take their place.

Those occurrences were rare, but they did happen.

They didn't always get logged in.

She should have thought of that.

"You couldn't have thought of that, and you couldn't have hiked down with every group." Steele held out his hand, waited for her to drop the phone in his palm. "You're not superwoman."

She studied Steele by the light of the phone he dropped into the console's cup holder. His hair was buzzed, as usual. He somehow managed to look like a fitness freak despite their hours on the job—him with the FBI, her with Homeland Security. Tonight, his face seemed taut. As for his dark brown eyes, they contained the worries of a nation.

Steele didn't glance away. He didn't have to hide his concern or his frustration. He didn't have to voice those things either. They both knew what was at stake. They both knew how much the success of this operation mattered.

He passed her the phone again, this time after opening a document stamped CLASSIFIED. As she scanned it, he caught her up on what had happened in the last week.

"We're looking at a Catastrophic Systems Failure in thirty-six hours and . . ." He glanced at his wristwatch. "Twenty-three minutes."

"Noon Friday."

"Basically."

"You've confirmed it will affect systems coast to coast?"

"As well as Canada. We've deployed all of our teams. There are a dozen places those kill codes could be, but one of our teams will intercept them before noon Friday."

"And Blitz?"

Steele clenched his left hand into a fist—the first sign of emotion she'd seen from him since getting into the car. "Honestly, I don't know. He could have the kill codes. He could be a decoy.

We'll proceed as if we are certain he has them, which is the same thing I'm telling every other team."

"Am I doing this alone?" She didn't mind working alone. Sometimes she rather preferred it.

"I have additional agents flying in. They'll position on the North Rim."

"An FBI team?"

"Yes, Quinn. The FBI is who I work for."

"And I'd rather have Homeland Security agents backing me up."

"We're pooling our resources, remember?" He dismissed her concerns with a wave. "I'll coordinate all teams from a secure location. Once we confirm who has the codes, we'll refocus our assets there."

It was unlikely they'd make that confirmation and still have time to move around personnel, and they both knew it.

"More details will be sent to your cell, but I need you down at Phantom Ranch. I assume you'll want to take a local on the hike down with you."

"Never hike alone." She'd been on enough rescues in the last six months to know that wasn't simply a slogan. There were a dozen different ways you could die hiking into the canyon.

"Once you confirm Blitz is there, wait until he's received the cancellation codes before taking action. If possible, and if time allows, I'd prefer you hold off his arrest until he passes those codes to whomever bought them. We suspect Blitz is merely the courier. The men involved on both the selling and purchasing end are almost as important as the codes—if we don't want to be right back in this situation six months from now."

"Got it."

She reached for the door handle, but Steele's hand on her arm stopped her.

"Be careful."

"Always." She flashed him what she hoped was a confident smile.

"Listen to me, Alli."

Her head jerked up at his use of her nickname.

They'd known each other several years, and he'd only called her by that name twice. The first time was when she'd woken up in a hospital room after having surgery. The second time she was trying to banish from her memory.

Interagency cooperation on cyber ops had begun the same year she'd been hired at DHS, when she was twenty-five, naïve, and optimistic. She'd just celebrated her thirty-fifth birthday. . . if you could call a phone call from her Aunt Polly and a piece of pie from Bright Angel Lodge a celebration.

Though they'd started their careers at roughly the same time, Steele was angling toward the managerial route. Allison needed to be in the field.

"I'm serious, Quinn. I need you to hear this. Be careful. Blitz isn't like most of our cyberterrorists. He doesn't spend all of his time in front of a computer screen. He isn't afraid of physical altercations."

Steele picked up the phone, but he didn't push the button to wake the screen. "He killed Mr. Harris with his hands, Allison. He didn't use a weapon. He didn't do it from a distance. He was looking in this guy's eyes when he choked the life out of him. Someone who could do that—"

"Is dangerous. I know."

"And I know that like every other mission you think this one can lead you to your father's killer."

When she didn't respond, he continued. "You're one of the best agents on the cyber task force, and I am convinced that's partly due to the fact that you have a personal vendetta to settle. Just don't allow that crusade you're so committed to make you reckless."

"I'll be careful." This time her smile was genuine. She'd been chasing Blitz for six months, and now he was close enough that she could practically smell him.

Game on.

Only as she hustled across the parking area to the staff headquarters, she understood that what they were facing wasn't a game. If Blitz succeeded in passing off the kill codes to the buyer, the situation could easily spiral out of control. The buyer might merely destroy the codes, then take credit for the impending cyberattack. Or the buyer could attempt to sell the codes back to the U.S. government for a hefty profit—which would take time, something they didn't have.

Whoever was behind the ransomware that had been inserted into the national grid had already proven what he could do. The document Steele had shown her established that the grid had begun experiencing debilitating fluctuations four days ago—a spike here, a brownout there. So far, they'd been able to keep the enormity of the looming disaster out of the news blogs, but she knew the story would eventually break. The mission clock was ticking, and there wasn't a single risk management specialist who doubted that the grid would fail—nationwide—in thirty-six hours.

Once that happened, all of the U.S. critical systems would crash, as well as much of Canada's. The worst-case scenario did not limit outage to the electrical grid. The threat had expanded to include medical, telecommunications, banking, even national defense.

Projections were that thousands of people would die.

That would only happen if she couldn't stop the man they referred to as Blitz.

She would stop him, and she'd have a private conversation with him before he was carted away. Arthur Quinn had been one of the FBI's first Certified Ethical Hackers, though they hadn't been called that back in 1996. The pool of computer criminals and hacktivists the FBI had chased was small. She hadn't found much regarding the operations her dad had been involved in, but she'd found enough to understand that he'd become something of a legend in the cyber world. Blitz would have heard of him, and whatever he knew about her father's death, he would tell her.

But she was going to need some help.

That wasn't something she enjoyed admitting, even to herself. Her mind wanted to sink back into memories of her early days as an agent, to her first partner who had been like a brother to her, but she shook those thoughts away. The next twenty-four hours would require all of her focus. Having a partner didn't mean she had to care about him, and she would not allow the person she had in mind put himself in danger. That was non-negotiable.

Fifteen minutes later she sat in Director Rivera's office.

Rivera was in her early fifties, stocky, and had a commanding presence. Her hair was raven black, long, fastened in a single braid down her back. Her cheek bones were high, her nose broad, and her eyes seemed to take in everything. She ran a tight ship, and the employees at the Grand Canyon respected her because of it. Nothing seemed to surprise the woman, not even Allison's latest request.

There was a tap on her office door, and Allison pulled in a deep breath. This would be the hard part.

"Enter," Rivera snapped.

Tate Garcia stepped into the room—all tanned six feet of him. At forty-nine, he remained ridiculously good looking, more like an actor walking onto a movie set than the Grand Canyon's most seasoned ranger. Allison had checked the schedule before she'd made her request. He was half way through his five day off rotation, and he'd spent those two and a half days up top. He'd be the perfect person to accompany her back down.

He held his ranger hat in his hands as his gaze bounced from Rivera to Allison and then back again.

"Have a seat, Tate. We have a rather unique situation."

Tate sat, placing his hat carefully on top of his knees. "What type of situation?"

Allison suspected by the look Tate shot her direction that he didn't approve of her. Of course, he didn't really know her either. What he was about to learn would be difficult for him to fathom. No doubt Tate Garcia thought he'd seen it all. She'd been there when he'd handled the relocation of more than one bear, rescued unprepared hikers, and tore into workers who had missed a shift. She'd been on the receiving end of that lecture more than once. As the most senior ranger in the park, he could have chosen any assignment. He chose Phantom Ranch.

"Allison needs to go back down to the ranch. Tonight."

"Tonight?"

"We need someone to accompany her."

"There's a storm arriving before morning, and you know as well as I do that night hiking is strongly discouraged."

"I'm aware."

Tate shifted in his chair, his attention firmly pinned on the director. Allison had the sneaking suspicion that he was avoiding looking directly at her.

"Kaia—"

Allison was surprised. She'd never heard anyone use the director's first name, not in the woman's presence.

"Look, I'm sure you have your reasons."

"I do."

"But. . ." He hesitated, his gaze sliding toward Allison and then back to the director. "As I said in my most recent report to you, I highly recommend that you discharge Miss Quinn."

"What?" Allison couldn't believe this guy. "I'm a good guide."

"You are a good guide, when you bother to show up for your shifts." Now Tate looked at her. His eyes, expression, and posture dared her to argue the fact. "You're not dependable. You're here for a week, maybe two at the most, and then you disappear."

Allison didn't know quite how to answer that succinctly, so she didn't bother. Instead, she waited.

Tate turned his attention back to the director. "I have no idea why you put up with it, Kaia. I don't want her guiding my groups down the canyon because I can't depend on her to be there to lead them back up."

"Whoever goes down tonight won't be guiding a group, and I

55

want to be clear about one thing up front. This is a request, not an order. If you don't want to do it, we'll find someone else." The director gave Allison a slight smile, then motioned with her hand. "Go ahead. You explain it."

Allison almost felt sorry for Tate Garcia, but instead of explaining, she pulled out her Department of Homeland Security ID and held it up for him.

Tate stared at it a moment, shook his head, and stuttered a response. "So, you're. . . I don't. . . that is to say. . ."

"She's with Homeland Security."

"I've been on a special operation here since March, watching for a cyberterrorist named Blitz. This morning, he hiked down to the ranch."

"Why would a terrorist want to be in the bottom of the canyon?"

"I need to be there before morning. I need to stop him before he leaves that ranch, or at the very least follow him when he does."

"Where would he go?"

"We both know that hiking alone, at night, isn't recommended."

"Either one of those things would be considered foolish. Together they would be—"

"Necessary, Mr. Garcia. They're necessary." Allison stood and walked to the large map pinned on the director's wall.

"We will soon have another team here." She tapped the map, the spot directly adjacent from them, on the North Rim. "By tomorrow, agents will also be positioned along the banks of the Colorado on the north side, and of course at every access road at the top. Our worry is that Blitz plans to raft down from Phantom Ranch, connect with one of his cohorts, and then escape off-road."

She turned to see if he needed more explanation. He was standing two feet behind her, staring at the map.

Finally, he dropped his gaze to her and said, "You didn't know he was coming, or you would have stayed down at the ranch."

"We didn't know when, but we had intel that indicated he would show up here eventually."

"How could you know that?"

Allison shook her head. She'd share what he needed to know, but she wouldn't tell him everything.

"Why not helicopter down?"

"Too loud and too noticeable. We don't want him to run, or worse, destroy something that he has—something we need." She waited for him to again meet her gaze. When he did, she added, "The clock on this cyberattack is already ticking. Cornered, he might speed up that timeline, which is something we cannot allow to happen. This has to be done with. . . finesse."

He studied her closely for a few seconds, though it felt much longer. Her mind flashed back to a science project where she'd pinned moths to a board. That was what it felt like to have Tate Garcia's attention locked on you. She was the moth in this scenario.

"You were the first person I thought of. You know the trail better than anyone, but if you don't feel up to it—" She let that hang in the air for a moment. "I'll find someone else, or I'll do it alone. As Director Rivera said, this is an optional assignment as far as you're concerned."

She almost felt guilty for baiting him, but while she might appeal to his pride, she would not downplay the danger of what they were about to attempt. "It's dangerous, and it's not in your job description."

Finally, he nodded once and turned to the director.

"Sam hiked up with me. He can lead tomorrow's group down."

"That's not going to happen. We'll come up with an excuse, offer them something else." Rivera nodded toward the window, toward the yawning canyon that had been her ancestor's home. The employee grapevine claimed Kaia Rivera's father was an engineer who had worked for the national parks. Her mother's lineage could be traced back to the Hopi Indians, or Puebloan Peoples as they were often called.

"I can't do anything about the people who are already down there. It'll be up to you and Quinn to keep them safe. We'll keep the ones up here out of harm's way." Her expression hardened. "This is my turf, and ultimately I'm the one responsible for our guests. You two need to protect the people on the bottom and stop this mad man."

She didn't blanch.

She didn't look afraid at all.

She looked angry. And determined.

Allison realized she wouldn't want to go up against the director. Perhaps she should have asked Rivera to accompany her. She had no doubt the woman would have agreed.

But there were other reasons that Tate Garcia was a better choice—reasons she had carefully considered before offering his name to the director. He had skills that she might need to draw on, and he knew the canyon better than any other person she'd met in her six months at Phantom. Tate was the partner she wanted, and based on the look of resignation on his face, he was willing to step into the fray.

As they walked out of the building, Allison could feel Tate studying her. She told herself she didn't care about his opinion. Then she remembered that he had suggested Rivera fire her. That was offensive, not to mention rude. She'd never been fired from a job.

"You hiked up Bright Angel Trail today?"

"I did."

"Even for a seasoned ranger—which you are not—hiking up, then down, the canyon in a single day is difficult."

"I'm aware."

"Combined, the two hikes total 19.2 miles, with an elevation change of 4700 feet each way."

Her patience snapped. She stopped, pivoted, and felt a glimmer of satisfaction when he took a step back. "I'm aware of the problems with this op, but *it is what it is.* Either get on board or walk away. I don't have time to convince you. I'm doing this."

He held his hands up in surrender. "I simply thought I should warn you."

"I'll consider myself duly warned, but it sounds to me like you're having second thoughts."

"Not exactly. Right or wrong, I consider Phantom Ranch my own personal territory. If someone is down there, if there's a threat to my workers and hikers, then I'm going with you."

"Fine."

"Fine." Tate nodded toward the all-night café. "Have you eaten?"

"No, but—"

"We need food."

"I'm not stopping for a cup of coffee, Tate." She had noticed that he had a parental attitude toward the other workers, but she was surprised to see it toward her. There was only a fourteen-year difference between them—not enough for him to lecture her on the dangers of anything.

She'd ordered a thorough background check on Tate Garcia months ago. He was forty-nine years old, came from a middle class, Baptist, midwestern family, and was employed by the national parks a few years after leaving the U.S. military.

It irked her that he was still looking fondly toward the café. "We can eat later. Right now, we need to catch a terrorist."

"We can't eat later unless we have food. I'll have the kitchen wrap up a couple of sandwiches. Also, we should take the time to grab stuff from the supply room."

Allison bristled, but nodded once.

He was right about the supplies and the food.

"Get the food and your pack," she said. "Meet me at the supply room in fifteen minutes."

Allison glanced around. It was pitch dark, so there wasn't much to see. They kept a low light presence around the complex. A few couples walked between the restaurant and the lodge. One or two others could be heard in the parking area. No terrorists that she could see and no one close enough to hear their conversation.

She stepped closer to Tate and lowered her voice to a whisper. "Get your pack and your weapon."

And that was when she knew that Tate was truly on board with what they needed to do. At the mention of his firearm, his shoulders pulled back and his expression hardened. She knew for certain at that moment that he understood the seriousness, the danger, of the next twelve hours. That relieved some of her own anxiety. She didn't like taking a local into an active op, but Tate was old enough and seasoned enough to make his own decisions.

He didn't bother arguing with her. "Twenty minutes," he muttered and walked off toward the lodge.

Tate Garcia.

Donovan Steele.

Both were good men, and both had her back. They might even both respect her in her role as a Department of Homeland Security agent. But neither knew what it was like to watch your father be gunned down, to live with the need to put the person responsible for that behind bars.

She would stop the cyberattack, but Blitz would also move her closer to catching her father's killer.

Chapter Two

J ohn Howard stood at the wall of floor-to-ceiling windows, staring out into the darkness. The clock on the wall behind him gave the time as a few minutes past midnight. Just under thirty-six hours until the ransomware he'd developed and deployed did its job.

Their headquarters was situated on the outskirts of Whitefish, Montana—a small rural town of fewer than seven thousand souls. Local residents were accustomed to living alongside famous singers, professional athletes, and Fortune 500 CEOs. People were polite but not overly friendly.

Situated in the far northwest corner of the state, the nearby Waterton-Glacier International Peace Park spanned the United States-Canadian border. The park offered quick access to Alberta and British Columbia. The border crossing within the park was a mere three-hour trip by car, much less by Cessna.

Stella had picked the location years ago. She had also chosen its name, Middle-earth. John hadn't read a lot of Tolkien and found the name rather prosaic and outdated. The location though? That was perfect.

John had risen up through the ranks of military intelligence then transferred to the Central Intelligence Agency. Nine years ago, he'd realized that he was on the wrong side of things. His first step toward that conclusion had been the passage of the Patriot Act, just six weeks after the September 11th attack. That single piece of legislation had significantly expanded the government's authority to conduct record searches, secret searches, intelligence searches, and trap-and-trace searches. The entire U.S. population was suddenly searchable. Anyone opposing the law would be blamed for further attacks.

The pivotal legislation passed with little to no opposition.

And John had been one of those sheep who fell obediently into line. The tragedies in Pennsylvania, New York, and Virginia had left a mark on their collective soul. The anthrax attacks that followed had convinced many who were opposed to the Patriot Act that it was necessary to protect America. As an agent who had already served in the federal government for nearly ten years, he'd felt the weight of both attacks.

Over his remaining years at the CIA, his opinions had slowly changed, much of that due to the world's dependence on technology. Every aspect of a person's life could be, and was, tracked. He'd known it was wrong, known that they were headed in a dangerous direction. The death of his family finally pushed him to the other side.

Now he worked for Stella Gonzalez.

She was ruthless and rich.

He'd dug up all that could be found out about her, which wasn't much. He wasn't comfortable with her fanaticism or intensity, but he could work with those things. More importantly, she was willing to fund and facilitate his mission.

Fifty years old, John could have been a doppelganger for the famous actor/director Ron Howard. Where Ron had starred in such iconic television comedies as *The Andy Griffith Show* and *Happy Days*, John felt that he balanced precariously on the edge of good versus evil. Ron produced films such as *Apollo 13*, *Frost/Nixon*, and *A Beautiful Mind*. John produced cyberattacks that would move the United States, and perhaps the world, from life as we know it toward life as it should be.

The transition would, necessarily, be a bloody one.

A tap on his door jerked John from his reverie.

"Enter."

Brett Lindstrom and Kate Jackson walked into the room. At sixty-four, Brett had developed something of a paunch and his bald head gleamed in the lamplight, but his eyes were as sharp as ever. He handled any personnel issues. Kate should have been a model with her dark skin, gorgeous hair, and tall, thin physique. Instead, she was in charge of the computer side of things. Kate was twenty-eight and a real whiz kid. She was, without a doubt, the best hacker he'd ever known, and he'd known a lot of them.

Brett had been with him since the beginning. Kate started two years ago and quickly worked her way to the top. Both had been aggressively vetted.

"We have something you need to see." Brett nodded to Kate who tapped a few buttons on the tablet she was holding.

The video display on John's south wall sprang to life. It was ten feet in height, eighteen feet in width, and offered a type of high-def resolution that the average consumer hadn't yet seen. John could view thirty-two different feeds on the individual panels or a single feed across the entire assembly. Kate chose to spread the "something" he needed to see across the array of screens.

"What am I looking at?"

"South Rim of the Grand Canyon. More specifically, the parking area outside the Yavapai Lodge."

Kate tapped her tablet and the CCTV footage rolled.

A tall man with an athletic build walked toward the sidewalk circling the hotel. As he reached it, a shorter, slighter woman bounded around the corner, nearly colliding with him. The man raised his hands to stop her forward progress, then nodded toward a black SUV. He entered on the driver's side. She sat next to him on the passenger side.

"With the dark tint on the windows, we can't see into the vehicle. They met for approximately nine and a half minutes." Kate fast-forwarded the footage.

The woman exited the vehicle, jogged off around the corner she'd originally appeared from, and the man drove away.

"Play it again."

He stepped closer to the video wall. The man definitely had a buzz cut, which could indicate that he worked for some arm of the government. Or he could be prior military. He certainly carried himself like someone who had spent time working for Uncle Sam, and not at a desk—more likely in the desert.

"I assume you've been through the reservation list at the hotel."

"Yes, and none of the names triggered a flag. Everyone was either a guest or a park employee."

"Show me our people at this site."

Kate again tapped the tablet, freezing the CCTV footage and relegating it to the left-hand side of the wall. Two additional feeds appeared on adjacent panels. Four green dots blinked on the feeds.

Brett stepped forward, like a professor about to address his students. "Blitz, Nina, and Lyra are all at Phantom Ranch."

"Cooper?"

"Here. On the South Kaibab Trail."

"And the diversion operations?"

Twelve other panels activated, showing the remaining teams they'd sent out. . . without kill codes. Those teams had a single job. They were to pull government resources away from the real operation. If they were successful, it would spread out the FBI, CIA, and DHS assets until they were thin and ineffective.

Stella thought it was overkill, but in the end she'd thrown up her well-manicured hands and scoffed, "We'll do it your way, as usual."

His way worked.

His way produced results.

In the last year alone, they'd breached data centers in New

York, Tulsa, Chicago, and Los Angeles. They'd hacked television stations, power plants, even GPS systems. Always, they had been able to shift the blame to others—the Russians or the Chinese or cybercriminals who were no longer useful to their cause.

With the current attack, they would achieve the outcome he had been chasing for far too long. Cyber Drop would usher in the changes that the world could no longer afford to wait for and shouldn't have to merely hope for. The time for action was now, and John Howard wasn't holding anything back.

Kate wasn't finished. "As you can see, the vehicle's plates were never clear. Whoever was driving knew where the CCTV cameras were located."

Which meant there was a better-than-even chance that whoever was driving worked for one of the various cyber task forces.

"Keep me posted." It was his standard phrase for "You're dismissed. Now get out of here."

Kate cleared her throat and Brett rubbed a hand over his bald scalp.

"There's something else?"

"We're not seeing any activity on the north side." She waved a hand toward the video wall, then at her tablet. "The buyers should be moving into place, but as far as we can tell, they're not. Our drones haven't picked up anything."

John walked over to Kate, close enough to peer into her eyes. She was able to hold his gaze for a few seconds, before glancing down at her tablet. "Sir."

"Maybe, Kate, they're as smart as we are. Maybe they know how to avoid your cameras."

"Actually, that's not possible because—"

Brett saved her by interrupting. "Regardless how well they can avoid our drones and satellite feed, there should be some movement on the North Rim. They can't just appear tomorrow. They have to make their way down to the river in order to meet up with Blitz, and we have no indication of that happening. No vehicles. No helicopters. Kate's not wrong. There's no one there."

Kate again tapped the tablet, having apparently regained her nerve. "The weather forecasts show a storm headed through the canyon. It's possible that our buyers are waiting until that passes, but it's a long hike down. If Blitz is going to pass them the codes tomorrow. . ."

"Our worry is that Blitz has made a side deal with the buyers," Brett added.

"Are you both finished?"

Brett and Kate locked eyes with one another, then both nodded.

"I appreciate your concern and your attention to detail. However, it's important to remember the overall picture. Don't lose sight of what we know to be true. Blitz doesn't have the nerves or the intellect to double-cross us. He's a hacker, nothing more."

Kate and Brett exchanged another look.

Neither contradicted him, something John was quite grateful for.

As they turned to leave Stella Gonzalez walked in. "A late-night meeting, and no one invited me?"

Kate and Brett both froze—near the door but not near enough to escape.

"And what is this we have here? Video surveillance. I love video surveillance." Stella sauntered to the wall and tapped the video panel with the blinking dots.

Kate jerked. She couldn't stand anyone touching a screen, let alone tapping it. Her OCD on that count was legendary. She did, wisely, keep her concerns to herself.

Stella turned to study the group.

She was seventy-two, tall, with skin pulled taut over fine bones and thin hair covered with a colorful wrap. She resembled a bird a little more every year—a hawk or falcon perhaps. Maybe a vulture. "Friends or foe?"

"Leave the tablet," John said.

Kate handed the tablet to Brett, who handed it to John, then the two fled.

"You scare the children when you make an entrance like that."

Stella laughed and dropped into a leather chair. "Brett is hardly a child. As for the girl, I'm not sure I like her."

John shrugged. It didn't matter who Stella liked. Personnel fell on his side of the duties roster, and he'd put Brett in charge of who was hired.

"Explain it to me."

He once again moved to the video wall. "This is CCTV that Kate captured from one of the lodges at the South Rim of the Grand Canyon."

He allowed the short video to play, then froze it when the car drove away, avoiding the direct line of sight of the cameras. "Probably it's a government team."

When Stella only settled her unblinking gaze on him, he added, "We knew they'd be there. It's not a problem."

"Tell me more."

He turned to the display showing the people they had on-site. "This dot is a man named Anthony Cooper who works with Blitz."

"Blitz isn't technically on our team, correct?"

"He's a contractor."

"And they both agreed to tracking?"

"They would have if they'd known about it, given the paycheck involved."

"Why aren't their dots together?"

"Cooper stayed on the trail, in case anyone follows Blitz down, which is doubtful. They would have left earlier."

"Okay."

"Blitz is at the ranch. He'll receive the codes from Lyra at daybreak."

Stella sighed heavily.

John braced himself for the argument to come. They'd already had it several times.

"Why do we need this girl Lyra? Why involve so many people?"

"Lyra has been in place at the ranch for more than a year. We slipped her the codes two months ago, before we had a buyer. She'll give them to Blitz. Blitz will take them to the buyer."

"Lyra couldn't do that?"

"No. She couldn't."

"Lyra is kitchen help." She waved a dismissive hand.

It was the wave that set John off. He had never been able to abide people who couldn't or wouldn't think things through. It irked him tremendously that Stella saw only *kitchen help* where he saw an asset.

Instead of throwing her out, which was what he wanted to do, he sat in an adjacent chair, his back ramrod straight, his eyes boring into hers. The only way to conquer a predator was to present yourself as a larger, even hungrier predator.

"Lyra is motivated," he explained softly. "Her brother was mistakenly killed in a drone attack when she was seven and living in a small village south of the U.S. border."

"Our government has used drone attacks in Mexico?"

"The war on drugs." John forced a smile. "The point is Lyra will do whatever we ask. That's why we're using her."

"Oh, John. You're so prickly." She shook her head but allowed her gaze to drift back to the video wall.

"And the last dot?"

"Nina Brooks. She's a relatively new recruit, but Brett is certain she can be trusted."

"But why do we need her?"

"Because someone has to watch Blitz after he receives the codes and as he delivers them to the buyer."

Stella stood, walked to the door, then turned. She put her hand on her hip—a posture that looked ridiculous on a woman of her age. "Do you know what your problem is, John? You still act like a spy. You think like a spy. I'll bet you even dream like a spy."

"That's why you hired me."

"No. I hired you because I believe you can get the job done, but sometimes it's just. . ." The wave toward the wall again. "Tedious."

John waited until she'd left, until the door had shut, and then another fifteen seconds. He trusted Stella. She wanted the same things that he did. It was in methodology that they differed. For that matter, he trusted Brett and Kate, but he'd learned long ago to always hold something back.

What he'd seen in the CCTV footage didn't bother him, but still he needed to check.

Walking to his desk, he opened the bottom drawer and pulled out what looked like a small gun case. Placing his index finger to the display pad, he waited for a beep, then opened the case. Inside was a tracking monitor. He pressed the *ON* button, then sat and waited.

First the screen turned blue, then it filled with an icon of the world. Fourteen dashes appeared, and he entered the passcode. The picture on the small screen changed again, and the program zoomed in to the northern hemisphere, then North America, then Arizona, the Grand Canyon, and Phantom Ranch. One green dot blinked—steady, healthy, strong.

He powered down the device, placed it in the case, closed and activated the biometric lock, then returned the case to his bottom drawer. Standing, he walked back to the windows and resumed staring out into the darkness.

Chapter Three

They grabbed energy bars and refilled their water packs.

"I should have guessed," Tate muttered.

"Guessed what?" Allison added a headlamp to an outer pocket of her pack.

"Looking back, it's pretty obvious you weren't some drifter looking for summer work, a woman in the midst of a mid-life crisis, or a thief hiding from the law."

"Those were the only three scenarios you came up with?"

"I didn't ask because I don't consider it my business to pry into employees' private lives." He put his hands on a collapsible emergency shelter, shook his head, and moved to the next shelf of supplies. "I wouldn't want anyone asking me personal questions."

"It's the same in my job," Allison admitted. "Seems rude to cross that invisible barrier that exists between co-worker and friend."

"On the other hand, your life is literally in the hands of the people you work with."

"Sometimes." Her mind wandered back to Steele. Did she want to know more about his personal life? How would that help? Shaking her head, she added, "I prefer to keep things professional. If that makes me a loner, so be it."

"I guess we have that in common." Tate grimaced. "I never would have suspected you worked for the federal government. And Homeland Security? Sounds like something out of a spy novel."

He reached for an extra emergency blanket, crammed it into his pack. "You're a senior agent."

"That's what my I.D. says."

"Could be faked."

"Not a chance. Rivera did a thorough background check before I started here."

He laughed, and Allison knew that she had chosen correctly. She needed someone steady and confident. Someone who didn't freak out easily. Although she was an excellent agent, she was at best a marginal hiker. She wasn't a fool. Hiking down the south trail in the middle of the night with bad weather bearing down on them wouldn't be easy. At night during a storm would be more than challenging.

Tate Garcia was the guy to get her to Phantom Ranch, then his involvement in this op would be over.

Tate stood there, looking around the room.

"Extra ammo," she said.

"Maybe we can shoot our way through the storm." He grabbed a box of shells for his Sig P220 and stuffed it in a side pocket. "We both have an emergency aid kit in our pack."

"An extra can't hurt, and put in a couple of emergency flares too, just in case." Though she had no intention of revealing their position. Still, *better to have it and not need it than need it and not have it*—the mantra of every hiking guide, and also a sentiment of most federal agents.

They were about to leave the supply area, when Tate stopped in front of a stack of tarps. "I prefer to pack light, but. . ." He pushed the tarp into his pack, zipped it up, and slipped his arms through the straps.

Allison did the same. Her pack was heavy, and that gave her a sense of assurance. Perhaps it was a false sense, but she'd take whatever comfort she could find. They opted to drive the short distance to the South Kaibab—she didn't need to add an extra three miles to her hike total.

Hustling out to the parking area, Tate stopped abruptly. "Where's your vehicle?"

"I hid it."

"Why?"

"They might have tagged it. I can't be sure."

"You sound a little paranoid," he muttered, but he led the way to his National Park vehicle.

Allison felt suddenly hyper-aware, edgy even.

Had Blitz left someone up top?

Was that person, even now, watching them?

They jumped into Tate's truck and drove east on Desert View Drive. The canyon on their left was a dark hole.

Another mile and Tate turned left on Yaki Point Road.

Allison continued to scan left to right then back again. When they reached the *Buses Only* sign and barrier, he shifted the truck into park, walked over to the keypad, and punched in a code. The barrier raised and they drove through.

"Wait." She watched in her side mirror until she was sure the arm had dropped back in place. She still had that sense of being followed.

"Who or what are you watching for?"

"Anyone and anything."

He parked in the far corner of the bus lot.

When she moved to exit the vehicle, he tapped his fingers against the steering wheel. She turned and looked at him in surprise. She couldn't read his expression. There wasn't enough light for that, but his posture was plain enough, and it said WAIT in capital letters.

When he didn't speak right away, she shifted, resting her back against the corner of the seat. "Say it."

"This is awkward."

"Chasing a terrorist?"

"No. Us."

As she waited, Allison realized that was another reason Tate had been her first choice. He never jumped in, never felt the need to break an uncomfortable silence.

"I don't even know what to call you."

"Call me?"

"Agent Quinn?"

She shrugged. "Or Allison. Either works for me. Look, Tate, it isn't like we're strangers."

She'd called him Mr. Garcia in the director's office, but they were about to hike into a canyon where someone's goal was national destruction. That same person wouldn't hesitate to kill two hiking guides. Any formality that had existed between them before tonight was best put behind them.

"We've been working together for months," she added.

"Yes, but I wasn't working with the person sitting in this truck with me tonight. I don't truly know you."

She spoke softly and calmly, resisting the urge to grab him by the shirt collar and pull him from the truck. "I don't have time to rattle off the details of my career and qualifications. You're going to have to trust me. I know what I'm doing, and I wanted your help because—"

"Why *did* you want my help? Why not another agent?"

"Another agent wouldn't know this canyon like you do. You may feel like you don't know me, but I do know you. I know how level-headed and capable you are."

"I'm not sure how much good I'll be against a terrorist."

"You focus on the hike down. I'll focus on the terrorist." In the last six months, during all those nights of waiting, she'd tried to envision every possible scenario. She hadn't quite pictured this one. "But also be prepared for whatever might happen. Your firearm is loaded?"

"It is, but—"

"Trust me, if someone threatens you, it won't be that hard of a decision. And it's not that different from shooting a rattler."

"You did that."

"You've done it before."

"How do you know about—"

"Rangers talk, Tate. Summer help, in particular, have done a lot to build the mythical reputation of Tate Garcia." She leaned forward and waited for his eyes to meet hers. "You're the real deal, and I need you with me tonight. But only if you're absolutely certain that you want to be involved."

He nodded once.

She hopped out of the truck, dragging her backpack behind her, then pushed her arms through the straps and adjusted them.

He did the same. As they prepared to hike down the canyon, Allison's mind drifted back to Donovan Steel.

Be careful.

She planned to heed that advice.

Looking at Tate, she offered, "Last chance to change your mind."

One quick shake of his head, but that wasn't enough. Suddenly, she remembered lying on a stretcher with a bullet lodged in her shoulder. She didn't think she would ever forget the concerned expression on Steele's face, the bright lights of the hospital corridor, the murmur of doctors and nurses, the pain of the wound. She didn't want to forget. That particular memory kept her sharp.

She stepped closer.

"You got any people, Tate? Anyone who'll miss you if this goes south? Because that's what you have to think about when you're in my line of work. Not how much you're willing to risk, but how much it will affect those you love."

"I'm a loner, Quinn. I thought you knew that. What about you?"

"Me? I live for this stuff." She hesitated, then added, "Make no mistake—Blitz is a psychopath, and he won't hesitate to kill anyone who gets in his way."

"Understood." Tate smiled. "Let's get your terrorist out of my canyon."

Allison was aware that this situation would be resolved—one way or the other—and then she'd move on to the next place, the next terrorist, the next op. While she appreciated the uniqueness of the canyon, her job was to stop a cyber thug, learn what she could about her father's killer, rinse and repeat.

Tate's situation was different. After tonight, he'd still be here, at the canyon, where he belonged. It was his home, and she couldn't imagine him living anywhere else.

She pushed those thoughts aside as they started down the trail. Tonight, they needed to focus on staying alive, on catching Blitz, and on protecting the guests and employees at Phantom Ranch. It rankled her that they were at risk. The canyon was a place of solitude, of unparalleled beauty. The fact that it had been invaded by a terrorist set her teeth on edge.

She needed to stop Blitz from handing off or destroying the kill codes.

She would capture him as well as the buyer he was supposedly meeting.

And she would learn what he knew about her father's murderer.

Once she accomplished that, this canyon—Tate's canyon—would be returned to its peaceful splendor. She sincerely hoped that when she left this assignment the canyon walls would not be smeared with the blood of good people.

The South Kaibab Trail dropped over four thousand vertical feet in six and a half miles. It left the rim on the west side of Yaki Point, descending immediately into a series of tight switchbacks. The trail itself was four feet wide and well maintained. The steep descent through rock ledges was known as The Chimney.

Allison had hiked it many times over the last six months. She preferred hiking down to hiking up. Though she considered herself to be in good shape, the hike up left her winded. Going down, she simply had to watch her footing. It wouldn't do to tumble over the edge and drop to the canyon floor below. Forget the fact that she could be killed. It would take Steele a full day to put another agent in place.

She stepped carefully, even slowed down at the switchbacks.

She'd never hiked the canyon at night, which had been a mistake on her part. She should have trained for this possibility. As her eyes grew accustomed to the darkness, starlight provided more light than she'd expected, allowing her to distinguish the outline of the North Rim. She couldn't see the Colorado River that had carved the floor of the canyon, but she felt it there—steady, constant, impervious.

On sunny days, when weather and terrorists weren't a factor, the average hiker took a little over four hours to reach the bottom via the South Kaibab. A glance at her watch told Allison that it was past one. They would need to pick up their speed if they were to make it to Phantom Ranch by five, which was when she wanted to be in place.

It was a mere 0.9 miles from the rim to Ooh Aah Point. Due to the trail's steep descent, it generally took hikers one to two hours to traverse. Allison and Tate covered the distance in forty-five minutes. During the day, Ooh Aah offered a breathtaking view, but Allison wasn't interested in sightseeing.

Tate dropped his pack and pulled out two energy bars. Tossing one to her, he asked, "Are you worried about getting there in time?"

"No. He won't make his move until daylight."

"Sunrise is technically seven minutes after six, though as you know sunlight doesn't reach the canyon floor until mid-morning."

"We need to be in position well before that."

"Then we have plenty of time. Let's sit for a minute."

She tried to quell him with a piercing stare, but it didn't work in the dark. Instead, she took a long pull from her water pack and sat on the boulder next to him.

"How long have you been an agent?"

"Ten years this fall. How long have you been a ranger?"

"Just celebrated my twenty-fourth year."

"You're practically an old man." She put a heavy emphasis on *practically.*

His laughter was soft and deep.

She liked the sound of it.

"Did you go to college?" She knew the answer to that, but apparently they were playing get-to-know-one-another.

"Nope. Straight into the military after high school. Served my country for six years, then drifted through a few jobs before landing at the NPS. I turned forty-nine this year. What about you?"

"Never ask a lady her age, especially one carrying a pistol."

"You got me there."

She could easily remember being a new recruit, Ryan by her side and the excitement of a new op, but that memory was invariably followed by the unfathomable pain of losing a partner.

Worse than that, she knew that her father's killer was still out there. She'd been nine years old the day he'd been shot. Some sleepless nights, it seemed to her that very little time had passed. When she was deep in a mission—like now—it felt as if an entire lifetime had slipped by since that fateful day. She was both the same person and a completely different one from the young girl who vowed to avenge her father's death.

The terrorist she'd killed that night on Hurricane Ridge, the night that she'd worked with Donovan Steele to stop a cyberattack, had sported a tattoo with Elfish writing—as in *Lord of the Rings*. Forced to take six weeks of medical leave, Allison had spent those weeks searching any tenuous treads between the works of J.R.R. Tolkien and cybercrimes.

The results had been hopeful.

Blitz couldn't have killed her father, but there was a possibility he might have been trained by the man she thought of as Gollum. She'd found that name in her father's papers, but she didn't know if it referred specifically to the man who had killed him. She'd didn't find a single reference to the name in an active op, which only served to deepen her conviction that Gollum was the man she was seeking.

"You're awfully quiet over there."

"Coming from you that's an interesting observation."

"What's that supposed to mean?"

She hesitated, then admitted, "Some days we count your words."

"We?"

"The hiking guides."

"You count my words?"

"Want to know your lowest number?" Instead of waiting, she said, "Twenty. Now that's a taciturn individual that can hike five hours with only twenty words."

"Maybe I didn't have anything to say that day."

"Four words a mile."

"If you wanted a chatter-box you should have picked someone else."

"You're well above your average tonight, and I'll stick with my first pick thank you very much."

They hiked the next quarter mile in silence. The trail to Cedar Ridge passed through slopes of red mudstone and siltstone said to be 280 million years old—older than man, certainly older than Allison's problems. She knew they were passing bright red rocks, but in the darkness she couldn't see their color. Instead, they loomed against the night sky like ominous shadows.

When they reached the portion of the trail that ran along the ridge with sharp drops on both sides, Tate paused to stare up at the sky.

She could sense the approaching storm to the west, though she couldn't see it yet. The sky above was a panorama of stars. "Worried about the storm?"

"Yes, I am, but I was pausing to look at the stars."

"Star watcher, huh?"

"Guilty."

Allison had never spent much time staring up. She'd been too busy watching her back. Plus, the few times she had paused to study the stars, she'd found herself drawing at least a dozen big dippers in the sky. She hadn't pegged Tate as a star gazer. This guy was full of surprises.

She could feel a change in the temperature preceding the storm. Steele had sent a weather update that she'd received up top. The storm would pass through fairly quickly and was projected to dump an inch on the South Rim. It shouldn't hit until after five a.m., and Allison was determined to beat it to the bottom of the canyon.

There was no way she wanted to be coming down the slope as the rain pummeled them. She certainly didn't want to be crossing the suspension bridge in the storm. The very thought of having to do such a thing caused her pulse to accelerate a notch, but she breathed deeply and forced it down.

They didn't so much as pause at Cedar Point—a large, wide-open area rimmed with cedar trees. Primitive bathrooms made it an ideal resting spot for hikers. Allison was grateful that Tate pushed on. The trail was less steep in this area and ran straight. She felt like they were able to gain some time. Approaching Skeleton Point, they had a three-hundred-sixty-degree view. Allison noticed the stars were now blotted out to the west.

The storm was barreling toward them.

"Let's stop here." Tate dropped his pack to the ground.

She knew there was no point in arguing, but at the same time she felt the restless urgency that came when she was closing in on a perp.

Allison sat beside him, stretching out her calves. She was undoubtedly in the best physical shape of her life, but she was feeling the effects of hiking up the canyon then down in the same day. "How many times have you done the roundtrip in one day?"

"Enough to know it's a foolish thing to do."

"Except for today." When he didn't answer, she added, "Today it's a necessary thing to do."

"Apparently." He stood and stretched. "Hydrate. Eat. Stretch. Repeat. You'll be fine."

Ugh. He could be so irritating.

What made matters worse was that he was fourteen years older and didn't seem to be struggling physically at all. He motioned to the left and disappeared into the darkness, leaving his pack next to her.

Maybe he was heeding nature's call. They'd both passed the toilets at Cedar Ridge. Or possibly he'd gone to star watch some more. Skeleton Point also offered an excellent view of the Colorado River, something they couldn't see in the darkness, but she could hear it. She was thinking of that, of the Colorado River, as she lay on her back and stretched her calf muscles—right then left, right then left.

Suddenly Tate was beside her in the dark, breathing hard and grabbing his pack. "Come with me."

Allison staggered to her feet, put her hand on her holstered Glock, and ran after him. When she came around the corner, he was kneeling beside a large shadow. She clicked on her flashlight, pointed it at the ground, and saw specks of blood in the dirt.

Then she heard a moan.

She was kneeling beside Tate before she spoke. "Where's he hurt?"

"Shoulder. Looks to be a stab wound."

Which would make sense. Blitz—or his associate, which was more likely—wouldn't risk using his firearm. Also, as Steele had pointed out, the perp who strangled Mr. Harris twenty miles from the park *wasn't afraid of physical altercations.*

She pointed her flashlight toward the injured guy.

Early twenties.

Hair pulled back by a hair band.

Scruffy beard.

She dug in her pack for her emergency bottle of water, helped him raise his head, and stopped him when he tried to drink too much.

"Let's see if that stays down," she said gently.

Tate had pulled out his med kit and donned latex gloves. He proceeded to cut away the guy's jacket and shirt. The stab wound had clotted somewhat, but it was swollen and an angry red. Allison had never been stabbed, but she had been shot.

She would never forget what that felt like.

This guy was in a tremendous amount of pain.

"What's your name?"

"Teddy. Theodore, actually. Theodore Payne."

"Ok, Teddy. This is going to hurt, but we have to do it." She positioned herself behind him, then pushed him into a semi-sitting position.

Tate had set out a roll of gauze and a package of wound clot powder. He tore the packet open. "Ready?"

"Ready," Allison said.

Teddy didn't say anything. She suspected by the way he was shaking that he'd gone into hypovolemic shock. She put two fingers against his carotid artery. His pulse was rapid and his breathing was shallow. His skin wasn't clammy yet. Possibly they'd found him in time.

Though he groaned, Teddy didn't cry out as Tate poured the powder into the wound. Tate wrapped the wound quickly and efficiently, as if he'd done so a dozen times.

"Let's get him on his side," Tate said.

The latest guidelines didn't recommend elevating a wound, but Allison didn't think turning him would make matters worse and it might ease his discomfort. They shifted Teddy onto his side. Tate pulled off his jacket, rolled it up, and put it under Teddy's head. Allison placed her pack behind him so he could lean against it.

She reached for his wrist, counted the beats. "His pulse is better."

Tate offered him more water as Allison pulled out an emergency blanket and covered him. If they could stabilize him, perhaps he could give them some details.

"Teddy, can you tell us what happened?"

At first Teddy shook his head, his eyes darting back and forth. Allison knew this was the work of Blitz, but she needed to understand exactly what had transpired. She glanced at her watch. A few minutes shy of three a.m. They had a little time. She sat down in front of Teddy, her legs crossed and her elbows propped on her knees.

Tate stripped off his gloves and put them in a biohazard bag along with the cut away pieces of Teddy's clothing. He re-packed his medical kit and stuffed it into his pack. Finally, he sat beside Allison. The only light came from Allison's flashlight, but it was enough for them to see one another.

"We're going to get you back to the top, Teddy."

Allison shot him a quick look at that, but Tate ignored it.

"I want to make sure your vitals have stabilized, and then I'll go for help."

"No, you won't."

"Yes, I will." He kept his gaze on Teddy.

Allison would win that argument later. She turned her attention back to Teddy. "We need to know what happened. Who did this to you?"

Chapter Four

Teddy swallowed visibly, squeezed his eyes shut, and pulled in a deep breath. After another minute, he opened his eyes and studied them, no doubt assessing whether they were friends or foes. Apparently, he decided on friends—after all they had helped him.

"Short guy. He looked like a gym rat. Pale complexion." He closed his eyes, then opened them again. "Blond hair."

Tate looked at Allison, and she shook her head once—not Blitz.

"Any idea why he attacked you?" Allison asked.

"I was taking pictures of the. . ." Teddy's teeth chattered, but he pushed through it. "Of the river."

"This doesn't make any sense," Tate said.

But Allison was ahead of him. "Did you pass the group headed down to the ranch? It would have been earlier in the day."

"Yeah, sure. That was around noon, I guess."

"And were you taking pictures then?"

"Probably. I've been doing it all day. I'm a student at Northern Ari—" He paused, pulled in another shaky breath.

"Northern Arizona. Multi-media major. I come out here a lot to hike and to. . . to take pictures."

"And when you stopped here, what time was that?"

"Sunset."

"Where's your camera?"

"He took it, along with my pack."

"Why didn't he kill you?"

Teddy shook his head as if he couldn't believe his luck. "I think he wanted to."

"Why did you think that, Teddy?"

"He was smiling, as he drove the knife into my shoulder. Then he seemed to like. . . remember something. He frowned when he pulled out the knife and put it back in his belt."

"What did he do after that?" Allison's voice was soft but insistent.

"He told me he was going to leave me to die slowly, that he didn't have time to properly finish what he'd started."

"Okay. Teddy, I need to talk to my partner." Those last two words nearly tripped her up, but she pushed forward. "We're going right over there, but we'll be within earshot if you need us. Okay?"

Teddy nodded to indicate he'd heard, but his eyes had already slid closed again.

Allison led Tate back toward the main trail. They stopped where they were close enough to still see Teddy, but far enough away that he couldn't hear their conversation.

"I'll go back up," Tate was saying. "You stay here. I should be able to have help here in—"

"No."

"What?"

"No. You're not going back up. There's a lot more at stake here than Teddy. You need to keep your focus on the mission."

"My focus is on that kid lying back there about to bleed out. Don't tell me that you're thinking of leaving him."

"Blitz is why I'm here, and my mission is to stop him. I'm sorry about Teddy, but we can't be distracted by this."

"Distracted?"

"Yes, Tate. Distracted. *This* is a distraction, and we can't afford to let it derail our mission. That's the way it is."

Tate stared at Allison in disbelief, as if he didn't think she was serious, but of course she was.

"Where is your compassion?" His voice had dropped to a low growl.

"I don't have the luxury of having compassion for every civilian that gets in the way of a terrorist." Her frustration spiked, teetered, feel back. "If we mess this up, thousands could die. You do understand that, right? You think you'd have trouble sleeping knowing that this kid didn't make it? How are you going to sleep if thousands die because we didn't stop Blitz?"

Tate stepped away and pulled in several deep breaths, giving his temper time to settle. She honestly didn't care if he agreed with her or not. She had seen things that he hadn't. She had experienced things he hadn't.

He walked back toward her, stopped mere inches away. His posture was rigid and his voice clipped. "I've recovered people from the canyon, sometimes days after they had died. I will not let that happen to Teddy."

"Think about what he said, Tate. The guy didn't have time to finish him off? That makes no sense. All he had to do was push him over the ledge."

"So why leave him?"

"Because he's a message—a warning—for us."

She had the satisfaction of seeing understanding creep into Tate's expression. "They know about us?"

"It's the only thing that makes any sense. Blitz is above all else arrogant. He's telling us to back off. He's telling us that he has someone out here, waiting and watching."

"And you're certain the person who stabbed Teddy isn't Blitz?"

"He isn't."

"Then how is this even connected with your mission?"

"You think it's a coincidence? That there happens to be a

terrorist at the bottom of the canyon and a stabbed hiker here? How could it not be connected?"

"I don't know, Allison. That's why I asked you to explain it to me." His voice rose in frustration. He turned away, then back toward her, waiting, willing to be convinced.

"My best guess is that Teddy caught Blitz on camera, or at least Blitz thought he did."

"Okay. He saw him snapping pictures when they passed each other at noon. A lot of people were probably doing that though."

"Teddy must have pointed the camera toward him—inadvertently."

"But Blitz didn't attack then." Tate looked up at the stars, then back at her.

She thought he was beginning to see the situation as she did, beginning to understand.

"He wouldn't," she explained. "He's in a group. He couldn't afford to draw attention to himself."

"He continued down to the canyon."

"Maybe. He could have waited until he reached the bottom and called one of his men." Even as she said it, Allison knew she was missing something. What, though?

"There's no cell service at the bottom."

"But there is a phone at the ranch."

"You think he'd use an unsecured line?"

"Maybe. Also, satellite phones will work in some places, if you have clear line of sight."

She felt like she had not fully anticipated all that Blitz might do. Of course she hadn't. If she had, Teddy wouldn't be waiting for paramedics. She couldn't prepare for every contingency.

No op was flawless.

No agent was perfect.

That was a standard she couldn't attempt to strive for because doing so would paralyze her.

Seeing what had happened to Teddy only served to strengthen her resolve. "Whoever Blitz is working for would be well supplied with both materials and personnel. We knew that. Our analysts are sure that Blitz will meet men who are determined to bring down the grid, and that he'd meet them downriver. We're prepared for both of those things."

"What do you mean. . . supplied with personnel?"

"Probably someone on staff."

"On my staff?" His voice rose in indignation.

"But I didn't think he'd have someone hiking down behind him." She shook her head, her eyes scanning left and right. "He could be at the bottom now, or he could be in the brush waiting to see if anyone else is coming down."

"Waiting for us."

"Exactly."

Tate ran his hands over his face in frustration, then made his decision. "I will not leave that boy to die."

When Allison started to protest, he held up a hand. "And I understand why it's important to stop Blitz, but maybe. . . just maybe we can do both."

She was already shaking her head.

He reached out, put his hands on both of her shoulders, and waited for her to focus on him. "Listen to me. A third of the way back up to Cedar Ridge there's a spot with good cell reception. That's half a mile. I'll hike up there and call in a rescue crew—"

"Not a helicopter. Blitz, or his guy, would hear. They'd know."

"Okay. Not a helicopter, but four paramedics can hike down and carry him out. I can hike up, make the call, and be back in thirty minutes if I hurry. It should only take an hour for the crew to make it down—they'll be fresh and move faster than we have been."

He had been slowing down for her, worried about her doing the roundtrip on little food and no rest. Allison caught that and wanted to be offended. Wisely, she didn't mention it. She was smart, in good physical shape, and resolute. But she couldn't have gone any faster, not after the day she'd had. Not unless she wanted to risk tripping over the edge.

"We can't wait for them," she argued.

"Okay. We won't wait. He should be stabilized by the time I get back. We'll leave supplies."

Allison glanced at her watch again. "It's past three now. How has this op gone so wrong in the first two hours?"

"Things took a turn well before that. We're just playing catch-up."

"All right. Go."

Tate hurried back to Teddy, pulled a few things out of his pack, and turned back toward the trail.

"Tate. . ."

He hesitated, then looked back at her.

And what she saw then seared itself onto the contours of her mind. Tate standing there alone, his world having been upended. An older guy who was nearly old enough to be her father. He'd adjusted to the op better than she could have hoped.

He didn't blink at the thought of going up against the likes of men who would stab a total stranger and leave him to die alone, leave his body to be ravaged by scavengers.

One untrained guy trusting a woman he barely knew.

Yet he was realistic, unafraid, and determined.

"Be careful." Her voice was a whisper.

"I will."

He turned and started back up the trail.

Where is your compassion?

Had she become immune to the suffering of others?

Or was she simply making the decisions that had to be made?

She didn't want the weight she was carrying. She certainly didn't stick with this job for the salary. She did it because someone needed to.

She did it for her father.

88

Allison sat in front of Teddy, watching and waiting and checking the time every few minutes. She'd thought he might fall asleep, but instead he studied her. His teeth had stopped chattering, and his pulse was strong.

"You're going to be fine," she assured him.

"Are you a doctor?"

"I'm not, but I've seen this sort of thing before."

He looked like he wanted to ask about that, but he didn't. "The guy who did this to me. . . who was he?"

"I don't know, Teddy."

"But you know something. You know something about him or why he's here."

"Yes, I think I do."

"So—"

Allison sighed. "I can't tell you everything, but I think you just got caught up in something that has nothing to do with you. Wrong place, wrong time."

"That's it?"

"Sorry, bud. Sometimes it comes down to that."

He again fell silent.

She glanced at her watch once more. It had been twenty minutes. Tate should be back soon and no matter what he said, they were leaving. They couldn't afford to wait any longer.

"He came up from behind." Teddy's gaze was fixed on something in the darkness. "I heard him, so I turned and that was when he stabbed me. No explanation, no threats, just the attack."

Allison nodded. The sort of people she chased—people like Blitz and Gollum—weren't big on explaining the things they did. Life was black and white for them. They didn't question their decisions.

She understood that.

Where is your compassion?

Tate's question had hit one of the few chinks in her armor. Was she becoming cold and callous, like the people she worked so

89

hard to stop? Was she losing her humanity? Could she still feel compassion?

As if to convince herself that she was a kind and feeling person, she leaned forward—toward Teddy.

"There are events happening here that I'm not at liberty to explain. The reason Tate and I were headed down the trail in the middle of the night is that we need to stop someone, someone who is already at the bottom. The guy who attacked you? I suspect he's providing backup for that guy."

"This guy you're talking about—he's a. . ." He couldn't seem to come up with the word. Finally, he simply shook his head and waited.

"Terrorist. He's a terrorist."

Teddy stared at her. His color had improved. Perhaps talking about what had happened was helping him recover from the shock of it, the violence of it.

"I've never heard of park rangers chasing terrorists."

Allison offered a smile. "Tate's a ranger. I'm not—not really."

"Oh. So, who do you work for?"

"Homeland Security." When his eyes widened, she added, "And that's all I'm going to say about that."

"Understood." He struggled to a sitting position, and she helped him.

She found an energy bar in Tate's pack and passed it to him. "Try to eat a little of this."

He nibbled at it, then seemed to forget what he was doing, staring at the small bar in his hand. "I think at first I was more shocked that he'd thrown my camera in the canyon than the fact that he'd stabbed me."

"You can buy another camera."

"Wasn't mine. It belonged to the university."

"They'll have insurance on it. Don't worry about the camera, Teddy."

"I guess." He took another small bite of the energy bar. "He didn't say much, other than the remark about not having time to finish what he'd started. Just stabbed me, threw the camera and my pack into the canyon, and left. I was lying on the ground, holding my shoulder. I tried to use my phone to call for help, but I couldn't get service down here. I guess the canyon walls block—"

"Your phone?"

"Yeah."

"You have a cell phone?"

"Yeah."

He reached and pulled the mobile device out of a zippered pocket on his right pants leg. "I keep it where I can grab it fast, in case I want to take a photo for social media and sometimes to set up shots for my camera."

"Teddy, did you take pictures with your phone earlier today? Did you take pictures of the group you passed?"

"I don't know. I guess. Maybe. I'm not sure."

She was already on her feet, crossing the small space between them, and then she squatted down in front of him and held out her hand. "Can I look at it?"

"Yeah. Let me just. . ." He typed in a passcode—5678—and handed her the phone.

She sat down beside him and clicked the photo icon. She ran her thumb over the top left corner of the screen which was a spider web of cracks.

"I busted the screen the first week I had it, and I haven't had the money to repair it yet."

She scrolled through pictures of geological formations, mule deer, an agave plant that looked to be at least ten feet tall, and the Colorado River. Again and again, Teddy had photographed the canyon walls, catching different shades of colors as the sun rose and then fell. Allison stopped scrolling when she reached photos that included people. She glanced at each one, then backed up, pausing on the third photo, the one that included the last of the group as they were making their way down the trail.

"They'd stopped for a break, I guess." Teddy used his good arm to rub his forehead. "I thought I'd set up some pictures while

I waited for them to move on, and then once they moved away, I pulled out my camera."

Allison pinched her fingers together on the screen, then spread them out. Her heart accelerated and her palms began to sweat.

Six feet—check.

Late 20s—probably.

Wiry build—without a doubt.

She'd studied the composite sketch of Blitz long enough to recognize him in an instant. But more than the familiarity of the shape of his face and color of his hair, she knew it was him by the look in his eyes. She couldn't have said how she knew, but she knew. She'd chased cybercriminals long enough to recognize one.

"Is that him? That guy? He doesn't look much like a terrorist."

"He could be the guy I'm after. Is he the one who stabbed you?"

"No."

Allison tapped the screen. "Do you remember anything else about this guy?"

"Not much. Like I said, I was waiting for them to move on so I could get some good shots. That guy, he turned around as they were leaving."

Blitz was at the back of the group. Ahead of him she could make out the back of Nina, one of the other park rangers. Nina usually worked with Jason and Todd. On most trips, Jason took the lead and Todd the middle. Allison remembered joking with Nina about how she always preferred to be at the back of the group. Nina had said it was so no tourist would bump into her and push her over the edge, but was it something different?

Was one of them—Nina or Jason or Todd—working with Blitz?

She didn't think so.

But neither could she rule out the possibility.

As for Blitz, he looked remarkably similar to the portrait their sketch artist had compiled, but also very different. Was it because of the glint in his eyes? No, the camera wasn't close enough for that, and Blitz was wearing a ball cap—shading his eyes, his black lanky hair jutting out beneath it and reaching to his shoulders.

He looked normal.

That was what was different.

That was what Allison found so disturbing. No matter how many times she did this, she always expected the monsters to look like what they were. This guy? This man could be any guy you saw at a gym, or along a trail, or in a restaurant. He hid his malevolence well.

A chill crept down her spine.

Then she heard the scattering of pebbles.

She pivoted suddenly, putting her body between Teddy and whoever was out there. In the same instant, she pulled her Glock, racked the slide, and held it steady, waiting, prepared.

Tate walked out of the darkness, raising his hands when he saw her. "Don't shoot. It's only me."

She pulled in a deep breath and holstered her weapon.

"Were you going to shoot him?"

"Don't put it past her, kid."

Tate dropped beside them. He'd taken a large two-liter bottle of water with him, but now he refilled it from the hydration bladder he kept in his pack. "Help is on the way. They'll be here within the hour. Now I'm leaving two liters of water, and I want you to drink what you can because—"

"You're leaving me?" Teddy's voice took on a note of panic.

Allison put her hand on his arm.

"Teddy, this guy. . ." She held up his phone. "The guy who is on your phone and the guy who stabbed you are both terrorists. We have to go after them before they hurt someone else."

Teddy began rocking, but he nodded that he understood.

"Three paramedics and a ranger are on their way down," Tate assured him. "I gave them very good directions for how to find you. What we need you to do is stay put and stay quiet."

"What if he comes back?"

"If he was going to come back, he already would have done so." Allison stood and picked up her pack, wound her arms through the straps. "Teddy, this guy left you to bleed out. He didn't hang around to make sure you were dead, and that's his mistake. Now we're going after him. I need you to stay here and wait for the paramedics. Can you do that?"

"Yeah. Of course."

"And Teddy, I need to keep your phone."

A look of dismay crossed his face, but then he nodded again. "I'll get it back though, right?"

"Sure. Of course. Give the paramedics all of your contact information. I'll bring it to you myself."

Tate looked surprised, but Allison didn't explain herself.

Instead, she said, "Let's go" and took off down the trail without looking back. It was nearly four in the morning. They'd already lost too much time.

"Getting soft on me, Agent Quinn?"

"I am not."

"You care about that kid. I saw it."

She didn't answer, wishing that Tate would drop the subject. She thought he might continue to tease her, but instead he simply matched her stride. As they approached the Tipoff, the trail was wide enough that they could walk side by side, but she knew from experience that it would soon narrow into a single- person track. When that happened, the switchbacks would also become precariously steeper.

"There's nothing wrong with caring about people." Tate's voice was soft, contemplative, as if he was maybe talking to himself.

"In spite of the opinion you seem to have formed about me, I do care about people."

"I never said you didn't."

Where is your compassion?

She stopped abruptly. "Please don't assume that you know how to do my job better than I do."

"I never said that either."

"But you act like it."

He sighed and shrugged his shoulders. "I have a tendency to come across as a know-it-all. I'm sorry."

She was surprised.

She'd expected him to deny judging her.

Instead, he'd apologized. There wasn't much she could do with an apology but accept it, and did his opinion even matter? She didn't care what he thought of her. She'd be far away from Arizona in another forty-eight hours, and Tate Garcia could have his precious canyon and hikers to himself.

Allison knew that wasn't fair.

She was tired, her adrenaline kept surging then dropping, and this was the easy portion of the night's scheduled events.

She needed to focus on the assignment.

Catch Blitz, apprehend both him and the buyer, acquire the codes that could stop the attack, question Blitz about Gollum, and then hand him over to the authorities.

"Let's see if we can make up for lost time."

Tate looked as if he wanted to argue. No doubt he'd remind her that hurrying wasn't something you wanted to do when descending into the canyon.

Then lightning flashed across the western sky and the wind picked up again, carrying with it the scent of rain. She thought of the bridge in front of them, then pushed it from her mind. She'd deal with that when the time came.

But nausea filled her stomach, and her palms began to sweat. She wiped them against her pants. If Tate noticed, he wisely remained silent.

The trail was less steep, and they were able to increase their pace. The roar of the river was audible now, even over the winds preceding the storm. Allison kept reminding herself that she knew this trail well, that there were no surprises ahead. She'd done this hike many times in the last six months, and she'd always made it across the bridge.

Tonight would be no different.

Fifteen minutes from the bridge that would take them across the Colorado and into the Phantom Ranch area, she stopped. Tate nearly barreled into her, but he didn't speak. Some well-honed instinct warned Allison against taking even one more step forward. The air had grown eerily still—literally the quiet before the storm. And then she heard it—the click of a rifle scope being sighted in for the kill.

In that split second, she didn't question what she knew.

She didn't hesitate at all.

Her training and her instincts informed what she did next. She turned and threw herself at Tate. They hit the ground, rolling toward the edge of the canyon, as the first bullet whizzed over their heads.

Chapter Five

Tate stopped their roll by throwing his arms around a protruding rock. Allison clung to his waist—too afraid to look down, too afraid to move. The entire bottom half of her body hung off the trail, dangling over the Colorado River.

"On three," he whispered. "One, two. . ."

With Allison still clinging to his waist, Tate heaved them up and over the edge. Allison rolled to her side and came up on her knees in a shooting stance, her Glock firmly positioned in her right hand.

She stared out at the darkness.

Listened for any human sound.

Became aware of Tate beside her, also holding his weapon, also waiting.

And that was why she'd chosen him. Tate was a decorated soldier who had served on Task Force 1-41 in Iraq. She'd counted on his training as a soldier being something he hadn't forgotten, even if he had been hiding out in Arizona the last twenty-five years.

She heard the barest of sounds to her right at the same moment that lightning split the sky. Their assailant had been closer than she'd thought. The sky returned to darkness, but she'd seen enough. She fired at the same time he did. She fired three shots. More would be a waste of ammunition. Fewer would be arrogantly confident.

Her ears rang from the fired rounds and reverberation. She crouched there half a minute longer—listening to her own breathing and Tate's.

But that was all she heard.

Their breathing.

Allison snatched her flashlight from her pack and splayed it across the ground. The man's body was sprawled in an awkward position. Her shots had hit him, then thrown him back and down. He looked as if he'd been kneeling, then toppled over backward. There was no movement.

"I'll cover you," Tate whispered.

She nodded once, then hurried across the ten yards and knelt beside the man's body. Two of her shots had found her target—one in the stomach, one in the upper torso. He'd hit the ground before the third could reach him.

"Clear," she called back to Tate.

She heard him holster his weapon, cross the distance in several long strides, and then kneel beside her.

"Is this one of your terrorists?"

"Do you know someone else who might be trying to kill us?"

Lifeless eyes stared back at them. Allison holstered her weapon as she replayed Teddy's description in her mind.

Short guy.

Gym rat.

Pale.

Blond hair.

Unless this guy had a twin, they'd found Teddy's assailant.

She quickly searched his pockets. Instead of questioning her further, Tate helped her roll the body on its side, held it there as she checked the back pockets, then rolled him back again. In his front pockets, she found three extra clips for the rifle. Each clip was filled with ammo. She also found a knife, still stained with Teddy's blood.

Nothing else.

No cellular.

"There must be something on him—some identification."

"The fact that there isn't tells us a lot." She stored the extra mags in her pack and pushed the flashlight into Tate's hand.

He pointed it where she indicated, and she pushed up the guy's right sleeve, turning his arm slightly to reveal the inside of his wrist. Though she'd known what she'd see, the image still caused her breath to catch in her chest.

Lightning again slashed the sky, momentarily illuminating the canyon, the trail, every rock around them.

Tate stared down at the guy, then glanced up, around, back at her. "We're too exposed here. We need to move."

Allison heard him, but she didn't answer. Why no cell phone? How had Blitz contacted him? How did this guy know about Teddy and the photographs he had taken?

"Lightning strikes within the canyon 25,000 times a year."

She patted down the man's pockets again, checked his ears for a communication device, and splayed her flashlight around the area in case he'd dropped the cell phone.

"Three hundred kilovolts, Allison. Heats the air up to 50,000 degrees Fahrenheit."

The lightning was now so continuous that she didn't need the flashlight. She stood, turned in a circle, surveyed the area one more time.

"It's a bad way to die—burns, ruptured eardrums, even cardiac arrest."

"I'm aware of the dangers of lightning strikes, Tate."

"Of course you are, because the information was part of your training." Tate leaned closer so she could hear him over the roar of the wind. "But until you're part of a recovery team. . . until you've located and carried back someone who was struck, you can't appreciate the devastation."

And then the rain started. The first few drops were large and hard, more like sleet than rain. It quickly turned to a downpour.

Reaching into her pack, she pulled out a device no bigger than a thumb drive, pressed the center button, and slipped it inside the dead guy's pocket. Then she picked up his rifle, made sure the safety was on and no rounds were in the chamber, and stuck it barrel-down into her pack. She could almost close the zipper over it, but not quite. Tate jerked the waterproof cover off his backpack and helped her place it snugly over the butt of the rifle.

"Let's go."

She didn't speak.

She couldn't even begin to form words.

Now that the danger of Blitz's accomplice was behind them, all she could think of was the bridge. As they reached the junction with the river trail and took a right toward Phantom Ranch, the rain increased in intensity. The trail instantly became muddy, slick, more dangerous. Lightning continued to brighten the sky, and at one point it hit so close that Allison thought it rattled the fillings in her teeth.

She could barely see Tate in front of her though they were hiking only a few feet apart. The rock face of the canyon wall was now on her right, the river on her left. She placed each foot carefully, terrified of slipping off the trail. She fought the urge to squeeze her eyes shut, but the terror—the old familiar dread—had begun to claw at the back of her throat.

The black suspension bridge had been built in 1928.

She had studied every aspect of both the black and silver bridges since they comprised the only two ways across the river. She'd hoped that knowledge would empower her. She had desperately sought to quiet her inner child.

The wind was now blowing the rain sideways, pushing them toward the cliff's wall. Steele's last report said that the storm would be intense but short-lived, skirting off to the north well before sunrise.

Through the haze of her fear, Allison had the ridiculous notion to blame Donovan Steele for the situation she was in.

Tate wisely did not slow down.

Perhaps he was still worried about the lightning strikes, though they'd largely moved off toward the north. She had made very sure that Tate understood the risks of accompanying her down into the canyon in the dead of night as she chased a terrorist and tried to outrun a storm.

She'd given him several opportunities to back out.

He hadn't, but she was fairly certain that he now regretted having signed on.

As for Allison. . . she had not had a choice.

So, she pushed on. What else was there to do?

If she died trying to stop Blitz, that was her job.

She should have felt calmer as they entered the tunnel that led to the bridge. The rock walls above and on both sides at least protected them from the bulk of the rain.

Too little, too late though.

She and Tate were both drenched.

The tunnel had been blasted through rock in 1928. It was quite narrow, forcing groups to walk through single file. Fortunately, Allison's problem wasn't claustrophobia.

Nope.

She would gladly wait within the confines of the tunnel until the storm raced away and dawn broke across the canyon, except for Blitz.

Blitz was at Phantom Ranch.

The handoff would happen at daybreak.

She would be in position before that happened.

Allison stood in the middle of the tunnel, trying to slow her heart rate and calm her rising panic. She reached out and placed her fingertips against the walls on her right and left. The rock was cold and damp. It did nothing to quell her fears.

The clamor of the storm was tremendous.

It should have helped that the tunnel provided a temporary reprieve from the pelting rain, but it didn't.

Tate turned on his flashlight. Its light splayed off the walls, the water dripping down, the trail turning to mud. "Maybe we should wait out the storm here. We're only thirty minutes from the ranch. Plenty of time to get there before daybreak." His voice bounced off the rock.

Allison shook her head. They needed to be in place before Blitz made his move. She couldn't let a storm—or her fear—stop them now.

Tate studied her. Sensing her resolve, he shrugged. "All right. At least let's hydrate, stretch, and eat something. Better to do it here where we're somewhat dry."

They weren't dry.

They were soaked, but at least they hadn't fallen to their death on the muddy switchbacks. The cave embraced them like a mother cradles a babe—safe and secure.

Allison paced back and forth.

Her gaze darted toward the far end of the tunnel, then quickly away. If anything, the rain had increased. Thunder rolled like the timpani section of an orchestra. Lightning flashed, revealing the horror waiting mere feet beyond the cave—her own personal nightmare.

"Trail mix?"

She pulled in a deep breath and extended her hand.

"You're shaking."

She didn't answer.

He dumped trail mix into her palm. When she wouldn't meet his gaze, he stored the trail mix in the top of his pack, zipped it closed, and crossed his arms. "What's wrong?"

She still didn't answer.

Instead of eating the trail mix, she stuck it in her pocket.

"You seemed to recognize the tattoo on that guy's wrist."

She tried to nod, but her neck muscles felt frozen.

Perhaps she was frozen.

Maybe this was as far as she was going to make it.

Tate was resting his back against the tunnel's wall, watching her, no doubt trying to figure out what was happening. Clearing his throat, he said, "An A inside of a circle means anarchy. Any kid with a game console knows that, but why was it etched on top of a tree?"

"They call themselves. . ." She attempted to pull in a deep breath, managed only a gulp of oxygen. "Anarchists for Tomorrow."

Sweat broke out along her forehead. She wiped it away with the soaked sleeve of her shirt.

"A somewhat arrogant name."

"The tree means. . ." She glanced toward the bridge.

"What does it mean, Allison?"

"Growth. It's supposed. . ." She tried to swallow, but her mouth was suddenly too dry. "It's supposed to represent growth."

Allison paced toward the far end of the tunnel, the bridge end, and back again.

Tate continued watching her.

"How did he communicate with your other guy? With Blitz? If he had no phone how did he. . ." His words drifted off as he shook his head. "I just don't see how that worked."

His question momentarily pulled her from her current crisis. That had puzzled her too. Apparently while her overactive amygdala had been busy paralyzing her, her prefrontal cortex had been solving the question of Blitz's accomplice.

"The AT group is careful—very careful—about when and where they use technology."

"Because?"

"They're aware of the government's eavesdropping capabilities. So they. . ."

She stared toward the end of the tunnel, toward the bridge waiting for her. Her stomach heaved, and she thought the little she'd eaten would come up. Would she become a vomiting, terrified mess in front of Tate Garcia?

Closing her eyes, she attempted to quell the rising tide of fear. She thought of her therapist—an older woman with gray hair framing her face and kind eyes. *You can't always avoid what you fear, but there are practices you can learn to help you through.*

Practices.

Routines.

Stopgap measures.

She placed the fingertips of her right hand against her left wrist and counted her heartbeats.

"They what? They have to communicate somehow."

"That guy back there, he must have been following the main group down. He didn't join them, because he didn't want to be seen." Her pulse was fast but strong. She wasn't dying. Her heart wouldn't stop because of her fear. "Blitz gave him some sort of signal."

"A signal that something had gone wrong."

"Yeah. Maybe he pointed at Teddy or stood directly behind him for a moment. Any pre-arranged gesture would be enough."

Tate stared at the ground and blew out a deep breath.

"The guy I shot must have seen the signal."

"Then he hung back and attacked Teddy."

"Right. Afterwards, he hiked a little farther down the trail and waited to see if anyone else would follow."

"Which we did."

"Yes."

She had refused to don her rain parka earlier, fearing it would slow her down if she needed to reach for her weapon. Now she fished out a small hiking towel and attempted to pat herself dry. Her hands were shaking so badly that she dropped the towel. When she bent to pick it up every fiber of her being wanted to simply sit on the floor of that cave, place her arms around her knees and wait until the storm had passed and daylight spilled across the canyon.

"And the thing you left on him? A sensor of some sort?"

"Yeah."

The military had been using those for many years. The *no man left behind* scenario often portrayed in movies wasn't always possible. When it wasn't feasible to carry out a fallen soldier, he was tagged and the body was picked up as soon as it was safe to do so.

It could also be used in the opposite scenario, when an enemy agent had been taken down but the body couldn't be immediately retrieved or disposed of.

"Someone will pick up his body?"

She nodded, trying to focus on his words but failing miserably. Nausea and dread fought her common sense. She'd been through this before though. She would not let it win.

Which meant it was time to move.

She stored the towel and picked up the pack. "Let's go."

"Wait."

Lightning again flashed across the sky, followed quickly by a clap of thunder that made her jump.

"Going out on that bridge in a storm, while it's lightning, is not smart."

"Fine. Stay here. Meet me at the meadow behind the main lodge."

"I'm not letting you go without me."

"Then let's move."

She didn't look back, simply squared her shoulders, trudged to the far side of the tunnel, and stepped out into the storm. The suspension bridge that connected the South Kaibab Trail to Phantom Ranch was a nice, solid structure. At 416 feet long and five feet wide, it was suspended sixty-five feet above the rushing water of the Colorado River. During a bright sunny afternoon, it was a lovely experience for most people.

It had never been that for Allison.

She had crossed it many times since going undercover at the ranch, but never at night. Never while a storm surged around them. She was aware of Tate hurrying to catch up, but she couldn't turn to look at him. She had to focus on the far side of the bridge.

She was halfway across when lightning again slashed across the sky. Glancing down, she saw the water churning like a giant whirlpool that would suck her under. The bridge seemed to sway and tilt. Allison stood, frozen, completely unable to move. Sweat dripped down her face and the muscles in her legs began to spasm.

All rational thought fled.

Her legs stopped moving.

Her mind filled with a slow reel of her tumbling, turbulent death.

Finally, she surrendered to her instincts, crouching, attempting to make herself as small as possible. With her arms covering her head, she could hear the beat of her pulse hammering in her veins. Bile rose in her throat. She squeezed her eyes more tightly shut, clamped her hands over her ears.

And then Tate was at her side.

The rain pelted them with such fury that talking was impossible. He maneuvered around her, stopped in front so that his face was mere inches from hers. His voice, when he finally did speak, was steady and convincing.

"Allison, I want you to hold my hand."

She shook her head, her teeth chattering, her gaze darting back down, which she immediately regretted. Better to close her eyes. Better not to see her death.

Tate's hands had enfolded hers.

She didn't pull away.

"Good. Now open your eyes."

She squeezed them shut more tightly.

"I know I'm an ugly, old guy, but look at me, Allison."

When she did, he smiled.

"Deep breath—with me. In—good. Out—you're doing great."

She began repeating her mantra. "I am bigger than my fear." She said the phrase over and over, eyes once more squeezed shut until it seemed as if there was only the storm, the bridge, Tate, and her words.

"We can't stay out here. I'm going to help you to the other side."

She shook her head again—a bobblehead doll completely unconnected from her common sense. Her brain had become a circuit board of fear. Her entire body trembled under the fury of the storm and the weight of her phobia. The gun on her hip was useless. The pack on her back held nothing that could save her.

"I am bigger than my fear."

"Open your eyes and focus on me. Focus on me and the far side. You can see it when the lightning flashes. You'll see that it's getting closer."

She didn't at first realize they were moving.

Slowly, oh-so-very-slowly, she became aware that she was in a standing position. She was placing one foot in front of the other. She was breathing and alive and walking across the bridge.

Tate continued coaxing her forward. "You're doing well. We're almost there. Only a few more steps."

Lightning split the night sky, but she didn't see the bridge or the water or her certain death.

She saw Tate, smiling, encouraging, leading her across the chasm of death.

"You're lucky that one didn't hit us. I would've pestered you with *I told you so's* for all of our lives."

Allison didn't laugh.

She wasn't sure she'd ever laugh again.

They proceeded slowly, but *slow and steady will get you there*, as her therapist used to say.

It did.

Unfortunately, there was no tunnel on the far side. They splashed along the muddy trail, not stopping until they reached the water station near the Bright Angel campground. Tate pulled her under the small roofed informational display, hesitated, then pulled her into his arms.

She caught the scent of his soap, aftershave, deodorant—the scents of her father.

Her trembling slowed, then stopped.

Her heart rate slowed to normal.

She pulled in another deep, cleansing breath and moved away from Tate—one step and then two, but she didn't leave the shelter of the kiosk. She wasn't ready to confront the elements yet.

"That was a brave thing for you to do."

She'd been staring at the ground—a part of her mind repeating her mantra, another part scolding herself for acting like a child. At Tate's words, her head jerked up.

Was he serious?

Or was he mocking her?

"I appreciate how hard that must have been." When she didn't respond, he pushed on. "How long have you suffered from acrophobia?"

"Since I was a child."

Run.

You shouldn't have tried to stop me.

Bang.

"Traumatic experience?"

"You could say that."

Tate dropped his pack on the ground and pulled out his water bottle. "What you just did took guts, Allison. I don't know of anyone with a fear of heights who would have attempted crossing a suspension bridge over the Colorado River at night in the middle of a storm."

"Probably because you don't know anyone else with acrophobia."

Her breathing had returned to normal and the tunnel vision had cleared. She reached into her pocket, found the trail mix and popped a few pieces into her mouth, then retrieved her own water bottle.

Tate had stopped studying her.

He was now looking out over the empty campground. "We

average a few every year—people who want to see the canyon but are worried they can't do it. Those inquiries are forwarded to me, and I work with them so they can have this experience in spite of their anxiety."

She hadn't known that—hadn't realized that he'd had any experience at all with people who struggled with acrophobia. "I usually can manage the symptoms."

"The combination of fatigue, adrenaline, and this storm probably made that difficult."

She nodded, her embarrassment fading nearly as quickly as her fear.

They stood there another ten minutes, backs against the information board, shoulders touching. Neither felt the need to say more about her panic attack. Finally, the storm moved on. She looked up, surprised to see that she could make out the surrounding area now. Starlight once again shone above them.

"Campground looks empty." Tate pushed his water bottle into a pocket of his pack. "Usually Bright Angel is full. The storm must have scared everyone off."

"Blitz probably picked tonight because of the storm."

"But how did he secure a place on the hike down? Those places fill up a year in advance."

"He killed a man who had a reservation, then he just happened to be at the visitor center when it was posted that there was one opening."

"He killed a man?"

"You can't be surprised. Terrorists have no scruples—anyone is fair game." She took a final pull from her water bottle, then stored it. "You saw what his accomplice did to Teddy and what he would have done to us."

"Thank you for that, by the way."

"For?"

"Saving my life." Tate glanced up at the stars, then back at her. "If you hadn't pushed me to the ground, I'd probably be bleeding out right now."

"Too bad I nearly knocked us both to our deaths."

Tate waved that away. "I guess we make a pretty good team. Kept each other alive and saved Teddy."

"Right."

Mentioning Teddy brought her mission completely back into focus. She needed to be at the ranch when the kill codes were transferred.

"I hope he made it out before the storm hit."

"Me too." She donned her pack, easily able to put the panic attack behind them. She'd dealt with her condition all her life. She'd worried it would keep her from being a field agent, but her superiors had assured her everyone had a weak point—at least she was aware of what hers was.

Awareness led to preparation.

Preparation helped you through.

Though this night, it had been the man standing beside her who helped her through.

They stepped back onto the path that led to Phantom Ranch, traversing the lowest part of the trail. The ranch was positioned at an inside bend where two hundred yards separated the canyon walls. Cottonwood trees, cacti, and scrub brush dotted the landscape, offering an unlimited number of places to hide.

Blitz wouldn't be here though. He'd be at the main building. Most cyberterrorists enjoyed their creature comforts. There was no way he would have spent the night in the rain.

"What's your plan?"

"Our intelligence suggests that Blitz will meet whoever has the kill codes before sunrise, behind the main building."

"Little risk of being seen then."

"Exactly."

"We're going to intercept him there?"

"We're going to watch and assess, and then you are going to slip inside and resume your normal job."

"What?" The word exploded from him.

Allison shot him a glare, then reached out and snagged his

arm, effectively stopping their forward progress. "Listen to me. I need you on the inside. You have a private room with a private entrance."

"What does that have to do with anything?"

"It'll be easy to slip in and pretend you've been there all night."

"And why would I do that?"

"I need you to resume your position and then feed me information."

"And I'm supposed to leave you out here? With a terrorist?"

"I also need you to shift as many people as possible out of Blitz's raft without drawing anyone's attention to what you're doing."

The sky had lightened just enough for her to make out his frustration, or perhaps she'd come to know him so well in the last twelve hours that she could imagine it.

"You're going to sit outside? How do you know there aren't more Anarchists for Tomorrow waiting? I'll admit that was a good shot back there—"

"Well, thanks, Tate."

"But waiting outside the camp alone is not smart."

"I am not alone. There are other agents above us on the North Rim trail as well as farther downriver."

"Which will do you no good if Blitz had more than one person hanging back."

"I can handle Blitz or any of his accomplices." There wasn't an ounce of doubt in her mind or her voice. "Now let's go. I want to be in position before the sky gets any lighter."

She understood that Tate was constantly playing catch-up. She'd gone from being frightened and vulnerable one moment to bossy and unreasonable the next.

He'd have to find a way to deal with that.

Nothing about her instructions was negotiable.

This was her mission, and they'd do it her way.

Chapter Six

Allison and Tate made their way past the stock barn, crew bunkhouse, ranger station, and amphitheater. Stretched across fourteen acres, the ranch lay at the bottom of a gorge which meant the high cliffs delayed sunrise by several hours and ushered in dusk well before sunset. The darkness didn't stop visitors from rising early. Most had been planning their visit to the canyon for two years, and they were determined to see all they could.

Phantom Ranch was abuzz with activity.

Eleven cabins and four dormitories housed ninety-two overnight guests. Electricity came from a buried line, and light blazed in most of the cabins.

Allison was counting on the fact that their park uniforms would give them a degree of anonymity. *Nothing to see here—just two rangers returning from a terrifying and deadly night hike.*

The breakfast bell rang as they found the perfect spot to position themselves approximately thirty yards from the back door of the lodge. Behind them Bright Angel Creek flowed at its normal rate. As predicted, the storm must have turned abruptly north after pelting them on the suspension bridge.

Allison and Tate took cover behind tall grass.

The area between them and the back door of the lodge was peppered with mesquite trees. Over the roof of the lodge, Allison could just make out the red rock face of the canyon wall rising abruptly. She turned her attention to the back door and peered through the rifle she'd taken from Blitz's guy. The sightline was perfect.

"You plan on shooting him?"

"I do not, but best to—"

"Be prepared. I know."

Allison thought the sky was lightening, but she could have imagined that. The night sky at Phantom Ranch was said to provide some of the best stargazing anywhere in the continental U.S. Indeed, what she saw was a riot of light. She was small and insignificant against the infinity of the heavens, and yet she had a job to do.

She was ready for this op to be over. Ready to intercept the codes, derail the coming calamity, learn about her father's killer, then go back to her apartment and sleep for thirty-six hours.

That wasn't going to happen anytime soon though.

Intercepting the codes would be tricky. If Blitz saw them coming, he'd destroy the codes. He had nothing to lose but money, and she suspected he had plenty of that.

"If I'm going inside, looking for information, I need more details." Tate's tone was low and steady.

She could tell he'd accepted the situation for what it was—messed up but necessary.

She studied him in the darkness, able to see only his darkened profile barely visible against the star-filled sky. *The night is darkest before the dawn.* Who had said that? Some theologian of a bygone era. Allison knew it wasn't always true. Scientifically speaking, darkness was determined by the phase of the moon, time of year, amount of cloud cover, and other factors. It was possible that the darkest moment occurred at the midpoint between sundown and sunrise. Still, she could appreciate the sentiment.

"Yeah, okay." When they were in Director Rivera's office, she'd been uncertain exactly how much she would share with him. They'd been through a lot since then, even if it had been only a few hours ago.

She had very little doubt remaining about whether she could trust Tate.

And he needed to understand what he was going up against.

"The Anarchists for Tomorrow are cyberterrorists that formed out of an eco-terrorist movement. Their stated goal is to create anarchy for a better tomorrow. They claim to be anti-government, anti-capitalism, and pro-democracy which is true at times depending upon whether it suits their momentary goals."

"You've dealt with them in the past?"

Run.

You shouldn't have tried to stop me.

Bang.

"Yes. Six months ago we received intelligence that they planned to bring down the entire U.S. electrical grid, along with a good portion of Canada's."

Tate considered that for a moment. She knew he understood the full scope and challenges when he asked, "Estimated casualties?"

"Tens of thousands. The most vulnerable in our society are often completely dependent on the grid."

"Elderly."

"Yes, but also those with chronic medical conditions that require daily care. Then there's an added death toll from a population thrown into a chaos they couldn't possibly imagine no matter how many apocalyptic movies they've seen."

The entirety of Allison's career passed through her mind, rewinding back through the ops and the training and the college classes until she was a girl standing against a tree, squeezing her eyes shut, hoping to make herself invisible.

"They represent a legitimate threat, obviously, or you wouldn't be here."

"They do. One problem with the AT is that they include a

broad swath of individuals. Many are well educated and success-ful. The monsters often look much different than we'd assume."

"And yet where there is a monster, there is a miracle."

"Huh?"

Tate smiled and waved away her look of concern. "Ogden Nash, an American poet."

Great.

She'd saddled herself with a partner who quoted poetry.

They were settled with their backs against two mesquite trees, watching the back door of the ranch and the meadow where the exchange was supposed to take place. The breakfast of eggs, sausage, bacon and biscuits was being served. She could just make out sleepy hikers slumping into their chairs in the main dining room.

"I assume this isn't the AT's first rodeo."

"Hardly. The grid failure on the west coast last year? That wasn't from the heat wave."

"Ah."

"They've hit a dozen cities since then."

"I don't know a lot about cyberattacks."

"Probably hasn't affected your job here in the canyon."

"Not before last night." He scrubbed a hand over his face. "But I do live in the twenty-first century. Even our infrastructure here at the canyon has some degree of dependence on the grid, and I don't mind telling you, we don't have much of a plan to deal with outages."

Allison nodded in understanding. "You're not the only place that's unprepared. Much of America doesn't have a valid, updated plan to deal with an extended outage."

"Yeah, but we have over five million visitors a year. A complete outage that extended to no electricity, downed cell phone communication, and inoperable GPS. . ." He blew out a breath. "It would be a problem."

When she didn't respond to that, he pushed on. "The attacks

you deal with, are you talking about ransomware and DDoS attacks?"

"Some. Other times, they creep in and steal information that they threaten to release to the public or sell. Then there's the attacks on specific targets that have technological vulnerabilities."

"Such as?"

"The dam failure in the northeast last spring."

"Killed quite a few."

"Yeah. The dam didn't fail, though it did experience an uncontrolled release. The AT remotely opened all of the gates. Forty-six tourists on the river were killed. There was no ransom demand that time. They were simply flexing their muscle."

She hesitated, but in the end decided there was no valid reason to hold back from Tate now. If he was on the wrong side of things, she wasn't telling him anything new. And he was very probably on the right side. "This attack is being masterminded by a terrorist called Gollum."

"You're kidding."

"We think Gollum connected with an older group—" Her mind flashed to the tattoo on the arm of the terrorist she'd killed on Hurricane Ridge—branches of a tree. Roots that turned into a sword. Writing in an Elfish language circling the top two-thirds of the image.

Not so unlike the tat on the terrorist she'd killed on the South Kaibab a few hours earlier. Not identical, but related. A group formed out of a group that she believed traced all the way back to the murder of her father.

"Not kidding. The prick is arrogant enough to slip lines from Tolkien into his code. We think that Gollum and the AT are two different groups. Gollum masterminded this plan, but needed someone to help carry it out. The AT wanted to be seen as a serious threat. They both were building up to just this sort of attack."

Tate seemed to consider that for a moment.

She let him think, let him come to terms with what they were facing.

"And you knew about this six months ago because that's when you showed up in my department."

"Right."

He shifted, rummaged in his pack, and withdrew his pistol. Placing it on the ground next to him, he studied it before speaking. "Cyberterrorists smart enough and self-possessed enough to work outside the scope of technology. That's a surprise to me. I would expect them to be fully in the cyber realm."

"It's also part of what makes them so dangerous."

"Where does your intel come from?"

"We have someone on the inside. Six months ago, the AT released a Memorandum of Destruction. It's not something they deliver to the *New York Times*. Mostly they posted it on obscure boards via the dark web. You'd be surprised how many people are cheering them on."

"I may live at the bottom of a 6,000-foot canyon, but I'm still aware of the state of the world at large. There are a lot of discontented, disenfranchised people."

"Yes, there are." She raised the rifle and again peered through the scope. Still no movement. "Gollum put the kill codes up for auction. Uncle Sam bid, but we didn't win."

"Who can outbid the US Government?"

"A very well-organized group of those discontented people you mentioned. Some of them stand to make a great deal of money if the market collapses."

"Which it would."

"Which it would."

"Your agent on the inside must be in pretty deep if he knew the location where the transfer would take place."

"Yeah." Allison hadn't been told who the inside person was, but even government agents had a grapevine. It hadn't been that hard to guess who was missing, who hadn't been seen or heard from in several months. There were only a few possible candidates. Allison hoped he or she made it out, because whoever it was had gone above and beyond the call of duty.

They had gone in knowing they might never come out.

"This group that outbid everyone else for the kill codes. . ." Tate shook his head, unable to continue to the obvious conclusion. "Once they get them, what will they do?"

"They'll destroy them, then take credit for the attack."

"And Blitz is behind it?"

"No. Blitz is a middleman. We think someone on Gollum's team wrote the code for the attack. That same person probably penned the kill codes. Gollum seems to have a very laissez-faire attitude toward civilization. He put the codes up for bid, chose a winner, then handed them off to someone in his organization. That person will give them to Blitz, who will pass them to the buyer." As if speaking his name could conjure the man, the back door of the ranch opened and Allison's target stepped out.

He stood in the shadows several moments—studying the field, Bright Angel Creek, and the north canyon walls. She suspected he was looking for the guy they'd killed. But he wouldn't necessarily arrive at the conclusion that the man hadn't made it. More than likely, Blitz would assume that he was still taking care of business.

The door that led to the kitchen opened, and Lyra Alonzo stepped out. Allison felt Tate tense beside her. Neither of them would have put Lyra on a possible terrorist list. She stood maybe five foot, four inches, and didn't top a hundred pounds. Twenty years old, with tattoos snaking up her left arm, she had always seemed shy and deferential.

That had apparently been a cover—and a fairly convincing one.

Lyra looked furtively right then left, then walked over to a tree stump. She stood there, glancing around nervously, when Blitz stepped out in front of her. Now that she could see him better, Allison was certain it was the same guy that Teddy had photographed. Peering through the scope, she realized that his facial characteristics were eerily similar to what the sketch artists had drawn.

Allison could hear the murmur of their voices, but not what they said. From where they were standing, no one in the dining room would see them. Blitz had chosen his hand-off spot well. Lyra pulled something out of her jeans pocket and passed it to Blitz. He stared down at it a moment, then zipped it into his jacket pocket—apparently satisfied it was the real deal.

Next, he pulled out an envelope that looked to be stuffed with money and handed it to Lyra. She shrugged once as she stuffed the envelope into her back jeans pocket. Blitz motioned to the door she'd come out of.

He was telling her to go.

The two had nothing to talk about.

They were vendors in a macabre market.

Lyra turned away, and Blitz attacked her with the ferocity of a panther. In a split second, he snapped her neck and let her fall to the ground. It seemed to Allison that the snap—the pop of vertebrae—carried across the meadow.

Tate had snatched up his pistol and started to rise, but Allison pulled him back. She felt the same rage that he did. Her heart rate pounded in her ears and adrenaline once again rushed through her body. But she understood that now wasn't the time to intervene.

Blitz looked around again, and that was when Allison understood. He was waiting for his accomplice to come and drag the girl away. He'd never intended to let Lyra live, but he'd counted on having help to dispose of the body. Accepting that help wasn't coming, Blitz pulled the envelope of money from Lyra's back pocket and returned it to the inside of his jacket. Then he reached under the girl's arms and proceeded to drag her toward the far side of the meadow. They lost sight of him when he disappeared behind a clump of rocks.

Allison turned to Tate. His complexion had paled, but he kept his anger in check.

"We couldn't have stopped him, Tate."

"You could have shot him."

"Yeah, I could have. But Lyra would still be dead. In case you didn't notice, Blitz was pretty quick with his pounce and kill." She took a deep breath, tried to will her heart rate down, fought to conserve her energy reserves. "A shot would have alerted everyone in the area to what is going on, and I'm not ready to do that yet."

"Why? He has the kill codes."

"Blitz didn't get those codes for himself. He's handing them off to someone downriver. We need to know who that someone is. Otherwise, this entire scenario will repeat itself in a month or a year or five years."

"And Lyra?"

Allison made a chopping gesture with her hand to quiet him as Blitz again appeared in the meadow. He brushed one hand against the other, as if he'd done a bit of early morning climbing and needed to wipe away the bits of rock and chalk from his palms. He strode confidently toward the door he'd exited and disappeared into the ranch, no doubt eager to enjoy his breakfast.

Allison and Tate crept backward, until they were standing at the banks of Bright Angel Creek. The babbling water would mask their voices, and the cottonwood trees hid them from view.

"I'll tag Lyra's body. As soon as Blitz is downriver, agents will come in and retrieve her."

"I guess that will have to do." Tate cleared his throat. "I don't like it, but I understand that's the way it needs to be."

"Do you think you can get into the lodge without being seen?"

"I'll circle around and come from the direction of the stables. It won't matter if they see me. They'll think I was out checking on the horses."

"Speaking of which. . . I'm going to need to borrow one."

"Any preference?"

"I'll take Bella." The three-year-old mare was a red roan.

Allison had ridden her half a dozen times. She was dependable and quick.

"Sure you don't want a mule?"

"Too slow, and I don't plan on going up to the rim. Blitz won't run that direction. He'll go downriver. We're certain of that much."

"You're taking a horse downriver?" He looked at her as if she'd lost the last shred of common sense she possessed.

"I seem to remember that southwest is the direction the river flows, Tate. Since Blitz is taking a raft, and my assignment is to follow him—yeah, I'm going downriver."

He was already shaking his head. "The river trail only covers the initial two miles."

"And Blitz will go farther than that—I'm aware."

"Have you ridden past that trail, Allison?" Now he was angry, and he wasn't even trying to keep his emotions in check. "I have, and there are areas where the canyon walls literally meet the river."

"I understand that it won't be easy."

"Won't be easy? I'm not sure it's even possible."

She stepped closer, lowered her voice, and allowed a little of her own anger to show. "It's going to have to be, Tate, because that's the only way to catch Blitz, the only way to intercept the buyers, and the only way to secure the kill codes. So I'm going down the river. Leave it to me to figure out how."

He turned and stomped away three feet, then pivoted back. "I expect you to return that horse."

"Now you're worried about the horse?"

"Just promise me that you'll see the mare isn't hurt, and that you will personally make sure she's returned."

Suddenly, she understood.

He cared for the horse, but more than that he took his responsibility as head ranger very seriously. There had been two deaths and one near-death in his canyon in twelve hours. He wasn't going to tolerate another—among his horses or his employees.

Instead of thanking him for his concern, she said, "I'll return Bella, Tate. You have my word."

"Fine."

"Fine."

And then his bravado deflated like a child's balloon after a birthday party. "I'll square it on the check-out sheets."

"Have breakfast, make sure you're seen, and do what you can to rearrange the tourists and workers away from Blitz's raft."

"I won't be able to move everyone."

"As many as you can."

"Rafts leave at nine sharp."

"Cabin Eleven is still being renovated and it's out of sight of the others. Meet me there at eight."

"All right." He stood and lifted his pack. "What if I can't get away?"

"If you can't make it, leave a note inside the nightstand of your room."

"Got it."

"And Tate. . . be careful."

His brow furrowed. He looked pale and tired, and Allison suspected that the shock of all they'd seen was beginning to sink in. But he also looked resolute.

He nodded, then strode off toward the stables.

Allison headed in the direction Blitz had taken Lyra's body. It wasn't difficult to find if you knew what you were looking for. Blitz had done nothing to hide the drag marks, but then people didn't walk around the bottom of the canyon looking at the dirt. Most people walked around staring up at the canyon walls.

She located the body behind a pile of brush. Blitz had tossed her there like yesterday's trash. Allison turned the woman's body over, swiped the hair out of her face, and straightened her clothes. She might not be able to carry her out, and she certainly hadn't been able to stop her murder, but she could give her body a modicum of respect. A part of her thought that Lyra deserved that.

Had she worked with terrorists? Apparently—yes.

But she'd been a young woman with her entire life ahead of her. She'd been redeemable.

Or so Allison needed to believe.

Pulling another tracker from her pack, she depressed the center button and slipped it into the front pocket of Lyra's jeans. Then she pulled a clean bandana from her pack and placed it over Lyra's face. It wasn't enough, but it was the best she could do.

Donning her pack, she checked her watch.

She had enough time—if she hurried.

Ten minutes later she'd found her spot—a place that she'd determined many months before—and dug out the SAT phone from her pack. She hadn't mentioned to Tate that she had one. She'd let him hike back up to call for help for Teddy. The parameters for when and where she made contact were strictly set.

Plus, there was the fact that she didn't completely trust Tate.

Mostly, she did.

She put her trust in him at a solid ninety-seven percent, but ninety-seven wasn't one hundred.

Steele answered on the second ring.

"Status." His tone was all business of course.

It wasn't like she'd expected, "Hi, honey. How are you?"

She covered the night's events succinctly, then waited for his reply.

"Teddy's stable and in surgery now. We retrieved the body of Blitz's accomplice, and we'll pick up Lyra as soon as Blitz is in the raft and headed downriver."

"Copy that."

"We've also located what we think is the accomplice's car. His name, by the way, was Anthony Cooper."

"That was fast."

"FBI has their resources."

She didn't rise to the bait. It was a constant contention between them—who worked for the better agency.

"In the vehicle was a cell phone. Cooper had placed two calls to the ranch—five and seven days ago."

Allison's mind tried to process that. The problem wasn't that she was exhausted. The problem was that she didn't want to believe the only possible conclusion. "He was in contact with someone at the ranch, but Blitz wasn't even there yet."

"Correct. This confirms that Gollum's organization had a man—or woman—placed within the staff of Phantom Ranch."

"Lyra?"

"Possibly, but I doubt it. There's no reason that Blitz or Cooper would have tried to contact her. She was handing off the codes, but he wouldn't need to remind her of that. We know from the communications we intercepted last week that she had received those instructions straight from Gollum."

"Then the phone call doesn't make sense."

"Our inside source says Gollum likes to have backups to his backups. That he. . ." There was the rustle of paper as Steele searched for something. "Here it is. He thinks and acts like a spy."

"Meaning what?"

"We don't know, but it could be that at some point he worked for the CIA. We have people on it."

Gollum worked for the CIA?

Her mind buzzed as she considered the possibility that he had killed her father, that he might have worked with her father. She pushed those thoughts aside. She needed to focus on the mission at hand.

So who had Anthony Cooper called?

Tate had been at the ranch earlier in the week. Was it possible that he was involved in this? She didn't think so—his shock at Lyra's murder and his confusion over the AT's plans had seemed genuine. It didn't have to be Tate though. With a staff of seventeen employees, various park rangers, and the regular allotment of guests, there were plenty of candidates.

Allison filed the information away.

There was nothing she could do about it now.

"We're sending agents down the north side. They'll take up position at all junctures along the river route."

"Good."

"Alli. . ."

There was a pause, and suddenly it was her friend on the phone, not her opponent from the competing agency. *Was* Steele her friend? She couldn't say, not for certain. But she did know that her trust in him was at one hundred percent. It had been, since two years before when they'd stopped an EMP attack in the Seattle area. Allison had been shot, and he'd stayed with her on a remote dirt track that led to Obstruction Point.

He'd refused to hike out for help, though he could have.

He'd refused to leave her alone.

"How are you holding up?"

"I'm okay." She realized that sounded curt, rude, insufficient even. "I think Tate's on our side. The hike down was fine—other than the guy trying to kill us."

"And the bridge?"

Like a cat brushed the wrong way, she snapped, "Fine."

There was a silence of several seconds, then Steele came back with his all-business tone. "Okay, Quinn. You're authorized to proceed downriver. Priority one is intercepting the person who has purchased those kill codes and retrieving the device. Secondary to that is arresting Blitz and anyone else involved in this operation."

"Got it."

"At any point that you feel priority one is in jeopardy, you abandon priority two. Questions?"

"No."

"Catastrophic Systems Failure is now twenty-nine hours away."

"I can do the math."

"Watch your back."

"Always."

"And Quinn? Once Blitz steps into that river raft, you are providing backup only."

"What?" She was staring up at the canyon walls, but her vision was immediately tinged with red. He made her so mad. How could he even think of busting her position to backup?

"Agents from the north side will take over primary."

"No. They won't."

"Wasn't a question, Quinn. It was an order."

She wanted to shout, "You're not the boss of me," into the phone, but that sounded childish. Besides, in this scenario, he was the boss of her.

"Are we clear?"

"Crystal." She punched the off button with a little more force than was necessary, shoved the SAT phone into the bottom of her pack, and headed back toward the ranch, back toward Blitz.

She needed to reach the barn before the stable hands showed up.

She had a horse to borrow.

Chapter Seven

John Howard rose early after only four hours of sleep.

He went through his ritual of one hundred sit-ups, one hundred push-ups, and fifty pull-ups using a bar installed in the doorway between his living area and small kitchen. He'd known many spies who had gone soft over the course of their assignments—mentally and physically. Either could kill you when deployed in the field—and in his case still could, though he was operating stateside and no longer in the employ of the Agency.

Breakfast consisted of yogurt, a single boiled egg, and toast with a cup of strong black coffee. He showered for two minutes exactly—the water hot and steaming. From his closet, he pulled out a clean black sport coat, black t-shirt, black pants and black shoes. It wasn't that he fancied himself a swat team member, or even thought he looked good in the color.

He'd switched to a minimalist wardrobe years ago.

He needed to save his decision-making ability for decisions that mattered.

The main computer center at Middle-earth had been set up in the basement level of the building. No windows to distract the computer geeks, not that they looked up often or at all. Their world was largely limited to what they saw on the screens in front of them. If this op was successful, and John was determined that it would be, then that would change. The hackers he employed, along with everyone else, would have to learn to live in the real world.

They'd be emancipated from the machines that held them captive, that recorded every word spoken, every item purchased, even every click of their mouse.

Sometimes John wondered if their computer specialists, programmers, data miners, and hackers understood their mission. Did they know that they were working to destroy the very thing that provided them employment? Most IT people were analytical in nature. Give them a problem, and they found a way in, over, or through it. They didn't always bother to think past the problem they were confronting. They didn't pause long enough to analyze what would happen after that problem was solved.

The daytime shift of "software engineers" consisted of six employees who sat in the middle of the room, three facing three. Equally split as far as gender, in every other way they were different—size, ethnicity, age, experience. Their monitors rose up between them, and the latest in headphone technology was affixed to their ears. They were content to exist in their digital bubble.

The wall at the far end of the room had been turned into a multi-media wall similar to the one in John's office.

Kate and Brett could watch what each hacker was working on through that bank of monitors, without lurking over the hacker's shoulder. At the moment, they were standing in front of the monitors, arms crossed, concern coloring their features. He was sometimes surprised to find that the two worked so well together. Brett was a generation older, and yet he was able to understand the most recent advances in technology. More importantly, he knew how to deal with any personnel glitches.

Kate, on the other hand, was a digital native. She was a true tech savant. More than once, she had found a problem with their code and fixed it.

John resisted the urge to clap his hands.

Today was the day that would literally change the course of human history. If he said as much outside the walls of Middle-earth, he'd be declared pathological, deranged, bonkers. He was none of those things, and he was not overstating the effect Cyber Drop would have. People would no longer be spied on, no longer be hunted and killed. They would be free of the machines that now controlled every aspect of their lives.

So why were Brett and Kate frowning?

"Problem?"

Brett and Kate looked up, startled. They hadn't heard him approach? If so, matters were worse than it looked, and they looked bad.

"Tell me."

Brett nodded toward a center monitor displaying a topological map. In the center of the contours blinked a red dot. "Anthony Cooper is dead."

"Dead?"

"As is Lyra Alonzo."

Kate pointed toward another display. "That's Phantom Ranch. As you can see, there are two green dots and one red."

John Howard didn't panic easily. He schooled his features and stepped closer to the monitor Kate had indicated. "The red one is set apart from the two green."

"Whoever killed her, moved her."

"How do you know it's Lyra's dot?"

She tapped the ever-present tablet in her hand and a square popped up beside the red dot. John found himself looking at Lyra's picture, statistics, and status—deceased.

He fought the urge to punch the wall of monitors.

This was his op, his brainchild, his dream of retribution.

Turning, he stared across the room and pictured a cool, clean river. He forced himself to imagine the sound it made—gurgling, rippling, splashing. The river was not polluted. It was pristine, unhindered, unwatched. That river and thousands of others just like it were what they were fighting for. The rivers, the people, the world. Those things depended on their success.

Therefore, they would succeed.

Turning back to Brett and Kate, he did not ask the obvious. He waited. Kate jumped in first.

"Cooper was on the South Kaibab trail when he died. Our best guess is that someone killed him."

"You think?"

"What I mean is that we can tell by the positioning of his dot that he didn't fall into the canyon."

It wasn't lost on John that the very technology they were seeking to destroy was the technology they were using to win this war.

Kate was still talking. "He could have died from any number of things—snake bite, lightning strike, even a mountain lion attack."

"But you don't think he did?"

More tapping on her tablet.

"The biometric tracer keeps a record of his vitals." One of the screens turned into a record of the man's blood pressure and heart rate. "As you can see there was a bump here, indicating that perhaps he was in some sort of altercation. Then his vitals stopped quite suddenly."

"Perhaps the mountain lion ate him."

"Cats will typically swipe once, slam the prey to the ground, play with it awhile, and then deliver a deadly bite. Cooper's vitals don't indicate that."

"How do you know the way a wild cat kills its prey?"

Kate looked up from her tablet, then nodded toward the group of workers. "Spencer, sir. He googled it."

John turned to see a thin guy peek over the top of his monitor and raise his hand. He didn't look old enough to legally buy a drink. He also didn't look as if he could do a single pull-up. Put him outside Middle-earth, put him in the wild, and he'd be dead before a mountain lion could find him. Instead of meeting John's gaze, he settled back into his seat and returned his eyes and attention to his monitor.

"Lightning?"

"Jasmine wrote a quick program to overlay weather data at the exact time Cooper died. No strike in that area at that moment."

This time John didn't bother turning around to see who Jasmine was. Did it matter? It did not. What mattered was that they had enough personnel in the canyon to complete the transfer of the kill codes.

John wanted the money that transfer would bring.

He had other plans that required financing.

"And Lyra?"

Brett took up the narrative. "Lyra died quite suddenly. The bio trackers keep a forty-eight-hour history." He nodded to Kate, who pulled up another feed. "As you can see, Blitz was with her at the moment that she died, then he apparently hid her body."

"Can either of you think of any legitimate reason Blitz would kill someone working on our side?"

"Maybe she was a double agent." Kate locked eyes with Brett.

"We vetted her thoroughly." Brett rubbed a hand over the top of his bald head. "But let's be honest here. We *can* accurately know everything—or practically everything—about a person's past. We *can't* know what's going on in their mind."

"Statistical odds?"

"Low. She didn't seem bright enough for such a deception."

"Could that have been an act?"

"No." Brett shook his head once, definitively.

"Seems unnecessary." If there was one thing John hated, it was capricious killing—killing because you can, not because you need to. Yes, people would die because of Cyber Drop, but they would be necessary casualties in the war against oppression.

He stared at the monitors. Two dots continued to glow green —Nina and Blitz.

"I want eyes in the sky."

Kate shook her pretty head. "A drone could scare off our buyer."

"A drone is going to tell us if our buyer is even in the vicinity, and it could also tell us just what Blitz is up to."

"It's a large canyon, sir. A drone zooming around could look for days and not come up with—"

"Someone has a cell phone turned on." He nodded toward the screens. "Someone who is headed down that river on one side or the other."

"It's doubtful they could use it."

"But we can track it, and then we can fly lower and grab a few photos. In and out—they might not even notice."

"But they might," Brett said.

"It's a chance I'm willing to take." He turned and looked directly at Kate, wanting and needing to be crystal clear. "Update me immediately regarding any changes. Don't think about it. Don't analyze it. Don't wait until you understand it. We are now within a twenty-nine-hour window, and I expect you to act accordingly."

"I will."

He looked across the room and studied the six people sitting at workstations. "Brett, walk with me."

Once they had ascended to the main level of the building, John walked out the front door and across the meticulously landscaped yard. At this point he wasn't worried about someone outside Middle-earth listening to their conversation. He was worried about someone inside listening to their conversation.

"I want you to look at the computer logs for all seven people downstairs, specifically at the time that Cooper died and the time that Lyra died."

"Even Kate?"

"Even Kate."

Brett shrugged. "You got it."

When John didn't say anything else, Brett blew out a breath

and crossed his arms. "Do you think someone down there is in contact with Blitz? Running him?"

"No. I don't think so, but I want to eliminate the possibility. This is it, Brett." John turned and stared back at the fortress they lived in, worked in, and might one day—if they weren't very careful—die in.

A drone strike was not out of the question.

He'd known the U.S. government to do far worse.

If their location was found out, anything was possible.

None of them had time to focus on that though. Everyone had been aware of the dangers when they'd signed on. Some worked for the money and some for revenge, but no one in that building doubted what they were doing. At least he didn't think they did.

"Today is the day we've been working toward since Middle-earth was built."

"Longer than that, actually. Since the day your family was killed."

Only Brett would have said that to him. John's family was not something that he spoke about. He'd gone so far as to have any reference to them purged from all public databases. He'd failed in protecting their lives, but he would succeed in protecting their memories.

John clamped his hand on Brett's shoulder. "We're David to their Goliath."

"Except we don't use stones."

"We don't need stones. Everything we need. . ." He waved toward the sky. "It's all there, in the network. We can bring them down with the very tools that they use to enslave, to endanger."

An image of his wife and daughter flashed through his mind, but he pushed that image away.

"Everyone will thank us, Brett. This will be the day of their emancipation."

Ten minutes later he was in his office. He walked quickly to his desk, opened the bottom drawer, and pulled out the small box.

Like the evening before, he placed his index finger to the display pad and waited. At the beep, he opened the case and pulled out the tracking monitor.

The screen powered on, a globe appeared, and he entered his passcode. The screen turned a reassuring blue. As it zoomed in to Phantom Ranch, John felt sweat drip down the back of his neck.

This was his ace in the hole.

This was the one person that no one else knew about.

Even if he had a traitor in his midst, the codes would be transferred and destroyed. He'd seen to that by offering the codes to a group that could bid more for the kill codes than anyone else. A group that was normally their enemy. But then these weren't normal times. The buyer would purchase the codes. He was one hundred percent sure that the buyer would then destroy those codes and take credit for the cyberattack.

Which was fine with him.

He didn't want credit.

He wanted the complete destruction of the grid, and he wanted the money.

Stella didn't know those details about the buyer. She didn't need to know those details. Why she'd insisted on offering them up for sale was something he still didn't understand.

He stared at the screen.

One green dot blinked—steady, healthy, strong.

Chapter Eight

Allison pulled the roan from her stall, tossed a saddle pad then a saddle over her back, and adjusted the cinches and stirrups while she spoke soothing words. "Good girl, Bella. I can trust you without a shadow of a doubt. Never had a horse betray me before, or tell me to stand down."

Providing backup.

She hadn't provided backup in years.

Yes, she was exhausted.

Agreed, it would be easier for agents on the north side to be in place to apprehend Blitz and whomever he was meeting.

But this was her op. She was determined to have a crack at Blitz before they took him away in handcuffs. She hadn't been able to stop the man who had killed her dad when she was nine years old, but she'd made it her life's mission to find out who did it. She would bring that person to justice, regardless of what she was *ordered* to do.

She was thinking of that, of the possibility that Blitz might know something about her father's murder. He wasn't old enough to have been involved, but he might have worked with the man who did. He might know more than she did about who and why. Those thoughts were spinning through her mind, which was why she didn't immediately notice the shadow stretching across the barn floor. Only when he shifted, did she look up. Fortunately, she had the wherewithal not to pull her weapon and shoot him.

"Zack."

"Allison."

"Beautiful morning."

"I guess."

She proceeded to bungee strap her pack to the back of the saddle, along with a grain bag and a basic equine first aid kit. Normally, trail rides were limited to less than a day. Those that went longer included a pack animal to carry extra feed for the horses. There was still summer grass to be had, but she would have to supplement that, especially if what was going to happen didn't happen on the first night.

She checked the cords one last time, then walked Bella out into the morning light. The mare was a red roan quarter horse that stood over fifteen hands high and weighed in at twelve hundred pounds.

"Taking my best horse?" Zack had followed her out into the sunshine.

"She's certainly my favorite." Allison flashed Zack a smile.

He was twenty-one, and from the way he interacted with guests and staff, he apparently thought he was God's gift to women. Blond hair flopped into his eyes, muscles strained at the long-sleeved Ariat t-shirt he wore, and his blue eyes remained trained on her. In his left hand, he held the clipboard with the day's list of guests who would be trail riding.

"Thought you were up top."

"Came back late last night. You didn't hear me? I tripped over Carl's shoes and nearly took a header into the pots and pans."

Carl Johnson was always leaving his shoes in the kitchen. She suspected his mom had raised him to take off his shoes when entering the house. Since he usually entered through the back door, his shoes were often abandoned somewhere between the back door and the refrigerator. Someone was always tripping over them.

"Aren't you off today?"

"I am."

"And instead of staying up top, you decided to take Bella for a ride?"

"I did."

"Big pack for a day ride."

"Maybe I'm meeting someone, Zack. Maybe I have a private rendezvous planned." She swung up into the saddle, mentally swearing because she did not have time for this conversation. "Check your paperwork. Tate approved it."

His eyes stayed locked on hers for a moment. Was he challenging her? Zack Lancaster was barely old enough to order a beer at The Tavern, and he was challenging her?

She eased up on the reins and allowed Bella to express her impatience.

Zack raised the clipboard, studied the paperwork, and finally shrugged. "You're right. Penned in right here."

He tapped the clipboard. "So, have a good day, I guess."

"You as well, Zack."

She felt his eyes on her as she moved away from the stables. When she glanced back, he was still standing there in the shadow of the roof's eaves. She waved a hand, wanting to appear unconcerned at his attention. Then she headed toward the trail that skirted the banks of Bright Angel Creek. She wanted Zack to think that she was going up canyon. After a quarter mile, she circled around, kept in the brush, and headed toward Cabin Eleven.

Five minutes later, she guided Bella out onto the trail and was stopped by a man she'd met the day before. He and his wife had been hiking down Bright Angel as Allison was hiking up it. Most people chose to hike down the South Kaibab. If the Mullins had done that, they would have been traveling with Blitz's group. They'd chosen the Bright Angel because they read that the grade was gentler, and it was. But Bright Angel was also several Brett longer.

Moose and Beverly Mullins were in their late fifties and had experienced some last-minute jitters in the middle of their hike down. They'd crossed paths with Allison at Indian Garden. Seeing her uniform, they expressed their concerns and asked her advice. This wasn't unusual on the trail. The canyon was intimidating, and the hiking was a challenge. Allison questioned them about their overall health as well as what preparations they'd made for the hike. In her opinion, the two would be fine, and she'd said as much.

"Miss Quinn." Moose Mullins waved a hand, then stepped out in front of Bella.

She had no choice but to stop.

Moose was a big guy, as his name suggested. He'd explained that his actual name was Marion, but he'd been a linebacker in high school and everyone had called him Moose. The name had apparently stuck. "Thought you were up top."

"Guess I missed this place." She gave the couple her brightest smile.

"Share a cup of coffee with us?" Beverly called from their campsite. She was the complete opposite of Moose.

He was six feet. She barely topped five.

He looked like a lumberjack. She looked like a runner.

Moose had a wild, dark brown beard. Beverly's gray hair was cut in a short bob.

Beverly turned over a piece of bacon in a pan on their campfire. The smell wafted toward Allison, and her stomach grumbled in response. She glanced at her watch. Twenty minutes until she was supposed to meet Tate, and the last thing she'd eaten was a handful of trail mix after crossing the suspension bridge.

"Are you sure you have enough to share?"

"We're sure," Moose said, taking Bella's lead while Allison dismounted.

"The eggs are instant, but the coffee is hot."

"That sounds, and smells, wonderful."

Five minutes later they were enjoying Beverly's breakfast as the Mullins recounted their evening.

Moose shoveled a forkful of eggs into his mouth. "Turns out we'd done the hard part when we met you at Indian Garden, just like you said. The rest was relatively easy."

"It was," Beverly admitted. "But I was still relieved to reach River Resthouse."

"And now we know what to expect hiking out."

A momentary silence followed. The peacefulness of the canyon, the calories she was consuming, and the two friendly faces in front of her all combined to help Allison draw her first calm breath since leaving Yavapai Lodge.

Moose looked up from his food, a smile wreathing his face. "We saw a mountain lion last night, just before dark. It was quite a distance away—"

"Thank goodness." Beverly offered a mock shiver, or perhaps it was real.

"I managed to take some pictures." Moose sopped up what was left on his plate with a piece of bread. "It was exciting."

"We're very grateful that you encouraged us to keep going. If we'd turned around. . ." Beverly craned her neck to take in the view of the canyon. "We'd have missed all of this."

"I'm glad you had a good experience." Allison finished off her breakfast, rinsed her plate and cup, and handed them back to Beverly. "What are your plans for today?"

"Thought we'd go and watch the rafters this morning."

Allison had been standing, scanning the camping area for anything that looked out of place. At Beverly's words, she froze. She didn't think there would be an exchange of gunfire when Blitz left on his raft. She planned to be watching, but she did not expect to intercede until he met the buyer.

Gunfire was unlikely, but it could happen.

Should she warn Moose and Beverly?

Lyra's lifeless form popped into her mind. Where Blitz was concerned, one couldn't be too cautious.

She plastered a smile on her face, then turned toward the Mullins. "I suppose that could be nice, but many of our guests prefer to walk up canyon a little."

"Up canyon?" Moose ran his fingers through his beard.

"Water is life in this canyon. You might be surprised at what you see."

"Like what?" Beverly tilted her head, interested but not convinced.

"If I remember the schedule correctly, a couple of the rangers will be going upriver to break out the handmade dams." When Beverly and Moose said nothing, she added, "It allows the flannel-mouth suckers, brown trout, and rainbow trout to swim upstream."

Beverly clapped her hands. "Let's do it, Moose. I can see river rafters in Colorado. Let's walk up canyon, just a little. I even have the makings of a picnic lunch."

Moose put his arm around his wife's shoulders. "If that's what you want to do, dear, we'll do it."

Allison felt a fraction of the burden she was carrying slip away. She walked over to Bella, pulled herself up into the saddle, said her goodbyes, and headed toward Cabin Eleven.

Her visit with the Mullins had done as much for her mood and energy level as the eggs, bacon, and coffee had. It helped to remember the people that she worked for. Her thoughts were very clear on the point. She worked for the American people. They were her employer, not the bosses back in Washington.

She had taken a vow to support and defend the Constitution of the United States.

And that Constitution existed for the people.

They were the faces that kept her coming back to this job day after day. She might go to sleep with images of Blitz, the AT, and revenge playing through her mind. But she woke thinking of the people that she was charged to protect.

She skirted around the corner of Cabin Eleven and had barely dismounted when she spied Tate walking toward her—casual pace, relaxed posture. He might make a good spy if he ever wanted to give up his ranger gig. Then again, he might *be* a spy for all she knew, but that was probably her paranoia talking.

"How'd you get away so fast?"

"I'm the boss, remember?"

Why was it that every man she came in contact with needed to reiterate his authority?

"Did anyone suspect anything?"

"Not that I could tell. You know how they are this early—"

"Barely awake and focused on finding caffeine."

"Exactly."

He handed her two sheets of paper.

"We only had seven signed up for rafting today. I've added myself—everyone knows even numbers work better in case we need to pair off."

"You added yourself?"

"Yes, Allison. I did."

She wanted to tell him that he wasn't going, that he had no training for this sort of operation, that he'd done enough. Instead, she stared at the paperwork he'd handed her and admitted to herself that having Tate with the rafters could be helpful. "And you don't think that your presence will raise any eyebrows?"

"I can't think why it would. I even filled out the paperwork for a few workdays off-site. I claimed that I needed to monitor and assess the river-rafting crew. By the way, our guy Blitz is listed under the name Brent Watkins."

She bristled at the word *our*, but then if there was anyone who had earned partner status, she supposed Tate was the man. He had survived getting shot at and nearly getting pushed off the edge of the canyon walls. He'd endured her panic attack and seeing one of his employees killed as he watched. The guy had *chutzpah*, as her boss would say. It could alternately be considered a compliment or an insult, depending on the mood and circumstances of the moment.

"Blitz has several aliases," she said. "First name always begins with a B. He's our guy, all right."

"As if there was any doubt."

"There wasn't."

The lower Grand Canyon rafting trips began at Phantom Ranch and ended at Whitmore Wash, Diamond Creek, or Pearce Ferry. Depending on which place you chose to exit, you were looking at five to seven days on the water, and that was with a motor trip. Oar trips took even longer. Private trips using the Grand Canyon staff could be gone for twenty-five days. Getting a place on those excursions required interested parties to apply through the national park's weighted lottery system. Getting your number pulled could take up to ten years.

Allison wasn't surprised that Blitz was going out on a motor trip, and she seriously doubted he planned to stay on the water longer than a single day. She suspected the first night they made camp, he'd creep away.

She continued to study the sheets, flipping back and forth between them. "Family of three, plus a couple in the lead raft?"

"Correct. If things go south, they should be able to easily move out of harm's way."

"Blitz, a twenty-three-year-old woman, and you in the second raft."

"Plus, two guides in each raft. Makes for a total party of twelve."

"I doubt this will be a party."

"Agreed."

She could feel his gaze on her as she studied the sheets. Then she spied the thing that was bothering her, the thing her subconscious had picked up on immediately. "Jason's a guide in the lead boat?"

142

"Yup."

"And Nina is in the rear boat?"

"She is."

"How does that happen? They work for the national park, not the private outfitter. . ."

Tate held up his hand in a halt gesture that was rather insulting. "They both applied for this months ago. They want the experience of riding with a commercial outfitter—either because it will help them better meet the needs of our guests on a national park rafting tour or—"

"Or because they're on Blitz's team and want to be there when the transfer happens."

Tate was already shaking his head. "It's more likely they're thinking of leaving the park service for a gig that pays twice as much. They wouldn't be the first to do so."

Allison thrust the papers back into his hands.

If he was going to work with her he needed to learn to be more suspicious of people.

Tate had somehow found time to clean up—splash water on his face, change clothes, probably even eat some breakfast and chug a cup of coffee. How else was it that he could look fresh and eager? He was forty-nine years old. He should look as tired as she felt, but then he didn't completely understand what was at risk here. He couldn't, because she hadn't told him everything.

She'd been trained to always hold something back—unless you're one hundred percent sure about the person you're colluding with.

Tate nodded toward Bella, whose lead rope was tied to the cabin's porch railing. She had enough leeway to chomp at the late summer grass growing nearby. "What's your plan?"

"I should be able to keep up with the rafts."

"Only because you're on Bella."

Allison shifted her weight from foot to foot. "Status of the river?"

"It's good. The storm we hiked through didn't drop much

water upriver, so the flow and water levels are still acceptable for rafting."

"I'll stay back in the brush, forge the river where I need to. Either way, I'll be watching. If you see anything that worries you, raise your right hand and point at something in the sky."

"Something?"

"A bird, Tate. An owl. A flying fish. Whatever."

"Gotcha." He smiled and hooked his thumbs through the belt loops of his trousers. "How will I know you've seen me?"

Allison cupped her hands around her mouth and produced a sound that she hoped resembled a bird of prey.

Tate laughed. "Great horned owl?"

"Supposed to be."

"Okay. We don't see many of those here, but I suppose your terrorist won't know that."

"As far as we know he's not a bird watcher."

Tate's expression turned suddenly serious. "So I see something, point to the sky, wait for your owl call, and then what?"

"I'll make contact. It might not be right away though."

"Got it." He studied her as if he was sizing her up.

Or was that concern in his eyes?

They barely knew one another, and yet there was something in his manner that so reminded Allison of her father. Then again, perhaps that was exhaustion and her imagination talking.

"Is that my only job?" he asked.

Allison glanced up at the canyon walls, then back toward the stables—toward Zack, who had been much too interested in her plans. Finally she looked across to the north side of the river. Her co-workers were over there somewhere. Steele himself was probably over there. He was a hands-on kind of senior agent. She'd never known him to run an op from headquarters.

The problem was that no one on that side of the river was as motivated as she was. This op had a personal angle for her. She'd been trying for ten years to make progress on her dad's case. This was the closest she'd ever been. She couldn't afford to depend on the men and women waiting on the north side to apprehend and secure Blitz and his cohorts.

Certainly those agents wanted to stop the attack, but plans were already in motion to mitigate the effects of the collapsed grid should it happen. Some agents even saw it as inevitable—a nice juicy target for any wannabe anarchist with a laptop.

Allison insisted on believing that it wasn't inevitable, that they could be stopped—if the agents involved were willing to sacrifice everything. If it came to that. Self-preservation was healthy, but only if it didn't jeopardize a mission.

She tossed one last look at Tate, then stood and walked toward Bella, anxious to be off. "If bullets start flying, you make sure that you cover the girl in your boat. Get her down and keep her down."

"I can do that."

It seemed insufficient though, and she knew it. Tate wasn't being paid to do this job. He'd been recruited, and though she'd given him every chance to say no, he stayed because he understood that she needed him.

Or because he was involved.

Could he be involved?

Could he be working for Gollum?

Why was it that she couldn't keep that vile thought from popping up in her mind? He'd done nothing to arouse her suspicions. . . which was suspicious if she thought about it too long.

Allison put her foot in the stirrup, grabbed hold of the saddle horn, and pulled herself atop Bella. The mare tossed her head, evidently as ready to go as Allison was. "Teddy's in surgery. Prognosis is good."

"And Lyra?"

"They'll collect her once we leave."

There wasn't anything else to say. Tate turned to go. Stopping abruptly, he pivoted back toward her and walked over until he stood right next to Bella. He dropped his pack on the ground and pulled out a small, brown paper bag he'd been carrying.

She raised an eyebrow and waited.

"Breakfast tacos—three of them. I thought you might be hungry."

She wasn't, but she would be. "Thanks."

He reached into the pack again and pulled out two large bottles of water. "Wasn't sure you had time to resupply." He pushed the bottles into the various pockets on her pack.

Allison thanked him with a nod, but she didn't trust herself to speak. How long had it been since someone had brought her breakfast? She was tired, and that made her emotional. She pressed her heels to Bella's side and started down the trail, moving in the direction of the boat launch. She looked back once. Tate was still standing next to the porch of Cabin Eleven. He offered a small wave.

Bella's steady pace, the creak of the saddle, and the beautiful morning should have calmed her, but they didn't.

There were too many unknowns in this mission.

Who had Anthony Cooper called? Which of the staff was a member of the AT? Why did Jason and Nina keep popping up on her radar? As for Lyra, how did one of Gollum's people end up working in the kitchen of the ranch?

And maybe that was what was bothering her.

With each turn of events, she was more convinced that this hadn't been a spur-of-the-moment plan thrown together to create havoc. This had been methodically thought out and put together well before those kill codes went up for auction on the dark web.

Gollum was still a few steps ahead of them.

If things went as she planned, that would change by nightfall.

Phantom Ranch was a busy place. At this point, none of their guests had realized anything was amiss. Director Rivera would see to it that no additional guests descended the trail, and once Blitz boarded that raft and headed downriver, the guests who were already at Phantom Ranch would be free to leave.

All lodging was filled up fifteen months in advance. That was why Gollum had put Lyra on staff. It was the only way he could be sure she'd be in place when he needed her, though why he'd chosen the Grand Canyon of all places to do this was beyond her.

Or maybe it wasn't.

Maybe he was thumbing his nose at modern technology and Uncle Sam's propensity to snoop.

The fully booked lodge and campground also explained why Blitz had killed Mr. Harris. Otherwise, Blitz would be sleeping in a tent at the campground, and even that filled up before most people made it down the South Kaibab trail. It was a standard saying among the workers that most visitors overestimated their own abilities and underestimated the canyon, which was a dangerous combination.

Approximately twelve people a year died hiking the canyon—most often from heat or dehydration. Few actually fell to their death in the canyon—a total over the years of only fifty-five according to an article Allison had read before going undercover. The disturbing part was that many of those deaths occurred as people posed for photos. A thirty-eight-year-old man from Texas was pretending to fall to scare his daughter when he slipped and tumbled 400 feet to his death.

People did not approach the canyon with proper respect.

People were unpredictable.

The other statistic that had stood out to Allison was that only one percent of the five and a half million people who visited the Grand Canyon annually hiked to the bottom. Most stopped at the rim, snapped a few photos, and left.

While few visitors descended the canyon, Phantom Ranch was still a busy place. As she rode Bella toward the bridge, she saw people stepping out into a perfect autumn morning, hurrying over to the second and last serving of breakfast, preparing for their day in the canyon. Campers were cooking over fires. Bird watchers and photographers set out on trails. She made her way past the last of the cabins, the employee bunkhouse, the stock barn, and the campground.

She couldn't possibly pass unnoticed, so instead she ambled as if she belonged there. She did belong there. It helped that she'd taken the time before harnessing Bella to change into a second set of clothes that were refreshingly dry.

What she didn't want was to be seen by the rafters, most especially by Blitz. So she circled around behind the boat beach, then moved upriver a half a mile. From there, and with the help of her binoculars, she had a clear view of the rafting company's boats as well as the folks putting on life preservers and storing their gear.

She waited until she saw Tate climb onto the rafts and the rafts pull out into the middle of the river. Then she pulled out her SAT phone and called Steele. "Blitz is on the river."

"Copy that. Catastrophic system failure is now less than twenty-seven hours away."

"I'm aware."

"Be careful, Quinn."

"Always." She hung up before Steele could remind her that she was now providing backup. That remained to be seen.

Tate had said there were twelve people, which included two commercial rafting guides, one senior park ranger, a family of three, a middle-aged couple, a young woman, two national park guides who might be on the wrong side of things, and one terrorist.

Considered that way, it was two—her and Tate—against eleven—everyone else.

No. It was one against twelve, because there wasn't another person in this canyon that she could trust one hundred percent.

She was fine with that.

She'd worked alone before.

Game on.

Chapter Nine

The only trail that paralleled the river was on the south side, and as Tate had made abundantly clear, it was less than two miles in length. Allison planned to simply keep moving downriver when the trail ran out. But first she had to get there, and that meant she had to retrace her steps from the night before—some of them anyway. Allison made her way past the Bright Angel campground and onto the 416-foot suspension bridge.

Her heart rate accelerated.

Her palms began to sweat and her vision tunneled.

But she wasn't incapacitated—not like before. Maybe she was too tired to care if she plunged to her death. But probably she was better able to cope with her acrophobia because of the bright sunlight and the absence of wind and rain and lightning. Or it could be that she was comforted by the presence of Bella, who had crossed this bridge many times.

Allison was even able to stare down at the water of the Colorado River. Tate had said that it hadn't rained upriver, but the storm had churned up the sand and silt sufficiently to give the water a brownish tinge.

Bella clomped off the bridge and through the cave.

The walls were so close that Allison was able to reach out and touch both sides at the same time. For the briefest of moments, they were in total darkness, then Bella turned slightly, following the contours of the cave and sunlight appeared at the far end. They came out the other side and branched down to the river trail.

She was now mere feet from the river. Instead of continuing south to the South Kaibab Trail, she took the right fork, which turned into the river trail. Soon she passed the Silver Bridge. The Black Bridge she'd just traversed was the only passage for horses and mules. The Silver Bridge, though newer, was too narrow for the animals. Combined, the two bridges offered the only dry crossing between Marble Canyon and Lake Mead. The distance was three hundred miles by road, and even farther when following the contours of the river.

The river flowed in a generally southwesterly direction, but the key word was *generally*. Allison had studied the maps enough to know what kind of ride she was in for. The river twisted and turned as it made its way through the canyon. The part of the river they would cover the first day traveled in a northwesterly direction with a few bends here and there.

She was happy to be traveling on a horse and not in a raft. The rafters would encounter Pipe Creek before her river trail ran out. The rapids there were classified a Class III, which was considered intermediate, containing fast currents and strong eddies, according to the websites she had visited.

The water to her right quickly became more fast-moving, and she knew the rafters had reached Pipe Creek when she heard their screams—what sounded like screams of delight rather than terror. Bella wasn't impressed, and Allison had no desire to experience the delights of river rafting herself.

The trail ended, and she let Bella pick the way forward.

It wasn't as if she could get lost.

All she had to do was keep the river on her right.

A mile farther, the rafts moved to the far side of the river to navigate Horn Creek—a Class VIII rapid that she knew would be challenging for Blitz, or anyone else inexperienced in the ways of rafting. The water had turned white and frothy as they entered Granite Gorge. She had read that the guides for the Grand Canyon/Colorado River rapids used a I-X scale, whereas most rapids only used a I-VI scale. She had yet to figure out why, but the foaming, churning mass of water to her right might be an indication.

For the first time, Allison wondered if Tate might have been right. Attempting to take a horse this far downriver, without a trail, was foolish.

But Bella somehow picked her way along the rocks. Allison pulled the horse to a stop, retrieved the binoculars, and tried to focus in on the rafting group. There were no screams this time. Apparently everyone was too terrified to make a sound. She dropped the binoculars, leaving them hanging from the strap around her neck.

Depending how the day went and how often the rafters stopped to stretch their legs and explore, they might also run the Salt Creek rapids, which were again a Class III. There were a few possible places they could stop for the night—Mile Creek, Trinity, Above Salt Creek or Granite Camp. She was rooting for either of the last two, as they were on the left side of the river—her side of the river.

Granite Camp was the largest of the four and it sounded like the most likely spot. The pull-in rested at the top of a pool above Granite rapid, another Class VIII. She didn't think the guides would want to take a tired group of rafters on a challenging rapid at the end of the day.

Allison ate her breakfast tacos, drank the water that Tate had given her, and tried to envision how the confrontation with Blitz was going to play out. On paper, it had looked entirely feasible that he would meet someone, pass off the codes, and confirm the agreed number of bitcoins were transferred to his account—all from the shelter of the canyon. In reality, she couldn't quite picture how he would meet someone on the other side of the river. How would he even know for certain where they would stop?

Then again, a thousand-dollar tip in the hands of a river guide could influence that decision. As far as the AT was concerned, a thousand dollars were mere pennies in a bucket.

Bella set a steady pace.

Allison was able to keep an eye on the rafters while staying behind them and relatively out of sight. The river and its banks were resplendent with life. A great blue heron landed just feet away from her. Prince's plume, four o'clock flowers, and Utah juniper trees dotted the landscape between her and the canyon wall. The sun warmed her face, and she found herself relaxing in the saddle.

Two hours into her ride, that changed.

Allison became convinced someone was following her.

Whoever it was seemed skilled at handling a horse. She never caught sight of the person, didn't even hear the sound of hoof-beats against the hard-packed trail, but she knew for certain that someone was back there. At first she hoped the person was motivated by mild curiosity or boredom and would turn back. Perhaps they had coincidentally picked the same area of the river and would soon branch off.

But the farther she rode from the Phantom Ranch campground, the less likely it became that any of those alternative scenarios were true.

Someone was following her, and it was time to confront them.

It was now late morning, and the area on her side of the river had broadened. The rafters were keeping to the right-hand side of the river. Allison was grateful for the curve that took them away from the south bank. She was certain that by this point agents on the north side would be watching them, and their circuitous route gave her time to stop and stretch her legs.

Instead of climbing back up into the saddle and continuing

downriver, she pulled Bella off into a small meadow and tied her lead rope to a mesquite tree branch. If anyone were to approach that clearing, they would assume either that she'd wandered off into the trees to heed nature's call, or that she was hiding behind the large boulder at the far side of the canyon.

She did neither of those things.

Instead, she circled back through the trees and came out nearly at the same point she'd stopped to eat, hydrate, and stretch. Then it was only a matter of waiting. She pulled her pistol from her holster and took aim at the spot the person or persons who were following her would round the bend.

She swore under her breath when she saw the Ariat shirt and blond hair, though most of the hair was now covered with a tan Stetson. Holding her pistol down and by her side, she crept behind him until she was within a few feet, and he had entered the clearing where Bella was cropping at grass.

Allison's pistol of choice was a long-slide Glock. It had the same durability as the standard Glock that police and military personnel carried, but it offered a greater distance between sights and fast target acquisition. The soft sound of her pulling the slide back caused Zack to freeze in his saddle. He didn't turn around, didn't move at all except to raise his hands in the universal *don't shoot* gesture.

"Dismount and don't touch your saddle bags."

He did as she requested, still silent but now facing her.

"What are you doing here, Zack?"

"Following you."

"I figured that, but why?"

"Because I wanted to know what you were up to." He glanced over at Bella. "I was worried about the mare."

"Sure, you were. So, you left your post at the ranch and moseyed out after me? I'm not buying it."

His eyes kept darting from the gun in her hand to her face and back again. Finally, he managed, "Who *are* you?" He seemed

153

more curious than afraid, which served to irk her even more than she already was—and that was a lot.

"Turn around, get on your knees, and interlock your fingers behind your head."

"Seriously, Allison?"

Instead of answering, she raised the Glock.

"Okay. Don't shoot me. Hell's bells, you're intense."

She walked forward, pulled a pair of zip ties from her pocket, and told him to turn around. Five minutes later, she'd secured his horse, removed the Smith & Wesson pistol from his hip holster, searched his saddlebag, patted down his pockets, and moved him out of the center of the clearing.

"Why did you follow me?"

"Because you weren't acting normal."

He was now sitting on the ground, his arms zip-tied behind his back. He fidgeted, trying to find a more comfortable position. She could have told him there wasn't one—not with his arms behind him. That position was specifically designed to be uncomfortable.

"You obviously weren't going out for a day ride or a rendezvous." He was sweating now, though the day wasn't terribly warm, and his eyes kept darting from his horse to Bella to Allison. "You'd added a grain bag and an equine first aid kit. Sure, every park employee knows to take an equine first aid kit if you're going out on a horse, but you shouldn't have needed the grain bag."

When she continued staring at him, he added, "I also noticed the rifle in your pack."

Allison tried to calculate back to when she'd last slept, decided it wasn't important, and sat on the ground in front of Zack—cross-legged, relaxed, like she had all day for him to spill his story.

She didn't have all day.

She needed to get back to the river within the next twenty minutes.

"Are you working for Blitz?"

"Who is Blitz?"

"Do you know about the kill codes?"

"What is a kill code?" His voice rose in exasperation.

"Did Gollum send you?"

"I don't know who that is."

She waited.

He finally added, "You're not making any sense."

Zack was shaking his head now, and he was starting to look a little afraid. That was good. Allison needed him to tell her whatever he knew, so she could do whatever she needed to do with him, and get back to the main objective.

She could kill him, but the situation didn't seem to quite rise to that level.

She could leave him here. A mountain lion might get him. He could dehydrate and die. It might be days before she'd be able to retrace her path, fetch him, and then turn him in for a thorough debriefing.

She could send him back to the ranch, but how could she be sure he'd go?

"I'm not going back, if that's what you're thinking." He seemed to be aiming for defiant but couldn't quite get there. Plainly, he was surprised and more than a little alarmed by what he'd stumbled into. "Something's not right at the ranch. Jason and Nina have been acting strange. Lyra disappeared this morning. You've taken off with my best horse, and I can't begin to understand why Tate would approve such a thing. Plus, I'm pretty sure—"

"Back up." She hadn't yet re-holstered the Glock. It lay on her lap, her right hand on top of it, practically begging Zack to give her one good reason.

"Huh?"

"Jason and Nina."

"Oh, that. I don't know. At first, I thought maybe they had a thing going and were hiding it from everyone, but then I heard them arguing last night."

The only reaction Allison allowed was a slight arch of her right eyebrow.

As if sensing her growing impatience, Zack rushed on with his story. "I was eavesdropping, I guess. Only because I was worried. And I heard Nina tell Jason that they had to keep their cool, that they couldn't afford to crumble now. She emphasized that word —*crumble*."

"Anything else?"

"He said something about not wanting to go, and she said it would solve their money problems."

"Were those their exact words?"

"Yeah. I think so." He closed his mouth and looked around, as if he'd find the answers to his questions in the river or on the canyon's walls. When Allison's silence began to wear him down, he added, "None of it makes any sense to me at all. Then Lyra disappeared. . ."

"Lyra's dead."

Those words had the desired effect on young Zack. All color bled from his face, and his gaze darted from Allison to her gun and back again.

"No, I didn't kill her, Zack. And I'm not going to kill you, *if. . .*" She paused dramatically and waited for him to look directly at her. "If what you're telling me is the truth."

"Of course, it's true. Why would I—"

"You're a snoop."

"No, I'm not."

"You're terrible at minding your own business."

"Okay. I guess that's true. Minding your own business is over-rated. I'm the generation that was raised to *see something, say something.*"

"Did you say anything, Zack?"

"What? No."

"Did you share your suspicions with anyone else?"

"No. I have no reason to lie to you. I haven't talked to anyone. As soon as you left, I went inside to give Tate a bogus story about a stomach bug only Tate wasn't there. Tate was on the rafting trip, which also made no sense. So, I found Todd Delaney—

"Is that who Tate put in charge?"

Zack's head bobbed up and down, causing the Stetson to wobble. "I told him I was feeling sick and going to lie down. Then I snuck out, saddled up, and followed you—which I might add, was pretty easy to do. You're not very good at hiding your trail, if that was your intention."

Allison weighed her choices. She didn't want to shoot him. It would be like shooting a Labrador. Finally, she sighed heavily and stood. Zack attempted to back away from her, but she'd placed him up against a rock and there was nowhere to go.

"I'm going to cut your hands free."

"You are?"

"Yes, but you're staying with me. I don't like it. I don't want you with me, but I can't trust you to go back to the ranch. So you'll go with me."

"Go with you where?"

"To intercept Lyra's killer."

"Are you going to give me back my gun?"

"No, Zack. I'm not."

His shoulders slumped, but he nodded in agreement.

She pulled out her pocket knife and cut the ties, then backed away three feet. In spite of his muscle, she had no doubt that she could take him down in a fight. She was quick, and she knew maneuvers he hadn't even seen in the movies. But why tempt him? Kids notoriously did stupid things like follow a Homeland Security agent down a canyon.

He stood there, rubbing his wrists.

"Get on your horse."

"Who do you work for?"

"I don't have time for this, Zack. Get on your horse."

"How do I know you're not a terrorist or something? I'm not going with you unless you tell me who you work for."

Allison looked to the sky, wondering what she'd done to

deserve Zack Lancaster. She couldn't pick him up and put him on the horse, so she pulled out her credentials.

He squinted his eyes, studied it, then finally looked up. "Homeland Security?"

"Yes."

"So, you're. . . what? You're on a mission?"

"Something like that."

"And those guys you asked me about—Blitz and Gollum. . . they're involved? There have kill codes? Who are they going to kill?"

"You're on a need-to-know basis, Zack. And right now, you don't need to know. You need to get on your horse." Keeping the Glock in her right hand, she fetched Bella. With her left hand, she grabbed the saddle horn and swung up into the saddle. Then she waited for him to do the same.

Motioning with the Glock, she said, "You go first. Back toward the trail."

"About that. . ."

"Just do it, Zack."

When they reached the river, the same spot where she'd had her lunch, the rafts were barely visible in the distance. They'd made it back in time. Allison knew there was another wide spot up ahead where they would again steer toward the far bank. She might lose track of them for a few hours, but seeing them gave her a measure of assurance.

"Let's go."

"Yeah, but, see, that direction is a bad idea."

Maybe she should shoot him, or duct tape his mouth shut. Why hadn't she thought of that earlier?

"This trail, it ends another half mile down. You end up surrounded by boulders, and then you have to backtrack."

She wasn't buying it.

For all she knew, he was the person that Anthony Cooper had called. She didn't think he was in on the unfolding cyberattack. He seemed too. . . stupid wasn't the right word. . . obstinate. That was it. Zack Lancaster was too obstinate to work for the other side. He'd argue with whoever was giving orders until they wished they'd never set eyes on him.

He'd probably argue until they pulled their weapon and used it.

But that didn't mean she trusted him.

Not one hundred percent.

———

Thirty minutes later the trail ended in a sea of boulders.

Allison had holstered her weapon, but she was a quick draw, and her temper was frighteningly short at this point. "Don't say it, Zack. Just turn around and head back the way we came."

He wisely didn't speak.

He did pull up on his mare's reins when they were halfway back to the lunch spot, stopped, and motioned to the right. There was a barely discernible trail.

Allison nodded once. "Lead the way."

If it was a trap, he'd be the first in and the last out.

But it wasn't a trap.

It was a nice loop that took them around the boulders and back to the river. Zack had obviously been at least this far down-river before. The walls of the canyon rose above them like sentinels guarding the Colorado. Allison had started the evening's hike with Tate at an elevation of 7,260 feet. Phantom Ranch sat at 2,560 feet. Everything in between rose above them.

It was while they were making that loop that a young man stumbled onto their path, followed quickly by a young woman. They looked haggard, ill-equipped, and lost.

Allison and Zack both stopped their horses and stared at the two who seemed to have appeared out of nowhere.

"Do you know where we are?" The guy looked to be approximately twenty years old with a scraggly beard, long hair that was pulled back and held with a band, and quite a few tattoos dancing down his arms-not enough to constitute a sleeve, but he was obviously working on it.

His eyes were wide and a bit glassy. He kept swiveling his head from left to right, then right to left. He didn't appear to be a threat, but neither did he appear anywhere close to normal.

The woman looked even younger, maybe eighteen. Her hair was dyed turquoise, and she sported a lot of hardware in her ears.

Allison had no problem with an individual's right to express their identity through body art, but these two looked as if they hadn't quite settled on that identity yet.

The woman stared at them with a shocked expression—as if they might be an illusion and disappear at any second, then she broke into sobs. "We're saved. We're not going to die—at least not today."

Allison and Zack both dismounted, and five minutes later, Allison had the basics of their story.

Brandon Ferguson and Skye Graham had started down the Bright Angel trail twenty-four hours earlier, while Allison was hiking up and out of the canyon on the very same trail.

Before she'd received the call from Steele.

Before the storm.

Allison didn't remember passing the two, which meant they'd inadvertently stepped off on a side trail at some point. Or perhaps they'd meant to. Hikers regularly thought they'd be able to find the main trail. That they'd only go a little ways. But invariably a better view always waited around the corner. By the time they turned back, nothing looked familiar. Such thinking accounted for most of the rescues the National Park Rangers did every year —that, and lack of preparation.

She wasn't surprised that these two had ended up lost.

Brandon squinted his eyes in an attempt to focus on Allison. "We zigzagged our way down to Indian Garden—started a little late maybe. I think it was afternoon. Was it afternoon, Skye? Anyway, I definitely remember Indian Garden. I guess that's where we took a wrong turn."

"We made it to Plateau Point. Remember? I snapped a picture." After an energy bar and a quart of water, Skye was perking up. "My phone's dead though, so I can't show you."

"You spent the night on the trail?" Zack tossed a look at Allison as if to say, *Can you believe how young and ignorant these two are?*

From Allison's point of view, he was only a year or so older than Skye and probably the same age as Brandon. Plus, Zack had been stupid enough to try and track a government agent. She thought it was a toss-up as to who had made the more foolish move.

"Yeah, we did spend the night on the trail. What choice did we have?" Brandon was nodding, and he seemed to be smiling at the memory of their harrowing evening. "We sheltered in this cave."

"We'd gone off trail to look at some rock formations, but then. . . then everything started looking the same."

"Suddenly there were trails everywhere—right, left, up, down. Even diagonal. It was wild, man."

"We couldn't figure out which way to go," Skye admitted. "Finally, we decided we were too fried to hike up, so we'd hike down. Going down was the ticket."

"Sure." Brandon's head was bobbing again, as if he were listening to music. "Thought we'd run into Phantom Ranch one way or another."

"But instead we ran into you." Skye smiled brightly, then widened her eyes and stared at the ground.

Allison was beyond grateful when they stopped talking.

"The canyon is two hundred and seventy-seven miles long, so the chances of running into the ranch aren't that great." Allison had spent enough time with these two. She needed to replenish their supplies, point them in the right direction, and get back to work. "Where are your packs?"

"Yeah, we didn't have one, but we did have some water bottles."

"Drank all of that."

"Yup." Brandon took off his right shoe—a regular, discount store, cheap tennis shoe, and not even a new one at that. He shook out a quarter cup of dirt and a few pebbles. Putting it back on, he glanced up and smiled. "Guess we didn't think this through too well. Should have at least brought a phone charger."

"A phone charger? That's what you think you should have brought?" Zack had apparently reached his breaking point.

He strode over to Brandon and stood over him waving his arms and gesturing first toward the canyon walls and then toward the river. "Eleven people a year die in this canyon—most from goofing around or not preparing. You two are lucky that you're not included in that number. Do you understand how stupid a thing you did? Do you realize we could have been finding your bones next spring?"

"Oh, we're pretty good hikers." Skye glanced around. Was she looking for a lost backpack or pair of hiking shoes? "I guess we were a little high when we started out, so maybe that explains why. . ."

Zack clenched both of his fists, brought them up to the sides of his head as if to ward off a terrible migraine, and stalked away. He stopped after a few yards and stood with his back to the group.

"What's his problem?" Brandon rubbed his calf. "It's not like we got lost on purpose."

Allison was kind of proud of Zack for speaking the truth. Plus, he'd somehow resisted reaching out and giving Brandon a good hard shake. That showed surprising restraint. Her impression of him went up another notch.

"I'll tell you what's going to happen next. I'm going to give you both another bottle of water and two more energy bars. Your job is to follow this path back to the main trail." She pointed in the direction she and Zack had come from. "When you reach the Colorado River, make a right."

"Okay." Brandon sighed, but he did manage to stand. "Take a right at the river. Got it."

Skye looked skeptical. "I'm not sure how much farther I can walk. Can't you just give us a ride?"

"No, Skye. We can't." Allison glanced toward her mare, who was possibly taking a nap. Then she turned back to Skye. "We're on our way to meet some people—in the opposite direction."

"Oh. Okay." Skye pooched out her bottom lip, but fortunately, she didn't seem to have anything else to say.

They accepted the supplies, offered a small wave, and turned toward the river.

Every operation had unexpected detours.

Although they doggedly tried to avoid involving bystanders, that wasn't always possible. Allison had been doing this job long enough to not be surprised by the twists and turns of an op, but she'd had it with detours and backtracking. The sun was now high in the sky, which meant dusk wasn't that far away.

She needed to be in position before darkness fell.

She needed to be ready to apprehend Blitz.

And one way or another, she would ask him about her father's killer.

Chapter Ten

Five minutes later, Allison and Zack were once again moving in the same direction as the rafters. She waited until they were out of earshot, pulled up on Bella's reins, dismounted, and dug out her SAT phone and a park map. Zack was watching her intently. When the phone connected with Steele, Allison walked away from the horses and made sure her back was toward Zack.

"Status." It was a bark more than a word.

Allison's annoyance level spiked, and this conversation had barely begun. "Just intercepted two hikers—a Brandon Ferguson and Skye Graham. I gave them emergency supplies and sent them toward Phantom Ranch."

"Why would you do that?"

"Do what?"

"You need to focus on your mission, Quinn."

"And leave them to die? Because that's what could have happened. People die in this canyon. They die from exposure or dehydration, falling, heart attack. . ."

Tate's words whispered through her mind. *Where is your compassion?*

Steele's sigh as well as his frustration traveled over the phone line. She envisioned him sitting in a diner, brooding over a cup of coffee and a warm piece of apple pie.

That probably wasn't fair.

He'd said he was going to a secure location. More than likely he was in a bunker somewhere—with plenty of stale coffee but no apple pie.

Still, the fact that she'd taxed his patience improved her mood a bit.

"What do you need me to do?"

"Contact the ranch and ask them to send out a couple of the seasonal workers on horseback." She studied the map, then gave Steele the location where the couple would reach the river.

"If our terrorists would stay out of the vicinity of the general population, things would be much easier." Steele's voice became suddenly very serious. "We're at twenty-three hours before. . ."

"Catastrophic system failure. Yeah. You mentioned that last time we spoke."

"What I didn't tell you is that some of the peripheral systems are already going offline. They have been all morning. Looks like it's going to be a cascade-type attack."

"But the kill codes will stop it. Will reverse it. Right?"

Instead of offering her any assurance, his tone returned to clipped, efficient, all-is-under-control. "We'll send someone for your hikers."

"If the NPS people ride out on horses, they should be able to reach Skye and Brandon and take them back to the ranch before dark."

"Fine. Anything else?"

She was still miffed about her bump to backup role, but she prided herself in being professional. No need to bring her grievances up now, though she would include a complaint about his unwise use of resources—aka her—in her operational report.

She didn't say any of that.

A gnawing worry had taken residence in her gut, brought on more by Steele's tone than his actual words.

Should she tell him about Zack?

But Donovan Steele had enough to worry about. He'd indicated that he was coordinating as many as a dozen teams. She understand that meant keeping track of a vast amount of details, agents, and resources.

She couldn't imagine the weight on his shoulders.

Plus, Allison didn't want to tell him about Zack. She would have a hard time articulating why she hadn't sent him back with the clueless hikers. She had her reasons, but they were difficult to explain, especially on a truncated phone call while she was standing in the middle of a canyon with a terrorist careening down the river.

Steele had grown tired of waiting for her answer, or maybe his coffee was getting cold.

"Agents on the North Rim are taking longer to get into position than we predicted due to last night's rains."

Her annoyance flared. What was their problem? She'd been able to get in position, and she had to cross a suspension bridge in a raging storm. She suspected they were about as experienced at hiking as Brandon and Skye.

"But they're coming."

"Yes."

"You're sure."

"I'm positive. Teams leaders have assured me they will be in place before dark. They're aiming for the area between Above Salt Creek or Granite Camp. It's doubtful Blitz will make a move before then."

"Fine."

"Fine—" It seemed as if he couldn't find the words to express whatever else he had to say.

She'd noticed that about him two years ago, when they were snowbound on Hurricane Ridge. He'd sometimes stop himself in the midst of a thought—to hold back the words that might hinder rather than help.

Your wound isn't worse ... it definitely wasn't any better.

They'll find us ... eventually, though we might be frozen corpses by the time they do.

We're not giving up ... don't give up on me, Quinn.

She always felt as if that experience on top of the mountain sat between them, as if it was this living thing that had become a part of their relationship. Except, they didn't have a relationship. They barely tolerated being thrown together on a joint op.

Steele cleared his throat. "Anything else?"

"Negative." She didn't need to tell him about Zack. It was trivial in the grand scheme of things. She'd pass Zack off to Tate, capture Blitz, and get out of this canyon.

Plus, Steele would argue with her, and she was not in the mood to defend her decisions.

"Be careful."

It's possible that he was going to say more, but she'd already pushed the END button. She powered down the phone, stuck it in the bottom of her pack, and walked back to Bella.

Zack was still watching her, but he didn't speak.

She tried to draw some measure of energy from the silence.

A great egret spread its white wings—slender, long neck stretched into a straight line as it flew beside them, low and close to the water.

A red-tailed hawk called from somewhere above.

They entered a wider section of river frontage where they could ride side by side.

Zack cleared his throat. "I'm surprised you didn't insist I go with them."

"Don't make me regret it."

"Trust me. It's better if I'm not on an extended hike with *Brandon* or *Skye*." He said their names as if it were painful to him.

Allison couldn't help laughing, but then she caught a glimpse of the river and remembered what she still had to do. She remembered the people who had already died on this op.

Mr. Harris—strangled.

Teddy—stabbed.

167

Lyra—impervious to the monster sneaking up behind her and lunging to break her neck.

"This isn't a game, Zack."

"I know it isn't."

"Good."

"Though. . . well, I don't know what we're doing or who we're after. Blitz, Gollum, kill codes—that's all you've told me. No matter how I turn those things around in my mind, they don't make any sense."

She flashed him a smile. "Excellent. They don't need to make sense to you."

They rode in silence for another quarter mile before she said what she would have said to Steele, what she maybe *should* have said. "Two reasons."

Zack shifted in his saddle.

"First, I'm not completely sure you would go back. You might go with our clueless hikers until you were sure they could find their own way, then circle back behind me. I can't be worrying about my back and my front."

One curt nod was all he gave her.

She'd guessed right. He was in this, whether she wanted him to be or not.

"And the second reason?"

"As much as I hate to say it, you're better on a horse than I am." Allison had never had illusions of being the smartest person in the room—or in this case in the canyon. It still pained her to admit that Zack might be useful, even critical to this mission's success. "You damn sure know this river trail better than I do."

"So you need me." The smile that wreathed his face caused Allison's stomach to hurt.

"You know this is dangerous, right?"

"I sort of guessed that when you pulled your gun on me."

"And you still want to stay? Because you can go back. You could probably catch up to Brandon and Skye in no time at all."

The trail was narrowing.

Allison pressed her heels to Bella's side and the mare broke into a nice jog. But Zack matched her pace, stayed close behind, and she still was able to hear his response. It again made her laugh.

"I'll choose danger with you over five more minutes with Brandon and Skye any day."

She fervently hoped that neither she nor Zack lived to regret their decision.

The rest of the afternoon proceeded without incident.

They skirted a few caves in the canyon wall.

She'd read somewhere that there were over four hundred caves within Grand Canyon National Park. Animal bones, some over ten thousand years old, had been found in them—bones of condor, mountain goats, camels and horses, even the dire wolf. Many held bat colonies, which roosted during the day. She had no desire to investigate them.

Occasionally she heard the splashing sound of a waterfall coming from far back in the chasms. She would have liked to ride back and see that. Her father had been an explorer of sorts, though he was a computer specialist by vocation. The days they'd spent camping had seemed to balance out his life and hers. They also helped soothe the heartache of a young girl who was learning to live without her mom.

However, this wasn't a sightseeing trip, and she had no reason to go south into the caves and chasms, streams and waterfalls.

Why would she?

The buyer of Gollum's kill codes had to come from the north. It was the only direction that made any sense.

Some of the cacti they passed had opened their pink, red, and yellow blooms. The rain had once again succored life in the canyon. Maybe too much life.

Bella jerked her head up and came to an abrupt stop, nearly jolting Allison from her saddle.

She peered ahead, trying to see what had spooked the mare.

"Rattler," Zack said softly. "There, in the middle of the trail."

They had both stopped a good distance short of the five-foot reptile.

Allison was well acquainted with rattlesnakes. Her father's only sister lived in Texas, where the western diamondback was fairly common. She'd seen her Aunt Polly use her shotgun on more than one rattler that had cozied up too close to the house. Allison had learned to freeze in place when she heard the distinctive rattle of a diamondback.

The Grand Canyon was home to the prairie rattlesnake.

Like the diamondback, most of the rattlers in the canyon reached five feet in length, though she'd heard stories of some reaching over seven feet. Pale in color, the prairie rattler blended perfectly into the dirt, rocks, and canyon walls. If she'd been hiking, she would probably have stepped on it.

Bella's instincts were significantly better than hers.

The snake lay in the sun.

From a coiled position, a rattler could strike a distance of over half its body length. The bites were rarely fatal, but Allison and Zack were a long way from any medical help. The recommended advice for someone bitten was to stay calm, call 911, and get to a hospital.

Those suggestions wouldn't help much given their location.

Venom from older snakes was more potent, and large snakes were able to store larger volumes. Allison couldn't tell this snake's age, but as far as size it was in the middling range. At the sound of their horse's hoofbeats, it had raised its tail to rattle a big, hard-to-miss, *stay away*.

Zack walked his horse back several more steps. "Can you shoot it? I could shoot it if I had my gun."

"I could shoot it, but Blitz might hear. If we alert him to the fact that we're here, we'll have a lot more to worry about than one snake." She glanced back at him.

He shrugged as if what she'd said made sense and hopped off

his horse. Making a sound in the back of his throat, he patted Bella's flank and she backed up until she was standing beside Denali.

"Impressive."

Zack smiled and handed Denali's reins to Allison.

Denali was a black and white paint with a sweet disposition and would have been Allison's second choice for this op.

Zack scooped up five small rocks and lobbed first one and then a second at the rattler. Initially, the snake continued to rattle, but by the third rock it surrendered and slithered away from the trail.

"Nice shot—with the rocks I mean. See? You don't even need that revolver."

Zack shook his head as if he couldn't quite figure her out. "You're different than I thought an agent would be."

"Huh. Because I'm not wearing a tasteless suit or men-in-black glasses?"

"Maybe." He laughed and pulled himself into the saddle.

They continued along the trail, Allison now alert for rattlers. The odds of seeing another were low. Plus, Bella had proven her ability to act as an early warning system.

"But also because you're crazy intense one minute and kidding around the next."

"You say intense. I say focused."

"Whatever."

"Operations like this take a lot out of you." She heard a buzz, glanced up, but saw nothing.

"What do you mean?"

"Well, for instance take my last twenty-four hours. I hiked up top yesterday, had a wonderful dinner, then fell asleep for two hours before I received the call."

"The call?"

"Then I hiked down."

"Last night."

Now it was Allison's turn to shrug. "You do what you have

to do."

"I guess, but I'm surprised you're able to sit up in that saddle. I've only hiked up and down in the same day once. I felt like I could sleep twelve hours afterwards."

Occasionally Allison could hear the voices of the rafters.

Laughter.

Screaming-which caused her to put her hand on her holster.

Followed by more laughter and calling out to one another.

Even when she couldn't see them, their voices bounced off the canyon walls. She again heard a high-pitched sound and looked up, wondering if she was imagining it. There was nothing up there—nothing that she could see.

Two hours later, when the rafters were again out of sight and they were riding closer to the river, she caught sight of something in her peripheral vision, and this time she was certain about the buzz she was hearing.

"Stop."

Bella obeyed immediately.

Zack was a little slower.

She shielded her eyes and studied the skies. When she spotted it, she swore under her breath and dismounted.

"Get off the horse."

Zack did, arching his back and pretending to be stiff. Allison didn't buy it. That boy was probably born on a horse.

"Where's your phone?"

"What?"

"Where's your phone, Zack?"

"What are you going to do with it?"

She focused on counting to ten. Made it to three. Swore and made it to his side before he had a chance to back up. Though he was taller and bigger, she had no doubt that she was the more intimidating figure. She had anger and resentment and justice to fuel her attitude.

"Where. . . is. . . your. . .phone?"

He squirmed under her stare. "I'm not going to tell you if

you're going to do something stupid like shoot it. We might need that phone."

"Give me your phone."

"You have one. Looked like some lame kind of satellite phone. Probably can't even get the internet, but at least you have one."

"Your phone is useless down here."

"Yeah, but it has a beacon, right? Like, the government could track our position if they wanted to, if they needed to."

"Give me your phone, Zack, or I swear you will be sorry."

Though Allison had tried to keep a calm and cool demeanor, they were now shouting at each other. She could hear Steele's mission clock ticking in her head. She did not have time for this.

"Last chance, Zack. Give me your phone." She put one hand on her weapon and held the other out between them—palm up.

"I'm not getting stuck out here with you without a beacon. You're at least halfway crazy. You could kill me and leave me here."

"You're counting on our government to find your body and send it back to momma?" She again thought of Lyra with a broken neck, Mr. Harris strangled, her own father shot.

Despite her irritation and exhaustion, her training kicked in. Zack was not a threat other than the fact that he was confused and scared, but confused and scared people did unpredictable things. What she needed was Zack completely on her side, Zack helping the U.S. Government with a capital G.

"Look up, Zack. Tell me what you see."

He'd taken a step away from her, but he did as she asked. "Canyons, sky, a bird—"

"Not a bird, Zack. That's a drone. It's following us because somehow it has locked onto your phone."

"It's turned off."

"Your phone is always on, Zack. Even when it's off, the microphone can be turned on."

She was simplifying things. Neither the government nor any hacking group that she knew of could turn your phone back on when it had been turned off. That technology didn't exist—yet.

But it could make your phone play dead—where you thought it was off but it wasn't. You'd see the slide-to-power-off button, be able to tap it, and watch your screen turn dark.

But if malware had previously been downloaded on your phone, the turning off part didn't actually happen. The only indication would be that your battery lasted a shorter amount of time, and most people wrote that off as not having the newest phone. The hackers, and the government, had every advantage when it came to snooping.

They could listen.

They could track.

They both had unlimited resources and the best programmers.

Drones were routinely used to apprehend terrorists and drug traffickers.

"That drone is following us, and it's because of your phone. I know that it's because of your phone because I'm not stupid enough to bring a phone that can be tracked."

"Well excuse me for believing that America is the land of the free." He stalked toward his mare. Reaching under the saddle horn, he extracted his phone and handed it to her. "Please don't—"

The phone made a nice plunk as it hit the water.

"Let's go."

She couldn't do anything about the drone.

It was flying too high to shoot. If it were merely tracking Zack's phone, it would assume it had lost the signal and return to base. If it was sophisticated enough to be able to see them, at that height, then it would continue following them. Another complication in an already complex op. She needed to focus on what she could control.

She needed to reach Granite Camp before the rafters did.

She needed to be in place and ready to intercede.

The welfare of the world—or at least North America—depended on it.

Chapter Eleven

John Howard sat back, hands clasped together behind his head, staring at the three monitors on his desk.

The far-left monitor displayed various news feeds.

The middle showed the stock market—including his position on certain stocks.

The last allowed him to keep his eyes on the workroom in the basement of Middle-earth.

At the moment, he was focused on the screen in the middle, and he liked what he was seeing. The stocks that he had shorted were all down, and though the markets would close in less than an hour, international and after-hours trading would continue.

His portfolio was up.

John's motivation in releasing Cyber Drop wasn't financial, but the monies earned from the impending collapse would go a long way toward building a new tomorrow.

A glance at the news monitor told him that the beginning phase of the cascade had garnered some minor attention. As he had expected, the government was working diligently to keep a lid on the story, but that didn't work long in their current age of information. Stories ignored by cable news channels often exploded on social media, gaining momentum until the official news outlets had no choice but to report on them. He had counted on that very thing, and was pleased to see it working exactly as he had expected.

Arm-chair investors didn't like losing money, and they were quite adamantly insisting to know what was happening and whether certain stock losses were tied to the "planned outages" on the East Coast. John knew that those stocks were currently only experiencing moderate losses. They were the same stocks he had shorted and would soon take a plunge, followed by a frenzied sell-off, and ending with a financial bloodbath.

So be it.

Once again, the very things that he despised about modern society were conspiring to help him move the country he loved toward a post-modern era.

Sometimes the stars aligned.

His cell phone beeped. The screen displayed the name *Brett*. He glanced at the monitor to the right and saw Brett and Kate standing near the video wall.

Pushing the speaker button, he barked, "What is it?"

"We have something."

"I'm on my way."

John put his computer into sleep mode.

He trusted the people inside Middle-earth, but why tempt fate? His password was a random selection of 27 characters, numbers, and symbols. It would take over two hundred years to crack, even using state-of-the-art software. No one would be breaking into his data.

He retraced his steps downstairs to the workroom. The hackers were no longer staring at their machines. Everyone had their eyes locked on the monitor wall.

"Talk to me."

"Our drone picked up a weak cell phone signal. It took us awhile to trace it as the signal would disappear whenever the canyon walls interfered." Kate's fingers flew over her tablet, pushing images to the monitor wall.

Each image was the same—two individuals, riding on horseback, moving slowly and methodically. John couldn't discern any particular trail, but then whoever this was apparently had one direction in mind—downriver. He supposed a trail wasn't necessary.

"Show me where they are in relation to Blitz."

The view widened and he could see two green dots on the river, indicating the position of the raft. Apparently Blitz and Nina were in the same raft. He knew from his tracker upstairs that the person he had planted was in the same raft as well. It was nice to see everyone together. He'd rather like to be present when the moment of transfer came, but he supposed he'd have to be content with watching it on the monitor.

Some things weren't worth risking his life for—idle curiosity being one of them.

"We called you as soon as the drone established a visual contact." Brett nodded to Kate.

"And then this happened a few minutes ago."

The second horse stopped. The rider looked to be a woman, though the drone wasn't close enough to give an identifying picture. She stared at the sky, shading her eyes with her hand.

The first horse stopped as well. Both riders dismounted. Definitely a man on the first horse, a woman on the second. And the woman looked to be in charge.

The drone was closer now, but still they could only make out the tops of the two persons' heads—a cowboy hat on his, a broad-brimmed hat on hers. What John would give to hear that conversation, but the drone simply wasn't close enough.

Then he was glad the drone wasn't any closer because the woman put one hand on her hip. . . on what looked like a holster. In all likelihood, she wasn't a good enough shot to shoot a drone out of the sky, but he'd rather not risk it.

Holding out her other hand toward the man, she waited.

When the man did nothing, she pointed to the sky, and then they both looked up.

"Can you zoom in on that?"

"We are zoomed in."

The man seemed to hesitate, then walked to his horse, retrieved something, and gave it to her.

She threw it in the river.

The vein in John's neck began to pulse and twitch. "That was a cell phone."

"It was. After she threw it in the river, they disappeared along the trail, and we weren't able to follow."

John could feel everyone in the room watching him.

What did they expect him to do?

Hold up his hand and declare the operation a disaster?

Call it off because their drone had been spotted?

None of those things were going to happen. They'd expected and planned for the fact that the government would be aware of their presence in the canyon, as well as their presence at the other twelve dummy sites. If all the government had sent were the two persons on horseback, John wasn't worried.

And yet, he was irritated that his team hadn't found a way to follow the two after the phone had sunk into the murky waters of the Colorado. "Do we know who the phone was issued to?"

Spencer bounced out of his chair. "The man's name is Zackary Lancaster. He works at the ranch, and is twenty-one years old."

"Any flags on his background?"

"Not that we've found."

"Then look deeper." He turned to look at the cybergeeks.

Planting his feet shoulder width apart, he rolled his shoulders and neck, practically hoping that one of them would challenge him. No one did. The room was eerily silent, the only sound coming from the fans that cooled the processors which ran their machines.

"I want to know everything about Zackary Lancaster—what elementary school he attended, who his parents work for, and what he's doing in my canyon. As for the woman, I want to know who she is. Work out a way to enhance that image. Once you do, start with what type of hat she's wearing, and find out if it's part of a uniform."

No one spoke.

No one moved.

John's annoyance gave way to fury.

"Don't look at me as if it can't be done. You're supposed to be the best. You're being paid generously, so do your job."

"Maybe we could if you'd picked a better drop spot. Maybe the bottom of a canyon wasn't the best place to do this."

The words were barely out of Jasmine Clark's mouth when John charged across the room with the fury of a bull headed toward a billowing cape.

His hands tightened around the woman's neck.

He lifted her out of the chair and slammed her against the wall. Her eyes bulged and her hands slapped feebly at his.

As for John, he saw red.

He saw the faces of everyone who had ever told him that he was a fool, that his concerns were ludicrous, that he needed to accept the changes of the twenty-first century with wide open arms. He saw defeat in this woman's expression, and he would not have it in his domain. He would wipe it from her face if it meant squeezing the last breath of life from her lungs.

"John. Stop. John."

He slowly became aware of Brett beside him, attempting to pull his fingers away from Jasmine's neck. The gall of the man caused John's anger to change course. He let go of Jasmine, balled his hand into a fist and slugged Brett in the face.

The force of the punch threw the older man against a computer monitor, which crashed to the floor.

Brett landed in a heap on top of the monitor.

No one moved.

No one spoke.

John forced his breathing into a slower, calmer rhythm. He smoothed the fabric of his sport coat, tugged on his sleeves. It had felt good to release some of the pent-up pressure, allowed for better clarity. These were the people he had to work with. For better or worse, at this moment, they were all he had.

Walking over to Brett, he reached out a hand and helped him to his feet. "You're going to want to put ice on that."

Brett nodded.

John straightened the man's clothing as he had his own.

He didn't look back at his employees until he reached the entrance to the room. Spencer was helping Jasmine to her feet. She looked stunned, as if she couldn't understand what had just happened. John knew from experience that a lack of oxygen could definitely mess with your cognition. She'd be fine, and in the future she'd watch her mouth.

Kate stood at the monitor wall, clutching her tablet to her chest—eyes wide but not meeting his. Instead, she stared at the far wall as if she might find answers written there.

The other hackers remained at their workstations.

He was the only one in this room who completely understood what was at stake. They were cogs in a wheel that they couldn't even begin to fathom.

No one met his gaze, which was fine with John.

Let them be afraid of him.

They had justifiable reasons to squirm under his leadership, but he knew they'd stay. Every person in this room drew a seven-figure salary.

Money could buy loyalty—for a time, and he wouldn't need them much longer.

Less than twenty-four hours.

Chapter Twelve

They returned to the trail.

Zack continued throwing glances her way—as if he couldn't decide whether she was very cool or very crazy. *Welcome to the club*, she thought. *Some days I'm not sure myself.*

Occasionally she used her binoculars to study the occupants on the rafts. There wasn't a single time as she watched that Tate raised his arm and pointed at something in the sky. Tate, the guests, and the guides all seemed completely relaxed. Every indication supported the notion that they were having the time of their life.

Blitz even laughed at one point.

Nina appeared to be completely at ease, though Allison did note that Jason rarely interacted with anyone. In fact, he looked quite morose. Good. If he had been stupid enough to sign on with Blitz or Gollum, then she hoped he lived to rue the day he'd taken a step onto that path.

The rafts typically pulled off the river in the early afternoon. By that time, the canyon walls hid the western sun, creating a prolonged dusk. Though they'd been on the river only seven hours, that was a long time for those new to rafting.

Tired tourists were dangerous tourists, and the rafting companies couldn't afford the bad publicity that came with an accident.

Allison was relieved when the guides continued past the Trinity and Above Salt Creek campgrounds. The Salt Creek rapids were only a Class III, which at this point would seem easy to the rafters. Now if they would only pull over for the Granite Campground, she could stop worrying about location and move on to worrying about how and when.

They did pull over at Granite Campground.

Relief eased the knot in her shoulders when the guide in the lead boat began shouting at the guide in the second boat and pointing toward a beachy area. The guide in raft two gave the guide in the first raft a thumbs up and pulled over.

Everyone immediately began to disembark.

What surprised and concerned Allison was what happened next. Instead of pulling in beside the second raft, the first raft continued around the corner and apparently beached there. She couldn't be sure, but she thought that was what had happened.

Why would they pull up in different spots?

Unless Blitz had told them to.

Or maybe the commercial guide in raft one was on Gollum's team. At this point, no one was above suspicion. Allison had been focused on raft two—the raft that Blitz and Tate were riding in.

She pulled up lightly on Bella's reins, and the horse stopped. Zack continued a few feet farther, noticed she was no longer behind him, walked his horse back and easily turned it around. Yup—he was a natural on a horse.

No doubt about it.

He'd spent his teen years winning buckles at the local rodeo, and now he was here—with her.

One of the most important skills of a Homeland Security agent was a person's ability to problem-solve. That's where Allison excelled. She had to be taught shooting, hand-to-hand combat, cyber terminology, and stealth tactics. But troubleshooting? That came naturally. She'd learned to figure things out for herself at the ripe old age of nine, walking alone, making her way on foot down from the old-growth forest campsite where her father had been shot.

Now she needed to carefully consider what to do with Zack.

And she needed to know what was happening on those rafts.

Maybe there was a way she could use his skills. Maybe there was a way she could turn Zack Lancaster from a liability to an asset.

Allison nodded toward the left—away from the river, and Zack turned his horse. They traveled through some grass, around a couple of boulders, and stopped next to a few scraggly trees. Bella and Denali both began to crop at what grass there remained in the area.

"The horses need a rest." Zack dismounted and reached for the feed bag.

Allison did the same.

"This is the farthest downriver I've been," Zack admitted. "Looks like a good campsite—sandy surface for their tents, probably even good trout fishing. I'm surprised no one else is camping there."

"My boss had a little to do with that." Allison shrugged when he turned to stare at her. "Director Rivera had a hand as well."

"You've met her?"

"You haven't?"

Zack shook his head. "What's she like?"

His voice held a note of awe, as if they were discussing the queen. . . which in some ways Rivera was, only she—and her people—represented a different type of royalty.

"She's remarkable. You'd like her, and she was quite determined to keep any guests out of harm's way. You won't see any other hikers or rafters. Not until this is over."

A plan was forming in her mind, but she needed to present it carefully so Zack would think it was his idea. It wasn't so much that she was manipulating him. There was little doubt he would agree to what she proposed, no manipulation required. But she wanted him to be all in. That would only happen if he thought the idea had been his.

"Since the rafts have beached for the night, we can stay here."

"All night?"

"I have to stay. It's my job."

"So this is as far as you're going?"

Allison shrugged. "Probably. Whatever happens will most likely happen here."

When he continued to tend to his horse, silently, she pressed. "Would you want to travel back to Phantom—alone and in the dark?"

"I'm not afraid of riding alone, and I don't mind riding in the dark."

"Uh-huh."

He looked up at her now. "Do you think Gollum or Blitz or whoever. . ."

She waited, let him work through his questions.

"Do you think they'd follow me back?"

"Honestly? Fifty-fifty chance. They might be aware of you."

"Because of the drone?"

"Yeah."

"I should have told you about the cell phone."

"Water over the rapid, Zack. Nothing we can do about it now."

"But the drone was theirs?"

"It wasn't one of ours." She pulled the equine kit from her pack, retrieved the horse pick, then walked over to Bella. She ran her hand down the mare's leg, then said softly "Hoof up." Using the pick, she proceeded to clean out rocks, dirt, and other debris from the frog of Bella's foot, then she traced around the inside of the shoe.

Zack was doing the same to Denali.

"Could have been anyone running that drone." She moved to Bella's other front leg.

"Except there's no one else here."

"Yeah. There is that." Allison finished with both front legs and patted the horse. Bella seemed to nod her head in thanks.

Moving to the right hind leg, she continued trying to cast bait in front of Zack. "Even if Gollum was flying that drone, they might wonder why you're this far from the ranch. Or they might not."

"They probably suspect everyone."

"People who are on the wrong side of things tend to be a bit paranoid, in my experience." She sighed heavily. "My problem right now is that the first raft has beached around the curve. The second stayed on this side. There's no way I can keep an eye on both of them."

"I could do it."

She almost felt guilty.

He looked for all the world like a hopeful pup.

"I don't know. I'm not supposed to put civilians in harm's way."

"Then give me my pistol back, and I'll sign a waiver releasing you of all responsibility."

She pretended to consider that, though she'd decided an hour ago that she'd return the Smith & Wesson to him. She didn't want to appear too eager though. Victories easily won were less sweet, and right now she needed Zack to feel like he'd won a victory.

She pulled his pistol from her saddlebag and walked over to him. He held out his hand, but she didn't release the pistol right away. Instead, she pulled out her Glock and held the two guns next to each other.

"Your Smith & Wesson is a sweet revolver."

"Thanks, I guess."

"My gun is a Glock 17L. It has a long barrel—8.86 inches to be exact. And a one-inch wide, accurately balanced slide. The magazine holds seventeen cartridges. It's a very precise weapon."

"So, what. . . you're a bad ass? Is that what you're telling me?" He smiled at her, and Allison saw something of the man he would one day become.

"Your words, Zack, not mine." She slipped her weapon into her holster, then handed him the S&W. "But yes, I am. I know a dozen ways to kill you—with or without this pistol."

She waited for him to meet her gaze.

His chin jutted out, as if bravado could pass for courage.

But his eyes blinked rapidly expressing his discomfort.

"I have no intention of doing that, Zack."

"Oh, so you're not going to kill me. That's a relief."

"Just don't mess with me. Okay? Don't do anything that would cause me to doubt you."

Zack jammed his revolver into his hip holster and stomped to the other side of his mare, muttering as he went. "Worse pep talk I've ever heard."

He tugged on the pad under Denali's saddle, making sure it was even on both sides. "As if I need a reason to be less on board with this."

Bending, he checked the girth buckles and cinch strap. "Now I have to worry about those guys *and* you. Little did I know that you're a psycho government agent. If this situation weren't so stupid it would make a radical movie—something produced by the Coen brothers."

Good.

He was unsettled.

If he were anxious, he would be careful.

He wouldn't take chances.

When he put his foot in the stirrup, she said, "Leave the horse."

He stared at her as if he couldn't believe his ears. But he took his foot out of the stirrup.

"There are a few things we need to go over first."

She walked him farther away from the river. She knew they couldn't be seen by the rafters, but she didn't want sunlight reflecting off his gun to give him away.

"Let me see you draw your weapon."

"Seriously?"

"Yes, Zack. Seriously."

He rolled his eyes, but assumed a shooter's stance and drew the Smith & Wesson.

"Not bad. Do you mind if I show you a few things?"

Zack shrugged, but she had his attention.

"Snatch it from the holster. Don't pull it. If you pull," She peeled off her jacket so that he could see what she was doing. "If you pull, the holster drags with you. You'll have a much cleaner draw if you snatch it."

"Makes sense."

"You give it a try."

He did, and a huge stupid grin blossomed on his face.

"Much better. Your grip is good from the beginning of the draw. That's critical."

"My dad taught me. He was a ranch hand in New Mexico, probably one of the last ranch hands since there aren't that many privately owned ranches anymore. That's why he encouraged me to hire on with the national parks."

"Smart man. I guess he was teaching you how to shoot in case of snakes, things like that."

"I guess."

"The bad guys in those rafts aren't snakes, though sometimes they act like them. One of the most important things I learned in training was not to look at the target."

"Huh?"

"It's tempting. You have this big, bad guy coming toward you, but it's very important that you look at the front sight of your weapon, not the target. Your gun is an extension of you. Got it?"

"I think so."

She holstered her gun, and he did the same.

"One more thing. Never shoot just once. Should you end up in a situation where you have to pull your weapon—and I sincerely hope you don't—then you empty that barrel. Don't wait and see if you hit the guy."

"Or gal."

That caused her to pause. She cocked her head and waited for him to meet her gaze. "Could you shoot a woman, Zack? If one was coming at you? If one was intent on killing you?"

"I guess."

His eyes told a different story, and Allison experienced her first moment of real doubt. What was she doing? Was she seriously thinking of sending this kid into harm's way?

She checked the time. Catastrophic Systems Failure in nineteen hours, thirty-five minutes. The impending event might as well be stamped on the face of her watch.

Yeah, she was going to do this, which meant she needed to be completely honest with Zack. Should something happen to him, the guilt would eat away at her—unless she'd been honest, upfront, and clear from the get-go.

"Look, Zack. This isn't fair to you. It really isn't, but I do need your help here. This thing we're trying to stop—it's big. Okay?"

"I don't even know what *this thing* is."

She studied him and came to the conclusion that he deserved to know the truth. "It's a cyberattack, against our infrastructure."

"The Grand Canyon's?"

"The United States. The entire United States, possibly part of Canada as well."

"Oh."

He nodded his head, as if what she'd said made sense, but Allison could tell that he was still processing her words. She waited, letting his mind and emotions catch up with the facts of their situation.

"So. . . no electricity anywhere in the United States?"

"If they're successful, that's exactly what will happen. Plus no communications—cell phones, GPS, air traffic control, emergency services. . . anything dependent on electricity would go off-line."

"But cities have generators."

"They do." She nodded, wanted to get moving, waited. "But those generators won't last very long."

"So people could. . . "

"Die. A lot of people could die."

"Then I guess we better stop them." Instead of looking frightened, Zack smiled.

It was a hesitant smile, but she was happy to see it nonetheless.

"If someone comes toward you in a threatening way, if someone draws on you, even if it's Nina, even if it's a woman or man you haven't met. . . shoot. Don't hesitate. You empty your revolver. Understand?"

He nodded, and he met her eyes when he did so.

Perhaps he wasn't as young and naïve as she had assumed.

"Make sure you're not seen. Stay low, keep your Stetson pulled down." She studied him critically. "Are you wearing anything reflective?

"No."

"Necklace?

"Nope."

"Earring?"

He shook his head.

"I want you to make your way quietly around to where you can see the first raft. Walk as if there's a mountain lion stalking you, because there might be. . . only his name is Blitz."

"What does he have to do with the attack?"

"Later, okay? Just proceed carefully, try to assess what's happening, and then meet me back here. In the meantime, I'll keep an eye on the nearest raft. Stay no longer than fifteen minutes."

"And the horses?"

"We'll let them graze here, take them down and water them after dark."

"Can we at least unsaddle them?"

"Huh-uh. Not yet. We might need them."

"For a fast getaway? Here? Doesn't seem very likely."

But he pulled out his water bottle, took a big swig from it, then slipped it back into his pack. He'd turned away and started to make his way past the small clearing toward the rocks when she called out to him.

"Zack."

He stopped, turned, looked back at her.

"Be careful."

He tipped the Stetson—a ridiculous gesture if there ever was one. And then he was gone.

Allison secured the horses by wrapping their lead ropes around a tree branch on the far side of the meadow. They seemed content to graze on the small patches of grass. She promised them a long watering as soon as Zack returned. Reaching into her pack, she pulled out the binoculars and a ball cap, then stuffed her National Park hat inside.

She made her way back toward the river, to her first reconnaissance point. As she walked slowly, careful not to disturb any rocks or make any sounds, she mulled over what she'd just done.

She wasn't sure whether it was morally acceptable to use a twenty-one-year-old civilian in a mission. Then again, what choice did she have?

Yes, she could pull out the SAT phone and call Steele again, but his people were trying to make their way down the North Kaibab Trail, which had an extra quarter mile of elevation change compared to the South Kaibab. The trail would be slick from last night's rain, and then they'd have to forge a path downriver in order to arrive where the rafts had stopped. There simply was no easy way for them to arrive in position by dusk. It would be a grueling day for experienced hikers, which those agents weren't.

And that was probably why Blitz had picked this place.

He'd predicted their moves, calculated the odds, and decided that he could get out before they reached the area where the codes were transferred.

But how was he going to get out?

That part, she hadn't been able to envision. A private guide on a power boat? Had they found a place to land a helicopter somewhere downriver?

She didn't need to tell Steele about Zack. She didn't need to bother him with a minor change of plans that she could handle herself. Considering the obstacles his team on the North Rim was facing, the other teams he was coordinating, and the cascading failures. . . she didn't think telling him she'd involved Zack would be welcome or necessary information.

Once those agents were in place, she needed them to stay on the far side of the river, blocking Blitz's escape route and intercepting the people who had purchased the kill codes. She didn't need them crossing over before the handoff was made. That would spook Blitz. It would definitely warn off whomever he was passing the codes to.

She didn't need to call Steele.

Things weren't that critical yet, and besides, she was still hoping for a few minutes alone with Blitz.

She reached the main river, turned left, skirted around a four-foot rock, and tugged down on her baseball cap. The cap would help to shield any reflection made by the binoculars. Since the sun was past the canyon wall, there shouldn't be any reflections, but she wasn't willing to bet her life on that—or Zack's. She scrambled to the top of a rock, dropped to a prone position, and glassed the raft.

At first, she didn't see anyone. The raft was beached in the same place it had been before. A pile of supplies had been set on the beach, back a good forty feet from the river.

Where had everyone gone?

Why had they left all their gear?

Then she heard the sound of a splash, followed by another. She moved her field of vision upriver and found them—splashing and playing in the water like a family of porpoises. In September? That water had to be freezing, but apparently they had found a warm shallow area.

It looked like the group from the first raft had joined the group from the second. So why park around the bend? It didn't make any sense. She quickly counted heads, but only came up with eleven.

How could there only be eleven?

Who was missing?

The two commercial guides were easy enough to pick out—they wore caps with neon orange stripes as well as their company logo. The couple from raft number one was standing a little to the side, slipping out of the river and drying off with a towel they'd left on a rock.

The family of three stood at the edge of the river, trying to coax their young daughter to stick her feet into the water.

Jason was by himself, sitting near the water with his arms wrapped around his knees.

"Struggling with your conscious a little late, my man."

Raft one occupants were all present and accounted for.

So the missing person was from raft number two.

Blitz was on the edge of the group, his pale skin covered by a black t-shirt. The twenty-three-year-old woman was submerged up to her neck, laughing at something he said, apparently clueless that she was speaking with one of the nation's most sought-after cyberterrorists.

Well, to be fair, he looked harmless enough.

It was what was in his brain, the skill in his coding, that was the problem. It was his lack of morality that placed them all in danger..

Which left Tate and Nina.

She glassed the entire area again—no Nina. Allison would recognize the woman anywhere. She'd been hiking with her for months, bunking in the same room as her. It was looking more and more as if Nina was compromised. How had she missed the telltale signs of that?

And then she saw Tate, and her heart did a flip. He stood nearly in the middle of the river, one hand covering his eyes as if to help him see better, and the other hand? The other hand was pointing to something high up on the canyon walls.

Only Allison knew that he wasn't actually pointing at anything. He was signaling. Something else had gone wrong. She cupped her hands and gave her best owl impersonation. Tate dropped his hand and made his way back to the beach area, laughing as he did so at something that one of the guides said.

She turned and scanned the canyon behind her, but saw no evidence of Zack. She needed to know what he'd seen around the bend, then she would find a way to meet up with Tate.

She backed away from the edge of the rock she'd been lying on, standing up only when she was sure she couldn't be seen. Then she quickly retraced her steps, making her way back to the small clearing.

The two horses were still cropping at the grass, but Zack was not there. How long had he been gone? What route had he taken? Should she wait here, or go looking for him?

She paced the meadow a little longer, her instinct telling her with each passing moment that something had gone terribly wrong. She knew which direction he'd left the meadow—to the southwest, so she set off in that direction. Ten minutes later she stepped between two boulders in full view of the river.

No Zack.

She hadn't passed him. He wasn't waiting here, scouting the rafting area, and he wasn't down by the raft—something he would have known not to do. It was as if he had disappeared.

She skirted a little farther west, then dropped to the ground and crawled to the edge of a boulder for a different view of raft one. No one there. Nina wasn't there, and everyone else was with the group around the bend. So what was happening?

She backed away from the edge and stood up, then turned in a circle. She looked around for any telltale sign that Zack might have been there—crushed scrub grass or the faint mark of a hiking boot.

Nothing.

She listened and heard—nothing.

But she hadn't imagined Zack Lancaster.

His horse was a couple hundred yards back, cropping grass next to hers.

She felt suddenly famished and tried to remember when she'd last eaten. Her eyes burned as if they were filled with grit. She fought the urge to pull her weapon and fire a few shots into the clear blue sky. That would be stupid. That was frustration speaking—as well as a good dose of sleep deprivation.

She needed to think, but worst-case scenarios kept popping into her head.

What if Zack were dead?

What if Nina had killed him?

What if their clock was wrong and the impending Catastrophic Systems Failure had already reached the point of no return?

Her stomach churned, and her throat was so dry she had a hard time swallowing. She wished she'd brought her water bottle with her. Why had she left all of her supplies back with the horses? She put her hand on her hip holster, needing to assure herself that she at least had that.

The gun's bulk brought a measure of assurance.

But she needed her supplies and the rifle and the horses. What had she been thinking leaving all of that unguarded? She'd thought that Blitz and Associates were all in front of her, but what if someone had held back? What if someone other than Zack had been following her from the ranch?

She made her way to the meadow, quickly, quietly, stumbling only once. She stopped—disbelief and dread and a good dose of fear darkening her thoughts. Leaving her unable to think what might have happened or what she needed to do. Her heart rate accelerated, and she fought the rising sense of panic that threatened to consume and paralyze her.

Allison stood in the center of the small meadow, turning in a circle, wondering how it had come to this. Where had she made the first mistake? Where had she made the critical one? And would the entire United States of America suffer because of her actions?

This meadow was where she'd left the horses.

This was where she'd left her supplies.

And this was where she was supposed to meet Zack.

She had not imagined the entire thing, but the meadow was empty.

The only sign that the horses had been there was a broken branch where she'd tied their lead ropes.

Someone had Zack, and that same person had stolen their horses.

Was it Nina or someone else? Whoever it was had all of her supplies—including the rifle she'd taken from Anthony Cooper's lifeless body. Including her SAT radio.

Chapter Thirteen

Don't panic, don't panic, don't panic.

The words Allison repeated in her mind were both a mantra and a prayer.

Her body wasn't buying it.

Her body was in full fight or flight mode, thanks to her brain perceiving a terrifying threat and her hormones responding to that impending danger. When she was in training to become a DHS agent, she'd had an instructor hammer home the fight or flight scenario including what could and what couldn't be done about it.

"You'll want to run or attack. It will take all of your will, all of your conscious choice to act counterintuitively." They'd all laughed at the example of a young mother, who upon hearing a tornado approach, had tried to run out the front door. Her husband grabbed her and pushed her toward the closet. "Running into the path of a tornado was not an active choice on the mom's part. She was doing what her body had insisted that she do —flee."

Allison understood that it wasn't an either-or scenario. The third possibility was to freeze. But she didn't plan on doing any of those things. She wasn't going to fight—not yet. And she certainly wasn't going to flee.

When had running from a threat ever worked?

Fortunately, her frontal cortex was active enough to recognize that freezing wasn't an option if she wanted Zack to survive.

Her mind understood all of that.

Physically, her hypothalamus had begun firing the nerves necessary to release adrenaline into her bloodstream. Her blood vessels were constricting, her heart rate was up, and her liver was converting glycogen into glucose.

Yup. Her professor would be proud of her withstanding that onslaught of biological treachery.

Even her stomach betrayed her by churning and rolling as if she were riding a skiff on the high seas. She could only control her physiological response to stress to a certain degree. So she didn't focus on that.

But her mind—her mind had been trained to analyze, assess, and plan her next move accordingly.

Steele had been quite clear with his instructions.

Priority one is intercepting the person who has purchased those kill codes and retrieving the device. Secondary to that is arresting Blitz.

Which meant that she could not break off surveillance of Blitz. She had to be there when he passed the codes which he probably wouldn't do until he had the cover of darkness. That gave her approximately. . .

Her watch read fourteen minutes after five. Eighteen hours and forty-six minutes until Critical Systems Failure. She had precious little daylight left. The sun didn't officially set until six forty-five, but their position was now deep in the canyon. They'd lose the light a good hour before sundown—at five forty-five. She had thirty-one minutes.

She skirted back to Zack's surveillance position, made her way down to the beach where she could see the camping site the group had chosen, and held back until she saw Tate head off between two boulders. She didn't know if he was trying to make it easier for her to make contact, or if he had to heed the call of nature.

She came up behind him as he was zipping up his pants.

He turned, saw her, and opened his mouth—then shut it before any sound escaped.

Pointing in the direction she had come, they backtracked a hundred yards, then positioned behind a large boulder.

"I wasn't sure you'd seen me, then I heard your terrible owl imitation, which no one else seemed to notice. I thought—" He stopped abruptly, reached out and put a hand on her arm. "What's wrong?"

"Someone's taken Zack."

"Who?"

"Zack. Zack Lancaster."

Tate stared at her in disbelief. "Zack's back at the ranch. I saw him this morning when I told him you'd be taking Bella."

"No. He's not at the ranch. He's here. It's a long story, and I'll explain later. Since Nina is the only one missing from your group, I suspect she has him."

"Has him. You don't think she would. . ." He stopped, apparently flustered and unable to voice, maybe unable to conceive, the worst-case-scenario.

But Allison had to face the worst-case scenario, even if it was her fault that it could have happened.

"Yes, she would. In my opinion, she wouldn't hesitate to kill him, but since I haven't found his body there's a chance that she's trying to draw me out."

"So you'll. . ." He ran a hand through his graying hair. "What? I'm lost here, Allison. I'm in way over my head."

"I'm not." She gave him a toothy grin, her adrenaline once again surging as a plan formed in her mind. "But I need your help."

"Of course. What can I do?"

"You have to stay with Blitz."

"I'm already with him, and let me tell you, that guy is a good actor. Other than the fact that he does not belong on a float trip down the Colorado, I would never have suspected him of being a terrorist."

"You have to keep your eyes on him at all times, Tate. If he leaves the group, you leave the group. At no point are you to let him out of your sight."

"Okay. And then what do I do?"

"If he's just going for a leak, do nothing, but if he's meeting with someone—meeting with Nina or someone you don't know, then you fire a shot into the sky."

"And what if I lose him?"

"Don't." She scraped a hand through her short curls and came away with a few twigs. Tossing them to the ground, she said, "He's more adept at this than we suspected. I certainly underestimated him, and it gives me no pleasure to admit that."

"You're being too hard on yourself."

"I thought he was merely a hacker looking to make some extra money, but there's more at work here. I should have understood that when he killed Lyra. We both need to assume that he's willing and able to do whatever he has to do in order to make the swap happen."

"The swap?"

"Money for codes. We saw Lyra hand him something. I suspect it was a zip drive containing the kill codes. That's why we can't lose him. We have to maintain surveillance on him at all times."

"And what if I mess up? What if I do lose him?"

"Same signal—a single shot into the sky."

"What good would that do?"

"You do not intervene. Whatever he has planned is not going to happen far from here. My bet is it's going to be on the water, either upriver or down. Blitz isn't going to go hiking any deeper into the canyons, especially after dark."

"Okay, so he meets up with someone to deliver these kill codes, I fire a shot into the air, and then you what. . . find us?"

"Yeah, Tate. That's exactly what I'll do. Hopefully, by that point I'll have recovered Zack. There's a small possibility that I'm reading this all wrong. Maybe Zack got spooked and moved the horses."

"But you don't think so."

She shook her head. Zack was young and naïve, but he wasn't stupid. He would know how she'd react to the horses being gone. He wouldn't have done that.

"You better get back to camp."

"Okay." He stepped away from her, then turned back. "I didn't tell you why I signaled. I overheard Nina talking with the river guide in boat one when we pulled over after a particularly challenging rapid. She asked if he could possibly park around the bend so that she and Jason could have some privacy later tonight."

"And he fell for that?"

Tate shrugged. "We all did. I mean, we fell for the person that Nina wanted us to see, so yeah...he believed her. Why would she ask him to do such a thing?"

"Asked and answered. She knew that splitting up your group would draw me out or—in case there were two agents following her and Blitz—split us up."

"Which it did."

"Yeah. I fell for it." She didn't waste time beating herself up over the miscalculation.

Nina would pay for her actions. Allison would see to that herself. She would find Zack, take care of Nina, and be back in time to intercept, then interrogate, Blitz. It wasn't that she thought of herself as a female James Bond. It was simply the only acceptable outcome of this situation.

At any point that you feel priority one is in jeopardy, you abandon priority two.

She clearly remembered Steele's cautious reminder. Priority one—intercept the codes and the buyer. Priority two—apprehend Blitz and any accomplices.

But she had more at risk than those two things. She had a

priority three, always humming in the background of her life. She would be there to arrest Blitz, and she would question him about her father.

Those thoughts were what had driven her mind to find another option than fight, flight, or freeze. Her desperation had coalesced into a plan.

She would find Nina, then circle around and surprise her. Nina Brooks was not a trained agent. She was a young woman who was in way too deep, though she might not realize that yet.

Tate muttered a worried, "Please be careful," then returned to the rafters.

Allison resumed looking for Nina.

She couldn't have gone far, not with two horses and a hostage.

Plus, where was there to go?

Fifteen minutes later, she saw the first drop of blood in the dirt. Had she not been searching for just such a sign, she would have walked past it. In fact, she had walked past it earlier—eyes on the horizon, searching for Zack.

The next drop was on a large boulder as she maneuvered through a narrow path barely wide enough for a horse. The blood mark was waist-high, which could mean that Zack's hand or arm was injured. That was the best possibility.

After that, she felt as if she was following bright neon directional arrows—horse manure in the trail, a small broken branch from a scraggly tree, more spots of blood, boot prints.

And then she heard the low murmur of voices, followed by a rather loud snort from Bella. Allison knew Bella's sounds, had ridden her enough to understand when she was contented and when she was nervous. The snort was definitely a sign of mild alarm.

She pivoted so that her back was against a rock, pulled her pistol, and quieted her mind so she could better listen.

"You should talk to me, if you don't want me to slash you again, Zack." Nina's voice was too calm, too matter-of-fact.

She sounded familiar and yet completely foreign to the woman Allison knew.

"I told you. . ." A cough, then Zack replied in a weak voice. "You've got this all wrong."

"You had two horses. You weren't riding both of them."

"I brought one..." He pulled in a deep, rattling breath. "An extra one for Tate. He's needed back at the ranch."

"And the rifle?"

Zack had no answer for that.

"I will find out if you're lying. You think your stomach hurts now? That wound is nothing compared to what I will do. I hope you understand that. You're smart enough to know that I'm serious, so why do you continue to lie?"

"I'm not."

"The truth will be known, Zack, when the person you're helping comes looking for you. I'll take care of them. Then I'll finish off what I've started with you."

There was a grunt from Zack, as if Nina had. . .

What?

Hit him?

Blocking out everything else, Allison became aware of another sound. Closer, much too close for her comfort, was the sound of ragged breathing—of Zack's ragged breathing. Zack and Nina and the horses were positioned on the other side of this rock. She was sure of it. Zack was hurt, and he was in pain, but he wasn't telling Nina what she wanted to know.

Instead of moving toward them, Allison silently retraced her steps and scouted a different path, hoping to come in from an unexpected direction. As she crept through the brush, a coyote howled in the distance and was soon answered by another and another. The long, rising then falling notes didn't bother her. Coyotes were a necessary part of the ecosystem of the Grand Canyon. The danger a coyote presented was certainly to be respected, but it was nothing compared against the likes of Nina Brooks.

Nina had been an employee at the ranch longer than Allison. There was no doubt that she knew this canyon well—knew the river, its curves, its paths. All of that was evident in the spot Nina had chosen—relatively high ground backed up against the canyon. No one could sneak up behind her, short of rappelling from the canyon's walls.

But it also meant that she would have one less direction to escape. Allison could use that to her advantage.

Allison had followed their tracks as she approached from the northwest. If she were to draw a straight line from the rafters to Nina's current position, that would be the direction she'd do it. But instead of barging in, she crept through the fading light so that she could approach from the northeast. It was a small difference, but it could prove critical.

When she'd gone as far as she could without climbing gear, she crouched behind another boulder and stole a glance into the small clearing. What she saw caused her heart to slam against her chest.

What she saw was straight from her worst nightmare.

Nina was holding a knife to Zack's throat.

Zack was seated on a boulder, slumping actually. He looked pale and his breathing was ragged. His hands were tied in front of him, and he was curled as far forward as possible—as if to protect his wounded stomach. He didn't look as if he had any fight left in him.

But he wasn't dead.

She took solace and found courage in the fact that he was still breathing.

The scene was improbable, something that would never be aired on a prime-time television show, because Nina was a good foot and a half shorter than Zack and thirty pounds lighter. And yet, the blood dripping from Zack's shirt told something of what had happened.

Allison was looking at the one thing that modern television and novels hadn't quite captured yet. It wasn't the person who was the biggest or strongest that won in fights between good and evil. It was the person who was the most desperate.

Nina's future somehow depended on facilitating the delivery of the kill codes. For whatever reason, Gollum hadn't trusted Blitz. So much for honor among thieves. He'd put Nina in place well before he needed her. Apparently, she was desperate enough or devoted enough—or maybe both—to take a life if that's what the situation required.

And Zack?

Zack was just a kid with a gun, who thought he would be brave enough to use it.

Chapter Fourteen

The horses were positioned between Nina and the northwest approach. Nina was counting on the fact that Allison wouldn't want to injure the horses, and she was right. She needed those horses to follow Blitz. She also needed them to carry Zack out of there. There was no way that she could support his weight all the way to the river. He plainly was in no condition to walk back.

With boulders of varying sizes to her left, center, and front, and the canyon wall to her back, it was as if Nina had positioned herself in a sort of cave. She'd wanted Allison to find her here. She'd chosen her battleground, and in many ways, she'd chosen well.

Allison felt confident she could disarm Nina, tend to Zack, and get him and both horses down to the rafting camp.

If he didn't bleed out and the horses didn't balk.

What she couldn't do a thing about was the crushed SAT phone that lay at Nina's feet. She'd apparently had time to go through the packs on the horses and retrieve what she wanted. The rifle lay close to her, but the knife clutched in her right hand and stained with Zack's blood was obviously her weapon of choice.

What was it with these people and hand-to-hand combat?

Mr. Harris had been strangled.

Teddy had been knifed.

Lyra had her neck broken.

Allison thought that it had to do with making sure someone on your team was indeed all-in. Asking Anthony Cooper or Blitz or Nina to shoot someone was one thing. Though it was a terrible and violent act, it was also cold, distanced, impartial. Cybercrime, by its very definition, was a hands-off type of violence.

Turning off the power to three hundred and fifty million people could be rationalized when you didn't consider the ripple effect of chaos and death. Pointing a weapon and pulling the trigger might seem like a video game when you could forget that what you were shooting was a living, breathing person.

But insisting someone to kill with their hands?

That called for an entirely different level of commitment.

Be careful. Donovan Steele's words whispered through her thoughts as she drew her weapon and stepped into the small clearing.

"Allison." Nina's eyes brightened, as if she was pleased to see a familiar face.

"Nina."

"I wasn't expecting you."

"Who were you expecting?"

"A man, I guess." She laughed though there was no humor in it. "We're conditioned to think both terrorists and government agents are men."

"And yet here we are."

"Yes, and you've arrived just in the nick of time. Old Zack here might not have made it another hour."

It was the same woman that Allison had known for months, and yet she looked so very different. Nina had always struck Allison as the quintessential American girl—blonde hair, Barbie doll figure, laughing blue eyes. The woman pressing a knife to

Zack's neck looked like someone Allison might take a wide berth around on a city street.

Her blonde hair was dirty, as if she hadn't attempted to brush it in several days. Her blue eyes jumped from spot to spot, unable to focus on any one thing. Dark circles beneath her eyes suggested she wasn't sleeping well—or at all. She looked a good ten years older than her age. She looked drugged.

Was she?

Had Gollum sent along a few pills to bolster her courage?

Had Nina been naïve enough to take them?

"How about we let the mares go?"

The horses responded immediately to the sound of Allison's voice. Bella again snorted and pulled on the lead rope, and that was when Allison saw the situation was even worse than she'd first assessed. Bella's lead rope was tied to Zack's right foot. Tied too tightly, with too short a lead. Denali's lead rope was tied to his left foot. She kept her head closer to the ground, shuffling her feet and trying to create space between herself and the smell of Zack's blood.

If the horses spooked, if they attempted to run, they would pull Zack with them. Allison's thoughts flashed back on the only path back to the river. The narrow gaps between the boulders. The horses couldn't pass through at the same time. They'd trample Zack if they even tried.

"I like the horses where they are."

"Cut the horses free. Let Zack go, then you and I can settle this."

Nina didn't seem to hear Allison. "Zack here has been pretty quiet, so I wasn't sure who he was working with."

"Why don't we keep Zack out of this?"

"Yeah. I'm sure you'd like that."

"I would, Nina. Because this is between you and me."

Nina shrugged, causing the blade she was holding to dig a little deeper into Zack's throat, though she didn't pierce the skin. His stomach was a different matter. She had slashed his abdomen from side to side at least once. The bleeding looked to have slowed, but then Allison had no idea how much blood he'd lost up to that point. She remembered the trail she'd followed to find him—drops of his blood in the dirt, a smear of his blood on the rocks.

She willed him to raise his eyes to hers, and he finally did. What she saw there brought a lump to her throat because his gaze was filled with misery and fear and pain. The innocence and arrogance of the young man who had followed her from Phantom Ranch were gone.

"Hey, Zack."

"I screwed up."

"Well, it wasn't a fair fight. Nina's been trained. Right, Nina?"

"Sure, if that's what you want to call two months in the New Mexico mountains."

"Is that where Gollum is hanging out these days?"

"He'd be pleased to hear you call him that."

"Not my goal, but okay. Let Zack, go. He's no threat to you."

"But he's such a nice piece of bait. He brought me you."

"I'm here. Let him go."

"I think he'll want to see this. He'll want to witness the breaking of a new dawn." Her smile widened and nearly reached her eyes. "Listen closely and you can hear it—the sound of a million computers shutting down. The sound of our government gasping as their tools of oppression are ripped from their hands. Listen and you can hear life returning to our Earth."

And that was when Allison detected something in Nina's demeanor that worried her.

Many assailants portrayed bravado, but Nina seemed disconnected from the reality around her. Her smile was almost playful, but the coldness coming from her eye was like an arctic breeze. The vibes pulsing from her were not drug-induced.

Nina was exhibiting symptoms of a psychotic break.

The madness was fighting for control here.

Allison focused on keeping her voice low, soothing,

nonthreatening. "The cyberattack isn't going to happen, Nina. You're doing this for nothing. Gollum knows that by now. He's probably packed up and moved on, leaving you and Blitz to take the blame."

Nina's countenance brightened. "You know about Blitz."

"I do."

"Gollum doesn't trust him—not completely." She lowered her voice conspiratorially. "That's why I'm here."

"Perhaps Blitz is here to watch you. Maybe Gollum is hoping you'll take each other out."

"Nope. You have it all wrong." She probably would have clapped her hands in delight if she hadn't been so determined to hold on to the blade. "That wasn't the plan at all."

"So what was it?"

Nina shrugged. "Why should I tell you?"

"If you're going to kill me, it won't matter. Satisfy my curiosity first. What did Gollum tell you was going to happen?"

"Blitz is meeting the buyer, on the river, tonight. He's going to pass off the zip drive with the kill codes, and in exchange the buyer will transfer funds into Gollum's account."

Allison knew Nina was telling the truth. She tilted her head to the side as if she enjoyed delivering the devastating news. She arched her eyebrows as if she were ever so slightly amused.

A glance at Zack told Allison she needed to hurry this along. "What if the buyer uses the kill codes, Nina? What if Cyber Drop is stopped?"

"It won't be. They want credit for the attack. They don't want to stop it."

"Are you sure?"

"I am. Gollum, myself, the buyer, and even Blitz. We're on the same side of this. We're on the right side of this."

"Why did Blitz kill Lyra?"

"He didn't kill Lyra." She shook her head vehemently. "Lyra ran. Gollum will catch her. He has more people than you think he does. They'll catch her before she reaches the rim. She shouldn't have run."

"She didn't run, Nina. I watched Blitz snap her neck. Then he walked back into the lodge as if nothing had happened."

"That's not true."

"It is true. I pulled her body into the brush. I covered her face so the animals wouldn't get to her before her body could be retrieved."

"We don't kill our own."

"Are you sure? From where I'm standing it looks like you do. Why don't you admit that this mission is a failure?"

"It is not a failure, and it's already happening." Her demeanor changed like a tornado reversing course. She spat the words, her expression becoming a mask of fury. "And it's your fault that it was even necessary. You government people—you are with the government, right?"

"Good guess."

"Electronic surveillance was the game changer. That's where you went too far."

"Then work to change the laws."

"You're in our personal lives and our homes, and you have to be stopped. You will be stopped."

"Who are you going to stop, Nina? Me? I'm not spying on anyone. I'm just doing my job."

"Don't play stupid. All the tech giants, all the social media platforms, even the telecom companies are party to it. Our phones are searched regularly. There is no privacy anymore." The smile returned. "But there will be. This time tomorrow, privacy will have returned to the American citizen."

While she'd been regurgitating the ideology of the Anarchists for Tomorrow, she'd tightened her grip on Zack. A speck of blood appeared where her blade met his neck. And finally, the sun dipped below the canyon wall, leaving the clearing suspended in a kind of twilight.

It was what Allison had been stalling for.

She raised both hands, loosening her grip on her pistol, palming it really, and then squatted and placed it on the ground. "Let's see how well Gollum trained you. Put down the knife."

"And what? Settle this with hand-to-hand combat?" Nina's lips pulled back over her teeth in a ghoulish grin. "You have no idea how much I'd enjoy that. You always thought you were superior to anyone else in the room."

"If by superior you mean better trained, I am."

"Did your training tell you to involve a kid? Did your training teach you to leave all of your supplies unprotected? You're at my mercy now. Your radio is busted, your buddy here is bleeding out, and those horses. . . one good thrust of my knife and you won't be riding them out of here."

"You might kill one of them," Allison admitted. "But I'll have my hands around your throat before you touch the second."

And there was the response Allison had been aiming for.

The hunger.

The uncontrollable need to prove that she was better.

Nina was a good ten years younger, more muscular, and probably quite agile. In height and weight they were a near-perfect match. But Allison was counting on the fact that she truly was better trained. Also, though Nina couldn't imagine it, she was more motivated. She would stop this attack, and doing so apparently would begin with killing the woman standing in front of her.

Allison made a come-and-get-me gesture with her hands, and Nina shoved Zack away from her. Allison heard a *whoop* of air come out of him as he hit the ground. Heard the horses shuffling, trying not to step on him.

Allison kicked away her gun with one foot.

The last thing she needed was Nina lurching for it.

When she kicked it away, Nina laughed and dropped the knife, also kicking it aside. With the lethal weapons out of reach, Allison's confidence soared. Taking down Nina would not be a problem.

The trick would be not spooking the horses.

She let Nina attack first. She was fast and furious, but it was rather like side-stepping a bully on a playground. Nina was all rage and very little finesse, and she landed against one of the adjacent boulders with a thud. Allison was able to turn and strategically reposition before Nina picked herself back up, indignation and hatred now distorting her face.

"Come on, Nina. You don't have to do this."

"I'm going to enjoy killing you." She raised her hands like a featherweight boxer, excited to be in the ring.

"Walk away."

"I'm not a traitor to my cause or to my country. I'm nothing like you." She bounced from one foot to the other, from side to side, preparing to attack.

"We'll catch you eventually, but today you can walk away, run to Gollum, maybe spend some more time in New Mexico at the training camp."

Nina charged again, and again she missed though she managed to knock Allison to the ground. The sound that came from Nina was guttural, almost animal-like.

They'd both landed perilously close to Zack and the horses. Allison had little room to maneuver, but she scrambled to the side though it boxed her in between Nina and a boulder.

Nina pulled back her arm, clenched her fist, and delivered an uppercut with all of her weight behind it. Allison managed to sidestep, avoiding a direct hit from the right punch and taking a glancing blow to her left jaw and cheekbone instead.

She shook her head, literally seeing bright white flashes of light. The pain was immediate, her adrenaline surged, and she sprang to a standing position.

Nina jumped back, dancing on the balls of her feet. "I was aiming to crush your nose."

"You missed."

Allison checked the left molar with her tongue.

Felt it wiggle.

Tasted blood.

Bella snorted again. Allison realized she was once more crowding the mares. Nina was purposely moving her closer to them. She waited until Nina charged again, feinted right, and brought up both arms, fingers interlaced together. One second before Nina would have crashed into her, Allison brought her arms down with all of her strength on Nina's left shoulder.

She heard the snap.

She felt the clavicle break.

Nina howled, danced back, and threw a kick as if she were a character from a martial arts flick.

The heel of her shoe caught Allison in the forehead.

Blood trickled into her eyes.

She swiped it away as Zack called out, "She has another knife."

Nina had, indeed, pulled another knife from her pants pocket —this time a switchblade stiletto with a black blade that looked to be approximately nine and a half inches—perfect for delivering a deadly thrust. It was smaller than the one she'd used on Zack but just as deadly.

Allison launched herself at Nina, knocking her to the ground. Nina brought up the knife, attempting to slash her with it. Allison's hands closed around Nina's throat.

"Drop it, Nina. Drop the knife."

Nina kicked and continued to slash at the air. Her eyes rolled up in their sockets even as her face turned red, even as her oxygen-deprived brain told her to acquiesce.

Instead, she continued fighting.

"Just drop it." Allison squeezed harder, heard the last of Nina's air swish out, and still the woman struggled.

With her last breath she fought.

Until suddenly, her body went slack.

Chapter Fifteen

Allison struggled to her feet and stared down at Nina.
"Is she dead?"
Allison nodded.
"Good."

She glanced up and saw Zack lying there on the ground, blood covering the front of his shirt, both horses shying away, but not too far. . .not too far.

She snatched the knife that had fallen from Nina's hand, strode across the clearing, and knelt beside Zack. First she cut the lead rope of Denali, then Bella's. She didn't dare take the time to mess with the knots Nina had so carefully tied. Once the horses were freed, she gathered their reins and walked them to the other side of the clearing. She spoke softly, touching their noses, whispering words of assurance, soothing them.

First Bella calmed, then Denali quickly followed suit.

They nudged her hands and nickered softly.

Praising them, she ran a hand down Bella's neck, made the way to her saddle bag, and pushed Nina's knife into an outside pocket. Then she pulled out her first aid kit, a large bottle of water, and a flashlight. The lens on the flashlight had a red tint, which she hoped would keep the light from appearing like a beacon in the darkness. The last thing she needed was more of Blitz's team finding them, and at this point she had no trouble believing there could be more.

She circled the clearing from left to right and used the flashlight to scout the perimeter. Finding her pistol, she retrieved and holstered it. Then she located Nina's original knife and Cooper's rifle and put both into her saddle bag. Confident that she'd done all she could to make the clearing safe, she hurried back to Zack, knelt beside him, and positioned the flashlight where she could see assess his injuries.

The wounds across his stomach were impossible to evaluate with shreds of t-shirt plastered to it. She cut the rope from his hands and massaged his wrists, encouraging the blood to flow more freely to his fingers.

His pulse was thready, his face drawn and haggard.

"I'm going to need your help."

"Okay." He nodded, but he didn't look at her.

She placed the flashlight into his right hand and closed his fingers around it. "Hold this steady for me. Focus the beam on your wound."

"I'm sorry." He looked directly at her then, and Allison saw a world of misery and regret, tinged with a healthy dose of embarrassment.

"Zack, you have nothing to be sorry about."

"This is my fault."

"It's not." Allison realized in that moment that she had been tainted by ten years in this job.

She had lost her compassion, as Tate had suggested.

In certain situations.

At certain times.

In order to save a life.

The body of the woman ten feet away proved that. "Nina had given her heart and mind over to this terror attack. It was the purpose for her existence. In her mind, stopping you and me was worth sacrificing her life."

"Which she did."

"Yes. She was a true believer—a zealot, a fanatic. You had no training to deal with that."

"You tried to train me. You told me. . ." He coughed, then grimaced. The effort caused a trickle of blood to seep from his wound. "You told me to pull my weapon and empty it, but I hesitated."

"You hesitated because you were confronted by someone you thought you knew. You didn't kill Nina the first moment you saw her because you wanted to believe it wasn't true, that she couldn't have become. . ."

"A monster?"

"A very confused and dangerous person." She wanted to say so much more to this young man whose life had been turned upside down and inside out—literally—in the last twelve hours. There wasn't time for that though. The mission clock was ticking in the back of her mind, the night growing darker, the moment of no return inching closer. Zack could and would deal with the trauma later, but only if he survived the night. "Let's lie you down. I need to take a look at your stomach."

She found a pair of latex gloves in the medical kit and snapped them on, then retrieved the scissors and cut away what was left of his shirt, pulling the fabric gently where the wounds had begun to clot.

Zack gasped, but Allison didn't slow or hesitate.

"I need to clean these, and it's going to hurt."

"Okay."

She didn't have saline, so she poured some of the fresh water over the wounds.

He jerked, but he didn't cry out.

She blotted his abdomen dry with a clean gauze pad.

"This doesn't look too bad." It looked bad enough, but there was no need to share that information with Zack. "The cuts aren't deep, but I need to close them."

She found the roll of medical tape, tore off several pieces, and carefully affixed them to the top of the first aid kit where they wouldn't touch the dirt. It was imperative she keep everything as clean as possible. He was as likely to die of infection as blood loss.

"Are you ready?"

"I guess."

She worked as quickly as possible, applying a strip of tape to one edge of the wound, closing the skin gap with the fingers of her opposite hand, then pressing down on the other edge of the tape—effectively sealing it shut. She completed the process for all three of the slash wounds.

In the dim glow of the flashlight, she could just make out Zack's face—terribly pale. His breathing was labored. He had clamped his jaws together and squeezed his eyes shut. Tears slipped down his cheeks, but he didn't make a sound.

"You're a tough guy, Zack. I have to say, I'm impressed."

"I was hoping. . ." He swallowed once, then again. "Hoping to impress you today."

"Mission accomplished." She covered the tape with several gauze pads. "I need to sit you up so I can wrap this."

He grunted, but pushed with his feet until he'd achieved a sitting position. It took two of the rolls of gauze to completely wrap the affected area, and by the time she was done he looked like something from a horror flick. Blood smudged his face, hands, and what was left of his shirt. His skin had a deathly pallor, and his eyes were a bit out of focus. But the wounds weren't bleeding through.

She checked his vitals.

Pulse—rapid.

Skin—cold and clammy though he was sweating profusely.

Pupils—dilated.

"We need to raise your body temperature, Zack. Do you hear me?" He nodded as if he understood, but Allison thought that maybe she was losing him. She stripped off the gloves and put a hand on each side of his face. When he still didn't respond, she locked his chin in her grip. "Look at me. Open your eyes. That's good. I need you to stay with me, Zack. Do you understand?"

His eyes met gaze, and where she had expected to see confusion and lethargy, she instead saw understanding.

He nodded once.

Allison stood, strode over to his horse, and checked his saddle bag. One extra shirt—of course it was an Ariat. Was it too much to hope he'd packed a plain old flannel shirt in there? She briefly wondered where his Stetson was, then dismissed the thought. Grabbing the Ariat shirt, she hurried back to his side.

"Let's put this on you. I know it hurts to move, but it'll help warm you up." She worked his arms through the sleeves and managed to fasten a few of the snaps at the top.

"Emergency. . ." His teeth chattered, so that his words were indiscernible, but he tried again. "Blan. . . blank. . . blanket."

Allison glanced around.

If there were any other assailants hiding among the rocks, an emergency blanket would be like a flashing signal. She hadn't seen any beams from a flashlight, but she'd been focused on Zack. Also, she had underestimated Gollum once—to Zack's detriment as well as her own.

She wouldn't do that again.

On the other hand, if there had been any additional members of Gollum's team hanging back they probably would have come to Nina's rescue while Allison was strangling her. They certainly would have attacked while Allison was occupied with bandaging Zack.

She retrieved the emergency blanket, reached around him, and snugged it under the shirt. The edges still showed, but at least he wasn't wearing it over his shoulders like a cape, daring someone to attack.

First-aid protocol was to lie someone down and keep them still when they were in shock.

But first aid protocol didn't take into account being shot, stabbed, or otherwise attacked by one of Gollum's goons.

"Better?"

Zack nodded, maybe because he felt better. Maybe because he understood it was what she needed to hear.

"You left quite a trail of bloody prints. Did you do that on purpose?"

"Yeah."

"Smart thinking. That's the only way I was able to find you."

She pushed the button on her watch. It read twenty-eight minutes past seven. Sixteen hours and 32 minutes until Critical Systems Failure. Armageddon was inching closer. On the plus side, she hadn't heard Tate give the signal. He definitely had not shot his Sig into the rapidly cooling night.

"I have to take you back to Tate."

"But—"

"Huh-uh. Just listen." She waited until she was sure she had his complete attention, until his gaze locked on her. "You did well, Zack. You didn't let her hurt the horses."

"She tried. That was how. . . I stepped in front. . ." His words trailed off.

"You protected Bella and Denali. I'm the one who messed up. I shouldn't have left them."

He glanced up at her admission, and Allison felt a surge of compassion for this kid—to her he was that, not yet a man, not a child. He was stubborn and arrogant and strong-willed. But he also held true when it mattered most.

She pressed her forehead to his, her hand on the back of his head. This was what it would feel like to have a little brother. In that moment she vowed that she would get him back to the rafting group, leave Zack where Tate could watch over him until they could escape this canyon and Gollum's sinister plans.

She pulled away and began repacking the first aid kit. "Tate will take care of you. I have to go after Blitz."

"Isn't Blitz. . ."

"He was, yes. He was with the group. But I suspect that to change very soon."

She pulled a tracker from her pack and walked over to Nina's body, splaying the beam of her flashlight across her lifeless form. Dark bruises circled her neck—bruises from Allison's hands. Pushing that thought away, she activated the center button of the tracker and placed it in Nina's jeans pocket. She didn't bother checking for the tattoo. She knew it was there, and at this point every second counted against them. Going to her backpack once more, she found an extra shirt and placed it over the woman's face.

While Nina had undoubtedly taken a wrong turn along her life path, she was still someone's daughter, a coworker of the people back at the ranch, and an employee of the National Park Service. Allison would give her the dignity that such a person deserved, regardless of the fact that she'd ended up on the wrong side of things.

As she stood up, her flashlight caught something tan that had been thrown up against the canyon wall. She reclaimed the Stetson. When she pushed it onto Zack's head, he rewarded her with a five-star smile.

It took her another fifteen minutes to prepare the horses and pack up the supplies she'd used. She donned a second pair of latex gloves, stuffed the blood-stained strips of Zack's shirt, her first pair of latex gloves, the bloody gauze, and all of the packaging she'd torn open into a biohazard bag. She pulled off the gloves she was wearing, crammed them in on top of everything else, and put the entire bag deep into her backpack where hopefully Bella wouldn't smell it, or at least wouldn't be spooked by it.

Next she attempted to boost Zack up into the saddle. She staggered under his weight, pushing with all her might. At the last moment—when she was sure he'd either fall on top of her or tip off the other side—he drew on some deep reserve and pulled, letting out a groan as he did so.

"Hopefully that's the worst of it. Are you okay?"

"Peachy."

"Are your wounds bleeding again?"

He reached under the shirt and the emergency blanket, felt the bandages, and pulled out fingertips tinged with blood.

"How bad?"

"It's not. . . not as bad as before."

"Okay. I think we can get back in twenty minutes—fifteen if we push."

"Thank you for saving me." He flashed her a smile that was small and shaky, but it held a glimpse of the young man she'd confronted earlier that day. "Now let's push."

She practically vaulted up into her saddle.

Bella and Denali seemed as eager to put the small clearing behind them as she and Zack were. They moved between boulders and the night sky opened up above and in front of them—four hundred billion stars in the Milky Way alone.

Allison looked up.

One of her father's favorite things about camping had been the night sky. "Philosophy, religion, science, and art have all been inspired by the stars, Alli. Never stop looking up."

So she did, and for a moment she was comforted that the night sky had not changed, the constellations were still in place, and some things were impervious to the plotting of humans. Some things were still as they should be and as they had been. She drew her first deep breath since discovering the horses were missing.

They passed through the narrow opening in the rocks that were stained with Zack's blood. Allison's feet brushed against the sides of the rock.

They made it through—barely, barely.

The horses picked their way down the game trail as if they understood their destination, and maybe they did. They were undoubtedly tired, hungry, and in need of water. Allison thought they were headed straight toward the river—some deep instinct guiding their steps.

Soon enough she saw a sliver of moonlight reflecting off water. They'd been riding side by side. When she thought they were almost in sight of the group of rafters, she held out a hand to Zack. It seemed to startle him, but then he understood, nodded, and slowed.

What was the best way to play this?

If she went charging in, Blitz would run for the hills, and his contact would probably be spooked into fleeing as well.

She could tell Zack to stop, to wait, but he looked as if he was barely managing to stay in the saddle. And she'd still have to extricate Tate from the group. Various scenarios popped into her mind —she considered, discarded, then went back over them again.

There was no good answer here.

She needed to stay focused on the primary objective.

Priority one is intercepting the person who has purchased those kill codes and retrieving the device.

Allison could practically hear the countdown clock in her head. She could see—she could literally envision—the scores of dead when major metropolitan areas descended into chaos. If that happened, she would be partially to blame. She had underestimated Nina's commitment to the cause. She had put Zack's life at risk by not sending him back to the ranch when she'd first encountered him. She had messed up.

But she would not jeopardize this mission because of further missteps on her part.

She also would not abandon the young man clinging to his saddle a few paces behind her.

Then the sound of a gunshot split the night.

The horses startled, but they didn't bolt.

"Hand me Denali's reins."

Zack didn't even argue. Instead, he tossed the reins to her and grabbed the saddle horn. Allison clutched Denali's reins in her left hand and held Bella's reins lightly in her right. Then she pressed her heels against Bella's side, told Zack to hold on, and they broke into a fast trot.

She heard the group of rafters before she saw them.

From the looks of things, they'd been sitting around a campfire, but a quick survey told her Blitz wasn't among them. So Blitz had left, Tate had stepped away from the group and fired his Sig, and now everyone was shouting at once.

"What the hell did you do that for?" The taller of the two guides was standing less than a foot from Tate, pointing his finger and demanding answers.

Several others in the group were also on their feet.

The family of three had pushed their daughter behind them.

The younger couple had stepped back, holding hands, apparently prepared to run if Tate proved to be a madman.

They were so enthralled with their own drama, that they didn't at first notice the sound of hoofbeats. But soon enough one, then another, and finally all of them looked up, mouths open, momentarily stunned into silence by the image of two horses and riders galloping out of the night.

Tate was the first to react.

He said something to the river guide, turned, and rushed to Allison's side, arriving at the same moment that Zack began to slide out of his saddle. "I need some help over here," he called, and both river guides hurried toward them.

"Get him near the fire. He's in shock. We need to stabilize his body temperature." Allison was aware of the murmurings from the rafters, but she ignored those for the moment. She dismounted and stepped back as Tate pulled Zack from the horse, staggering under his weight. She jumped forward but wasn't needed. Both river guides were there to keep him from falling, and together they and Tate carried Zack toward the group.

"We need blankets."

The young couple was the first to react. "We have two." They disappeared into a tent and returned with two sleeping bags.

"Unzip them as far as you can. Let's put one under him and one on top."

As they did so, Tate stepped closer to Allison and lowered his voice. "Was he shot?"

"Knife wounds—three slashes to the abdomen. I cleaned and bandaged the wounds, but riding on the horse didn't help. I think they've busted open again."

The mom in the family group must have overheard. She stepped forward. "I'm a nurse practitioner. How can I help?"

She had long auburn hair that was probably curly when let loose. She wore it pulled back with a band and a blue bandana tied over the top. The woman was approximately Allison's age, but had a softer build—not fat, but not ultra-thin. A family woman, a mom, and apparently a health professional.

"What's your name?"

"Eleanor. Eleanor Bonner."

"All right. Eleanor, I need you to keep him stable until medical help can get here, which will probably be morning. Zack has been slashed with a knife three times across the abdomen. They looked to be relatively shallow cuts but did bleed heavily. I cleansed the wounds as best I could with water, then taped them closed, applied gauze pads, and wrapped the entire thing. Some of that tape came loose in his ride here."

"Got it." She called out to her husband to fetch her medical kit, then walked to where Zack was lying and knelt beside him.

Allison looked behind her. Bella and Denali were standing where they'd left them—patiently waiting. "Can you get someone to look after these horses? I might still need them."

Tate turned and called out to the young couple. "Bryce, Mia, can you take care of these horses? They need water and feed—"

"There's feed in the saddle bags," Allison confirmed.

"Bring them back as quickly as you can."

The couple hurried toward the horses, grabbed the lead ropes, and led them toward the river.

The rest of the group's attention was split between the medical drama in front of them, Tate's unexplainable behavior, and Allison. The river guides seemed the most agitated, probably because the safety of this group was their responsibility.

Tate touched her arm. "You're hurt too. You should let Eleanor—"

"I'm okay, Tate."

"But—"

"I'm okay. I appreciate your concern, but I don't need medical attention at this moment. What I need is to go after Blitz."

He might have argued, but the two guides were walking in their direction. The taller of the two was the first to confront them. "I don't know what's happening here, Tate, but you need to start talking."

He had his hand in the jacket of his pocket, and Allison had little doubt that he was gripping a gun, trying to decide whether to pull it.

Allison stepped forward and thrust out her hand. "I'm Allison. Allison Quinn. And you are?"

He shook her hand, but rather tentatively. "Pete Johnson, and this is my rafting group. Whatever's going on, I have a right and a responsibility to know." Pete was older, maybe closing in on fifty. He'd no doubt seen a lot of things on the Colorado River, but he'd never seen this.

Allison pulled her credentials from her pocket and held them out for Pete's inspection, then flashed them at the group that had gone suddenly silent. "I'm a senior agent with the Department of Homeland Security, assigned to the cyber task force. Tate fired his weapon a moment ago in order to signal me."

"Signal you about what?" Mason Hobbes, the younger of the two guides, stepped forward. "And I'd like a better look at that I.D. if you want me to believe you."

She almost laughed, but she was too tired. Mason had flirted with her several times in the last six months. He knew her, but he knew her as a park worker.

She tossed the identification to him and said, "I'm going to need that back."

He studied it in the glow of his penlight, then handed it back to her. Turning partly toward the group, he said, "Looks legit."

Then he turned back toward her, his gaze taking in both her and Tate. "What was the signal for?"

Pete stepped closer, though at least he'd taken his hand out of his pocket. "What exactly is going on here?"

"Someone in your group is part of an imminent cyberattack." Allison didn't bother lowering her voice. "I'm here to stop him. I've been following your group since you left Phantom Ranch."

"On horses?" Pete shook his head. "I didn't know it was possible to travel this far downriver on horseback."

"It was my only choice."

"And you're saying that you've been following someone in this group?"

Everyone began looking around, mentally checking off the people they'd been with all day. Allison heard the words *Brent* and *Nina*, but of course Nina wasn't who anyone was concerned about. She was a park employee. She might be an oddity on the river since most river guides were men, but she had already earned their trust with her park uniform.

Mason arrived there first. "Are you talking about Brent? Brent Watkins?"

"That pale guy? I can't imagine. . ." Pete ran his hands across the back of his neck, looking lost, looking like he'd found himself in the middle of an unfathomable situation that he was being asked to believe was true.

"Yes, it is the man that you knew as Brent Watkins." Allison held up her hands, palms out. "I'm not telling you anything else about that. Tate was watching him as I searched for Zack."

Mason was shaking his head. "How did Zack even end up in the middle of this?"

"Long story, and I don't have time."

"So we're just supposed to believe you?"

"Yes. You are."

But there was something she was forgetting.

"This is just. . . unprecedented." Pete once again asserted his leadership role. "I'm going to need to call back to base—"

"Do you have a SAT phone?"

"Yeah. Of course." Pete glanced over at Mason, who nodded in agreement. That they had phones? Or that they were admitting they had phones? She sensed that they still didn't trust her, but she didn't have time to convince them. Every moment that she delayed, Blitz moved farther away. Every second she spent here with these people, she risked losing the codes.

"Get the phones," Pete said, and Mason jogged off toward their supplies.

Allison tugged on Tate's arm and motioned away from the group, but the young couple—Mia and Bryce—had returned with the horses. They made their way to the front of the group and were trying to get Tate's attention.

"It's okay," Allison said. "See what they need."

As she waited, she tried to mentally flip back through the key components of this mission, but her mind was twirling like the colorful and hated circle of death on a computer screen.

Five minutes later Mason came back empty-handed.

Blitz had stolen the phones.

Blitz, or Gollum, had thought of that too.

The gravity of their situation hit Allison with the force of a hurricane's winds. They were completely isolated with no way to make contact. Possibly, they were surrounded by an unknown number of Gollum's people. Zack was in critical condition. Women and children were at risk. Civilians were firmly standing in harm's way, and the mission clock was ticking.

The situation had finally reached the point that if she had a phone, she would have called Steele. Since she didn't, she was going to have to handle things herself. It was her responsibility to stop Blitz, or these people might die and the entire North American grid could collapse.

Chapter Sixteen

Pete and Mason seemed to understand the seriousness of their situation.

"What now?" Pete demanded.

"How could you let this happen?" Mason had turned the corner from feeling surprised to placing blame. "How could you have any kind of operation that would put innocent people at risk?"

"I didn't put these people at risk, Mason. In fact, I'm trying to ensure that everyone gets back home unharmed. I'm trying to keep Zack from bleeding out after Nina—who none of us suspected—attempted to gut him." She wasn't sure that anything she said was getting through, but Nina's name brought him up short.

He opened his mouth to argue with her, then shut it.

"What I need you to do, Mason—what I need all of you to do —is stay here, stay calm, and wait for morning."

Pete made a sound of disbelief, so she directed her next words to him.

"Do not proceed down the river. Do not attempt to go back to the ranch, which I'm pretty sure would be impossible anyway. It's a long walk and Zack's horse can only take one person back, maybe two. Plus, moving Zack might kill him. Just wait here, and we'll have agents come and give you further instructions."

There were groans and murmurings all around.

And still she couldn't remember the thing, the important thing that was slipping through her sleep-deprived brain like water through a sieve.

"Are we safe?" This from the nurse practitioner's husband, who was now holding his daughter's hand.

That image—a father and a daughter—pricked at Allison's heart.

It was too close, too dear, too familiar.

"Yes, you are. These terrorists have no interest in you. Their attack is aimed directly at the heart of the U.S. government and big corporations. Stay together. Stay here. Wait for help."

Pete said something to Mason, then he stepped closer and lowered his voice. "We're not the kind of people who sit around and wait for help. We especially don't wait for the government to help us. If we're in danger, you need to say so, because we can and will protect ourselves. We *will* take care of these people."

Allison resisted the urge to headbutt the guy.

She still hadn't recovered from her fight with Nina. Her tooth hurt, her cheek was swelling, and when she reached up and touched her forehead her fingers came away with sticky half-dried blood. She didn't need to add to her current pain level by getting in a scuffle with a river guide.

She tried for an understanding expression. "I see what you're saying, but the danger here has passed."

"How can you be sure of that?"

"Because I've been tracking this guy for the last six months. I know everything that can be known about him." When their expressions remained skeptical, she tried again. "The guy you knew as Brent Watkins had a job to do. He had something to deliver—and no, I won't tell you what that something was. My point is that he did not stick around. He fled, and I intend to go after him. If you're worried about the safety of this group, I suggest you set up rotating shifts through the night."

Mason pulled Pete away. As they worked out what they were going to do, Allison turned to Tate, finally able to ask him what she needed to know.

"Tell me what happened. How did Blitz manage to sneak off?"

Tate crossed his arms over his chest. "We were all sitting around the fire. I'd kept my eye on him since you and I last talked. He might have noticed. A couple of times, he looked up as I was watching him."

"He'd be on high alert, especially since Nina was gone."

"I still can't believe she attacked him with a knife." He glanced over at Zack, then back at Allison. "Just like Teddy."

"Yeah."

Allison thought of Nina, her face covered with a shirt, her body lifeless. It was hard to reconcile the person who had fought her so viciously with the person she'd worked beside. She could relate to Tate's confusion, but she didn't have time to indulge it. "Back to Blitz—"

"Right. I looked up and Blitz was gone, just like that. I asked the person who was sitting next to him, Pete Johnson, where he'd gone. Pete said he saw him walk out going east—thought he needed to relieve himself. So I guess he went upriver, or maybe that was a ruse."

"How long ago?"

Tate glanced at his watch. "I'd say thirty, maybe thirty-five minutes."

She thought of taking Bella, but the horse was plainly exhausted. And what if the mare ended up being more of a liability than an asset? Allison could scramble over rocks or wade the river. If Blitz had gone east, he'd followed the same trail she'd taken to get here.

Allison knew that trail.

She could catch up with him.

But if he'd gone west, trying it on foot would be dangerous and slow. The horse could pick her way in the dark. Allison might have to backtrack in places because the trail petered out, as it had done when she was first riding with Zack.

"Denali can stay with you. I'll take Bella. Also, get Denali's saddle off. She's been through a lot."

"Got it."

"Watch over Zack."

"Of course I will, but..."

Tate didn't have a chance to voice his reservations. A scuffle broke out on the other side of the campfire, and then Allison looked up to see Jason holding a gun to Eleanor's head.

The thing she hadn't been able to remember.

Jason Faulkner.

Her mind flashed on the argument that Zack had overheard.

They couldn't afford to crumble now.

He said something about not wanting to go.

She said it would solve their money problems.

Jason was Nina's partner, but Jason had been left behind. Had Nina even told him that she was leaving? Had Nina told him that she'd trained in one of Gollum's camps? From the way that Jason was holding the gun, from the way his hand was shaking, she would bet that Jason hadn't been trained.

Allison approached Jason in calm, measured steps until she stood five feet in front of him. Eleanor's daughter was screaming, and the father was trying to calm her. The rest of the group was completely silent—so much so that she could hear the crackling of the fire, a hawk crying out, even the whisper of the river.

Eleanor looked alarmed but steady.

Good for her.

Maybe she worked at an inner-city hospital. Maybe she'd dealt with unstable people before. One look at Jason told Allison that's what he was—unstable, scared, and out of options. He had none of Nina's arrogance, none of her madness.

"Put the gun down, Jason."

"Why? So you can shoot me?"

Allison's raised her hands, shoulder height, palms toward him. "No gun. See?"

He glanced past her, and Allison hoped that Pete and Mason and even Tate had the presence of mind not to push this man. Jason was not a man who wanted to die.

He was a man who needed a way out.

"I don't want to go to prison." His voice trembled and his hand shook.

"Put the gun down, Jason."

"I didn't even know what she had planned until last night, and then. . . then it seemed. . . it seemed too late."

"Let Eleanor go, and you and I will talk about this."

"But you work for the government. You said so yourself." He began thrusting the gun toward her for emphasis.

Allison worried it would go off by accident. He wasn't aware of the position of his trigger finger. He wasn't aware of much except for his own desperate situation.

Tate had somehow crept around and now stood behind Jason. Allison could see him at the edge of her vision, but she couldn't risk looking at him. "Eleanor, are you okay?"

Eleanor nodded, a small gesture meant to assure but not threaten.

"Jason, I'm going to ask you, one more time, to put the gun down. I'm going to give you to the count of three. One, two. . ."

She never made it to three. At the moment where she would have said *three*, Eleanor gave a little jump and stomped as hard as she could, throwing all of her weight on Jason's foot. At the same time, she dropped to the ground and rolled away.

Jason howled, his arm jerked up, and Tate was there, snatching the gun from his hand.

Allison had pulled her weapon, racked the slide, and assumed a shooter stance. Her pistol was less than three feet from Jason's head.

"I will not miss."

Hands shaking, he interlocked his fingers behind his head. "Don't shoot me. Just don't shoot me."

Allison tossed a set of zip ties to Tate, then holstered her weapon. Tate quickly subdued the young man, arms tied behind his back, and frog-marched him to a camp chair near the fire. Eleanor flew into her husband's arms.

"You really are. . ." Mason had walked up beside her. Now he blew out a breath, shaking his head. "You're everything you said you are."

"Yeah." Allison patted him on the back, then jogged over to check on Eleanor.

"I'm okay."

"You're sure?"

"Yes."

"That was a sweet move you pulled on him."

"Learned it in a personal defense class. Guess I'll have to thank my instructor when we get back home."

Her husband stuck out his hand. He was thin and tall, wore dark wire-rim glasses, and had the air of a professor. His black hair had a simple cut and his clothing wasn't exactly designer labels. The term *salt of the earth* came to Allison's mind.

"I'm Steve. . . Steve Bonner. Thank you. Thank you, for saving my wife."

"Your wife saved herself, Steve."

The little girl who had her arms wrapped tightly around her mom's waist, glanced up at Allison. Eyes wide, tears drying on her cheeks, the sight of her felt like a knife plunge to Allison's heart.

"This is Piper. She's nine." Steve placed a hand on the girl's head. "She wants to be a botanist. That's why we're here. Why we decided to raft the Colorado. She's been studying about the canyon's plant life for a year, maybe more."

Allison squatted in front of the little girl. Perhaps she shouldn't take the time to reassure her, but something in the girl reminded Allison of herself. Her age? Her love for nature? Or maybe just the look of confusion in her eyes. "Piper, maybe when you get home you can do some drawings about the plants you've seen."

Piper nodded and pushed her red, curly hair out of her eyes. "But not the bad guys. I don't want to draw them."

"I don't blame you one bit. Don't worry about the bad guys. Okay?"

Piper glanced toward the fire, where Mason, Pete, and Tate all stood in a semi-circle around Jason. Then she looked back at Allison. "Are you, like, a cop?"

"Something like that."

"Good." She turned to her dad and threw her arms around his legs. "I'm tired."

"Okay, pumpkin. Let's get you to bed."

Which left Allison standing beside Eleanor. She needed to be on the trail, on Blitz's trail, on the path to bringing all the events of the past twenty-four hours to an end. But she also needed to ask.

"Zack?"

"I'm as confident as I can be that he's going to be okay. He lost a fair amount of blood, but I think he's stabilized."

"Thank you."

Eleanor nodded toward Allison's forehead. "Want me to take a look at that?"

"No. I'll be fine." She'd make time for medical aid later, after she'd caught Blitz and put him in either a body bag or a government vehicle. At this point, it made no difference to her. "Thank you, for helping him."

"I'll continue to monitor his vitals." Then she added, with more compassion than Allison felt she deserved, "Be careful."

Allison wanted to check on Zack one last time, but she needed to do so quickly.

She squatted next to him, reached for his hand, and squeezed it. He opened his eyes and looked into hers. In that moment an understanding passed between them. Allison thought it was like that sometimes. You could become incredibly close to another person in a very short amount of time. The intensity of a moment could bind you together.

"You're going to be okay. Help will be here by morning. Eleanor and Tate will look after you until then."

He nodded, then said, "I think I lost my hat."

"Not a chance. I tied it to Denali's saddle."

He closed his eyes, but the smile remained.

She walked back to Bella. The mare tossed her head as if to say, "Rehydrated and ready to go, boss." Pulling herself into the saddle, Allison felt every one of her thirty-five years.

The struggle with Nina had done more than leave her with a wound on her forehead, a swelling jaw, and a loose tooth. Her body hurt from the slams to the ground, or maybe from the coiled tension, and a deep exhaustion was working its way through her bones.

"Allison."

She turned back at the sound of her name, looked at Tate, and waited for him to jog over to where she was.

She hoped it wasn't more bad news. The river rafters had been through a lot. The vacation they'd looked forward to for months, maybe years, had become their worst nightmare. It would be up to Tate to calm everyone down, to explain anything else they needed to know, but not too much. She trusted he could do all of those things. At that moment, she knew that Tate was her partner as much as Ryan had been.

A partner wasn't merely someone assigned to you.

It was someone willing to step in the path of danger for you. It was someone who had your back, or maybe someone who talked you across a suspension bridge in the middle of a storm.

Tate didn't speak until he was standing right beside her, one hand on Bella's neck, the other on Allison's arm. In a low voice, he said, "Blitz isn't the only one who is gone. The young woman in our boat—her name was Sophie—she's gone too. I don't know if she's his partner, or if maybe she saw something she shouldn't have."

"Got it." She put her hand on her pistol, assuring herself that after all she'd been through it was still there.

"If she's on his side, it'll be two against one."

"Which means the odds are in my favor." She flashed him a smile, and then she was gone.

Allison tried to picture the river map as she let Bella pick up the trail that headed back east, back toward the ranch. For Bella, it was a simple matter of returning home. They moved quietly. The horse seemed to sense that they were headed toward rather than away from danger. She stepped carefully and moved at a steady pace with no direction from Allison.

The night enfolded them.

The sliver of moon reflected off the water.

Above that, the canyon wall stretched like a yawning black monolith. On her right and her left it rose so tall that she had to tilt her head back or pin her gaze on the distant horizon to see above it. But there. . . over the darkness. . . the stars remained. She allowed her mind to rest on that thought for a moment, but no longer.

Then she pulled her attention back to the problem at hand.

Blitz would need to pick a spot that was accessible from the north side of the river. How was this hand-off supposed to happen? How did he expect to get away with it? Would the buyers come over in power boats, take possession of the codes, then help Blitz escape? How?

She chewed on the problem but came up with no reasonable answers. Eventually, her mind again wandered. Her muscles relaxed as she became attuned to the sound of the river rushing by, night birds calling to one another, and the occasional sound of a fish slapping the water. Bella would alert her to danger well before her own senses could. She'd read that a horse could smell fifty times better than a human. Not that anyone had ever created a test for such a thing. But it was well established that humans had 350 olfactory receptors while horses had 1,066—a piece of trivia she could probably afford to forget in order to make space for more important facts.

Why was she even thinking about olfactory receptors?

She needed to focus.

Allison patted Bella's neck, who slowed, then stopped. Allison didn't bother dismounting. She turned in the saddle, giving a satisfying pop to her back, and reached into a side pocket of her pack. She retrieved two caffeine tablets, an energy bar and a bottle of water.

She pressed her heels lightly to Bella's side, and the mare resumed her steady walk. Not too fast—they wouldn't want to trip over Blitz in the dark. And not too slow—she had to personally ensure that he didn't escape.

He couldn't escape.

She had to stop this attack.

She had to capture Blitz.

She had to learn about who killed her father.

Allison was fully aware that finding her father's killer wouldn't bring him back. The hurt she had endured for so long wouldn't suddenly ease. The sense of loss for the childhood that she'd never had would remain. She didn't remember her mother, who had died in a car accident when Allison was only two. But she remembered her father.

She remembered that he was a good man.

That he took care of her.

That with him, she felt safe.

She would have justice for her father's killing.

And if she died in the process, so be it. That wasn't depression. It was simply a place of acceptance that she'd reached long ago.

Blitz and maybe the woman named Sophie had a forty-minute start on her, but they were on foot. Certainly they wouldn't have planned over an hour hike. Even that seemed like a stretch to Allison.

So with a forty-minute lead, and with Allison making quicker time on horseback...

She yawned and glanced at her watch. Two minutes after nine. Slightly less than fifteen hours until Gollum unleashed his chaos. What was his game plan if he were to succeed? He wouldn't, but what was he thinking? Would there be any more cyber-attacks after that?

What would still be working to attack?

What would be left?

Where would Gollum send all of his hatred when he no longer had a cyberworld to rail against?

She heard the hoot of an owl and smiled, remembering Tate's evaluation of her bird call. The owl's hoot did sound better than hers. It *was* better than hers. She needed to work on her signals.

But not tonight.

Tonight she needed to stay upright in her saddle until she found Blitz. Then she needed to finish this.

Chapter Seventeen

Allison stopped Bella in the middle of the trail.

Her left cheekbone throbbed, and she was pretty sure she had at least one loose tooth. The bleeding on her forehead had stopped, but when she touched the wound it felt as if a goose egg were lodged in her skull. That might explain the blinding headache. In the grand scheme of things, those injuries were all inconsequential.

Her vision and trigger finger were fine.

That was what mattered.

She had to be close to Blitz's location. The man wasn't exactly a specimen of athletic prowess. He'd hiked down the Kaibab Trail the day before, risen before daylight to kill Lyra, and ridden a raft downriver all day. He must be exhausted and missing his computer. He must be nearly as ready to be done with this as she was.

Allison put a hand to the mare's neck. She didn't say the words, but she thought them. *Easy girl, real quiet now, not a sound.*

And Bella? Bella stilled completely.

They stayed that way thirty seconds, a minute, then two.

Nothing. No human sounds at all. A lizard scampered to her right. The river flowed to her left. Ahead—only silence.

She pressed her heels lightly against Bella's side, and they moved on. But what were they moving toward? How exactly did she expect to find Blitz in the middle of the night? In the darkness of the canyon? There was only a sliver of moonlight to guide her. She looked up at the light of an infinite number of stars, but that light wasn't enough. How could it be?

She wasn't even positive he'd gone this direction.

At this point she was running blind, fueled only by instinct.

She glanced toward the river and tried to see something— anything on the other side. Hoping, praying even, that she would spot some sign of Steele's team, but there was nothing. There wasn't a single light.

No team of agents waiting to forge the river.

No helicopters in the sky.

No one on this path except for her.

She stopped again, listened, then moved on.

Twice she nodded off in the saddle, but not for long. Her head drooped, she let up on the reins, and the sound of Bella grazing on the scant grass found along the trail pulled her back to her present nightmare. They both needed sleep, but that wasn't going to happen anytime soon.

She blinked her eyes several times, sat straighter in the saddle, and squeezed her right earlobe until tears stung her eyes. She thought of her bunkbed at the lodge and her hotel room at Yavapai. She allowed herself to consider how it would feel to put her head on a pillow, to let her body rest on a mattress, to snuggle under the covers and pretend the world wasn't out there.

She even closed her eyes for just a moment and pictured her apartment in Virginia.

A scream splitting the night woke her.

Jerking upright, Allison put her hand on the butt of her weapon.

Bella stopped, tossing her head, but quietly, as if she understood the real danger didn't come from the wildlife. Allison calmed the mare, then rubbed at the muscles around her jaws and along the back of her neck.

"Only a bobcat," she whispered. "Not even that close."

Bella needed water.

Allison stopped when the trail inched close to the river and hopped off the horse. As the mare drank her fill, Allison pulled more emergency rations from her saddlebag—two more caffeine tablets, a swig of water, and another protein bar. The tablets felt as if they stuck in her throat, and the protein bar tasted like sawdust. She chased it down with more water, then forced herself back into the saddle, though the first time she tried her foot missed the stirrup.

Bella turned her big head and nuzzled her once. Allison climbed up, pulled in a deep breath, and assured herself that she could keep going.

Could she keep going?

The only sounds around her were natural ones—the river, a raptor, wind rustling through the trees, the plop of a fish.

Three more times, she stopped in the middle of the trail to listen. Three more times she heard only the sound of nature. How long had it been since she'd left Tate's camp? Had she overshot Blitz and Sophie's location? That wasn't possible. The only other possibility was that he'd gone the opposite direction. If that were the case, she needed to turn around.

Should she turn around?

And then the mare's head jerked up, and she stopped. Allison became aware of the sound at the same time Bella did. It wasn't much to go on, but she was sure it was Blitz. Maybe a shoe against rock. Maybe the brush of fabric against fabric—someone walking. Maybe.

She focused all of her attention on her hearing. She even closed her eyes, and when she did, she heard the other thing—a light clinking.

The sound a carabiner makes against a metal water bottle.

She was suddenly more alert than she'd been in hours. Her senses seemed supercharged. And then another sound, below the sounds of walking. So nearly out of range that she might have imagined it.

Two voices, arguing.

They couldn't be to her left. This woman—Sophie—and Blitz weren't walking on water. They weren't in a boat. She would have heard the sound of a raft, of oars slicing through water.

Could they be to her right? There was little space between the river and the canyon walls here. Blitz did not seem physically fit enough to climb those walls. If he were, she'd hear heavier breathing. Plus they weren't climbing, they were walking. She was sure of that.

So, they were in front of her.

And not far.

Allison slid silently off Bella and walked the horse to what looked like a patch of grass. She allowed herself a moment to press her forehead to the mare's forelock. Bella had risen to the occasion. She had seen Allison through a long and difficult day and an even more demanding night. Bella was a good horse.

I'll be back. Wait for me. Rest.

Her pack would make too much noise—like Blitz's. Instead, she touched the Glock on her hip. It would be enough. It would have to be.

She followed them for another ten minutes.

Now that she knew what she was listening for, now that she was attuned to their presence, they sounded like teenagers walking through a dark tunnel—speaking loudly to assuage their fears. They weren't speaking loudly. And they might not have any fears. But she could hear them now. She knew she was on the right path.

Her legs felt heavy, and she worried she'd stumble.

Then her stomach started growling.

Why was she so hungry?

Exhaustion increases hunger.

She could eat later. She could rest later. She was so close now that she could practically smell them. It wasn't a human smell. It was something much worse than the odor of unwashed bodies. It was greed and callousness and a disregard for all else.

It was the scent of danger.

She didn't realize she was getting too close until she could suddenly make out their words. They'd stopped around the bend in the trail. Boulders rose between where they were and where Allison stood. She froze in place, her heart slamming into her chest.

She'd nearly stepped out in front of them.

She'd nearly blown it.

In that moment, exhaustion fell from her like a cloak she no longer needed. Her confusion was replaced with decisiveness. Her worry morphed into enthusiasm and a driving desire to see this mission through to the end—the only acceptable end. She would stop Sophie and Blitz. She would intercept the codes, and she would find out any minute detail Blitz might know about her father's killer.

She crept up behind one of the boulders—carefully placing one foot in front of the other, moving with her breath, sliding through the night as if she belonged there. She stopped behind a boulder and realized it was blocking their words.

Slowly—slowly and carefully—she moved around it until she was peering between two of the rocks.

She couldn't have said what she'd expected to see.

She knew nothing of the woman, Sophie. She'd seemed young and easily amused. She'd seemed clueless. Clearly, based on what was playing out in front of Allison, that was not the case. At the moment, Sophie was quite obviously the one in charge.

Why did it startle her to hear Blitz whining and trying to persuade this woman? Why should that surprise her? She knew firsthand that men often responded meekly to authoritative women—some did. Blitz apparently did. And she harbored no doubts that a woman could be as immoral and dangerous as a man. Nina's lifeless body in a clearing near the canyon wall attested to that. Zack's wounds bore testimony to the fact that a woman could be every bit as cruel as a man.

She drew back, out of their line of sight and slowly, gently, pulled out her Glock and waited.

"I don't understand why we had to come this far."

"You wanted to do this in front of the rafting people? You were being watched back at that group."

"No, I wasn't."

There was a pause, and then Sophie said, "Gollum had someone keeping tabs on you—from the moment you made it to the ranch."

"No, he didn't."

"Nina."

"Nina wasn't watching me."

"Yes, she was."

Another pause.

"What happened to her?"

Allison could practically hear the woman's shrug. "Doesn't matter. Maybe she ran. Maybe someone took her out."

"Who?"

"I don't know, Blitz. There is no telling how many sides there are to this. There's no telling how many people want you and me dead. Now give me the codes."

"How do I know you won't kill me once I hand them over?"

"I'd like to, if I were being honest, but for some reason you've caught Gollum's eye."

"Meaning what?"

"Meaning he has other plans for you."

"I don't know. This didn't play out quite as I had imagined. I might go back to simple DoS attacks. They pay less, but at least there isn't any hiking involved."

"Do you always whine this much?"

"I have blisters on my feet from that hike down the South Kaibab Trail. Do you want me to show you? I have quarter-sized blisters on the back of both ankles. They hurt like a mother—"

There was a brief flash of light, and Allison peeked around the boulder in time to see the woman staring down at her watch. It was just a tiny spot of light. Allison couldn't make out much about her. She certainly hadn't paid attention to the woman when she was spying on the rafters earlier. Sophie had looked like a twenty-something adrenaline junkie, and maybe she was.

Maybe she was in this for the thrill.

But Allison didn't think so.

Allison thought this woman pressuring Blitz for the codes might be the real deal. Sophie might be in deeper than Nina had been.

How was it that people were so easily able to hide their true identity?

"You said the buyer's boat would be here at thirty minutes past ten. We only have a few minutes. Hand over the kill codes, and I will make the transaction."

"Why you?"

"Because it's my assignment."

"No. It's my assignment. I don't even know that you are who you say are."

"You know that I saved you back there. You heard the gunshot right? That older guy...what was his name?"

"Tate something. He's the big kahuna of this place."

"He was watching you, and when you left he fired his weapon. He signaled to someone that you were gone."

"You don't know that."

"He also probably took care of Nina."

"Took care of her?"

"Killed her." The woman's voice became soft, mocking almost. "You don't know anything about killing, do you? I'll bet the boldest thing you've ever done with those fingers of yours is tap a few keystrokes to bring down a town or an organization or a person. You cyberterrorists are all the same—soft, limited, afraid."

"That shows what you know, because I am capable of killing. In fact, I killed Lyra. You know why? Because she could identify me, and I'm not stupid. I'm not taking the blame for whatever might go wrong."

"This is too big for you." Sophie's voice grew softer. "Give me the codes. I'll take care of the transaction, and I'll make sure you receive the agreed-upon price."

"If I did that, and I'm not saying I am, but if I did. . . How am I supposed to get out of here?"

"Not my problem."

"I'm not walking back to Phantom Ranch alone, not out here in the middle of the night. There are mountain lions out here. You heard that wild animal before—"

"That was a bobcat."

"Maybe. But bobcats can attack too."

"All the more reason for you to rejoin the rafting group."

"Huh-uh. Not going to happen. Plus, that guy Tate is back that direction."

The woman laughed. "About those rafts. . . a military drone that Gollum acquired is going to hit them a few moments after daybreak—it'll be a nice sunrise surprise for everyone."

Allison froze, her breath caught somewhere between her heart and her throat.

"Hit them?"

"Pow. Blow them up. There will be nothing left."

"Why would he do that?"

"Why do you think? He'll wait until he's sure that everyone is in them. It's better if there's no one alive who can identify you or me. You took care of Lyra. Gollum will take care of them. As for the people back at the ranch, they'll think that you and I perished with all of the others on the rafts. We'll be in the clear."

Allison's mind tried to catch up with what she was hearing— what she hadn't imagined even in her worst-case scenarios.

They were going to blow up the boats.

They were willing to kill the men, women, and even the child —Piper, who had red, curly hair like her mother and dreamed of being a botanist.

Her mind was sluggish. She had to work to figure out what was bothering her because her thoughts wanted to scramble ahead at the same time they were lagging behind.

Better if there's not anyone alive who can identify you or me.

The woman who was meeting with Blitz was definitely the twenty-three-year-old who was in the second raft. But what side was she on? She wasn't on the buyer's side, because she hadn't known what time the meet was set for. At least, she'd acted like she didn't know that information until Blitz told her.

But if she was a part of Gollum's team, why was she on the raft with Blitz? Why did Gollum need two people—three if you included Nina—on the raft, headed downriver, assigned the task of handing over the codes? It didn't make sense that she was working for the buyer either. She'd been staying at Phantom Ranch. Blitz could have handed the codes to her there, and he could have hiked out instead of rafting downriver. He could have let her make the transaction—except he hadn't known about her.

Gollum had backups to his backups, and now they were in conflict with one another.

Allison couldn't make sense of it.

Then she realized she didn't have to make sense of it. Steele could figure out the details, but only if he was alive to do so. If any portion of his team. . .

Her team.

She could finally admit that to herself.

It didn't matter if they worked for the FBI or DHS. What mattered was that together they were going to stop this madness. If those agents attempted to rescue the rafters, there was a risk that everyone could be taken out by Gollum's drone.

Steele could be taken out by Gollum's drone.

Maybe it didn't even matter whether Steele's team was attempting to intercept the buyers or rescuing the rafters. The fact was that they were all hunkered down in a fairly small region of this canyon. They'd be sitting ducks for a military drone.

And there it was.

That was the point of the exercise.

The entire thing had been a trap to destroy the team that had become quite adept at tracking Gollum and averting his diabolic plans. In one sweep, he could take out the buyers, the government team, and everyone associated with Operation Cyber Drop.

Were the kill codes even real?

Sophie seemed to think so.

Blitz certainly believed they were.

Allison forced her attention back to the two people on the other side of the boulders.

There was more arguing back and forth and then Blitz began shouting, finally reaching the end of his patience—or possibly understanding the predicament he was in for the first time.

"You can't blow up the rafts. How will I get out of here?"

"Definitely not my problem. You are not going with me, that's for certain."

"I'll tell you one thing—I am not walking back to Phantom Ranch. Even supposing I could make it, which is doubtful, don't you think it would look kind of suspicious if I were the only one to survive a rafting explosion that killed eleven other people?"

And then Allison heard the sound that she'd been expecting—the cocking of a hammer on a revolver.

"Give me the codes, or I'm going to shoot you and search your body and take them."

"I thought Gollum wanted me for another job."

"Gollum doesn't always get what he wants."

Allison didn't know if the woman was stupid enough to fire a weapon. The sound would echo off the canyon walls and be heard for several miles. It was the reason Teddy had been stabbed. It was the reason Blitz had broken Lyra's neck, and Nina had slashed Zack. It was the reason she hadn't shot Nina—that, and the fact that it would have spooked the horses. Firing her weapon would have been akin to signing Zack's death warrant.

There were plenty of silent ways to kill a person.

Why risk drawing attention?

Would Sophie take that sort of risk?

It wouldn't be a risk for Allison though. Her situation had changed in the last ninety minutes. What did it matter if she drew anyone's attention? In fact, she wanted Steele to know where she was, not that he'd be able to exactly pinpoint the spot. Still, it would give him a chance. It would draw his team away from the rafting group.

It would also attract the attention of the buyers and anyone else coming for the woman. She seemed to think she would be able to leave with the buyers.

Allison only knew that firing her weapon would draw everyone out of their hidey-holes.

So be it.

Her decision made, Allison circled around the rendezvous spot and came up behind Blitz and his accomplice.

Chapter Eighteen

J ohn Howard stared at the bank of wall monitors and tried to reconcile what he was seeing with what he had expected to happen.

They were not the same.

They were nowhere near the same.

He'd sacrificed so much for this—years of his life, most of his finances, and all of his friendships. He'd sacrificed his future. Now the dream of an emancipated citizenry was slipping through his fingers.

Had he made a mistake with the people or the location? They'd run the simulations from every angle. The canyon was one of the few places left in the continental U.S. that had very limited surveillance by Big Brother.

Yes, there had been risks.

Yes, he was aware that it might not work. The latest simulation had calculated a 69.4 percent chance of success.

But it had been their best choice.

As for the people, he'd run a risk analysis based on their personality profiles. The results of that analysis had been the reason for the backups of the backups. Every person had a weakness. Every backup negated that weakness with their strength.

Blitz was the cyberstar—strong with analytical coding, weak with anything regarding physical strength.

Anthony Cooper was the answer to that weakness.

The simulation had also computed a 32 percent chance that Blitz would either be unable or unwilling to do what needed to be done.

Nina was the answer to that weakness.

Jason Faulkner and Lyra Alonzo had been no more than chess pieces—useful to a point and then expendable.

Sufia Alshedri had been his ace in the hole. The analysis program had yet to find her weakness. She was the real deal and the solution to every possible complication they might face.

This mission should have been a success.

Now he watched the monitors as his dreams and hopes for Cyber Drop crumbled, or very nearly so.

Brett and Kate had been the first to arrive at his office, followed a moment later by Stella. He'd rather have endured this defeat alone, but that wasn't to be.

Stella sat in the leather armchair and crossed her legs. "Someone catch me up." It wasn't a request.

She had changed into a tight, black dress—reinforcing in John's mind the image of a vulture. Her head was covered with a black wrap that had the faintest bit of silver thread running through it. On anyone else, the outfit might have looked elegant, but on Stella it emphasized the lack of curves or softness of any kind. She steepled her long red nails and waited for someone to answer.

Brett and Kate looked at him.

"Nina's tracker turned red several hours ago," John explained.

"The person you had watching Blitz?"

"Yes."

"She's dead?"

"Yes."

"And Blitz?"

"Still alive." The answer popped from Kate's mouth, and she

pressed her fingertips against her lips—as if she could shove the two words back in.

"Explain it to her," John said. He continued to stand, back ramrod straight, eyes on the monitors.

"Blitz's tracker is still green."

"Did he kill Nina?"

"Not possible. Blitz was at the river when Nina died, or rather when she was murdered. I suspect she was murdered. Like Lyra and Cooper, her heart rate and blood pressure experienced a sudden change. But with Nina, she didn't die immediately. Either she fought back, or whoever did it took a little time with her."

"Explain that to me."

"Biometrics show a spike in her heart rate for a full six and a half minutes, then nothing. A completely different scenario from a fall or anything like that."

"Who murdered her?" Stella's questions came out flat, as if she were requesting more information regarding a restaurant's fresh catch of the day.

Brett placed both hands in his pockets. "We don't know."

"Why?"

"Because we haven't tracked every person in the canyon."

Stella stood, walked to the beverage cart near the door, and poured herself a scotch over ice. After taking a sip, she turned to face the group.

"Anthony Cooper's dead, Lyra's dead, and now Nina's dead. It would seem that our band of merry men—" She tossed a glance at Kate. "Excuse me—men and woman—aren't faring very well."

"There's still Blitz," Kate pointed out, then firmly shut her mouth. It seemed she hoped by pressing her lips together she could convince herself not to speak.

Brett glanced at John, then returned his gaze to the monitors. Clearing his throat, he said, "There has been a lot of activity on the north side of the river. We aren't able to precisely track the individuals, but we are picking up the movement with our drones. What we don't know is whether they're the buyers or the government—or both."

Stella cast a long look at John.

He sensed that Stella was losing faith in him, wondering if she'd chosen the wrong person for the job. As much as he hated to admit it, even to himself, he needed her. Or rather, he needed her money if he was to see his vision come to fruition. He'd made quite a bit of profit on the stocks he'd shorted, but he'd need that money for the second phase of his plan, the phase that Stella didn't know about.

And if the cascade affecting the North American grid didn't continue, if Cyber Drop did not happen, then he'd need to pull back his original investment or risk losing it.

His plans hinged on what was happening in the canyon at this very moment, and it galled him that he wasn't there. He'd never been one to find contentment in sitting back and watching. He'd rather be the one calling the shots—or taking the shots—whichever the situation required.

He would be successful—maybe not tonight, maybe not tomorrow. Soon though. He wouldn't give up until he'd seen this through. He couldn't give up. If he did, what would his life have stood for? How would he avenge the deaths of his wife and daughter?

No.

He refused to let that happen.

Failure was always an option, but it wasn't one he was willing to embrace.

"This might still work." He clasped his hands behind him and rocked back on his heels. "The two most powerful warriors are patience and time."

Stella's brow furrowed. "Sun Tzu?"

"Leo Tolstoy."

Everyone continued looking at him skeptically—in particular, Stella seemed unconvinced.

"We have more than Blitz." John walked to his desk and

pulled out the small tracking device. Once he'd navigated past the biometric authentication and entered the fourteen-digit password, he waited. When the device successfully zoned in on Sufia —when he saw that her dot was glowing a healthy green—he pushed the image on to the wall monitor, in the box next to what Kate had displayed.

"This is Sufia Alshedri, and as you can tell by the color of her tracker, she's alive and well. She's also a Saudi-trained operative. I personally interviewed her, and I can assure you that she has a passionate devotion to our cause. I employed Sufia to make sure that this transaction between the buyer and Blitz took place, and according to that green dot, that's what she's doing."

Kate tapped on her tablet and succeeded in overlaying John's tracking information with hers.

"They're together," Kate murmured.

"Her instructions were to follow Blitz and to intervene if she felt the situation called for it. Plainly the situation called for it."

Stella rattled the ice in her glass. "And when is this grand event supposed to take place?"

John didn't need to look at his watch. "Now. A fifteen-minute window began at thirty minutes past ten."

Stella stood, walked over to John, then reached up and brushed a piece of imaginary lint off his shoulder. She lowered her voice enough to suggest it was for his ears only, but she was obviously quite aware that everyone in the room could hear her. He had no doubt that she wanted everyone in the room to hear her.

"I believe in personal responsibility, John. Don't you?"

He didn't bother with an answer.

Every nerve in his body warned him that a cobra was within striking distance. Any move or motion could be the one that would lead to his death. He clasped his hand around the gun in his pocket. He wouldn't go gently into that good night.

Stella pivoted and turned her attention toward Brett and Kate. "John is ultimately responsible for the success or failure of this mission. But you, Kate. . . John tells me that you're now the reigning leader on the technical side."

Kate nodded once, definitively. She also met Stella's gaze without blinking or cringing or crying out for mercy. The girl had a little backbone, more than John had expected.

"As for Brett." Stella walked back to the beverage cart and refilled her glass, taking her time, drawing out the moment in order to receive the attention she craved. "You're responsible for the human side of things, and it looks to me like that's where we're having a problem."

Before Brett could answer, John jumped in. "How about we wait and see how this plays out before assigning blame?"

"Excellent idea." Stella returned to her seat and crossed her too-thin legs. "What do you say we all watch it together? That way if things don't go as planned, the person that I need to hold responsible will be right here in this room."

John was grateful for the small Ruger he kept on his person every day. He'd learned long ago that you couldn't anticipate the twists and turns twenty-four hours might take. He understood the importance of being able to defend himself. He didn't think Stella would be foolish enough to physically challenge him, but he had seen her kill before.

She'd done so without blinking.

The woman was a psychopath.

The sooner he could be shed of her the better.

But first, he had to see this mission through to its intended conclusion.

Chapter Nineteen

"**D**rop the weapon." Allison's voice was quiet, barely more than a whisper. She stood completely still, the barrel of her Glock pressed against the back of Sophie's neck. She thought the gun sort of spoke for itself, but she gave the command anyway, in case there was any doubt what she expected from the woman.

"In general, that's not something I'm overly eager to do."

Allison put a little more pressure on the gun.

"But if you insist." Sophie raised her hands and let her pistol fall to the ground.

"Now move over there, beside Blitz."

Blitz had been sitting on the ground, attempting to put his shoes back on over his blistered feet. At Allison's appearance, his eyes had widened, as if he couldn't believe this night had gone from terrible to terrifying. He stumbled to his feet, nearly tripping over the shoes that he hadn't tied securely.

Sophie did as Allison had instructed.

It didn't pass Allison's attention that she'd given up a bit too easily, which meant she had a backup piece. That was okay. At this distance, Allison could kill her before she retrieved it, let alone fired it.

Allison kicked the pistol away, heard it rattle up against a rock. In her right hand, she held her Glock, in her left, she shone a small penlight at the ground. As before, the red lens muted the light and allowed her to retain her night vision. It provided enough visibility for her to see them, but maybe not enough for them to adequately see her since they were looking into the light.

"Who hit you in the face?" Sophie's eyebrows arched in something like amusement. "Looks as if your forehead and your cheek are going to be sporting a nasty bruise."

So they could see her. Allison didn't care. She had a feeling that all three of them weren't going to walk away from this, but the choice was theirs to make. She directed her questions to the woman. "What's your name? Your full name?"

"Why does it matter to you?"

Still all attitude. Her breathing was normal, her eyes calm, her gaze steady. She wasn't rattled one bit by Allison's appearance. Maybe she'd even been expecting it.

Whoever Sophie was, one thing was certain.

She was a professional—and maybe she wasn't twenty-three. Allison thought she was probably a good five years older. She had long black hair, a model's figure and stood a solid five foot, ten inches. Her physique wasn't muscular exactly, but she was wiry— as if once coiled she could strike with impressive strength.

"Name."

"Sufia Alshedri."

So not Sophie. Allison wasn't surprised. She would, of course, use an alias. Sufia Alshedri might be another false name, but Allison didn't think so. She thought it had the ring of truth, plus there was the defiant way the woman had raised her chin and looked straight at her.

"And you are?" Sufia's tone suggested they were two strangers, meeting for coffee.

"What's your signal?"

"I don't know what you're talking about."

"Your signal to the boat. What is it?"

Allison racked the slide on her Glock and raised it an inch higher—center of mass would be an easy target. And though Blitz had killed a woman with his bare hands a mere twelve hours before, she didn't think he would rush a loaded gun. Nope, the woman would be her first target. Blitz would be her second.

They all knew it.

He was inching backwards, as if he could disappear into the night.

"Don't try to run, Blitz. That won't end well for you."

Sufia laughed. "I'm not sure he's capable of running at this point. Didn't you hear? He has blisters." She shook her head and grimaced, as if to say *Can you believe this guy?*

"What is the signal?" Allison repeated. She was running out of patience, and she let that creep into her voice. Let them think that she was tired, cranky, maybe impulsive. Let them worry.

"Blitz hasn't told me. That's what we were arguing about. You probably heard us as you were lurking about in the dark, and if so then you know as much as I do—which isn't much at all."

"No, you were arguing about the kill codes. I want to know how you're supposed to signal the boat on the north shore."

Sufia allowed the smallest of smiles to cross her face.

"When is the swap supposed to take place?"

"We're in the window now." Sufia shrugged. "Less than fifteen minutes. If we haven't made contact by the time the window closes, the buyers will skedaddle back to their lair."

Allison flicked the gun in Blitz's direction.

He jerked as if she'd pulled the trigger, held his hands in front of his face and started talking fast. "Flashlight, three bursts pointed toward the north bank, then leave the light on."

"Okay." She pulled two zip ties from her pocket and tossed them on the ground. "Sufia, secure his arms behind his back. Do it quickly and quietly."

Sufia seemed amused. Definitely not twenty-three. Definitely a professional. But who did she work for? Gollum? That's what she had told Blitz. Allison wasn't so sure, and the only way to know for certain was for the buyer's boat to land on this side of the river. Her instinct told her that when that happened, many of her questions would be answered.

Blitz sputtered, "I'm not letting you put those things on me."

"You want her to shoot you?"

"I don't even know who she is."

"She's the government, Blitz. She's the big bad wolf, the one that you anarchists work so hard to defeat."

Blitz's swagger left him like air from a punctured balloon. He meekly put his arms behind his back, staring down at the ground as Sufia did as Allison had instructed.

"And who do you work for, Sufia?"

"Me? I work for myself." The woman smiled broadly. "There. Just as you asked. He's trussed up like a Christmas pig in days of yore."

"Blitz, turn around and walk back toward me." Allison wanted to make sure Sufia had secured the ties correctly. She kept the gun trained on Sufia, reached down with the penlight, and tugged on the ties once.

"Ouch."

Yup. Nice and tight.

"Move back over beside Sufia."

She gave him a light push in the right direction. Blitz stumbled, but he moved next to Sufia, then turned to face her. He might be a good actor, but Allison thought what she was seeing was genuine. He certainly appeared subdued.

Killing a helpless woman you outweighed by fifty pounds was one thing.

Being held at gunpoint in the bottom of a canyon where no one was going to come to your aid was something else entirely.

"Now what?" Sufia was plainly not worried.

Did she still think that she'd come out on the sunny side of this? Perhaps she was counting on the buyers coming to her rescue, counting on the fact that then Allison would be solidly outnumbered and outgunned. Allison almost pitied the woman because what Sufia hadn't figured into the equation was that she was going up against someone who had literally nothing to lose.

That was Allison's greatest asset and biggest stumbling block.

In her formal evaluations she'd been called both exceedingly courageous and dangerously reckless—often in the same report.

"Make the signal. Now."

"Are you sure you don't want to creep away into the night first? These guys. . ." Sufia nodded toward the river. "They don't mess around. Plus, you look like you could use an ice pack and a couple Tylenol. Or something stronger?"

"Do it now."

Sufia shrugged as if to say *Fine, but don't say I didn't warn you.* "Mind if I fetch my flashlight?"

"The flashlight. Nothing else."

Sufia laughed at that. Her long black hair fell over her shoulder as she reached into a pocket of her trousers. Her eyes relaxed, lids half closed. Allison didn't watch any of that. She watched the woman's hands.

"Slow, Sufia. I'll only shoot you if I have to." When Sufia glanced up, Allison added, "Don't make me have to."

"You government types are all the same—full of fury and indignation. It's tiresome." But she did as she'd been told.

For all Allison knew, three bursts could be an SOS signal. *I'm being held at gunpoint.* But it hadn't sounded as if they'd been colluding before she revealed herself. She couldn't imagine a scenario where these two were bosom buddies working on an op together.

She couldn't imagine one trusting the other with their life.

"Now help Blitz sit down, right there."

Blitz let out a big *oof* when he landed on the ground, but he didn't move. Was he as utterly defeated as he seemed? Or was it all an act?

Allison wasn't taking any chances. She stepped back into the shadows between two of the larger boulders. "I'm right here, and I'm accurate at two hundred yards. I'd estimate you to be seven yards from me. Am I clear?"

"Yup." Sufia raised her hands again, eager to show her compliance. "It doesn't have to happen this way though. I'm willing to share."

"Share?"

"The money of course. You can't make that much working for the U.S. government, and I'm not talking pennies and nickels. This is a big payday. You might want to at least consider—"

"I don't want your money."

"What do you want? To save the world? I'm afraid it's too late for that. If this plan doesn't work, another will. Why not take the money—I'm willing to give you half—"

"Hey. That's my money."

Sufia shot a pitying glance at Blitz, shook her head in mock consternation, then turned her attention back to Allison. "You could enjoy what little time you have left before Gollum finds you. We'll make the trade, I'll split the money, and you can scurry away."

"Not happening. Send the signal."

"She's supposed to be standing near the water with the flashlight pointed down." Blitz drew back when both women turned to look at him. Shrugging his shoulders, he added, "Just saying."

"Do as he said, and Sufia—" Allison waited until the woman turned her gaze toward her, wanting to be sure she had her complete attention. "Don't put your hands near your pockets for any reason."

"You are so intense."

Which echoed what Zack had said earlier. Allison's mind wanted to go back over that, to think of the boy and what Nina had done to him, and how she had killed Nina. Her mind wanted to process those things. She needed to process those things, but she wouldn't go there right now. She couldn't go there right now.

Fifteen minutes.

Probably less.

The ticking of the clock had grown louder, drowning out all other thoughts. The countdown to the world's annihilation.

Sofia sauntered closer to the water, clicked on the flashlight, and pointed its beam down—toward the water. She clicked it on and off three times, then left it on.

A small point of light in a very dark canyon.

A beacon of sorts, but not the type that would save anyone.

Allison became gradually aware of a change in the sound of the water and realized there was a boat approaching. Its motor was nearly silent—some new tech thing that DHS didn't even have. Unless it was DHS. Hope blossomed in her chest, until she noticed a change in Sufia's stance.

Her shoulders relaxed a fraction of an inch.

Definitely not Department of Homeland Security then.

What was surprising was that the woman still thought she could walk away from this.

Allison stepped behind the shoulder-high rock, breathed in and out, then assumed her shooting stance. She'd long preferred the Weaver Stance to the Isosceles. The Weaver allowed for more pivot of her torso. Best to assume that Blitz would try something and that she'd have to shoot him after she took out Sufia and whoever was driving the boat.

She thought her left eye had swollen a little, but she used her right for peering down the gun's sight. Her injuries weren't severe enough to affect her accuracy.

Allison wasn't afraid.

More than anything, she had the sense that she'd been moving toward this moment since her phone rang in her room in the Yavapai Lodge up top. Maybe she'd been moving toward it since the fateful night her father was killed.

Run.

You shouldn't have tried to stop me.

Bang.

She wasn't a child. She wasn't running. She would stop them. She was filled with a sense of purpose and righteousness and hope that the disaster Gollum designed could be averted. Now that the moment of truth had arrived, any remnants of fatigue fell away.

Her hearing sharpened.

Her eyesight cleared.

Her aches and pains and disappointments evaporated in the presence of what needed to be done.

She was Allison Quinn, a thirty-five-year-old woman with little family, no close friends, and zero life outside of her job. She was also the government agent who had gone through eighteen months of training followed by ten years of ops. She was as ready as an agent could be.

The entire situation went to shit within the first ten seconds.

The boat drew near.

Sufia called out something in Arabic to whoever was piloting the boat.

The pilot raised a weapon. Allison hit him with her first bullet and her second. As he splashed into the water, someone else in the boat shot Sufia—center of mass, kill shot. She fell back—her torso half in and half out of the river, flashlight still on and piercing the darkness. Blitz screamed and tried to flip over and crawl behind a rock. The person in the boat shot him too.

He didn't shoot Allison.

He still couldn't see Allison, though she now understood he was wearing night vision goggles. She was sheltered behind the rock, her gunsight barely clearing the top of the stone. By the time he turned her way, she was emptying her magazine.

She saw his body jerk back.

She saw red blossom on his chest, then his arm.

Somehow, he still managed to turn the boat and hit the throttle. Allison pulled another magazine from her pocket, ejected the first, slammed in the second, and continued firing. She emptied her second magazine into the raft. She heard the air hiss out of it, understood that the water was deep there, and heard the man sputtering and gasping as he went under.

And then she didn't hear anything else except for the ringing in her ears.

Chapter Twenty

An unnerving silence cloaked the room as they watched the monitors. Sufia's vital signs plummeted from strong and steady to lifeless and flat. Her dot changed from green to red. John's words, uttered only a few minutes earlier, echoed back to him.

Sufia Alshedri . . . alive and well.

She's also a Saudi trained operative.

I personally interviewed her.

Kate remained standing in front of the wall of monitors. She glanced up at the images displayed there, then down at the tablet, up and down, as if by checking one more time she would see something different.

Brett groaned and dropped into a chair. He ran a hand over the top of his head, but he didn't speak.

No one dared to speak.

John wanted to point out that Blitz was still alive, but his vitals were also changing, as if he were in distress. In all likelihood, his dot would change from green to red very soon.

John Howard wasn't one to linger over a disaster.

There would be time for an operational post-mortem later. First, he needed to pull back his stock positions. He needed to salvage what he could of his funding. Then and only then would he turn to analyzing what exactly had been the fatal blow for operation Cyber Drop.

Stella wasn't that patient.

Her expression had hardened into a thing devoid of any emotion.

Not monstrous.

Cold. Mechanical. The reaper dressed in Armani.

She stood, smoothed the fabric of her pants, touched her hair covering, and dabbed at the corner of her mouth. She placed the glass of ice and whiskey on the table, careful to set it on a coaster.

Her moves were slow and deliberate.

Every action the very picture of repressed rage.

John waited, suspecting that she would scream, perhaps push and shove, possibly even throw something in the hopes that shattered glass would soothe the beast welling up inside of her.

Stella surprised him though.

She didn't do any of those things.

Instead, with the speed and agility of a much younger person, she reached into her pants pocket, withdrew her pistol and fired it, sending blood and bone into the wall of monitors.

John's heart rate doubled. Almost unaware of what he was doing, he'd pulled his Ruger, placed his finger on the trigger, and raised the weapon.

But Stella didn't turn toward John.

She wasn't watching him or the other remaining person in the room. She gave no attention to the body splayed on the floor. Without a single word or glance, she pocketed the pistol and left.

Chapter Twenty-One

Allison slammed another full magazine into her Glock and waited, gun pointed toward the river. Her ears felt clogged, as if she'd taken a deep dive underwater. She was hyper-aware of the sound of her heart thumping in her chest and the feel of the pistol against her palm. The pressure in her ears caused a slight dizziness, but she fought it, waited, and gradually her hearing returned.

First, she was able to make out the sound of the Colorado River, still rushing past, then the wind in the trees, the shell of the boat slapping against a rock, whimpers from Blitz.

No other boats appeared.

No one else shot at her.

The danger—for the moment—had passed.

She went to Sufia, snatched her penlight off the ground, turned it off, and pocketed it. Squatting, she put both of her arms under Sufia's—then lifted and pulled her body from the water. Allison didn't make it far, but she was able to leave her in the grass, staring up at the night sky. Not that she was seeing any of it. The hole in the middle of her chest had ended Sufia's stargazing, as well as her terrorist activities. Allison couldn't spare any remorse for her. Sufia had, very plainly, chosen her path.

Next, Allison turned to Blitz.

He'd stopped trying to crawl away and was curled into a fetal position, rocking back and forth though his hands were still tied behind him. Blood drenched one pants leg.

She knelt beside him. "I'm going to cut your ties and attach new ones in front. Don't try anything, Blitz, or that bullet in your leg will be your first wound but not your last."

He didn't respond in any way. He seemed to be in shock. The guy was either a great actor or a complete mess.

"Tell me you understand what I said."

"I understand."

She cut the ties, and he rolled over. She didn't have to tell him to put his wrists together. He did it before she could ask. Allison slipped new ties on him, then tightened them enough that he wouldn't pose a threat.

She used the pen light to get a better look at his wound. It was bleeding significantly, but she thought he'd survive it.

"We need to get away from this clearing. There might be a second boat."

"Second boat?" He looked at her blankly and finally managed, "Of buyers?"

"Of people who want to kill us."

That seemed to pierce the cloud of bewilderment hovering over him. He began nodding his head vigorously. "Okay. Yeah. Let's go."

And now she could hear that his teeth were chattering.

Had he lost enough blood to be in shock?

She flashed the beam of light up to check. His skin appeared clammy, and his lips had taken on a blue tinge. She had five, maybe ten minutes to stabilize him, but she couldn't do it out in the open.

Moving him proved very nearly impossible.

He couldn't or wouldn't put any weight on the leg. Finally, she told him to lie down on his back. She grasped him under the arms as she had Sufia and pulled him out of the clearing. They weren't going to make it far that way, but maybe a little distance would be enough.

By the time they stopped, a mere forty yards from where Sufia's body still lay, his breathing was ragged and Allison's arms felt as if they were made of mush rather than bone and sinew.

What Allison did next wasn't out of compassion or some misguided sense of regret.

She felt no sympathy for this man.

She simply needed him alive—at least for a few more minutes.

She pulled her belt from her pants, placed it above the wound and tightened it until Blitz cried out in pain. Like her triage instructor had said. If it didn't hurt, the tourniquet wasn't tight enough.

Next she pulled off her jacket, then yanked off her overshirt, wadded it up, and pushed it into his wound. When he screamed, she hissed, "You need to keep it together, Blitz, unless you want one of Sufia's friends to find us and finish what they started."

He stared at her, nodded, then asked, "Why are you doing this? Why are you helping me?"

"Because I have questions, Blitz, and you're going to answer them. Now keep quiet, and don't try anything stupid. You need to be very aware that if you do try anything stupid, I will put a bullet in you, and this one won't be in your leg. Got it?"

"Yeah."

"Say it."

"I've got it. I understand."

"I'm going to fetch my horse, my pack, and my first aid kit." She added as an afterthought, "Keep that shirt pressed to your wound unless you want to bleed out before I get back. And don't go anywhere."

Which was a pretty ridiculous statement, because honestly, where was he going to go? How far could a man with a bleeding femoral artery crawl?

Not that far.

And he'd leave a pretty obvious trail if he tried.

She'd fired two full magazines of bullets. The guy in the raft had fired at least six shots, maybe more. She didn't remember the noise, but it had to have been terrific. Steele would have heard the volley of gunfire if he was anywhere in the area. She wouldn't be surprised if the guests back at Phantom Ranch had heard it.

The cavalry was coming.

She hoped.

In the meantime, she meant to have a little private Q&A time with Blitz.

If everything went well, she'd still be able to hurry back to Tate and warn the river rafting group to stay away from the water before Gollum's sunrise drones arrived.

Just maybe, this op wasn't a total loss after all.

She jogged back along the path she'd crept over only a few minutes earlier. The distance seemed shorter now that she wasn't listening so intently for any sound of Blitz. She found Bella exactly where she'd left her. The mare swung her big muzzle around. She'd apparently been frightened by the gunfire and had attempted to pull her lead rope loose—had almost succeeded.

Allison untangled it from the tree. "Sorry, babe."

Bella nuzzled her hand.

"I didn't bring any treats." But there was still grain in the grain sack she'd packed. She'd get her answers from Blitz, then tend to her horse. She hoisted herself up into the saddle and urged Bella into a fast trot.

She scouted out the last few yards for a better hiding place and found one on a slight rise. Getting Blitz there wouldn't be easy, but where he lay now wasn't acceptable. She needed to be able to keep an eye on the river, Sufia's body, and the trail. She needed to monitor all three. She'd find a way to get Blitz to the rise if she had to drag him.

Tying Bella to yet another scraggly tree, she whispered, "You're a good girl. Wait for me."

She jerked her first aid kit from her backpack. Holding it, her mind flashed back to Zack bleeding through his shirt, Zack tied to both horses, Zack looking up at her and apologizing.

Had he made it?

Or had he died?

Were Eleanor Bonner and Tate still sitting by his side?

She pushed those questions from her mind and hurried back to Blitz. He looked marginally better when she knelt beside him. The tourniquet had slowed the bleeding, and his lips had lost their bluish tint. His teeth still chattered, and when she felt for his pulse, it was rapid. There was no use checking to see if the bullet had exited. There was nothing she could do about it either way.

She opened the medical kit, found the clotting powder, and tore it open with her teeth. "This is going to hurt."

"It already hurts."

But he didn't cry out when she poured it into the wound. She covered it with a pressure bandage, then wrapped the entire thing tightly in gauze. It didn't bleed through immediately, which she took as a good sign. He'd either make it or he wouldn't. Honestly, she didn't care. All she cared about was that she'd at least guaranteed herself ten minutes of conversation.

Was that callous?

Was she becoming as heartless as the people working on the other side of this thing?

Had she lost her compassion?

She didn't think so. Blitz had chosen his side, and he'd chosen badly. That was on him, not her.

She found a bottle of water and insisted he drink.

She thought his color improved a little more, but it was hard to tell in the glow of Sufia's penlight.

"We have to move."

He didn't have the energy to argue with her, or maybe he finally realized it was futile to do so. He even managed to throw an arm around her shoulders when she cut his hands free. Five minutes later, she had him settled on the small rise, his back against a rock. She stood straight, feet planted shoulder width apart, hand on her holster, her eyes scanning—river, Sufia, trail, Blitz, repeat.

Blitz coughed, caught his breath, and asked, "Who were those guys?"

"In the boat? I'm not sure, Blitz. Don't you know who you were doing business with?"

"Apparently not." He took another drink from the bottle, then added, "It wasn't supposed to happen like this."

"They were highly trained. That much was obvious. I'm sure they had a night scope. They hit Sufia with their first shot. The shooter might have been former military."

"Why did they kill her?"

"Why did you kill Lyra?"

He stared at her, his eyes two large orbs revealing nothing.

Allison shrugged. She hadn't expected an answer to that particular question. "They suspected that she'd been compromised. It wasn't personal."

"Okay."

She didn't ask for the kill codes. She'd seen him zip the small device into his jacket pocket. She retrieved it, and he didn't put up any resistance. The bullet wound seemed to have quelled his querulous attitude. She tucked the small flash drive into an inside a pocket of her own jacket—one that fastened securely, one that anyone would have to kill her to get to.

"Explain it to me."

He shook his head, but then he started talking, as if he needed to bare his soul, as if she could absolve him from his sins.

"Gollum contacted me a year ago. Said he had an easy job. He'd call and tell me when. I was to have a bag packed, be ready to go when I got that call."

"Which you received, two days ago."

"Right. He was able to disable that guy's car up top. It was a hybrid of some sort. He hacked into the on-board computer system and turned it off."

"You're talking about Mr. Harris."

"I guess." Another fit of coughing and his breathing became more labored, but he continued talking. "Yeah, his name was Harris."

"Did you strangle him?"

"No. I'd never killed anyone. Before Lyra, I mean. I knew how. I'd practiced, but actually doing it. . . I'm not that fond of touching people. You know?"

"So then who killed Harris? Your guy Cooper, did he do it?"

Blitz nodded. "Is he dead?"

"He is."

"Okay." His eyes darted past her then back. "Did you. . ."

"Yeah."

"Okay."

She didn't need to know all of this. Someone on Steele's team would get the full story, and Blitz seemed to be fading in and out of consciousness.

"Hey." She snapped her fingers, and he jerked awake. If she had to, she'd use the ammonia tablets in her first aid kit. "When did you become a member of the AT?"

"I don't know who that is." His voice was soft, feeble, totally unconvincing.

"Anarchists for Tomorrow." She pulled up his sleeve and found the same tattoo that had been on Anthony Cooper. These guys weren't exactly subtle about their political leanings. "What do you know about Arthur Quinn?"

"Who?"

"Arthur Quinn. Think, Blitz. It would have been twenty-four years ago."

He blinked rapidly, then murmured, "I was a kid then."

"But you've heard of him. You've heard that name. I could tell by your reaction."

Blitz nodded once, then raised the water bottle to his lips. His hands were shaking, and he spilled more than he swallowed. He didn't seem to notice.

"What? What did you hear?"

Blitz was staring at her now, realization dawning. "You're her. You're the kid."

"Tell me what you know about Arthur Quinn, Blitz."

He tried to laugh, coughed, then winced in pain. "You're the legend, not him."

"I don't know what you mean."

"All AT members have heard of you."

"Why me?"

"A tough government agent with a vendetta against cyber. . ." He pulled in two more short breaths. "Against cybercriminals, hell bent on bringing us all down because her old man was popped when she was a kid."

"Popped by whom?"

He shrugged, then looked at her with a bit of defiance in his eyes. "Ask Gollum."

The power between them had shifted, or at least Blitz thought it had. She'd revealed her weakness. She'd asked for the one piece of information she'd give anything to know. And she could tell from the gleam in his eyes that he understood the predicament she'd placed herself in. Even lying there, bleeding out in that great canyon, he reveled in the fact that he had something she wanted.

It wasn't kill codes.

It was answers.

She could make him tell her. A bullet could be pretty convincing. Or the pressure of two fingers against a gunshot wound. But if she did that, if she allowed herself, what would separate her from the likes of him?

Where is your compassion?

She suddenly became aware of the sound of motor rafts, several of them. Not quiet ones like the buyers had arrived in. Big, noisy rafts.

High powered rafts large enough to carry a team.

Steele was coming.

Allison stood and prepared to walk away, but Blitz called her back. She didn't go to him, but she did turn in his direction.

"He was one of us."

"Who was?"

"Your old man."

She had the surreal idea that she was listening to him through a very long tube. His words were both clear and at the same time incomprehensible. She felt light-headed and her thoughts scrambled in a dozen directions.

Finally, she managed a weak, "No, he wasn't."

"You asked what I heard. Story is he was one of us, and he got cold feet—so they killed him. Left a kid, all alone in the woods of northern California. Left you."

She stood there, but she didn't meet his eyes.

She didn't want to look into his face.

Blitz was a despicable piece of humanity whose life she had just saved. She didn't trust herself to move one step closer. And she didn't believe a word he said. In fact, she knew that he would say anything if it gave him the upper hand. He'd lie, cheat, sell his own mother—if he'd ever had a mother. He might have been raised by wolves for all she knew.

"Don't believe me? Search the dark web for references to Frodo, 1995-1996." He coughed again but pushed on. "You'll find a few answers, though I doubt they'll be what you hoped to find."

She wasn't aware of walking back to him, or kneeling down beside him, or grabbing him by the throat. But suddenly that's where she was, that's what she was doing, and for a split second, she lost all control of her emotions.

Losing control had never felt so good.

It was what she wanted to do.

What she needed to do.

"My father did not leave me. He was murdered. And he was not one of you."

Blitz struggled, his feet kicking out hopelessly, his hands slapping at hers.

"My father was nothing like you."

Later, she would wonder what she would have done given another ten seconds. But she wasn't given another ten seconds. Fate or luck or God saved her from murdering a man who had not earned the right to live. Suddenly the area was awash in floodlights, and Steele's team was pouring out of the rafts.

Allison Quinn stood, brushed off her pants, and walked away —grateful that Donovan Steele had arrived in the nick of time.

Chapter Twenty-Two

S teele strode toward her.

Tall and handsome and his eyes full of concern.

"You're hurt." He reached out to touch her face, but she jerked away.

"I'm fine. Two in the water, one on the beach, and Blitz is back behind that rock hanging on by a thread."

"Okay."

"The rafting group is downriver several miles, on the southside, at the Granite Campground."

"Got it."

"Also, a woman named Nina is southeast of the rafting group. I tagged her body."

"We'll recover her."

"One of the National Park employees—Jason Faulkner—might have been in on it. Might have been Nina's unwitting partner. I'm not sure how much he knew about the operation. He's with the rafters."

"Okay."

"Zack Lancaster, another park employee, is also with the rafters. Tate's watching over him. Zack was stabbed. . . slashed. He needs medical attention stat."

Steele raised his SAT phone and barked a few orders into it, but he never took his eyes off her. He never stopped studying her, and the worry in his eyes was enough to cause her undoing.

She couldn't let that happen.

Not here.

Not now.

She waited until he ended the call, then retrieved the zip drive from her pocket and dropped it into his outstretched palm. "The kill codes."

Steele called another agent over and handed her the zip drive. The young woman took off at a jog and hopped into a boat that was manned by yet another agent. Together they headed across the river. The lights of the boat became a dot in the darkness. It looked to Allison as if Steele had brought the entire DHS department with him.

Not that it had done her much good an hour earlier.

Where had they been when Zack was bleeding out?

Why hadn't they intervened as the buyers opened fire on her position?

That wasn't fair, and on one level she knew it. Knowing didn't stop the mind from questioning why.

"Anything else?"

"According to Sufia, the dead woman on the beach, Gollum has a military drone and is planning to hit the rafters at daybreak."

"That's not possible."

Allison shrugged. She was no longer the one in charge. "He had a military-grade river craft, and I'm pretty sure that guy shooting at me had military-grade weapons, but it's your call."

Steele issued more orders into his phone, then crossed his arms.

"What aren't you telling me?"

He was one of us. Frodo, 1995-1996.

She stared at him. In her exhaustion, for a few seconds, she thought of baring her soul to Donovan Steele. Then he flicked his glance to the right, and Allison came to her senses. The man standing in front of her didn't care about her unresolved childhood issues. He was in charge of a government operation to stop a domestic terrorist event.

He wasn't here to be her friend.

So, she didn't answer him.

She turned and strode toward her horse.

But he wasn't letting it go. He followed, throwing questions at her like darts at a board. "What happened back there? Why didn't you call in? What were you thinking, going off on your own?"

She turned on him with a fury borne from all of the doubts and injuries and heartbreaks of the last twenty-four hours.

"I was doing my job. That's what happened back there."

"You were supposed to provide backup."

"I realize that."

"It literally means you are to step back."

"Step back?"

"It means you call us. You check in. I don't have to tell you this, Alli. You're a better agent than—"

Her temper flared when he would use her first name, as if this were personal. As if they meant something to each other.

She thought about punching him but decided she was too tired. "I was ready to step back, *Donovan*."

His head jerked up.

The look in his eyes should have warned her to back off. The practical side of her brain begged her to shut her mouth and act like a professional. The commonsense voice in her head screamed for her to stand down.

The voice of a seasoned operative.

The voice of her father.

Like the times before, she ignored that voice. When had she ever backed down? That wasn't the way she did things. She was full throttle regardless of the consequences, and she had the bruised face to prove it.

"Do you think I wanted to go through the last twelve hours?

Are you suggesting I wanted my face to look like this or that maybe I was looking forward to killing four—count them, Tate—four people?"

The adrenaline was surging, but she didn't have enough of it left. She crashed before she could adequately express her indignation. She sank onto a rock and covered her face with her hands.

"Hey. Look. I didn't mean—"

"Yes. You did." She scrubbed her hands over her face. An exhaustion that reached to her bones threatened to consume her, but she couldn't let it.

Not yet.

Raising her head, she squared her shoulders and met his gaze. "I was providing backup. Reconnaissance only, as you had instructed. Then I discovered Zack following me. . . a twenty-one-year-old kid who might be bleeding out right this minute because by the time I figured out what to do with him, Nina appeared on the scene."

Now she was back there, seeing Zack with blood dripping from his shirt, seeing her SAT phone smashed and lying on the ground, seeing Nina's smile. She was in that small clearing and realizing she was completely alone—again. She was overwhelmed with the scent and the sight and the terror of the two mares tied to Zack and shying away, but not too far. . . not too far.

Her hands began to shake and she crossed her arms, tucked her hands under her armpits, attempted to literally hold herself together. "The fight with Nina didn't go well, for either of us. But I had to stop her. You understand that, right?"

"Of course."

She dropped her defensive position and held her trembling hands in front of her. She stared at them and tried to forget the feel of Nina's larynx crushing beneath her fingers. She thought of Steele warning her about Blitz, about the dangerous nature of someone who was able to kill with his bare hands.

He didn't use a weapon. He didn't do it from a distance. He was looking in this guy's eyes when he choked the life out of him. Someone who could do that. . .

A tremor started in the center of her being, and she feared she would lose her composure completely, disintegrate there in the middle of the killing field.

She didn't.

She stiffened her spine and forced herself to stare at a place over Steele's right shoulder. "Nina had busted my SAT phone. There was no way to make contact."

"Okay." He held up his hands, attempting to stop her, but it was too late.

"I loaded Zack onto his horse, and we made for the rafting group—made for Tate. Together we moved Zack to a place by the fire. But I still wasn't done, right? There was no way to signal you. So, I manned up, and I handled it." Now she was standing, scowling at him, begging for a fight. "I did what I was trained to do. I took care of Blitz and neutralized Sufia. I stopped whoever the guys were in that boat. And I got the kill codes."

"Look, I was just worried. I'm sorry."

She walked to her horse and fought the urge to put her arms around the beast's neck and draw some comfort from the steadiness of Bella's presence.

She was a Homeland Security agent.

She should start acting like one.

"Alli, at least stay long enough to get looked at by a medic."

She pulled herself up and into the saddle. Bella stood there steady, stalwart, patiently waiting for a signal. Allison considered turning and looking at Donovan Steele, but what was the point? He wasn't her boss, not really. This was a joint operation.

Maybe they'd work together again.

Maybe they wouldn't.

So instead of turning or acknowledging his last words in any way, she pressed her heels firmly against Bella's side. The mare shot down the trail at a gallop. It would seem that Bella was as ready to be done with this night as she was.

By the time Allison made it back to the Granite Campground, another raft full of Steele's team was there securing the site. Floodlights had been set up, and agents were working their way around the camp.

She handed Bella off to an agent. Running her hand down the horse's neck, she tried to convey her gratitude to the mare. Bella had been faithful, smart, and patient.

How many humans could you say that about?

"She needs watering and feed. Also, someone should check her hooves before attempting to ride her back to the ranch."

"Will do."

She ignored the looks tossed her way from other agents and walked over to Tate. He stood there, waiting for her—his ranger hat in his hands and a look of relief on his face. Five yards past him, she could see a young, female medic kneeling beside Zack. Allison thought he looked better than he had earlier in the evening.

"How's he doing?"

"Weak, but he asked for her phone number, so I think he'll make it."

The laughter felt strange, but oh, how she needed it.

"You look worse than the last time I saw you." He paused, waited, then gently asked, "Long night?"

"You could say that."

"Heard the gunshots. Sounded like a shootout at the OK Corral."

"It was a shootout, but I'm still standing, so there's that to be grateful for."

"Good. That's real good." Tate smashed the hat onto his head. "I somehow managed to keep everyone here. They wanted to help, but I convinced them otherwise. I did what you asked."

"I appreciate that."

"You had me worried, Allison. I wanted to take Denali and

find you, but I was afraid I'd come around a corner and get the mare killed. You were pretty emphatic that I wasn't to. . ."

She was already shaking her head. "I was able to do what I did last night because I knew you were here, helping these people."

Tate stepped closer and lowered his voice, though no one was paying them much attention. "Did you get the codes?"

"I did."

"So, you can stop the attack?"

"Hopefully. I think so."

Gollum was many things, but he wasn't a man who failed to deliver. The codes would work. They had to, or his negotiating price would take too big a hit. Allison had no doubt he was already moving on to his next fiendish scheme.

"Blitz?"

She held out her hand, palm down, and wiggled it back and forth. Tate stuck his thumbs in his pockets and blew out a breath.

She walked over to Zack and knelt beside him. His eyes were open, his gaze was clear, and he even had a bit of the old goofy smile on his face.

"This one's a real cowboy," the medic said.

"You should see him on a horse."

The medic smiled and wiggled her eyebrows, then said, "I'll give you two a minute."

"Saw you brought Bella back."

"She's a good mare."

"The best."

His gaze darted around, but his breathing was steady. His color was much improved from when she'd first brought him back to the camp. Physically, he seemed as if he was going to make it.

"How ya doing, Zack?"

"I'm okay." His eyes searched hers. "How are. . . things?"

"Good. Very good, in fact."

He nodded as if that was all he needed to know. "The medic

said I'm going to be all right. She said you saved me. . . you and Eleanor Bonner."

Allison reached forward and brushed a bit of dirt off his forehead. Zack's right arm had an IV running from it, and with his left hand, he grasped his Stetson.

"It's my fault you were hurt tonight, Zack. I want to say I'm sorry. I should have insisted that you return to the ranch the minute I became aware that you were following me."

"We've already been through that. It's not your fault. It's mine. I didn't think things through. I could have jeopardized your entire mission."

Their eyes met and an understanding passed between them. The past was the past. The important thing was that they'd both survived—damaged, but still breathing.

"You are pretty good on a horse."

"Thank you, ma'am."

"Try to stay out of trouble."

"I will." This came out a little shakily. Zack dropped the Stetson and brushed at his eyes with his left arm.

She wanted to tell him it was okay to cry. She wanted to join him and weep for the people who had chosen the wrong path and were now dead. She wanted to take the time to apologize to every person in this rafting group that their once-in-a-lifetime vacation had become an unforgettable nightmare.

Instead, she hugged him awkwardly, stood, and turned back toward Tate. They walked over to a rock and perched on it.

Steele's team was busy assessing injuries and interviewing witnesses. They had moved everyone back, away from the river, and under the cover of a few trees. They would be safe from Gollum's drones, though in all likelihood Steele would be able to stop those. Another agent walked through the group checking people's names off a clipboard. When the agent arrived next to Jason Faulkner he stared at the ground, then stood and allowed himself to be led away from the group.

Tate followed her gaze. "They'll take him in for questioning?"

"Yeah."

"I talked to him a little. I don't think he was aware of the attack plan. He was definitely in over his head, but he didn't seem to have any knowledge of what was actually happening."

"They'll figure it out."

Steele's team would. One thing the FBI was very good at was investigating, pulling someone's background apart until every infinitesimal part was laid out on the table. Within forty-eight hours, they would know everything there was to know about Jason Faulkner. They would know whether he was an active accomplice or a clueless bystander who found himself caught up in the unimaginable.

As far as Allison could tell, the group of rafters seemed frightened and tired, but physically okay.

Eleanor, Steve, and Piper Bonner were accepting extra blankets. Eleanor and Steve snugged one around Piper nice and tight. That image might carry Allison through the next forty-eight hours—a family still intact, a mom and dad who would watch their daughter grow to adulthood, a child who might one day become a botanist. Eleanor glanced up, saw Allison, and gave a thumbs up—the universal all-is-well symbol.

The young couple, Bryce and Mia, who had helped with Allison's horses, were answering another agent's questions. At one point they turned and pointed at Tate. He offered a small wave.

Allison cleared her throat. "They'll want to talk to you, too, before the night's over, though I vouched for you."

"You did?" He seemed surprised, then laughed when she ducked her head and gave him a you-must-be-kidding look. "I feel kind of honored. If I'm not mistaken, you had your doubts about me."

"Maybe a little." After the thirty-six hours they'd spent together, Tate had now been placed on the Trust One Hundred Percent list.

It was a woefully short list.

"You doubted me because you take your responsibilities seriously. I know a little about that." His voice had taken on a more somber tone. "You care about the people you're called to protect. It makes you very cautious."

She didn't answer that.

She didn't think she could.

Those were the words she'd wanted to hear from Steele, who probably didn't know how to deliver a compliment or atta-boy, atta-girl in this case.

The commercial guides were also being grilled, but Allison knew that was just a formality. Steele's team had no doubt thoroughly vetted Pete Johnson and Mason Hobbes since the rafts had left Phantom Ranch. The fact that they weren't already handcuffed said that their background checks had come back clean.

She didn't tell Tate about the possibility of a military drone attack. She suspected they were safe now. Steele had issued a no-fly zone and called for military backup. Any helicopter or drone coming within ten miles of them would be escorted out or shot down. Pilot's choice.

"According to the Hopi clans, two brothers created the Grand Canyon by tossing lightning bolts and piling mud to build the canyon walls and create a path for the river."

"Two brothers, huh?"

"Pokanghoya and Polongahoya."

"I don't know what that means, Tate."

"Who does? Maybe it just means that the history of this place stretches back far before the misadventures of man."

"There's some comfort in that, I suppose."

"I love this canyon." Tate tipped his hat back and stared up at the stars. "Love its remoteness and peace. Love that the river flows on no matter what people do. I wouldn't want to be any place else."

Allison forced her gaze up—to the river flowing past the small group, the canyon wall on the opposite bank rising five thousand, five hundred and fifty feet, the North Rim stretching to the horizon in both directions, and above all of that, starlight as far as she could see. She tried to think of a single place she cared about the way that Tate cared about the scene in front of her, but she came up blank. Possibly, she could plant Tate's canyon firmly in her mind, and remember it when she needed a momentary escape.

She certainly didn't look forward to returning to her apartment in Virginia, but where else was there?

Her aunt's place in Texas.

It wasn't home, but it might be the place to start looking.

He was one of us. Frodo, 1995-1996.

She didn't for a second believe that what Blitz had said about her father was true, but there was something about that phrase. *Frodo.* Something she'd read or seen before. She'd give it a few days and see if her memory could bring it up. If it didn't come to her, she'd go to Texas and go through her father's things one more time.

Steele would insist that she be evaluated by a doctor, and the DHS doc would recommend she take some time off. Allison had been through this before, and she knew that arguing with the doc was an exercise in futility.

An agent called out to her, then nodded toward one of the rafts. It was time to go.

She stood and stuck out her hand.

Tate shook it, then enfolded her in a hug.

She remembered crossing the suspension bridge, crouching there in the middle as the rain fell in sheets around them, the terror of lightning striking nearby. She remembered Tate talking to her, coaxing her safely to the other side, pulling her into his arms. Like before, she was painfully aware of the smell of soap, aftershave, deodorant—the scents of her father.

She pulled away. "Thanks again."

"Of course."

She walked toward Steele's team, but Tate called after her so she turned around and walked backward.

"If you ever need a job. . . "

Allison laughed, then turned back toward the other agents.

She had a job, and despite all that had happened in the last thirty-six hours, she knew she was good at it. She had other cyber-criminals to catch, and she had a personal mission that she would see through to the end. Though she'd initially been shocked at Blitz's answers to her question, she now thought that she could work with what he'd said. There was a good chance that she was one step closer to finding her father's killer.

Game on.

Chapter Twenty-Three

At Steele's insistence, Allison received emergency medical care on-site.

Jeremy, the FBI medic, was tall, stocky, and entirely too cheerful. He cleaned the wound on her forehead and applied Steri-Strips. "I hope you like green, yellow, and purple. The bruise on your forehead is probably going to extend to the bruise on your jaw. The good news is that it appears as if nothing's broken."

At his insistence, she promised to schedule an appointment with the DHS doc once she was back in Virginia.

"How's your balance?"

"I was just riding a horse, and I didn't fall off."

"Nauseous?"

"Nope."

"Blurred or double vision?"

"Not at all."

"Memory problems?"

When she didn't answer, he pushed. "Can you recall recent events and details that led up to and included your injury?"

"Yeah. I remember all of that quite clearly." The images were pushing into her consciousness—images that she would rather forget. "Honestly, I'm fine."

He looked up from his tablet and gave her a you-might-as-well-say-it look. Plainly, he wasn't going to let her leave until he'd ticked every box on his digital form.

"I have a severe headache, and I think my tooth is loose, plus there's some ringing in my ears."

"The ringing should stop in the next hour or so. Were you in close proximity to the gunfire?"

"Since it was aimed at and came from me, yes."

His eyes filled with compassion, and Allison looked away. She didn't have time for this.

Jeremy's demeanor returned to all business. "You took a pretty solid hit."

"More than one."

"Okay. I suspect you have a concussion." Jeremy typed something into his tablet, something that probably went straight to Allison's boss. "Don't drive, and see your doctor as soon as possible."

She was the first agent out of the canyon, at Steele's insistence. A rafting crew ferried her to a short trail on the north side. That trail led to a clearing where a helicopter was waiting. The helicopter took her to the South Rim.

She walked into her room at Yavapai Lodge.

Everything was as she'd left it. Covers tossed back from when Steele had called. Extra set of clothes hanging in the closet. Toiletries still on the bathroom counter. She took a hot shower, laid down on the bed, and passed out for seven and a half hours.

On waking, she ordered room service, then packed her belongings. She did not hike back down to Phantom Ranch. She'd done enough hiking to last her a while. The few things she'd left in her locker back at the ranch could be put in the "Someone left it, you can take it" box.

A glance in the mirror caused her to flinch. The medic had put three butterfly stitches on her forehead. The skin around her left eye and cheekbone had turned a dark purple. Her jaw felt as if she'd been slugged, and the tooth hurt. She certainly looked like she'd been in a fight—which she had.

A fight for her life.

A fight for America.

It sounded a bit sappy, but the truth bolstered her mood.

Fortunately, her face looked worse than it felt. Three Tylenol were enough to keep the headache at bay, and she couldn't jiggle her tooth with her tongue anymore. Maybe she wouldn't need to see a dentist.

She hated going to the dentist.

She'd gladly face a terrorist rather than lie prone in a dental chair and listen to the sound of a drill. Though to be fair, she had one of the nicest dentists in Virginia. He even offered to give her a sticker when she managed to show up for her appointments, grousing and hoping that the doc would have left on an impromptu vacation.

Her cell phone that she'd left on the charger in her room binged with a message from Steele. She was booked on the first available flight out of Arizona. Glancing at her watch, she calculated she had just enough time to do one more thing. It would entail driving the rental that she kept up top, which meant going against the medic's orders. If pushed, she could claim that she forgot what he'd forbid her to do.

The ninety-minute drive to Flagstaff helped her decompress. She pulled her rental into the first big box store, made her purchase, and then she stopped by the medical center to visit Theodore Payne.

"How ya doing, Teddy?"

His eyes widened, and he dropped the cup of Jell-O he'd been focused on. "I can't believe you came to see me."

"I told you I would."

"Yeah, but. . . I can't believe you did."

They studied each other for a minute.

Allison was remembering finding Teddy on the trail, her argument with Tate, and him leaving to call for help. She was seeing

Teddy wrapped in the emergency blanket—shivering, in shock, in danger of bleeding out.

"Did you get the guy who stabbed me?"

"Yes."

"So, he won't like. . ." He plucked at the hospital blanket. "He won't come after me again will he? He won't find out that I. . ."

"He's dead."

"Oh." He glanced up now. "Did you kill him?"

"I did."

"Wow. Okay. Well, thanks."

"I also spoke with your doctor in the hall. He expects you to make a full recovery. Says you won't be pitching in a baseball game, but—"

"I never did that anyway." Teddy smiled for the first time since she'd walked into the room. "Never was much of an athlete."

"I brought you something." She dropped the shopping bag on his bed.

When he pulled out the latest smartphone, his eyes lit up like a kid at Christmas. "Sweet."

"Try not to crack that one."

She stood to go, but waited when she realized Teddy was trying to find the words to say something.

"Take a minute, Teddy."

He nodded, pulled in a deep breath, and ran his thumb over the box holding the new phone. Finally, he looked up at her. "I just want to say thanks. Sometimes people don't do that. They think they'll have time later or maybe that it doesn't need saying. Like it's understood."

"I do understand."

"Yeah. Okay. But I need to say it. If you and that park ranger hadn't come along, I would have died on the South Kaibab Trail. Who knows how long it would have taken someone to find my body."

She could tell he'd spent a lot of time thinking through this, a lot of time staring out his hospital room window trying to make sense of a world that was often nonsensical.

"I'm not brave like you." He brought a shaky hand to his forehead, rubbed a spot there, then let his hand fall back to the blanket. Closing his eyes, he forced himself to continue. "I have no idea what career I want to pursue. I certainly don't want to be. . . to be an agent or anything."

"It's not a super popular job choice."

"But I do understand how important your job is and also how valuable life is. I understand those things now, and I won't forget."

"Finish your degree, okay?"

"Yeah, sure."

"Make them give you a new camera."

"Okay."

"Take care of yourself, Teddy."

She eventually found the airport car rental return drop, though she drove past it the first and second times. "Definitely not operating on all cylinders, Quinn."

By the time she boarded her flight, she was nearly asleep on her feet. She dozed most of the way back to Virginia, and she kept the appointment to see the DHS doc the next day.

"I can't seem to get enough sleep."

"Your body is catching up with all that has happened." He confirmed that she had a concussion—something she already knew, did x-rays of her face—which showed nothing was broken, and assured her the medic's butterfly stitches were adequate.

She saw the DHS shrink the day after that.

"It's good to see you again." Dr. Michie smiled warmly, as if the words were heartfelt, and maybe they were.

To Allison, she looked more like a lab scientist than a counselor, with her large glasses, no-nonsense hair, and lack of makeup. Very little about the woman had changed in the years that Allison had known her. For some reason, she found that comforting.

In this room with this person, there was a steadying sameness.

"It's been a while."

"No offense, doc, but this isn't my favorite place to visit."

"Understood." She crossed her legs and waited. Dr. Michie was very good at waiting. Beside her were a notepad, a pen, and a folder that probably held Allison's entire life history. "Maybe we should begin with what happened on your last assignment."

"Aren't all the details in that folder?"

"Some of them are, but I'd like to hear it from you."

Allison sat forward, elbows propped on her knees, fingertips pressed together, and stared at the floor.

"We've been here before, Allison, and you know this is a safe place. Take your time. I have no patients or pressing engagements after you."

She was silent a few more minutes, but finally the details of all that had happened began to pour out of her—things she hadn't told Steele or included in her official reports. The majesty of the canyon. Facing her acrophobia every time she hiked up or down the trail. Seeing the younger brother she'd never had in Teddy and Zack.

She described shooting Anthony Cooper in the dead of night, strangling Nina with her bare hands, and killing both of the men in the boat.

She admitted that she still hoped to find her father's killer.

She told Dr. Michie almost everything, because, as the good doctor had said, they had been here before. Allison understood that the odds were likely that she would find herself here again. This was the one place where she could bare her soul, where she could afford to be vulnerable. Doing so felt like setting down a very heavy rucksack and slowly unpacking the rocks that she'd been carrying for far too long.

The only thing she held back was the final conversation with Blitz.

He was one of us. Frodo, 1995-1996.

She couldn't speak that out loud. Not yet. Maybe not ever.

Both her physician and Dr. Michie agreed that she needed to take off a month. She didn't have the energy to argue. Instead, she went back to her apartment, turned off her phone, and slept for another fourteen hours.

Her bruises turned from purple to yellow.

Her tooth stopped hurting.

Her body, much more quickly than her mind, began to recover.

She lasted four more days at her apartment in Virginia—forcing herself to eat the meals she ordered, taking hot showers, sleeping, and generally avoiding the news. She watched a few old movies and tried to read the books on her nightstand—but the headache returned, so she gave up on that.

She stared out her window at the life flowing around her, and she had absolutely no idea how or if she wanted to rejoin that race.

He was one of us. Frodo, 1995-1996.

Finally, tired of pacing her three small rooms, she called her Aunt Polly, who said, "Come on."

Chapter Twenty-Four

John Howard wasn't looking forward to a final debriefing with Stella, but she'd been very clear that it wasn't optional. He made his way up to her office, surprised to see suitcases waiting near the stairs.

Stella had chosen the third floor of the lodge for her personal domain. Boasting an open floor plan and large windows on all four sides, the views were stunning—the Flathead Valley, Whitefish Lake, even Glacier National Park could be seen on a clear day. John looked out those windows and saw the world as it could be, as he was determined it would be.

"John, I'm so glad you could make it."

He gave her an obligatory smile.

"Don't just stand there. Sit. I want to talk."

He walked across to the area that looked like an aristocratic library and sat in the leather chair. Something told him if he sat on the couch, she'd perch beside him. He wanted to keep as much distance between himself and this venomous creature as possible.

"Let's talk about last week."

Today's costume was a designer pants suit made from an expensive-looking royal blue fabric, with a matching head wrap. Maybe she was undergoing chemo, and he didn't know it. He couldn't think of any other reason she'd insist on wrapping her head in cloth every day.

"I sense that you're not pleased with the way things progressed."

"You didn't have to shoot Brett."

"Oh that." Though it was only ten in the morning, she walked to a drink cart, poured a splash of scotch over ice, and held the bottle up in his direction—one perfectly penned eyebrow arched.

"No. Thank you."

"You need to loosen up more, John. We don't need you sinking into despair and deciding to jump off a bridge. A little drink and a long vacation might be just what you need."

He didn't bother answering.

She returned the bottle to the cart, picked up her drink, then perched on the couch—carefully crossing her legs, her eyes intent on something outside the window. When she turned to him, it seemed to John that he was staring into a black abyss—one nearly as disturbing as the U.S. government.

"I did have to shoot Brett. When there's failure, someone must pay, and I didn't want it to be you, John. Or the girl. What is her name?"

"Kate."

"You seem interested in Kate."

"Interested?"

"Romantically perhaps?"

"She's young enough to be my daughter."

"I didn't want to take that away from you. But Brett. . . well, I trust that you will find an adequate replacement for him."

John nodded once. He had, in fact, already found a replacement for Brett Lindstrom. He kept a list, of course he did, of possible personnel should anything untoward happen. He just hadn't thought Stella had it in her to shoot Brett in the head while he was standing in front of a fifty-thousand-dollar video wall.

She'd been surprisingly quick with the PSA-25, a small pistol that packed a lethal punch.

He had almost shot her then—with Brett on the floor, Kate attempting to staunch the bleeding from the hole in his head, and Stella checking to see if she'd broken a nail.

He had very nearly shot her.

Then he'd remembered that he needed her—for now.

It had taken longer to repair the wall than it had to replace the man. Another sad indication of the state of their society.

"What's bothering you?"

"We shouldn't have created kill codes," John said. "That entire scene in the canyon could have been avoided, and what was its purpose anyway? Why create a program that can finally bring down the entire nefarious system, if we're also going to create a way to stop that program?"

"There are at least two good reasons why."

"Such as?"

"The money."

"What money? The buyers pulled out when their men were killed and the codes weren't delivered." The buyers had been funded by John, but he wasn't going to bring that up. He'd taken a big hit when he'd had to pay the default fee. Not to mention what he'd lost in the market when stocks had returned to their normal highs the next day.

Stella shook the ice in her glass, taking her time in answering his question, probably just waiting to see how much agitation he could endure. But John had waited out much worse than Stella Gonzalez. The Russians could teach her a few things in tactical maneuvers of personnel.

"First of all, I made quite a bit of money. When the stocks went down, I bet on them taking a dead cat bounce, and they did. We have more money than ever to fund our little enterprise."

John felt the beginning of a headache forming at the base of his skull. She had bet that Cyber Drop wouldn't succeed? Why had she done that? Had she been instrumental in the demise of their operation? Had she leaked details to the government?

That couldn't be it.

Stella was guilty of breaking at least half a dozen federal laws, not to mention murder. She was in this as deeply as he was.

"We created chaos. That's our goal. Yes, we could have simply inserted Cyber Drop into vulnerable critical systems, let the cascade run, and watched the lights go out from Calgary to Texas. Instead, we had two—maybe three—entities of the U.S. government running around in circles." She finished the drink and flashed him a genuine smile. "It was marvelous."

He didn't respond.

Their goals were as far apart as Canadian cities were from the Mexican border. As far apart as the east was from the west.

"The kill codes also served to prove to the government what we are capable of doing and what we're willing to do."

"Why do we care if they know what we're capable of? If we'd simply act, then they'd see. Then we could move on into—"

"Into your bright tomorrow. Yes, you've mentioned that." She placed her glass in the palm of her hand, uncrossed her legs, and looked directly at him.

John understood that what she was about to say was the true reason for this meeting.

"Tell me about the agent—the woman that Blitz wrote you about."

"You saw the text."

"I did."

"Having people within the prison system certainly pays off, or he wouldn't have been able to get that message to us. He certainly isn't allowed access to email, and anything written and mailed would have been confiscated. Now sources tell me that he's been transferred to the witness protection program, which could work to our benefit as well."

She motioned for him to get to the point.

"Allison Quinn, age 35, is a senior agent with the Department of Homeland Security assigned to the cyberterrorism unit."

"And?"

"And she's the daughter of Arthur Quinn, known to the AT movement as Frodo."

Stella ran a finger around the top of her glass, something she only did when she was holding back. She cocked her head left, then right. "And what do you know of Frodo?"

"Only what's in our files."

"Right." She stood and reached for his hand.

He managed not to grimace at her touch.

"We have big things ahead of us, John. This little exercise served another purpose. It proved to me that you have what it takes to lead my movement."

One last saccharine smile, and then she dismissed him.

Instead of going back to his office, he walked outside, down the trail, to the overlook. Once there, in the one place he'd confirmed that her cameras couldn't reach, he pulled out his wallet and removed the picture of Lillian and Penelope. He ran his fingertips over their faces, trying to remember Lillian's voice and the feel of Penelope's arms around his neck.

For one moment, he let the grief and loss and loneliness consume him.

Only for one moment.

Then, he tucked the picture back into his wallet and the wallet back into his pocket.

He surveyed all that was in front of him, what would be the location of the New Government. He could see the buildings and the homes and the camera-free streets. He could see the future that he would usher in for America's better tomorrow.

With a smile, he turned and walked toward the Lodge.

It was time to get back to work.

And this time, he wouldn't fail.

Chapter Twenty-Five

Polly's reply encouraging her to "come on" was all the encouragement Allison needed. She packed a single carry-on bag, hopped a flight to Austin, rented a car, and typed her aunt's address into the GPS system.

The capital of Texas grew more congested every time she visited her aunt, which was at least once a year. Now the eleventh most populous city in the United States, it reminded her too much of D.C. She clutched the wheel, gritted her teeth, and fought her way through the gridlock.

The cars and lanes and mass of humanity fell away as she drove, until there was only her car and an occasional pickup truck pulling a cattle trailer. She ended up behind one that held two goats, hunched together, drawing comfort from one another. From Austin-Bergstrom International Airport, it was only two hours to San Saba, Texas—*Pecan Capital of the World*, always written with capital letters.

Only two hours.

But oh, what a difference those two hours made.

The hills stretched out to the horizon and seemed to call to her. They practically whispered a promise of some small token of peace.

Her aunt's "little place" encompassed nearly five hundred acres of farmland with a four-thousand-square-foot main house, a swimming pool large enough to swim laps in, and riding stables. Allison stayed in the guest house. It was a mere eighteen hundred square feet of living space—nearly twice that of her apartment back in Virginia.

She drove through the gate, up the lane, and parked under the portico where Polly was waiting for her. Aunt Polly was a young sixty-two years old. She wore bedazzled jeans and a western shirt. Like Allison's father, Polly was tall, and her six-foot frame hadn't bent at all to the ravages of time. Her gray hair was held back with a band, and the makeup she wore was minimal.

Polly was the real deal, at least in Allison's eyes.

She clasped Allison's hands, then softly touched the bruises on her face. "It's good to see you."

They sat on the porch and drank sweet iced tea.

Polly talked about new kittens in the barn, the goats in the east pasture, and her newest gelding. "Dante is feisty, but I think you'll enjoy riding him. And don't look at me that way about the name—it was Edward's doing."

Edward was Polly's property manager. He'd been there for as long as Allison could remember, had little to say, and always offered her a big smile.

"Let's go to the guesthouse, before you fall asleep in that chair."

Walking to the adjacent building, Allison paused, closed her eyes, and basked in the warm Texas sun. Maybe this was what she needed. Maybe here she could find a measure of peace.

They stopped on the smaller porch of the guest house.

"No need to lock the door," Polly reminded her. "If anyone shows up on this place who shouldn't be here, Edward will take care of them. The kitchen and bath are stocked with anything you might need."

Polly pulled her into a hug, kissed the top of her head, then walked away.

Allison slept and walked and avoided the news.

Three days of that and she felt her strength return.

Four days and the yellow bruising on the left side of her face began to fade.

On the fifth day, she poured herself a cup of coffee, sat on the couch, and covered her lap with a hand-sewn quilt. She ran her fingers over the seams, turned the quilt over and saw the embroidered label.

Rosalynn Quinn. 1928.

Her great-grandmother had hand-stitched the fabric together. This land had been in her dad's family for three generations. There was continuity here—a sameness that Allison found wonderfully healing.

She turned on the television for the first time and sat there not watching it, though she was mildly curious as to what was going on in the world. She could check the news on her phone, but she opted to sip the coffee and wait for the early morning report. Through the window, she could see dawn creeping across the farm, revealing pecan trees, a field of baled hay, and a herd of goats.

This was a good place.

This was what she'd needed.

Something changed on the television screen, and she looked up to see the National News banner flash across the bottom. When she saw Ken Langston standing in front of a bank of microphones, she reached for the remote and turned up the volume.

"Kenneth Langston, the Director of Homeland Security, testified on the hill yesterday. He assured senators that the national power grid was no longer in danger—referring to a terrorist event that had been foiled earlier this month. Seven were killed in that event, including two civilians whose identities have been withheld."

The picture of Ken was replaced with a driver's license photograph of Nina. Allison's finger went to her temple and traveled down her cheek bone. She again remembered her hands closing around the woman's neck, remembered Nina slashing at her, remembered the defiant look in her eyes that had held firm to the very last breath.

"Nina Collins had confirmed terrorist ties. In addition, the dead include three international terrorists who were here on student visas. Sufia Alshedri held a Saudi Arabian passport."

She's the government, Blitz. She's the big bad wolf, the one that you anarchists work so hard to defeat.

"Jayron Neal and David Johnstone were both from the U.K."

Allison could hear the boat coming out of the darkness, taste the adrenaline, feel her finger on the trigger.

"Anthony Cooper was a California resident and was also killed by a DHS agent during the operation to thwart the cyberattack that reportedly would have taken out two-thirds of the national grid."

Anthony's mug shot appeared, apparently from a previous arrest. He looked less monstrous than he had coming toward her in the dark of the night. She flashed back to throwing herself at Tate, rolling toward the edge of the cliff, coming up with her weapon pulled and shooting toward the single small sound that might be—that was—him.

"The location of the joint operation between Homeland Security and the FBI has not yet been disclosed, though two different sources have stated off the record that it happened in one of the national parks. Meanwhile in the stock market. . ."

Allison muted the television, then turned it off completely. She sat there, both hands wrapped around the mug of now-cold coffee, and allowed the tremors to pass. It was simply the reality of all that had occurred catching up with her. The flashbacks and memories and voices of those people and events would eventually fade.

They had before.

She walked to the kitchen, poured the coffee down the drain, and grabbed her ball cap. The Texas sun could be relentless, even in September. She'd found that she could walk a little farther each day before the headache and nausea returned. The hike back was often taxing, but that didn't stop her. She was determined that by the end of her month-long forced sabbatical, she would be free of any symptoms and easily pass the concussion protocol.

Physically, she knew that she could pass the required exam in order to be reinstated.

The mental assessment might prove a bit trickier.

She could now go five or even ten minutes without thinking about the canyon, but invariably her mind would slip back. When that happened, her left arm would begin to shake or her heart rate would accelerate or sweat would bead on her forehead. Each time it happened, she was instantly back in the canyon.

As she began her walk across Polly's field, she again felt the memories pulling her back. This time though, those memories were framed with the newscaster's words.

The location of the joint operation between Homeland Security and the FBI has not yet been disclosed...

Tate would be happy that his park had not been named. They didn't need the bad exposure or the lookie-loos that such publicity could bring.

Mr. Harris and Lyra Alonzo were obviously the two civilians mentioned. Allison liked that Lyra hadn't been tagged a terrorist. She might have made a mistake, but she'd given her life for it. At least her family could bury her with dignity. Mr. Harris had very simply been driving the wrong vehicle at the wrong place during the wrong time, and it had cost him his life.

Allison had killed four of the seven—Anthony Cooper, Nina Collins, Jayron Neal, and David Johnstone. She didn't even attempt to forget their names. In fact, she wanted to remember them. She didn't ever want killing to become matter-of-fact, routine, forgettable. It was no small thing to take a life, even when doing so was the only action that could save others.

The review board had determined that all four kills had been justified and necessary, but she understood that those kills were also as responsible for her banishment as the concussion. DHS had long ago accepted that agents needed time to process traumatic events, and they were traumatic no matter how *justified and necessary* they were.

As she worked through her emotions, Allison realized that she was okay with the fact that she'd taken those four lives.

Fewer recruits on Gollum's side meant a safer America.

She didn't regret a single one, and she didn't have nightmares over them.

What did keep her awake in the middle of the night was the nagging fear that the DHS and FBI were merely putting fingers in the holes of a leaking dam. There seemed to be no lack of people willing to work for the Anarchists of Tomorrow—both Americans and foreigners. Plus, there were many more groups like them.

How had Anthony Cooper gone from the beaches of southern California to carrying a knife and rifle on the South Kaibab Trail? At what point had Nina Collins decided to join the other side? What had motivated Jayron Neal and David Johnstone to pilot a raft across the Colorado River in the middle of the night and open fire?

Sufia was the one terrorist involved in Cyber Drop that she understood. The Saudi people had a tumultuous history with the United States going back generations. It was possible the woman had been raised to despise America and Americans from a very young age. Her dedication to a cause, while misguided in Allison's opinion, was at least something she could grasp.

But Nina was a puzzle to Allison.

How did a young girl with an Ivy League education end up working for terrorists? Both the DHS and FBI were still digging into her background, trying to determine the extent of her terrorist ties, but Allison hadn't heard anything definitive.

She hadn't answered the three phone calls from Steele.

She wasn't ready to speak with him.

Anything he had to say could be sent through her director or typed into an email. Deep down, she suspected the calls were of a more personal nature, and she most certainly wasn't ready to face that. He didn't leave a message.

She'd received one brief email from Steele, but he hadn't mentioned Nina. He did say they'd determined that Jason Faulkner did not understand the full scope and intent of what he was involved in. He thought they were training to become river rafting guides, and he'd already told all he knew about Nina which hadn't been much. In the end, Jason had asked to be reassigned to a different national park—somewhere without water.

She had talked to Tate twice.

Both times he'd called, he had told her how Zack was doing, updated her on Bella and Denali, and described the stars. Allison thought that a real friendship was developing there, and she welcomed that. She'd spent too much of her life alone, using her job as a shield to protect herself from other people. She wanted to remedy that, but she had no idea how. Perhaps Tate would be a good place to start.

As for Blitz, he'd been placed on the witness protection list, which meant he'd turned on Gollum. She wasn't surprised to hear it. She was, however, haunted by his last words to her.

He was one of us. Frodo, 1995-96.

Returning to the guest house, she hung her ball cap on a hook by the door and poured herself a glass of water from the Brita pitcher in the fridge. Her hands began to shake, and she pressed them flat against the granite counter.

She counted and took deep breaths, and the tremors passed.

They always passed.

Allison looked out the window at the hills and the sunshine and Dante grazing in the field, and she was filled with a strength and energy that she hadn't thought possible a week ago. It was time. She could do this. She was strong enough now—recovered enough.

She walked to the small office whose door she'd yet to open. Stored there were the only items recovered from her father's home office twenty-six years ago. Nearly everything related to his work had been taken by authorities and investigators, kept, probably destroyed.

But she remembered an old laptop that her Aunt Polly had mentioned finding in the attic. What it was doing there was a mystery.

Allison had seen it once, years ago—when she was still in college.

She'd spent an entire week of spring break at Polly's, had stumbled across the laptop, and had even turned it on. Of course it had been password protected, so she'd created an excel chart and proceeded to try a dozen, then two dozen, then a hundred different variations per day.

After the fourth day, she'd stumbled across the password —alLicat7891.

Alli Cat was his pet name for her.

7891 was the year of her birth backwards.

And he'd always emphasized the importance of giving things not one, or two, but three tries. When she'd capitalized the third letter, she'd been rewarded with a screensaver that was a picture of her and her father standing in front of one of the giant sequoia trees.

The hard drive, however, had been blank—wiped clean.

Ten years with the Department of Homeland Security's cyber force had not turned her into a hacker. Her training had been focused on target acquisition, but she had learned a little about computers.

Nothing was ever completely erased.

She opened the door to the office and walked into the room.

Ten minutes later, she'd located the laptop, plugged it in, and powered it up—a little surprised that it even started. She typed in the password, smiled at the picture of her and her father, and finally clicked the cursor in the search bar.

She stared at the blinking cursor.

What if Blitz had told the truth?

What if her father wasn't the man she thought he was?

What would she find when she typed *Frodo, 1995-1996*?

She shook those fears away. She would find that her father was a patriot. She would find that he was the man she had always loved.

Allison's heart lifted with something. Not hope. Nothing that bright. Maybe expectation. Belief that the answers, or maybe the path to the answers, was here.

She stared at the blinking cursor, and then she began to type.

The End

Thank you for reading, **Support and Defend**. I hope you enjoyed the story. If you did, please consider rating the book or leaving a review at Amazon, Bookbub, or Goodreads.

Keep reading for a preview of ***Against All Enemies,*** Book 2 in the Allison Quinn series.

Afterword

Author's Note

Albert Einstein said, "Logic will get you from A to B. Imagination will take you everywhere." I sought to use the former and relied heavily on the latter while writing this book.

To my knowledge there is only a very short trail that runs parallel to the Colorado River along the south side and within the borders of Grand Canyon National Park. For the purposes of my narrative, I've created one that begins on the south side of the Bright Angel Suspension bridge and continues to Diamond Creek. Also, though horses are provided through private outfitters, it's much more common to use mules when traversing the trails into and out of the canyon.

While much of the technology described in this book has appeared frequently in news reports and major motion pictures, part of it is only rumored to be possible. I'll leave it to the reader's judgment as to which is which.

Against All Enemies
  An Allison Quinn Thriller
  Book Two

Allison Quinn stood in the middle of the Dallas Mixmaster and had to quell the urge to pull her firearm and shoot someone.

Drivers of cattle trailers and eighteen wheelers honked angrily at Mercedes, BMW and Tesla drivers. Hyundai, Ford, and Cadillac also made cars with self-driving features, but the bulk of the disabled vehicles blocking lanes on this fine April morning were BMW and Tesla. The backup stretched as far as Allison could see in every direction. Tempers were flaring, and it wasn't even ten in the morning yet.

Her newest partner, a young man sporting three earrings and long hair pulled back in a band, hustled over. Malik Elliott was all enthusiasm and zero experience, which is why the powers-that-be had assigned him to Allison.

"Tell me something good, Elliott."

"TXDot and Highway Patrol are both onsite." He adjusted his designer glasses. "They're working on getting enough wreckers to move the disabled vehicles, but it's going to take some time."

The highway interchange connected Interstate 35E and Interstate 30. Once among the top 20 most congested roadways in Texas, it had been constructed in the early 1960s and saw over a half a million vehicles per week. "What sadist conceived a place like the Mixmaster?"

Elliott stared at the ground, trying to hide a smile.

She hated when he did that.

"What?"

"Nothing, boss."

"Just say it."

"Hasn't been called the Mixmaster since 2017."

"Really?"

"Seven hundred-million-dollar improvement. It's the Horseshoe now."

"The Horseshoe?"

"I didn't name it, boss."

Allison tried, without success, to hold in a sigh. "Do you have any good news to report? Anything helpful?"

"The event is trending on Twitter. No one has tied it to cybercrime—yet. And Tesla stock has dropped 12 percent."

A trooper wearing a Texas Highway Patrol uniform approached somewhat hesitantly. He looked old enough to be her grandfather and cranky enough to be her twin.

"Problem, Officer Sanchez?"

"I have a driver—a Mrs. Kincaid—who is insisting on talking to the person in charge. You are the person in charge, right?"

"Yeah. That would be me."

Allison instructed Elliott to get an update from the car manufacturer on exactly what kind of cyber breach took place and followed the officer to where Mrs. Kincaid waited. She was elderly, impeccably dressed and without a doubt wealthy.

"Are you the person in charge, or is Officer Sanchez simply trying to hand me off to someone else?"

"Senior agent, Allison Quinn, and yes, I'm in charge."

She didn't specify that she worked for Homeland Security, JCTF Division. In an attack like this one, the Joint Cyber Task Force that consisted of FBI and HS agents worked hard to fly under the radar.

Allison held out a hand which the woman shook with a surprisingly strong grasp.

"Nice to see a woman in charge."

Allison didn't respond to that. She'd worked with plenty of less-than-competent men and women. Allison assured Officer Sanchez that she would take it from there.

Once he'd moved out of earshot, Mrs. Kincaid lowered her voice. "Before my vehicle shut off, a symbol displayed on the screen."

"A symbol?"

"Yes."

"A malfunction symbol?"

"No. It was a tree of sorts."

Allison's pulse picked up a notch. Thirty thousand websites were hacked worldwide every day. It was estimated that 300,000 pieces of malware were written every day. DDoS Attacks—Distributed Denial of Service attacks—were expected to grow to 15 million in the current year. Until that moment, until Mrs. Kincaid said the word *tree*, there had been no indication that this was anything more than your garden variety attack.

"If I gave you a sheet of paper, could you draw me a picture of what you saw?"

"I can do better than that, Agent Quinn. I took a picture with my phone. Let me airdrop it to you."

Quinn walked to the side of the highway, pulled out her cell phone, and punched the contact button for her boss.

Kendra Thomas answered on the first ring. "Talk to me."

"I'm sending you a photo just shared with me by one of the Tesla drivers."

"Okay."

"This symbol appeared on her vehicle's screen before everything shut down."

There was a moment's silence, then Thomas came back. When she spoke, her voice, was resolute. Not surprised. Certainly not frightened. More like a general who was ready and prepared to enter the next battle. "It's them."

"That's definitely the symbol for the group that very nearly carried out an EMP attack in Seattle. As you know, we're fairly certain they are a branch of the Anarchists for Tomorrow. Whether it is actually them or someone pretending to be them—"

"Circles within circles with these people."

"I recommend we elevate this to a Level 2 threat. This could be just the beginning."

Technically the DSH had only two types of advisories. Bulletins and Alerts. Bulletins usually dealt with critical terrorism information not indicative of a specific threat. Alerts were more specific about the nature of the threat. The two types of alerts were elevated and imminent.

That was technically how terrorist events were handled.

The color-coded system of the post 9-11 era had been replaced in 2011.

In truth, within the JCT they still used a number system. Five was a vague threat with little actionable intelligence. One was imminent risk for persons or systems within the United Sates. Currently they were at a level four.

"I recommend we move to a level three."

"Done." Thomas's voice was steady and definitive. She didn't waste time questioning the agents on the ground. She also didn't hesitate to inform them of the bigger picture when they needed to know. "We have agents in Galveston now on what we thought was an unrelated op. I will update them and get back with you."

Thirty minutes later, Allison received instructions. "Galveston. Terminal 2, Pier 28. Leave Elliott in charge of the Dallas site."

Which said a lot.

If an agent with Elliott's lack of experience could be put in charge of a site, there was no further threat there. Allison had worked under Thomas in Seattle—an op that still caused her pain in her shoulder when the temperature fluctuated. A gunshot wound could do that to you. Thomas was decisive, efficient, and she did not broker fools. If she was sending Allison to Galveston, to Pier 28, then that's where the threat was.

She caught a ride on a helicopter, which was the only path out of the Mixmaster—the Horseshoe—other than walking. The copter took her to the downtown Dallas federal building where the task force had set up camp. There she requisitioned a vehicle and drove out of the underground garage, passing the Sixth Street Book Depository as she made her way out of downtown.

She wasn't yet born when John Kennedy was assassinated in 1963, but she knew the details—both what had been made public and what hadn't. Unlike some of her co-workers, she didn't think the world had grown more dangerous, more deadly.

The world had always been dangerous and deadly.

Ask John Kennedy.

Ask Jackie.

You could go back in time all the way to Lincoln in the Ford Theater. The world had always been dangerous.

What had changed were the tools of war.

The war itself—that had stayed the same.

And she—Allison Quinn—had taken a solemn vow to protect this country. To fight this war. Privately, she'd also vowed to catch the persons responsible for her father's murder.

Since the AT was involved, with this op she just might be able to do both.

Game on.

You can purchase *Against All Enemies in ebook or print*, exclusively from Amazon.

Also by Vannetta Chapman

DEFENDING AMERICA SERIES
Coyote's Revenge (Book 1)
Roswell's Secret (Book 2)

KESSLER EFFECT SERIES
Veil of Mystery (Prequel)
Veil of Anarchy (Book 1)
Veil of Confusion (Book 2)
Veil of Destruction (Book 3)

ALLISON QUINN SERIES
Her Solemn Oath (Prequel)
Support and Defend (Book 1)
Against All Enemies (Book 2)

STANDALONE NOVEL
Security Breach

FOR A COMPLETE LIST OF MY BOOKS, VISIT MY
Complete Book List

Contact the Author

Share Your Thoughts With the author:
Your comments will be forwarded to the author when you send
them to vannettachapman@gmail.com.

Submit your review of this book to:
vannettachapman@gmail.com or via the connect/contact button
on the author's website at:
VannettaChapman.com.

Sign up for the author's newsletter at:
VannettaChapman.com.

Printed in Great Britain
by Amazon